SOUND & FURY

We can no other answer make but
thanks, and thanks, and ever thanks.

Jeffrey Cook

WRITERPUNK Press

Published in the USA by Writerpunk Press
Layout and typesetting by Lia Rees
Cover designed by Elizabeth Hamm

Fonts used: **SHORTCUT** by Misprinted Type
Kingthings Trypewriter by Kevin King
Rafale by Suleyman Yazki/Svet Simov/Vasil Stanev
Cardo by David Perry
SENANG BANYOL by Adien Gunarta
Angst Dingbats – ✺❂✿◙⊕ – by Angst

ISBN: 978-0692386132

This book is dedicated to, necessarily, WILLIAM SHAKESPEARE, for his consummate skill at putting words on the page. To JOHN WESLEY HAWTHORNE, for his consummate skill at bringing together people who put words on the page. And ESAIAS MAYO, who will doubtless be stunned to see his name mentioned in the same place as the Bard's. Together, they are the heart and soul of the Writerpunk Project.

- **Jeffrey Cook**, on behalf of the collected punks

All profits from this book go to support PAWS animal shelter and rescue in Lynnwood, WA. PAWS is a champion for animals - rehabilitating injured and orphaned wildlife, sheltering and adopting homeless cats and dogs, and educating people to make a better world for animals and people. http://www.paws.org

paws.
people helping animals

Foreword
What Is Punk?

To me, punk is about being an individual and going against the grain and standing up and saying 'This is who I am.'
– Joey Ramone

SO, WHAT IS PUNK? There's an awful lot of genres out there with a word, and then "punk" attached. So what makes, say, cyberpunk different from mainstream science fiction? Why isn't just anything some type of punk?

When it comes down to it, punk is about an aesthetic. Whether the defining thing is a technology, as is the case with cyberpunk or steampunk, or something more general, like splatterpunk, the thing has to reshape the world into the path not taken, or the path that shouldn't be taken. If you look at, say, steampunk cosplayers, yes, the base of their wardrobe is Victorian in most cases, but there's brass and gears and goggles everywhere. The real Victorian era had quite a lot of color to it, as new dyes were being discovered and experimented with – but in Steampunk, the world looks a lot like what we see in old photos and clippings, with sepia tones everywhere. Likewise, that technological enlightenment comes with a changing in historical attitudes. You see female mechanics, doctors, and front-line fighters in a lot of settings, many of whom are also perfectly at home in fancy corsets and gowns, right up until they go to work.

In splatterpunk, for another example, you don't just have horror and graphic violence. You have Tarantino-esque blood sprays, dying enemies who contain way more blood than they should, and highly stylized violence. Meanwhile, the existence of the horrors that populate it shape and inform not just the immediate story, but the entire setting. *Night of the Living Dead* isn't punk. You can see the normal world, and normal teens. The evil is unleashed, and then it ends. *Zombieland*, on the other hand, might be. There, the horror defines the entire setting, and people's lives, personalities and style are shaped by the horror's existence – and while "Shoot for the head" can work, people make sure to pack chainsaws and hedge clippers too.

The mainstream is what you would expect, for good or ill, in any genre. In cases of historical-based punk tropes, like Steampunk, Dieselpunk or Teslapunk, technologies that were never explored become defining parts of the setting. For some of the more modern or futuristic punk genres, the expectations are twisted, and then the style elements are turned up to 11.

So it is with the works you see here. All of the stories here are familiar, or could be, if you read enough Shakespeare. They're then given a twist or three, letting the storytellers add elements of their chosen genres along the way to making the stories their own.

Jeffrey Cook

Introduction
Who We Are

The whole is greater than the sum of its parts.
— Aristotle

WHAT HAPPENS WHEN stay-at-home moms, business people, students, freelance dilettantes and all in between gather to discuss writing?

Let me ask you another way.

What do you get when writers – some published, some haven't written in years, some completely new to the craft – discuss cyberpunk and steampunk works?

Well, if the right mix of people find each other, you get a group like Writerpunk.

We are a group of writers who are not only passionate about storytelling, but love to imagine new worlds. We're the kind of people who sit back and think "What if?" before spending hours over our keyboards tapping out dieselpunk, clockpunk, and cyberpunk stories. We like to delve into the past, change one event, and watch how the ripples will change the future – and we scribble down the results. We look toward the future, envision what cybernetics will do to mankind, and bring that vision to the present. We're the kind of people who see a picture of Abraham Lincoln with a machine gun grafted to his forearm and think, "Yeah, I could work with that."

But before any of us put pen to paper, fingers to keyboard, or quill to parchment, we were all readers. We read books like *Do Androids Dream of Electric Sheep?*, *Neuromancer*, or *Mirrorshades*, and came away with a love of cyberpunk. We saw movies like *The Rocketeer* or *Sherlock Holmes: Game of Shadows* and walked out of the theater with the wheels of our minds turning, eager to create our own worlds.

Above all, we are a community. We started as individual writers interested in cyberpunk and steampunk and associated genres, and together we became more. While some of us had written in those genres for years and others were sticking a toe in to test the waters, we all benefited from being Writerpunks.

And now we have written a book.

J. Sarchet

Preface
Why Shakespeare?

FIRST, BECAUSE A LOT OF THESE STORIES ARE TIMELESS. Sure, kids still groan at the difficulty of reading all the thees and thous and the rest when he comes up in school. Despite that, there's still regular references made to *Romeo and Juliet* in pop culture. People still know a lot of the quotes. From "To be or not to be, that is the question" to "Friends, Romans, countrymen..." the stories are about broad themes that still resonate with people. A lot of them have been adapted for different settings in movie and theater.

Secondly, because we suspect Shakespeare would approve. Some of his stories are very old stories, or based upon old stories that were well known in his era. Then he took those events and dramatized them. His stories persist, and stand out from others, in part because of his willingness to challenge some of the accepted order of his day. His work includes mad rulers, incest, betrayal, falling in love with the enemy, and, of course, Puck. Very little was off limits if it would get the audience in the theater.

Also, everyone who contributed to this book was a reader first. We all admired Shakespeare's craft and way with words. We appreciated just how much depth there was to these stories, and with it, how readily all those elements could be made at home in different settings.

Finally, Shakespeare is one of the foundations of

literature. *Romeo and Juliet* and *Julius Caesar* are taught in a lot of high schools. His stories are major pillars of a lot of college English classes. His plays are still performed on stages around the world, from poor little school stages to major productions. So if punk literature is about taking the expectations of literature and twisting it, then punk Shakespeare is only natural.

Jeffrey Cook

EDITOR'S NOTE: The works of Shakespeare are part of the public domain, so creative people are free to use them as inspiration for new works of art or fiction – exactly what has been done in this anthology (and future volumes!). Some stories follow the source play and echo some of the dialog closely, while others use the Shakespearean work as a beginning and head off in a fascinating new direction:

- "Mac" by Carol Gyzander – Cyberpunk, inspired by *Macbeth*

- "The Green Eyed Monster" by S. A. Cosby – Dieselpunk, inspired by *Othello*

- "Prospero's Island" by H. James Lopez – Teslapunk, inspired by *The Tempest*

- "A Town Called Hero" by Warren C. Bennett – Dieselpunk, inspired by *Much Ado About Nothing*

- "The Winter's Tale" by Jeffrey Cook – Steampunk/Clockpunk, inspired by *The Winter's Tale*

See <u>www.punkwriters.com</u> for a short synopsis of each play.

People To Blame, Part 1
The Writers

CAROL GYZANDER writes under her own name, even though few can spell or pronounce it (think "GUYS and her"). She was a prolific reader of classic science fiction and Agatha Christie mysteries in her early days; since they moved every two years, she had lots of time on her hands as the perpetual new kid. But she became adept at people-watching in order to fit in at each new school, and followed this up by studying anthropology – the study of people and their culture – and lots and lots of English literature at Bryn Mawr College. Now that her kids have flown the coop, she has gone back to her early loves with an amateur detective novel and more science fiction in the works. See what else Carol is working on at:

www.CarolGyzanderAuthor.com

S.A. COSBY is an author and poet from Gloucester, Virginia. He has had his short fiction published in several magazines and anthologies including *ThugLit* and *Crackedrearview*. His fantasy trilogy *Brotherhood of the Blade* is published by HCS Publishing, with volume 1 available on Amazon and volumes 2 and 3 to follow in the spring and summer of

2015. When he isn't writing S.A. is an avid collector of knives, swords and comic books. He lives in Gloucester with a lazy pug named Pugsly and a cantankerous squirrel named Solomon. You can check out his work at S.A. Cosby Author on Facebook or at his blog:

thewalkingbook.WordPress.com

H. JAMES LOPEZ was born on a Navy ship in the Caribbean Sea outside of Barranquilla. He is a construct of too much sun, too much alcohol and not nearly enough time on land. Since 2009 he has been writing fiction in all the forms which come to mind. Current works include two books on Military/Urban fiction, a High Fantasy novel in review and a book about steam warfare in Texas at the time of the Republic.

Keep up with his future works on his Facebook page, H James Lopez. A sample of his novel *The Blue Star Workaround* can be found at:

www.jukepop.com/home/read/1880

The life of WARREN C. BENNETT is comprised of many experiences. He is a traveler that has lived in the wilds of Yellowstone, the deserts of the Southwest and down the street from Mark Twain's grave. He is a gamer that seeks products that are both fun and thought provoking. He has been playing the guitar for over half his life and is contemplating learning the banjo. He is a voracious reader that understands that the power of words can hurt or heal a human heart. His faith underlines everything he does regardless of how light or dark life becomes. The spark that ignites his desire to write combines all these areas and pushes him to spin tales of wonder and imagination for the world. He is glad to speak to anyone that has a question, though he doesn't always have the right answer. He can always be reached via Twitter @warrencbennett or at his home on the web:

warrencbennett.net

JEFFREY COOK is quickly becoming a Steampunk veteran. He is the author of the emergent Steampunk *Dawn of Steam* trilogy. (*Dawn of Steam: First Light, Dawn of Steam: Gods of the Sun,* and *Dawn of Steam: Rising Suns.*) He has had Steampunk stories published in the anthologies *Steampunk Trails 2, Avast Ye Airships, Free Flowing Stories,* and *A Cold Winter's Night.* In a much less steam-powered vein, he is also the author of the YA Science Fiction-Mystery *Mina Cortez: From Bouquets to Bullets,* and will soon release the first book of the Fair Folk Chronicles, *Foul is Fair,* co-written with his normal editor, Katherine Perkins.

He lives in the wilds of Maple Valley, Washington now, but after a start in Boulder, CO, he moved all over the United States (and a little bit of Canada). His mother insists he's wanted to be an author since he was six years old, but he didn't get his official start until 2014. In addition to the novels and anthology projects, the life-long gamer has contributed to Deep7 Games out of Seattle, WA. When not reading, researching, writing or gaming, he is also a passionate football fan. (Go Seahawks!)

http://www.authorjeffreycook.com/about.html

KATHERINE PERKINS is Jeffrey Cook's co-author, having worked with him not only on The Winter's Tale, but also served as the editor on the *Dawn of Steam* series. (*First Light*, *Gods of the Sun*, and *Rising Suns*.) She lives in Coralville, Iowa, with her husband and one extremely skittish cat. She was born in Lafayette, Louisiana, and will defend its cuisine on any field of honor. When not reading, researching, writing, or editing, she tries to remember what she was supposed to be doing.

People To Blame, Part 2
Editing, Design + Related Mischief

ESAIAS MAYO is a nomad of the best kind. A college biology major, his love of literature has freed his soul to follow the trail left by the winds of his creativity. This very thing is what caused him to birth the brain child that grew to be this particular anthology. The Bard being his first great love, and Punk literature being his newfound soulmate, it only made sense. He gives an eloquent bow and hopes that you will enjoy the familiar, yet uniquely portrayed, themes of murder, deceit, and passionate love that you shall dive into.

JEFFREY COOK originally jumped on board this project as a writer, then realized it was lacking something: namely deadlines and organization. Having already finished The Winter's Tale, and with experience writing for anthologies before, he boldly put on another hat (he likes to think it was a pirate hat), and took over. A lot of effort went into organizing a bunch of punks. It turned out that they didn't just need excited writer punks - the group needed editing punks, formatting punks, artist punks, and even a few cheerleading punks for good measure. (He also likes to think Victoria and Elizabeth had amazing punk cheerleader outfits). He's currently working with the primary charity (PAWS of Lynnwood) to coordinate donations, and setting up the release party... and, despite all the work, already looking forward to the next one of these.

T.J. FORD, J. SARCHET and CAROL GYZANDER were originally responsible for editing. T.J. and Carol also stepped into the breach (aptly enough) for some last-minute proofreading.

She's just a girl who can't say no, which is how T.J. FORD found herself Editrix of the first *Shakespeare Goes Punk* anthology. An aspiring writer and lover of both steampunk (especially corsets) and the Bard (especially *Macbeth*), she's found it rather a fun project on which to work. In between rescuing dangling participles and saving serial commas, T.J. is a mind-body therapist with bicoastal practices in New York City and in Portland, Oregon, where she lives with her food-scientist husband and their increasingly deaf cat Scamper. In her spare time T.J. has a penchant for running long distances of 20 or 50 or 100 miles, preferably on the trails of the Hobbit forests in the Pacific Northwest.

J. SARCHET was born on the day before yesterday with holes in her shoes and crying the blues. No, wait. That was the Scarecrow from *The Wiz*. Well, despite her mysterious origin story, J. has been writing all her life. In fact, she often remarks that she likes words more than most people (present company excluded, naturally). The first story she ever wrote was scribbled in a small spiral notepad and stashed behind her family's piano for safekeeping. Although she has spent most of the last 26 years filling notebooks with stories and not letting anyone read them, more recently she has begun sharing her work with others. Though she has seen the most success as a poet, she has also written one-act plays. Currently she is hard at work on a speculative fiction novel she hopes to self-publish. When it is completed, J. won't be hiding it behind a piano, but rather shouting the news from the rooftops.

Carol's biography can be found in the writers' section!

LIA REES is a creative dilettante living in London (England) who is currently engaged to an American anarchist. She is laid-back and amiable, if a bit self-absorbed, and has the sense of humor of a 12-year-old. Her taste for design led her to volunteer for the layout and typography of this book; she was also involved in proofreading and cover art. She loves music and has been known to crochet, make jewelry and explore papercrafts. Lia supplies independent authors with design and publishing services, which include video trailers and everything demonstrated in the book you're holding. Lately she finds herself making posters, business cards and merchandise too. Her business, Free Your Words, can be found at the unsurprising location of <u>freeyourwords.com</u>

ELIZABETH HAMM created the cover. Born in California, raised in North Dakota, and probably never going to get a proper tan, Elizabeth has been interested in the graphic, video, and written arts since she could form tangible memories. Closing in on finally finishing a dual degree in Broadcasting and Multimedia Studies, she continues to combine the two worlds together along with her love of writing. Being creative and passionate about the world of fiction brought her to volunteering her growing knowledge and time to design the cover of this book. In her spare time, she writes novels, shoots short films, and does her own video news program weekly. Elizabeth can be reached at lizziebelina@gmail.com for all things cover design, graphic design, or video.

VICTORIA L. CANNY was an official cheerleader for the project. But no one knows who she is, or if that's even her real name. For all we know, she could be an eighty-six year old recluse, living off the Oregon coast and babbling on about shadow people trying to steal her cats. She could just be an average person struggling with eighteen credit card payments and two mortgages taken out on her Florida condo. Or, she could just be some random chick that sort of appeared one day, waving a manuscript in the air and proclaiming herself to be the next great 'maybe this book will be better than the last one' author. And it wasn't the best manuscript in the world, but leaps and bounds better than her previous attempts.

Gentles, perchance you wonder at this show;
But wonder on, till truth make all things plain.

MAC

Carol Gyzander

CHAPTER ONE
Fair is foul, and foul is fair

THE PRECISION CASTINGS FACTORY MANAGER, Cawdor, stepped into the darkened production bay, his footsteps echoing down the empty hallway behind him. Stopping just inside, he frowned and looked around the empty room for the source of the blue glow he thought he had seen. The hulking machines of the production line stood still and silent. The area was lit only by the safety lights at the perimeter of the bay and the yellow work lights of the cleaning bots. He had no idea these would be the last things he would ever see.

FM Cawdor shook his head; the shift time wasn't complete, yet there was no one working on Mac's assembly line. Again. Raising his arm, he consulted the data display linked to the moddy chip at the base of his skull, and his frown deepened. Moving to the transport area at the end of the production bay, he saw twelve pallets of completed product snugly bound and stacked, ready for transport at the end of the shift.

He looked up at the short, spiky black hair and piercing eyes of Mac, the day Shift Supervisor of this production line, shown in the group of photographs hanging on the wall. He didn't understand why Mac kept changing things.

He shook his head again and shrugged. Mac had instituted procedural changes that made things more efficient, and Mac's workers left before the end of the shift when they had attained their quotas. No other production lines in the factory even met their quotas, much less finished early. Cawdor didn't get the point.

The whirring sound of a pair of cleanup bots approached from the other side of the pallets. Bots were ubiquitous; his consciousness barely registered the faint sound as he walked around the row of pallets with his pocket light, idly double checking the count. One bot swept the floor, and the other scooped up the pile of debris and extended its scoop to dump it into the refuse bin on its back.

Coming around the corner of the stack of pallets, Cawdor startled when he finally saw the bots; he tripped over his own feet and fell directly into the path of the scooper bot that towered above him. It stopped abruptly when it detected the presence of a human within its perimeter, but the unbalanced weight of its extended scooping arm caused it to topple forward and fall onto Cawdor, trapping him beneath it.

His cry rang out and echoed across the empty production bay, abruptly silenced as his head struck the floor. No people were nearby to hear, but the scooper bot's emergency beacon came on immediately, sending a signal to the Corporation's home system that was passed through the factory network.

The last thing Cawdor saw was a series of bots coming toward him out of the storage bay, drawn by the emergency beacon. The sweeper bot extended its squeegee to trap the blood that pooled across the floor from his head.

When they no longer detected his pulse, the bots paused momentarily then continued their cleanup activity. Two bots extended arms with cutting tools on them, and proceeded to dismantle the scooper bot that had been responsible for the human's death. Another one scooped up the dead body onto a rolling cart, straightening his arms and legs with gentle care. He looked as though he was sleeping.

A specialized bot with a red emblem on its side rolled down the hall into the factory bay and stopped by the body. Extending a narrow arm, it felt along the back of the dead man's skull and inserted a thin probe into the back of his neck. Pulling out the small moddy chip, it inserted the chip into a slot on its own console and sent a signal to the home computer.

Within a matter of minutes, the entire scene had been cleaned and scoured. The bot responsible for the forbidden death of a human had been dismantled, Cawdor's family had been notified of his death, and a message had been sent to the home office. The body of Cawdor was rolling down the hall on the makeshift gurney. The room looked as though he had never entered it.

Moments later, a blue glow shone through the darkness. Three women were standing in a circle in the production bay. A rumbling sounded, like thunder.

"When shall we three meet again? In thunder, lightning, or in rain?" asked the first.

"When all the change has come," replied the second.

"That'll be before the day is done," said the third.

"Then, to the Fringe," added the second woman.

"There to meet with Mac."

All three joined hands and threw back their heads as they laughed. "Fair is foul, and foul is fair. Let us away through the smog and filthy air." They disappeared, and the blue glow faded.

CHAPTER TWO
Cattle car

Two hours before his 12-hour shift was technically over, Mac punched out of Precision Castings and dashed through the sudden electrical storm for the commuter pod, nimbly sidestepping the people-pusher bots that crammed extra workers onto already-full pod cars during shift changes. *Like a bunch of cattle,* thought Mac.

The factory staggered the shift start times of different production lines in order to move the workers most efficiently. This meant the trains were constantly full and in use, and one would usually only run into workers from the same shift. Mac had discovered that he could ride with his friend Banks if he got his production shift to end early.

Making his way through the crowded pod, he threaded his way through the mass of utilitarian gray jumpsuits with blue shoulder patches like his own, indicating the wearer worked on the production lines. The black circle around his own blue patch indicated his status as a Shift Supervisor.

There he is. Mac slid in next to a man who was leaning against the door on the far side of the car, absently snapping his fingers as he waited. The dark red of his shoulder patch clashed with his bright red hair.

"Finished early again, I see," said the waiting man. The doors ground shut and the pod lurched into motion.

"Yeah, well," said Mac. "Just can't see the point of doing it the way they have it set up. Makes me crazy, Banks."

Banks raised his eyebrows. "Most Corporation workers don't care, Mac." His voice dropped as a worker near him idly turned to look at them. "They do their shift as required, then go home to their boring little houses to eat their boring food and watch their boring entertainment box shows with their boring little wives."

"Well, guilty as charged for the rest of it. I'm always amazed at the things you say, Banks. You've been more interesting than everyone else since we were kids. Is that why you got selected for the Science Lab to work with the moddy chips?"

Banks stared at Mac intently for a moment, then his face relaxed and he shrugged. "Hey, who knows? I just do what I'm told." He looked around the car to see if anyone had taken note of the conversation. Pulling the collar of his uniform up around his neck, he leaned back against the door, closing down further conversation as he stared at the floor.

CHAPTER THREE
Anomalous readings

As the pod clattered back and forth, Banks let his mind drift to an earlier time when he was still a child, and therefore not yet subject to emotional control through his moddy chip. His family had just finished the celebration after he had survived the installation procedure and come home; he would not start the compatibility testing until he was further into puberty and his brain had been shaped by the ensuing hormones. His older brother was nearing the end of the compatibility testing period, and the whole family anxiously awaited the results.

Coming home from after school play, Banks had slammed the door but stopped suddenly, brought up short by the sight of his mother's tight, drawn face. "Mom? What's up?" The door to the office was closed. It was only because of his father's Science Lab job that they even qualified to have an office.

She looked up from staring at the table. "Hush, child. Your brother is undergoing the final section of his compatibility test. He's in there with your father and the team." Allowing his father in the room during the testing was a measure of respect for his status as a scientist. Of course his mother had no such status.

"So, how is it going? Can I go in there?" The door to the office opened a crack, and Banks could see his father gesturing to him and holding a finger to his lips. Leaving his mother behind in the kitchen, he slipped through the door and stood with his father at the back of the room.

His red-haired brother was sitting in a chair. Two men were looking at a small console display that they had brought with them, with the red emblem of the Science Lab on the side, and thin silver wires connected to the moddy chip in the back of his brother's neck at the base of his skull.

Banks moved closer to his father, and slipped his small hand into his father's large one. The same hand Banks had seen carefully manipulating tiny instruments, when he was repairing things that he had brought home from the Science Lab to work on. Hands that Banks had thought could fix anything; now those fingers tightened on his own.

His father gestured to the console and whispered, "It's calculating the percentage of compatibility that your brother shows for the moddy chip, Banks. He has to make at least 80% to get a job here with the Corporation, and hit a certain aptitude score to get a job in the Science Lab like mine. Not everyone can score that high. If he doesn't score well enough, they'll decide that he is not a good risk... to keep..."

The man's voice caught for a moment. "He wouldn't be a good enough match to keep as a Corporation employee." The big fingers nearly crushed his small ones.

"But what happens to him if he's not compatible, Dad?" Banks had been trying to avoid thinking of that scenario. He couldn't comprehend any alternative to living in Manufacturing Division.

His father looked to be sure the technicians were not listening to them, and still lowered his voice. "Well, son, he would have to leave. There are other jobs and other places to live outside of here. It's just a very difficult and dangerous life, to be honest, and not one that I would ever wish for either of you. Unfortunately, your brother has been showing some, shall we say, anomalous readings, and I asked them to rerun the last test. They've been staring at that display for a really long time now."

A red light blinked onto the console. One of the technicians looked up from the console, and nodded at the other one. "Well. Right. That's it, then. Not acceptable. On behalf of the Corporation, we express our regrets and condolences that we will not be able to offer you a job with the Corporation here on ManDiv. You will be required to leave Corporation housing, since you are now of legal age. Today." The other technician started disconnecting the wire from the moddy chip at the back of his brother's head.

Banks could hear the wailing that sprang up from the kitchen, and realized that his mother had been listening at the door. His father gave his hand one more squeeze, then dropped it and rushed to the boy in the chair. Kneeling down, he wrapped his arms around his oldest son and held him still. "You're going to be all right, son. You're ready for whatever comes."

Disoriented, the boy sat quietly in the chair. The technician pressed a button on the console, and a long, thin arm extended from the testing bot and plucked the moddy chip out of the back of the boy's head. The older boy slumped forward into his father's arms. The father straightened up quickly, in the process bumping into the thin arm extension holding the chip. His hand flashed out and caught the chip before it hit the ground.

Flicking his hand over, his father palmed the chip and passed another one that had been hidden in his sleeve to the technician. Banks could see the whole maneuver. His eyes grew large, but he knew to keep his mouth shut.

The technician nodded his thanks and installed a new chip to indicate his brother's changed status. "Again, he needs to be out of ManDiv housing by the end of the day. Transport will arrive at 14:00 to pick him up and take him to an alternate Division for reassignment based upon his test scores."

The two packed up their equipment and left the housing unit, ignoring the mother crying desperately in the kitchen as they passed her on the way out.

Banks came back to the present with a start as the pod screeched around a curve. Rubbing his face with his hand, he looked around a bit wildly until he saw Mac; then he relaxed and smiled.

CHAPTER FOUR
The Fringe

Rocking with the motion of the pod as it hurtled down the track, Mac checked the time on his arm display. "Huh. I'm not expected home for two hours yet. What on earth am I going to do now?"

Banks smiled slyly. "What say we take a different way home?"

Mac looked at him with interest. "Wow, I didn't know there even was another way home."

When the pod arrived at the stop before theirs, near the Wall, the thunderstorm had stopped, leaving puddles on the ground. They slipped out the door with the rest of the crowd, then moved diagonally across the platform to the edge and down a narrow alley. When they were out of eyesight, Banks stopped and stuck a small disk on the back of Mac's neck, over his moddy chip, and another on his own.

"What's that for?" asked Mac.

"It masks your signal; we don't want any prying eyes from the Corporation noticing where we're going. Remember to take it off when we get back."

Mac raised his eyebrows but said nothing. Mac followed Banks as he turned again and went through a narrow doorway. They walked through a large, empty warehouse that was built into the stone face of the Wall, the cliff that marked one end of ManDiv.

At the back of the huge room, Banks triggered a hidden latch and a small door in the stone swung open, revealing a narrow rough-hewn tunnel. Coming out at the end, the smell and the sound stopped Mac in his tracks for a moment as he adjusted to the energy of the scene.

They stood on a natural ledge at the edge of a huge, crowded stone chamber. From their vantage point, they could see the ends of narrow streets criss-crossing the space. Lights, images, and holographic displays assaulted the eye from every angle; signs hung over store doorways, and banners were displayed over booths and stalls that lined the streets on multiple levels.

And the sounds: merchants, some in rags, pushed carts along while shouting their wares. Machinery droned and screeched somewhere in the distance, and several different types of music assaulted their ears at once, coming from bars and stores all around them.

They walked down the narrow ramp from the ledge to the floor level and entered one of the streets. Scantily dressed women leaned out of upper level windows, shaking their shoulders at passersby while calling out provocatively. Mac stood and stared at them. "Banks, I've never seen a woman act that way."

"I know, Mac. It takes a little getting used to. Just don't make eye contact and try not to engage with anyone. People in here have unusual abilities." He indicated a passing man with what appeared to be razor blades protruding from the knuckles of one hand.

As they walked down the street, Mac and Banks dodged oncoming vehicles and sidestepped the piles of manure left by unseen beasts of burden. The far end of the street ran down into a large body of water in the underground cave, and Mac caught sight of a fishing boat unloading its catch at a decrepit pier. Sunlight from an external entrance glimmered across the water.

"Ah, the Fringe. How I miss it when I'm not here. And how I want to leave it when I am," murmured Banks.

Mac nodded. "Strangely compelling. What is this place?"

"This is the Fringe, where people actually wind up when they are rejected from the compatibility test. You remember that my older brother didn't pass?"

"Of course, Banks. I remember how upset you and your parents were. But you told me and Lydia that they transferred him to another Division that matched his testing profile. This place is, well, astounding." Mac looked around with bright interest.

"Well, what they really do is shove people through another door in the Wall onto the cliffs, prepared or not, and they just leave them. And then when the transport reps from ManDiv have gone, the Fringe residents come out and get the person, bring them into the Fringe caves, and try to get them to assimilate. This place is mostly invisible from the outside, and the Corporation doesn't bother with it much."

Banks turned and pointed at the door on the ledge. "This is a back door, in a way. But you can't get back in without setting off alarms unless you have a moddy chip of some kind."

Mac stood open mouthed, gaping at his childhood friend. "Banks, you're kidding! Your brother wound up here? This place is fascinating. Why don't more people come in here?"

"Well frankly, Mac, most people who work for the Corporation have no idea this place exists. And even if they did, they would have no interest in coming in here. It's the moddy chip that controls their curiosity. Intriguing that you find it appealing in here, even though you have your chip in. I thought you might. But don't get too attached to this place. It's not as great as it seems."

"Do you come in here much?"

"Only now and then, when I can't stay away. Trust me, Mac, it's not all goodness and light in here. Most people don't transition into this life very well. And you don't live to an old age; people would as likely kill you as look at you." Banks put out an arm to stop his companion as a pair of brawling drunks poured out of a drinking establishment to their left, a man and a woman.

The young man was wiry and dressed in what had once been a Corporation jumpsuit but was now several years outgrown, and had been patched and modified to stay on as he grew. His arms and shoulders were exposed and Mac could see multiple scars across one shoulder. For her part, the woman was even more scantily dressed. She wore a short leather skirt and sleeveless tunic, cut low in front to expose most of her cleavage; she had tattoos down both arms. She was sweating, her chest heaving with anger and exertion as they faced one another, each waiting for an opening. Mac was mesmerized.

Banks started pulling him down the street through the gathering crowd. "Come on, trust me. We don't want to be here." Over his shoulder, Mac watched the woman circling the man, looking for her opportunity, and heard the onlookers starting to take sides in the argument.

"Hit him!"

"Hit *him?* Hell, hit *her!*"

Banks pulled on Mac's arm to keep them from getting involved as the two hecklers turned on each other, knives drawn. Stepping to the side to avoid the crowd, they walked on, occasionally buffeted by the throngs of people who were moving along the narrow street.

A rich spicy aroma reached their nostrils, stopping them in front of a small food stand that featured some sort of fish on a stick and dishes of rice with sauce. The vendor's gaze flicked to Mac and back; his face broke into a sly grin and he nodded at Banks. Banks tightened his lips at the innuendo, but nodded in return.

"Hungry?" asked Banks.

Mac turned and stared at him. "I want that. It smells so good I can feel my mouth water. What kind of fish is it? Wait, I don't want to know. But what do they use as currency? I can't imagine they take Corporation credits."

"They do," Banks said. "You just don't want to have the Corporation know you spent any credits in here." Mac again raised his eyebrows.

Banks dug in the pocket of his gray jumpsuit and pulled out a small bit of electronic equipment. The vendor eyed it for a moment before snatching it from his hand and tucking it away in his apron. He then dished out two large servings of fish and rice, gesturing to a bench in an alcove next to his stand.

"Come on, sit down," said Banks. "I want to tell you about how this place got here; nobody in ManDiv knows the history except Science Lab personnel. We can eat while I talk, but I'm afraid that later you're going to regret eating it."

They sat down and Mac tore into the spicy meal. Banks laughed at the look on Mac's face when he took the first bite of the skewered fish. "Oh my god, this is the best thing I've ever had. I had no idea food could have so much flavor. So much better than what Lydia dials up on the food box. Uh, how do you eat the rest of it?"

"Scoop with your fingers. Eat slowly, Mac. And you probably don't want to eat the whole thing until you're sure how it's going to sit with your stomach." Banks smiled as he watched Mac ignore his advice and devour the food, scooping the greasy rice with his fingers after only a moment's hesitation. *That's still the Mac I knew,* he thought. "Careful, this is a bit different from Corporation food."

CHAPTER FIVE
The story of ManDiv

While they ate, Banks told Mac the story his family had passed down for generations from working in the Science Labs; about how the Manufacturing Division had come to be established, and why the Corporation used moddy chips. They had started out as simple access badges and communication devices so that people could connect to the Corporation's network, but were used for more and more control of the population as time went on.

Life was different in ManDiv from on the Mainland, he explained. In the breakdown after the war, during which much of the planet had been devastated, the Corporation had taken control from the government. They had separated a group of dirty, dangerous manufacturing jobs from the rest of the society; the manufactured components were sent back to the Corporation.

This new Manufacturing Division was created on the British Isles, which had been mostly destroyed during the war. ManDiv thus had the advantage of being on an island where the factories would be secure, the rest of the society was protected from the hazardous facilities, and the blue collar worker population could be controlled more strictly than on the mainland.

The Corporation built the factories and rebuilt the minimum housing facilities needed on the island, keeping the few large houses that still stood; they then moved the remaining blue collar workers and their families to the new ManDiv location.

In an economical move, they sent just the necessities needed for production; no books, no art, no history. School lessons were limited to what needed to be known to do the blue collar jobs; children had been raised in ManDiv for generations to be slotted into factory positions. They were fitted with a simple moddy chip that allowed data communication and regulated security access.

The Corporation had deemed the unpredictability of human beings as one of their most dangerous features, and found that it impacted production. They gradually upgraded the moddy chips so that they tied into the human nervous system and suppressed human emotion and desire. This made human behavior easier to regulate, and the Corporation workers attained a certain regular level of productivity.

Workers were given jobs suited to their abilities and intelligence, as determined by testing when they reached puberty, as well as housing that matched the status of their job and the size of their family. However, something began happening in the Manufacturing Division that made it much more difficult for women to conceive and carry a baby full term; radiation, pollution exposure - no one really knew.

As the birth rate dropped in ManDiv, women were required to take more and more care to promote their role as child bearers. No longer allowed to participate in the workforce, they were relegated to safeguarding their health by staying at home, trying to get pregnant, and raising the children. The Corporation again used the moddy chips to increase the control they had over people's lives. Now the chips were used to keep people happy with their lot in life, and to regulate female behavior by hormonal control to increase the chances of pregnancy.

However, the mental function of some outliers was not compatible with the use of the moddy chips. For whatever reason, whether neurological structure, or personality factors such as lack of impulse control, the person's brain either rejected commands from the moddy chip, or accepted them sporadically, or misinterpreted them.

This, of course, produced aberrant behavior that threatened the larger good, the Corporation's good. It was deemed acceptable to exile those who did not fit in, and who could not be controlled by the moddy chips.

CHAPTER SIX
Factory bottleneck

Back at Precision Castings, the workers in Production Line C were standing around, waiting for the workers at the front of the line to complete their task and pass more units up to them.

The Line C Shift Supervisor walked up the line, chatting with the waiting workers.

"How's it going?" he asked.

"Fine," said the worker leaning against his station. "No complaints."

"All right, then," said the Shift Supervisor. "If you don't get any more units out of the front end by the end of the shift, we'll just have you pick up tomorrow wherever the night guys leave off. No biggie."

"Right, boss. You got it."

The Shift Supervisor walked down to the front end of the assembly line. "Hey, what's up?"

"Same as usual, boss. The bot can only do so many of these per hour or it overheats."

The Shift Supervisor nodded. "Yup, that's what I figured. Okay, when the shift is over, just turn it off and it'll cool down. Night guys will power it back up when they get in."

"You got it, boss. Normal procedure."

"Yup."

CHAPTER SEVEN
It was all about a woman

Banks ended his story, "So the Corporation said, 'What point is there to regulating everyone but a few? We can't leave some people unregulated.' And that's what happened to my brother."

"Whoa!" said Mac, listening spellbound to the end of the story, his fingers still in the rice. "So they did to him what you said before – they just turned him out?"

He scooped up the rest of the food and then wiped his fingers on his jumpsuit without even hesitating; he was so enthralled that he didn't even notice Banks smiling at his action.

"Yeah, it sucks. Here, dump your dish in this bin and we'll keep walking. I have someone for you to meet."

As they headed out to the street again, a large man came in who wore a sleeveless tunic. One arm was completely covered with intricate tattoos, which only served to call attention to the other arm which was smooth and perfect, and had no decoration; it was an oversized mechanical arm that looked human, except for its immense size. And the metal fingers.

Mac was staring, and Banks elbowed him in the ribs to make him look away. The large man leaned in at Banks and licked his lips as he walked by; Banks simply nodded as they passed.

"Who – or what – was that, Banks?" Mac leaned in closely so as not to be overheard.

"He's a cyborg. A combination of human man and mechanical parts; something bad apparently happened to his arm, and he managed to get a replacement made. From the time I've spent with him, I'd say it's quite a bit stronger than a typical human's arm. And he's pretty ruthless."

"You KNOW him?"

"Let's just say that he will do anything, or, uh, anyone, for a price. Also that he's a person who can be hired to get a nasty job done. He generally hangs out here near the food stand."

Mac looked at Banks, who refused to meet his eye. Mac shrugged, and they continued walking down the street, dodging a vendor pushing a cart full of vegetables.

"So, Banks, how does your family know all this? I've never heard the history of ManDiv before. At least, not told like that."

"My family has been working in the Science Lab for generations. It seems that we have good analytical capabilities that are passed on. It was one of my early relatives who was put in charge of instituting the change when the Corporation instructed the Science Lab to install moddy chip units that extend farther into the brain and exert more control over the individual. And he didn't like what he saw it doing to people. So he found a way to alter the chips to get around the control, and managed to keep his children from being controlled as well. And we've passed the history down for generations, now."

"You know, this is way over my head; I don't even understand how the moddy chips do what you say they do."

"Okay, let me explain it in a way that will work with what you probably DON'T know about brains. Now, remember what I said about the moddy chips being used only for communication and security clearance, but then they changed?" He looked inquiringly at Mac, who nodded.

"The thing that made the new version possible was the development of the applicator mechanism, in Corporation labs on the mainland. It's a little device that is implanted in the back of the skull, where the moddy chips are located. You have to have reached a certain growth threshold before it's put in so that your brain is developed. You remember, we were all about the same age when we had the procedure."

Mac nodded. "Yeah, of course I remember."

"The applicator grows a bunch of probes that reach into the pre-frontal lobe, searching out the right spots to attach. Then once the child reaches puberty and all the new hormones have started shaping the brain, the moddy chip is plugged in and it sends a continuing series of electric impulses through the probes. This causes certain neurons to fire which, in turn, prevent other neurons in certain areas from firing, effectively inhibiting human initiative and the use of good judgement. It turned the ManDiv workers into compliant sheep."

"My god, Banks, I had no idea the moddy chips do all that. I thought we were just getting, I don't know, old, like our parents."

"Indeed. So you can see how horrified my relative was with the whole thing, and why we've kept our family clear of them. We have all had the applicator installed, but we've altered the chip so it doesn't connect to our brains and it simulates passing the compatibility test."

Mac slowed his walking, and turned to face Banks. "So what happened with your brother when he took the test?"

"Well, we still have to live in this stunted society. My father knew that he himself had been at the farthest edge of being accepted for a Corporation job, although his traits also made him a good scientist and qualified him for a job in the Science Division. So, he planned ahead and kept an eye on the testing for us both. And my brother was showing signs of being far outside the acceptable parameters. He had too little impulse control."

"Wow, it was lucky that he knew to look for that, Banks."

They had stopped in front of a little booth under some stairs leading to a balcony with a blue glow emanating from it. The only furniture in the booth was a table with two chairs. A woman sat at the table facing the street, her hands hovering over a large glass orb; a fat woman sat facing her, her attention on what the fortune teller was saying, while her man hovered behind her, a scowl on his face.

When the prediction was finished, the fat woman abruptly pushed the chair back and turned on the man who was looking over her shoulder, hitting him over the head and screaming, "You've been with my sister? What kind of a rat are you?"

As they tussled, the fortune teller smiled directly at Mac and, with a gesture, invited him to take the empty chair. But Banks again pulled Mac down the street and continued talking.

"Father knew that my brother's impulse control was so poor that he would never be happy in the Corporation world, even if the altered chip showed him to be moddy-compatible and the Corporation allowed him to stay. So Father learned more about the world outside, about this place, and helped my brother stash enough money and materials in the Fringe to try and make it on his own when he was exiled."

"That was good – to plan ahead. So he was all set when they turned him out."

"Yeah, well, as best as he could be."

They came to a shop in a building made of stone walls, with a tiny window covered with bars in the metal door. Banks pressed a small button, and a face appeared at the door to peer through the window. One side of his face was metal, the eye mechanical; he lit up with a smile when he saw Banks through the window and opened the door. The smile did not reach his mechanical eye.

"Banks, how good to see you!" He looked at Mac, then back at Banks with his head tilted to one side. Banks nodded in affirmation, but as to what the question was, Mac had no idea. They entered the store; Mac looked around to see the tables and shelves crammed with mechanical devices and tools.

"Mac, this is Otto. My family has worked with his family for generations. He has, shall we say, multiple lines of business and can get anything you ever thought you wanted. We can trust him as much as we can trust anyone in here."

"Please, look around," said Otto. "If anything special you need, just let me know." And he disappeared into the back room.

"So anyway, about my brother," said Banks as he walked up and down the tools and goods on display. "My father had been bringing my brother in here for a while before the test, and set him up as Otto's apprentice. Otto also has a thriving back room business in repurposed electronics. Whenever I stop in, I bring him a little something from the lab that I know he'll be able to use."

"So you come in here to see your brother? You've kept in touch?"

Banks paused. "Well. I did. After my brother was exiled, our father started teaching me and bringing me in here, too."

"Come on, where is he? Can I see your brother?"

Banks looked down at his hands. He was silent for a moment. "No, Mac. He's dead. Been dead for over ten years. He didn't last more than a couple of months in here. Most exiles don't. The ones who live to be adults in the Fringe are the ones who were born here and grew up in an environment with free will."

"Oh god, Banks. What happened to him?"

"It was all about a woman. My brother fell in love, heart and soul, with a woman whose partner took exception to the relationship, brought two guys with him, and surprised my brother in bed with the woman. My brother – remember the poor impulse control? He took all three of them on. One smashed him over the head with a chair and then the woman's partner stabbed him. My brother never stood a chance."

"Jesus, Banks. I'm sorry. But what about you, then? You tested as moddy-compatible?"

"Oh, hell no. Well, I wouldn't have, except that Otto repurposed my brother's chip for me so that it would make me pass the test. Then we switched them. Now I work with all different types of chips in the workers, and the bots, and I have a special project that I'm working on at Birnam Welding Factory.

"Mac, I'm an outlier and I have no emotional control from my moddy chip. I do what I want and when I want, simply working within the parameters of my job in the Science Lab."

They stood in silence for a while, until Mac said, "Wow. All these years I've known you and you haven't mentioned a word about your family. I only saw you at school or at play. So why are you telling me all this now?"

"See, right there - the fact that you're even asking questions is an example of why. I have no spouse, no friends except for you. My parents have both passed away. I started to realize that I don't like being alone, and I missed you, the real you; the reason I've always liked you is that you're different, too."

Mac felt a thrill run through himself at these words. Different. Different was dangerous. That's what they'd been brought up to believe, told to feel. But, wasn't it true? He was always trying to do things differently. Look at the way he had changed the procedure at his production line at Precision Castings. He himself would have been happy to work the full shift and overproduce their quota, but the other workers simply didn't understand the concept.

Mac wanted to become the top producing Shift Supervisor in the factory. Then they would have to promote him. He could have made changes in the procedures, in the whole Division, making it more efficient; but the other workers had insisted on stopping when they reached quota.

He looked at his companion. "What are you saying?"

"Mac, I've known you since we were kids, you and Lydia. I know you're different, like I said. And I couldn't figure out how someone like you could pass the test and be working in the Corporation. You just don't seem like you would have been moddy-compatible. So I did a little digging in the Science Lab records. You know the electrical storms that we have now and then? One hit during the final compatibility testing for our age group, and caused some kind of power surge during our final test. The techs recorded it, but nobody ever thought to think that there was a problem."

Mac sat, digesting this information for a moment. "Okay, so you're suggesting I never should have been approved as compatible for the Corporation?"

Banks took a deep breath. "Yes. That's exactly what I'm saying. Neither you nor Lydia. Think about it, Mac. Are you happy? Every day, doing the same thing the same way?"

"Well, no. I hate all the procedures. I guess I have a good partner in my wife, Lydia; you know we all had fun when we were growing up, but these days she – well, she's always preoccupied by the entertainment box. She used to be more fun and interesting before we were married, but not now. And she's only receptive some of the time to – you know." And the image of the fighting woman with the heaving chest appeared in his mind. He couldn't help the quickening in his loins at the image. Lydia never provoked these thoughts anymore.

"Yes, Mac, I do know what you mean. She's programmed by the moddy chip to only be sexually responsive during her ovulation time. Without that control, women in here are much more, shall we say, dynamic."

"So what are you suggesting? That I leave home, abandon Lydia and move in here to the Fringe?"

"No. I don't think you'd last in here, Mac. Just like my brother didn't. But if you want, I can have our friend Otto here alter your moddy chip."

"Alter. As in what, exactly?"

"Like mine. He can remove the ability of the Corporation to limit your human emotions and control your responses. And then you can live as your own person in the Corporation world, just as I'm doing."

"Huh. Sounds dangerous."

"Well, my father trusted him. And I've turned out all right."

Mac sat for a while, thinking. He noticed his insides starting to rumble. And wondered if that was the new food, or the enormity of the decision facing him.

CHAPTER EIGHT
What the hell, let's do this

"What the hell, Banks. Let's do this."

Banks leaned over to his companion. "Okay, you're sure, now? I don't know that it can be changed back."

Take a deep breath. I can do this. "Yes. Because I'm miserable right now. And I agree, I don't think I'd last long in here."

"What about your wife? Do you want to change Lydia?"

Mac shook his head. "No. I won't draw her into this yet. Let me see if this works first."

"All right." Banks signaled to the shop vendor in the back room, and nodded his head. Otto came out and pulled the curtain across the window in the front door, effectively screening them from prying eyes; he confirmed that the door was locked. The vendor embraced Banks and they quietly exchanged a few words. Banks shook his hand and turned to Mac.

"Mac, he can make the change right now. He says he can update the chip in place."

"What do I have to pay?"

Otto spoke up for the first time. "No charge for friend of Banks. He told me he might bring you one day. I feel bad about brother all these years. I help no charge. Sit, sit here. Takes just a minute."

Otto walked into the small room at the back of the store, returning with a small device, and connected it with a thin wire to the moddy chip at the back of Mac's head. Pressing a button, he initiated the software update to the chip. Banks watched the process with care. After a few minutes, a green light came on the device's screen and Otto disconnected the wire.

"Sit, sit here for a while. You feel okay, right? Nobody else has ever asked for this except for his family." Otto shone a light into Mac's eyes, checking his pupils.

CHAPTER NINE
Where have you been, sisters?

"Where have you been, sisters?" Standing on the balcony, the fortune teller looked over her shoulder at the other two approaching; the blue fog billowed around their feet. Her flowing dress morphed into a tightly fitted gray jumpsuit.

"Killing dogs," said the second.

"Sister, what of you?" said the third, her beard rippling long and then short as she spoke.

"Ah, a plump sailor's wife in the Fringe had a basket of apples and yet refused to share. So I sent a wind to blow her husband off course."

The second clapped her hands with glee. "I'll give you a wind!"

"And I'll send another," added the third.

"As for myself, I'll hold back the rest of the winds."

Holding hands, the three circled one way and then the other. "Thrice to thine, thrice to mine, thrice again to make up nine," they chanted together.

The third sister said, "The charm is done. He'll never get back to port. We'll teach her to refuse us."

"And look! Mac is on his way," said the first.

CHAPTER TEN
Hail to Mac

It had started to get damp, with fog rolling off the body of water in the cave. Walking along the narrow street, Banks had his collar pulled up but Mac simply strode along, taking in everything they passed with delight.

"So foul and fair a day I have not seen. I want things. I want everything, Banks."

Mac felt overwhelmed by a million new sensations. He wanted to stop and see every shop and vendor stand they passed. Where before, he had been willing to observe the Fringe with interest, now he wanted to experience it headlong. It was all Banks could do to keep him headed for the exit, to get him back towards his Corporation housing.

"What's this one, Banks?" He stopped in front of a man with a little table covered with various pieces of shaped wood.

"It's some sort of game. You fit the pieces together as fast as possible, and if you go faster than the vendor can, you win a prize. I think they're all rigged."

"It can't be that hard. I'm sure I could do that. We do similar things on the production line at Precision Castings. Let me try!"

"Never mind, friend," Banks said to the vendor and tried to push Mac along the road. "Come on! You need to get back within a reasonable time."

Mac wrenched his arm out of the Science Lab worker's grasp. "Don't tell me what to do!" he cried with immediate fury. Then, looking at his friend's shocked face, he calmed himself.

"Sorry, Banks, I'm feeling a little funny. Like I'm special. I don't know, like I could fly."

As if to demonstrate, he broke into a grin and ran across the road, leaping up the stairs onto the blue lit balcony over the empty fortune teller's booth and holding his arms up to the sky. "Ha HA!" he cried.

Three scantily clad women with veils were sitting on the balcony, and looked up at him. "Ah," said the first. "Now here's Mac. We've been waiting for you. Hail, to the Shift Supervisor above all others!" Mac turned to look at her with surprise.

The second woman rose, and draped her arms around his neck and shoulders. "Hail, to the Factory Manager of Precision Castings!" Without thinking, Mac drew her into an embrace, kissing her neck.

The third stepped behind him, wrapping her arms around his waist and running her hands down his belly. She pressed herself against his body. "Hail to Mac, the Manager of the Division." He half turned, and slipping one arm back, he cupped her buttocks and pulled her against himself. Her veil slipped aside momentarily, revealing a full beard.

Banks stepped toward the balcony to address the women. "Ladies, and I opt to call you ladies as I don't know what other term to use, are you imaginary or are you truly real? You seem to know things of the future, and you offer him such great predictions of hope that he is enthralled. But don't you have any words for me? If you can look into the seeds of time, and say what will happen, then speak to me, who neither begs nor fears your favors nor your hate."

"Hail, Banks!" said the first woman, echoed by the other two. "Lesser than Mac, and greater."

The second one leaned away from embracing Mac, and extended a languid arm in his direction. "Not so happy, yet much happier."

And the third lifted her head from where she was kissing Mac's back, looking directly into Banks' eyes. "You shall beget the Corporation leaders, though you be none. So all hail, Mac and Banks."

"All hail!" repeated the women.

Mac pulled himself away from fondling the one in his hands. "What are you, you three? I already know I am the Shift Supervisor. But what do you mean about being the Factory Manager or Division Manager? Where do you get this information?"

The three women vanished.

"What the hell?" Mac spun around, "Where did they go?"

"Vanished." Banks shook his head. "Were they ever here?"

"But you saw them too! Right?"

"Indeed. I did."

Mac rubbed his chin, and stared at his friend. "Your children will run the Corporation, Banks."

"Huh. I have no children. Yet. You will be Division Manager, Mac."

They continued walking in the direction of the exit out of the Fringe, each absorbed in his own thoughts. Mac began moving slower and slower, then rubbed his belly. "I don't feel so good, Banks." And he turned to the side of the road and vomited.

Wiping his mouth with the back of his hand, he sat on the ground and slumped back against the wall of the building. "Well. I guess that's better."

Banks chuckled. "Told you not to eat all that spicy food, Mac."

"Yeah, I guess that's it." Then his mouth dropped and he sprang up, suddenly invigorated. Both men checked the data displays on their arms. Mac gasped and then showed Banks the message:

PRECISION CASTINGS BULLETIN: REGRET TO INFORM THAT PRECISION CASTINGS PLANT MANAGER CAWDOR KILLED IN ACCIDENT. SHIFT SUPERVISOR MAC PROMOTED TO PLANT MANAGER. REPORT AT USUAL TIME.

Mac whistled low. "My god, it's coming true just as they said. I'm taking over from Factory Manager Cawdor. That means your children are going to run the Division someday!"

"And you're going to be the Division Manager, my friend," said Banks.

Mac stood stock still and shook his head as if to clear his vision.

Banks checked his own data display. "But there's worse news, Mac. Cawdor was killed by a cleaner bot."

"What? How can that be? Bots can't kill humans. They're prohibited. My message says it was an accident."

Banks grimaced. "There's an internal hobble switch in all of the bots that keeps them from taking any action that will endanger or kill a human being. I'm being called into the Science Lab but I can only imagine that this was an unfortunate accident. Anyway, let's get you home. I imagine there's some cake in your future tonight, as you have some celebrating to do about your promotion, otherwise I would stop by and fill you in on what I find out."

"Banks, I'm planning to celebrate with something more than cake."

CHAPTER ELEVEN
Lydia discovers Technicolor

Mac followed Banks out of the hidden passageway and back to the station. Banks reached up and peeled the patch off the back of his neck. Mac did the same, pocketing his own patch.

Waiting on the platform, Mac stood quietly, looking around. Every little thing caught his gaze, and Banks watched him see things for the first time.

"So, how are you feeling, Mac?" he asked, quietly.

"I think I'm getting the hang of it. I still get the data messages through the moddy chip onto my arm display, but I feel different in my body. And in my, I don't know, in my soul. I feel alive, Banks. Thanks to you." He leaned over and wrapped one arm around Banks' shoulders.

Banks stood in the embrace, stiff and unyielding. "Uh, thanks, but that's the kind of thing that people don't do in here. Remember? You're going to need to keep it together, man. Keep a low profile."

Mac pulled his arm back. "Yeah. I get it. No emotion."

"At least not in public. At home with your wife, that's a different thing."

"Oh yeah. My wife." Mac's lips tightened, and he raised his arm and keyed a message on his data screen to Lydia about the promotion. "I don't know if she's even going to care about it, Banks."

Banks grasped his shoulder tightly, just for a moment. "Of course she will. I know Lydia from the old days, remember?" Mac looked down and shook his head.

But when the next pod pulled in, Mac jumped on and twirled once around the center pole. He waved to Banks, who was waiting for one in the opposite direction to head back to the Science Department. Banks nodded, with a slight smile.

As he rode the pod to his stop, Mac rocked along with the motion of the car. His eyes started to close with the rhythmic motion, and then he was eleven years old and playing with his friends Lydia and Banks, on the street outside his apartment block. They had built carts out of scrap material they found in the dumpsters at the end of the street, and were racing along the sidewalk. Mac was almost in the lead, neck and neck with Lydia and Banks trailing behind, until they came to a narrow section. Both of the lead carts wouldn't fit through the opening in the wall.

Mac had debated about slowing down so they wouldn't both crash, but Lydia reached up and grabbed his cart and pulled hard, shoving him back and propelling herself forward in front of him through the gap. She laughed over her shoulder as she rolled off in the lead, arms raised over her head in victory.

Then he drifted into when they were thirteen, and the three of them were walking home from school. Their age group had just been tested for their moddy chip compatibility; their specific job training would begin the next week. They were sneaking into the rubble pile to read some of the old books of plays that they had found buried in there, full of stories of passion and war and love.

Lydia had tripped and grabbed his arm, and when he reached to catch her she turned and trapped him up against the wall and pressed herself against him with her arms around his neck.

Mac had stroked his arms up her sides and slipped his knee between her thighs, then reached down and pulled her body against his. She shivered, rose up on her toes and touched his lips lightly with her own, then pressed harder.

*

What Mac had not seen at the time was that Banks had stood and watched them for a moment, then turned and shuffled off down the street, his head down and his hands jammed in his pockets, leaving the two of them alone. Banks had stopped once to look back at his friend Mac, who had been too involved to notice the departure, much less the tears in his friend's eyes.

Mac's head jerked up as the pod ground to a stop at his station; he got off and walked along with the surge of bodies heading in the same direction. He passed a series of similar cement block buildings and turned in at his own entrance, differentiated only by the number on the gate. He took the elevator to the fourth floor, and walked down the hall lined with identical doors. Stopping in front of his own door, he looked back down the hallway, noticing the drab uniformity for the first time. He opened the door and entered the small rectangular space he shared with his wife.

"Lydia! I'm home!" She was not in the room, but came out of the washroom drying her hands.

"Hello." A bland smile.

Mac couldn't hide his excitement. "Lydia! I've been promoted to Factory Manager!"

"Yes, so you said in the message. It seems out of the ordinary."

"Well, apparently there was an accident of some sort, and Factory Manager Cawdor was killed. Banks said he was killed by a bot, if you can imagine."

"What? No. Bots can't kill people."

"Well, yeah, that's the strange thing. Apparently there was some kind of a weird accident." He looked down, pulling his chin. "Huh, if that can happen, I wonder what else they can be made to do."

Lydia turned to the controls of the entertainment box.

"Lydia? Aren't you – what's the word – excited about the promotion? There are so many things I want to change to improve the factory!"

"Well yes, of course, Mac. Very nice. I dialed in a special dinner to celebrate, as you requested. I added gravy to the meat."

Mac stepped up behind her, sliding his arms around her waist in the same way that the third woman had done to him in the Fringe, drawing her close.

She stepped away. "It should be ready in fifteen minutes, Mac."

"I was hoping we could have a more special celebration tonight, Lydia."

She frowned. "Should I have ordered cake?"

He tried again, leaning forward and stroking her hair. "I meant in bed, Lydia."

She looked puzzled. "But it's not the right time of the month, Mac. What would be the point of that?"

He sighed and stepped away, and sat down in front of the entertainment box. "Never mind. Cake would be nice."

Mac sat and thought for a bit, then keyed in a private message to Banks on his data display. "Please stop by on your way home. Will save you some cake."

At the knock on the door, Mac jumped up and let him in. "Hey! Glad to see you! Banks, of course you know Lydia. Lydia, you remember Banks."

Banks came in and looked around. "Lydia, it's wonderful to see you! Nice place, Mac."

"Thank you," she said. "It is nice to see you again, Banks."

Mac said, "Banks, it looks like every other module for married workers my level. We aren't going to get assigned to a larger unit until, I mean, unless we have a baby. That's one of the main things that Lydia talks about."

"Right. What was I thinking?" Banks hid his chuckle with a cough.

"Lydia," Mac said. "Why don't you keep watching your show? Banks and I are going to sit and talk for a little bit in the kitchen area."

"All right, Mac. That would be fine."

The two men moved to the other end of the room, and sat to talk in low tones.

"How are you, Mac? Is everything okay?"

"Yes, fine. But I'm a little disappointed. I feel so excited about the promotion, like I have so many changes that I want to make to improve the factory, and I'd like to share them with Lydia but she has absolutely no interest in hearing about it. She can't imagine why I would want to change anything. And I tried to get her interested in – well, let's just say those three ladies put some ideas in my head. But she's programmed to not respond. I never noticed how much it bothered me before. So, Banks, I wanted to take you up on your offer. See if you can help Lydia the way you helped me."

Banks sat and looked at him for a long moment.

"You know, I was wondering if this would make things better or worse for you. I've never found anyone that I consider compatible. That's why I'm alone, and why I have no children."

Well, one of the reasons, he thought.

"So, I borrowed the control device from Otto when we left," said Banks. "And I took a look at Lydia's test scores just now when I was back in the lab. They show some similarity to yours, Mac. At the far edge of acceptable; no wonder we were all friends when we were young. But she certainly seems much more integrated into the Corporation lifestyle now than you did. I wonder if it isn't the hormonal aspect that's involved as well."

Both turned their heads to view Lydia, sitting on the couch watching the entertainment box with her hands folded in her lap, a placid expression on her face.

Mac said, "She liked to play games and she played hard, to win. So, can't we do anything to change her back too? Like she was? I miss my Lydia, Banks."

"Let me think. We have to account for the hormonal control." And his voice trailed off as he pulled out a pocket device, similar to the data display on his arm, and did some calculations.

After a long period of consideration, during which time Lydia was completely absorbed in her show, Banks looked up. "I don't see any reason why this wouldn't work for women as well as for men. I just need to make one minor change to the override algorithm to negate the hormonal control as well. So. Do you want me to try it?"

Mac exhaled deeply. "Yes. Banks, she was so much more interested in life before we were married. I feel like this system has buried the woman I knew. I didn't realize that the young Lydia was the woman I loved, but I feel it now, Banks. I miss her. I'm starting off on a new adventure now that I've changed, and I want to do it with her."

"The question is also how she would feel about it, Mac. Is this what she would want? It's not like we can get an informed opinion from her since she's so far under."

"I've been sitting here and trying to think about that as well. I truly think she would. When we were young, she used to be more alive, more interested in the world."

Mac turned to Lydia. "Lydia, Banks needs to do some maintenance on your moddy chip."

"Yes, dear. Should I come over there?"

Banks moved his chair to sit behind her. "It's okay, Lydia. Just rest there for a few minutes." He threaded the thin wire into her moddy chip and triggered the device. After a few minutes, the green light blinked and he disconnected the wire.

"Lydia?" asked Mac. "How do you feel, honey?"

She turned and looked at them. "Well, fine of course." And frowned. "Oh, my – I feel – oh, Mac. Banks?"

Mac came around in front of her, kneeling down. "I'm right here, Lydia."

"What's going on, Mac? Did he just change something? You said I needed maintenance on the moddy chip." And she reached out and held onto his forearms.

"Let me fill you in, Lydia." Mac drew her close.

Banks stood up, tucking the device back in his pocket. He looked at them for a long moment. "I'm going to head home and leave you two to talk, Mac. I think you've got this under control. So to speak."

*

Later, Lydia and Mac cuddled under the blanket, their bare skin pressed together. "I've missed you, Lydia." He stroked her hair and nuzzled her neck. "That was fabulous."

She rolled onto her back and stretched her arms over her head. "Mac, this is just astounding. I feel like the whole world is bursting with color where it's been black and white for so long. It wasn't always like that, though, was it?"

"No, I don't think so. I know we both had our emotions regulated as we got older, and especially after we were married, but it seems like the change was bigger for you. I remember you when we were young, and you were exciting and adventurous. I think that's what drew me to you, Lydia."

She dragged her fingertips lightly down his chest, towards his belly.

"But not recently, my husband?" she asked.

"Well, it seems like you've just been lost in the entertainment box. When I came home with things to talk about, things I'd tried to improve at the factory, the most I got from you was 'that's nice, Mac,' and then you went back to watching the box."

"Well, tell me now, then. What is this promotion going to mean to us? Are you going to have to work longer hours? Or a single shift?" Her fingers continued to move, circling his navel.

"Huh, I don't know. I mean, the old Factory Manager just did things the same way every day. He punched the clock like the rest of us. Of course, he never cared about the quotas or quality control or anything, as long as it was within the range that the Corporation defined. But I know I can make it better."

"Wow. I wonder how that's going to go over, making that many changes." Her fingers were slipping even lower now, stroking back and forth across his abdomen and following the lines of muscle downward. At the look on his face, she chortled. "Come on, keep talking. You're the one who wanted to tell me things."

"Um, what? Uh, I guess I'll have to keep track of it as I go and see what the reaction is from upstairs. You know, there are some other things that are going to change for us as well. We're going to get larger living quarters."

"Yes, you're right – I hadn't even thought of that. I guess I can take care of that while you're working. What are we entitled to? Larger than just this one room?"

"I should think so, Lydia. Probably the same as if we already had several children, that's my guess."

"Wow, think what we could do with the space. Oh, Mac, this is exciting!" Forgetting the task at hand, she sat up in the bed, the covers falling from her shoulders.

"Hmm, let's worry about that a little later, Lydia. Come here." And he pulled her down on top of him as she giggled.

CHAPTER TWELVE
The new Factory Manager

The next day at Precision Castings, Mac entered through the large metal gate, punched in as usual and went to the office of the Factory Manager. His office, now. He walked in, sat down in the big chair, and put his feet up on the desk. Looked around at the wall of monitors showing various parts of the factory. *Okay,* he thought. *I can get used to this.*

His first move was to examine the data on the workings of the various production lines. He went through the quotas and production statistics. Some simple analysis told him that the allotment of bots and manpower was all wrong. There were backups in the production system; some stages of the assembly process were kept waiting for other parts to be produced. Yet it hadn't occurred to the prior Factory Manager to change the setup and use more assembly bots to relieve the bottlenecks.

Well, that would have to change. He'd have to see how to get his hands on more bots; maybe talk to Banks about what their real capability was. Between that, and using the human workers more efficiently, he estimated he could double the output of the factory.

Later that day, Mac called Lydia with the details of their new housing. They were now entitled to move into Inverness House, the residence dedicated to the Factory Manager's family. The previous Factory Manager's family was already being relocated.

"I'll get right on it!" she answered immediately. "I feel glorious! I went out for a walk, and the sky was showing a bit of blue through the haze, and I started thinking about how to pack up our stuff. I mean, I knew we'd be moving because your job entitles you to a much larger residence, and we don't have so much to move since we were in such a small place. I'm so excited! Mac, I've seen Inverness House from the street but I never paid attention to it before! I can't believe the Factory Manager's house has its own name. It's so huge! How are we even going to furnish it, Mac?"

"Take a deep breath, Lydia. Relax. I believe it comes already furnished and there's a staff to run it and do the cooking and such. Everything stays with the house. His family is being moved to a smaller place."

"Huh. A staff? Well, we'll have to see if the house suits us, Mac. We'll see."

"Lydia, the movers will be on our doorstep tomorrow morning."

"What? Tomorrow? Okay, I've got to get busy!"

In the afternoon, Mac got a message on his data display that Division Manager Duncan was coming to visit from the mainland. DM Duncan was bringing his son, Malcolm; as his Assistant District Manager, Malcolm had recently been named as the future successor for Duncan's job as Division Manager. Now that the previous Factory Manager of Precision Castings had died, they were taking a tour of the various factories in the Manufacturing Division.

Well, thought Mac, *this is an interesting stumbling block to advancement. The DM's son is now next in line for his father's job – the one I want.* He sat at his desk and steepled his fingers in front of him, lost in thought.

So. Just how did the bot kill the Factory Manager? And could it be replicated? He pulled up the data console on the desk surface and started studying the report of how the accident had happened. After a while he put the papers down.

Duncan and Malcolm will both have to go.

CHAPTER THIRTEEN
Guess who's coming to dinner

Mac gave his coat to the doorman and walked into the foyer at Inverness House, the Factory Manager's residence. *My new home,* he reminded himself. Built of stone, with ornate carved trim around the windows and doors, the mansion had a front door that opened into a large foyer with a huge curved staircase.

Crossing the foyer, he entered the Great Room, which was quite large and open with a double height ceiling. Two boxy modern sofas flanked by a pair of arm chairs stood next to the entertainment box. One section of the room was filled by a huge dining table, ringed with high backed chairs. A massive fireplace filled one wall, flanked by empty shelves. *Well, if I could locate some of those old books that we found in the rubble as kids, we could put them on those shelves.*

He sank into the sofa next to Lydia. She was leaning back against the cushions, wearing a soft dress that clung to her curves and accentuated her breasts. She handed him a glass of wine; she had apparently started without him, as the bottle was nearly empty.

It was already dusk when he had arrived home. Mac had been working long hours at the factory, and had in fact triggered the alarm bot by leaving many hours past his regularly scheduled shift. He had reprogrammed the system to allow him to come in and out at any hour, something that the previous Factory Manager had never felt the need to do.

"Well," he asked, "how has all the unpacking been going? Anything broken?" The move had actually occurred with a minimum of difficulty, and Lydia had accomplished the unpacking in a short time; of course, they didn't have much to move.

"Yes, Mac, we have all of our stuff and nothing is broken. I've moved some of the furniture around, and I found some artwork in the attic and had the staff hang it where I wanted it. And some really cool looking displays of old daggers and knives. It's all been settled for days, but you're hardly ever home. I know you're working hard so that's all right, but all I have to do now is sit around. And I have to say that I did the best I could, but I don't really care for the decor in this place."

Mac shook his head at the rush of words, and looked around. "The decor? You mean the furniture and stuff?"

"Yes. The furniture looks just like our other apartment, except more of it because we have more rooms. But it should be more grand looking, Mac. I mean, you're the Manager of the whole Precision Castings Factory, for crying out loud. People should know you're important." She snuggled up to him on the sofa.

Mac put his arm around her and kissed the top of her head. *She's adorable.* "Well, Lydia, I do want to make my mark with the Corporation. I've been studying how to make the factory run more efficiently, and I think the changes I've been making will double our production numbers. I'd like to be in line for Division Manager at some point, although it's always been someone from the mainland. I guess it's because they're not controlled like everyone else here."

"Oh Mac, yes! I can see you doing that. I'm sure your natural abilities will shine through now that you're no longer under moddy chip control. I mean, if you think about it, who else better? How do we help you do that?"

"I just found out that Division Manager Duncan will be coming in to visit. His office is on the mainland and he hasn't been here in years."

"That's a wonderful opportunity, Mac. Wait until he sees the changes that you're making. Where does he stay when he comes in?"

"Here."

"What? HERE? Are you kidding? We just moved in! I can't be ready. When does he get here?"

"Tomorrow afternoon. He's bringing two staffers and his oldest son, Malcolm, the Assistant District Manager. They'll be here overnight. And there will be a meeting of all the Factory Managers from this Division."

"Where do I put them? This is insane. I've never done this before, Mac!"

"Now we know why the house is so big, Lydia. The extra bedrooms will work fine. We can put Division Manager Duncan in the large guest room at the top of the stairs, and the two assistants can share the room with multiple beds right next door. His oldest son Malcolm goes in the room down the hall. His wife and their two younger children aren't coming; they'll be staying at home on the mainland."

"Oh, of course she'll want to stay with them. So lucky to have THREE children. That's amazing!" And she clapped her hands together and smiled dreamily for a moment.

Lydia shook her head and sighed. "Now, he hardly ever comes here? So this is our only chance to impress him? That's just not fair."

"Well, really," Mac said, "I would think that being named as successor to the Division Manager should be based upon criteria from the job. I met him years ago when he came to Precision Castings for a review. I think he's coming back just because he has to, after the death of our previous Factory Manager. But DM Duncan has named his son Malcolm as his intended successor."

Lydia raised her eyebrows. "How old is this Division Manager? When is he likely to retire?"

"Interesting that you should ask that. I had the same thought and looked it up. He's not slated to retire for another seventeen years."

Mac picked up the bottle of wine and tried to pour another glass, only to find it mostly empty. "Hold on, I'm going to go look in the wine cellar and talk to the staff about what we have on hand for tomorrow. I'll bring up another bottle for us, too."

CHAPTER FOURTEEN
Give me strength

Lydia jumped up from the sofa as soon as he left and paced around the large room.

So, my husband, you want to be Division Manager. And I can see you in the job; who else will have the capabilities that you do now?

She picked up a steak knife from the table as she paced and toyed with it in her fingers.

You have the ambition to want the job, but you want to do it the right way; I don't think you have the heart to do what it takes to get it. But really, seventeen years? I know the way to make this all happen quicker. What to do, how to convince you?

She paused, stopping in front of the massive fireplace. The flames stirred something deep within her, and she raised her arms high and cried out, "Give me the strength of a man! Let me be the one to help push this along. Take away my feminine form, and fill me with resolve from the top of my head to my toes. Come, dark night, and hide the blade of my knife."

Lydia had calmed herself by the time Mac returned with another bottle of wine; she had replaced the knife on the table and was standing quietly by the fireplace, staring into the flames. She tilted her head to look at him. "Come on, seventeen years?"

Mac chuckled and drew her back down onto the sofa with him, pouring each of them another glass of wine.

"Mac, that's a long time to wait for a chance at a promotion. If he were out of the way, I would think there is a good chance that you'd be named his successor, right?"

"Out of the way, huh?" he said. "Well, assuming they use production numbers for promotion criteria, I am going to outperform all the other factories in the Division. And I can't see why they wouldn't name me. I don't know much about how the Divisions work, but that seems to me to be the reasonable way to choose the next Division Manager."

Lydia sat up on her knees on the couch, looking down at him. "I can't help but think about how the Factory Manager was killed by the bot. Would that work?"

"Huh." He was silent for a long while, holding his glass, and finally asked, "What? Would what work? Have the Division Manager be killed by a bot? You know that was a freak accident. Bots can't kill humans."

"Mac, I know, but ever since you and Banks set me free from the moddy chip control, I've been wondering if you set that accident up on purpose."

"Lydia! What a thing to say."

They sat together in silence for a time. Mac was the first to speak.

"It couldn't be the same thing. Not bots again. People would know that something weird was going on. And the other one truly was an accident."

Lydia started, and looked at him.

"What?" he said. "I'm not suggesting we should kill him."

"Oh, you're not? I thought you were."

"Because there's no way we could get away with that," he said.

Quiet again.

"Because we'd be caught."

Lydia was still quiet. A thin crease had appeared between her eyebrows. Mac realized she was thinking furiously.

"All right," she finally said, sitting back against the sofa cushions. "I've got it. Leave it all to me."

CHAPTER FIFTEEN
The DM visits

The sleek car pulled up in front of Inverness House without a sound, bringing Division Manager Duncan and his party from his private pod car at the station. No walking for a Division Manager; his time was considered too valuable. The driver got out and opened the door. Duncan stepped out and looked around, followed by his son Malcolm. The accountant got out of the front passenger seat with a sleek briefcase under his arm.

Staff members from Inverness House met them outside and unloaded the baggage, escorting the party into the large front foyer. Lydia and Mac stood at one end of the echoing hallway, Lydia a half step behind her husband.

"Welcome, Division Manager Duncan!" Mac's voice boomed out. The party crossed the foyer and Mac and Duncan shook hands.

"Mac, it's good to see you again. Except for the circumstances, of course. I remember your avid participation the last time I was here for a ManDiv review conference, and I am thankful to have an employee such as yourself to fill the Factory Manager's shoes."

Mac inclined his head. "You are too kind, Division Manager Duncan. May I present my wife, Lydia." She curtsied briefly, and he grasped her hand for a moment without shaking it.

"My pleasure, Lydia. My oldest son, Malcolm, the Assistant District Manager." More handshakes ensued.

"Let us show you to your rooms, gentlemen, so you can get settled before dinner," said Mac.

*

Mac paced up and down the length of the foyer. His hands twisted together behind his back, and he shook his head as he walked, occasionally stopping to rub his chin and then resume his pacing. The sound of voices came from the table in the adjacent Great Room.

Mac was talking to himself. "If it were simply all done when the deed is done, then it would be good for it to be done. If his death had no consequences, then it would be a good thing for him to die."

He walked a bit more, then stopped.

"But it doesn't likely end with just one killing. Who's to say that if I were to kill Duncan to become the District Manager, there wouldn't be someone waiting in the wings to kill me for the same reason? If I poison him, wouldn't someone likely poison me?

"And he's here in double trust. First, I work for him and should owe him my respect and allegiance. And second, I am his host and as such I should be protecting him and closing the door against harm, not inciting it myself in my own home. The only thing motivating me is ambition."

Lydia opened the door from the Great Room and slipped into the foyer.

Mac stopped his pacing. "What?" he said.

"Mac, Duncan has almost finished his dinner. Why did you leave?"

"Why, did he ask for me?" Mac asked, almost eagerly.

"Of course, you know he did."

He shook his head. "Lydia, we will go no further with this business. He has honored me with this promotion. I owe him too much to take his life."

"What has happened to your hope of a bigger future? I thought you a better man when you were willing to do what you proposed. Are you afraid to actually do what you want? Or would you prefer to live the rest of your life thinking 'I should have' instead of 'I did'?"

Mac drew himself up to his full height. "Give it a rest, woman. I dare well enough to do all that is needed to be a man; look what I've done for us already. He who dares more is no man."

"Ha. What was the idea of suggesting it to me, then? When you dared to do it, then you were a man. And if you would be willing to take the chance, then again you would be more of a man. But look at you; now that we have the opportunity, you're losing your nerve."

Mac looked down and his shoulders drooped. "But Lydia, what if we should fail?"

Lydia smacked him in the arm.

"We fail? Screw your courage to the sticking point, Mac. I'll give the driver and the accountant a drug in their wine. Tonight when Duncan has gone to bed, they'll be so passed out they won't hear a thing. Take the antique dagger from the display in the hallway outside their room; after you stab him with it, all you have to do is bloody them up and everyone will blame them for his death."

"Woman, you should only have male children, because this ruthless nature of yours should never be tolerated by girls. All right, I am convinced. Let's go put on our best faces to hide the deceit that is in our hearts."

*

Later that night, after all had gone to bed, Mac sat in the home office of the new house, looking at the frowning face of Banks on the communication screen on the wall.

"How are you doing, Mac?"

"All right, I guess. And you?"

"Well, I'm sorry to call so late. But I've been having trouble sleeping. I got to sleep all right, but then I woke up dreaming of the three we saw in the Fringe. And what they predicted."

"Ah yes," said Mac. "What do you think of their predictions? Your offspring will rule the Corporation, Banks."

"Well, yes, that is an interesting thought, but since I'm unlikely to have any offspring I've been concentrating on other things."

"Oh come on, Banks, of course you will, but in order to have that prediction come true, you would need to have Duncan out of the way. Have you considered that?"

Banks sighed. "Mac, I can't picture it when I'm awake, but that is indeed what I have been dreaming about tonight. I want some kind of a family again more than anything."

"Well then. Would you support me in the action, if I were to undertake it?"

A silence as the two men regarded each other. Finally Banks spoke slowly. "No, Mac. I have no love for the Corporation, but I want to keep my reputation clear. I risk too much already, having an altered moddy chip, as well as what I've done for you out of friendship."

"I understand, my friend. So much has happened so fast. I hope you can get some sleep tonight." And Mac cut the connection.

Walking into the hall, he suddenly stopped short and stared at the space in front of himself. "What is this I see before me? I'm supposed to take the dagger from the frame on the wall. Why do I then see it here in front of me – floating in mid-air?"

He reached out a hand. "Should I take this one instead? Is it real?" He drew his hand back. "Gaah, it is already bleeding now, dripping blood. It draws me down the hall. I will follow."

*

Lydia stood at the window of the master bedroom, looking out the window at the night, swaying a bit as she stood and talked to herself. "Ha, I must have sipped a bit of the wine with the sleeping potion that put Duncan's two staffers out cold. It made them sleepy but made me bold."

The door to the master bedroom crashed open and Lydia startled around, gathering her white nightdress about herself.

Mac staggered into the room holding an ancient dagger, his hands bloody. "The deed is done. But as I passed their room, the accountant and the driver were trying to wake, talking in their sleep. One cried out, 'Mac has murdered sleep, and will sleep no more.' And I couldn't make the words come out to tell them that all would be all right. How could it ever be all right again?"

She came across the room to him. "Darling, you can't think like that or you'll go crazy. Go and wash the blood from your hands."

She looked down at what he was holding. "Oh Mac, why did you bring the dagger in here? You were supposed to leave it in the room with his assistants so everyone will think they have done the deed. Take it back, and smear them with blood."

"No. Lydia, I can't go back in there and look at what I've done." He shuddered.

"Infirm of purpose! You can't give up now. Give me the dagger." She took it from his hands and left the room.

Mac shivered. "What is it about this thing that makes me shake so much? And how do I clean this blood off my hands? I could turn the ocean red with this blood."

Lydia came back in a few minutes, holding her hands out in front of her, also covered with Duncan's blood. "I planted the dagger by the driver and the accountant, and smeared them with Duncan's blood to make it look like they did the deed. My own hands are the same color as yours, now, but I'm ashamed to have such a pale heart." They stared at each other, trembling.

They heard a knocking noise somewhere in the house. "Come on," she said. "We need to clean ourselves so nobody sees us and suspects anything. A little water clears us of the deed."

Mac shivered again. "If I must know what I've done, it would be better to not even know myself. That noise again! Wake Duncan with that knocking, whoever you are – alas, I wish you could."

CHAPTER SIXTEEN
The new District Manager

The sun was barely up when the doorman finally opened the door to Duffy's insistent knocking. "Sir?"

"Is DM Duncan awake yet? He is expecting me."

"No sir, but I can get the Factory Manager for you."

As he said this, Mac came down the stairs drying his wet hands on his robe, followed by Lydia. "Yes? Wait, you're Duffy? The Factory Manager of Birnam Welding?" *What is he doing here?* Mac wondered.

"Indeed I am. The DM asked me to stop in and join him for an early meeting. Is he not up yet?"

Mac glanced at Lydia. "No, not as far as I can tell. You think he wants you to wake him? He's in the room at the top of the stairs."

They waited in the foyer as Duffy went up, and heard a soft knocking on the door, followed shortly thereafter by a commotion and cry. Duffy came out of the room with blood on his hands. "Duncan is murdered!" he said. "Wake the house!"

Mac ran up the stairs and looked into the room, then burst through the door into the neighboring room where the driver and accountant were still lying in a drugged stupor. The people in the foyer heard him cry out in anger, and then he reappeared in the doorway with a bloody dagger, and blood splattered on his face and hands.

"I found them with the murder weapon on the floor next to one of their beds, and Duncan's blood all over them. I... I lost control and I stabbed them. I couldn't help myself. But how could they have killed the Division Manager?"

Duffy looked at him. "And the other question is, why?"

Mac paused. "The one was the accountant for the Corporation. I suspect there was some sort of anomaly or error in the Division accounting that he needed to cover up."

Duffy raised his eyebrows at this.

Duncan's son Malcolm had reached the hallway by this point. "What's happened?"

"Your father is dead, apparently killed by the accountant," replied Duffy. "But Mac has killed him in turn." And Duffy studied Malcolm for a long moment.

*

Mac stood to the side at the head of the conference table at Precision Castings as Duffy addressed the small group of Factory Managers in the Manufacturing Division.

"Gentlemen, as you know we have gone through a period of major and unusual change in the last weeks. I would like to introduce to you our newest chief, Division Manager Mac." He bowed slightly to Mac, and sat down. The small group applauded politely as Mac moved to the head of the table. He held his hands up to quiet the room.

"Thank you, Duffy. Your work as Factory Manager at Birnam Welding has been very good, and I am delighted to say that your line of bots will play an important role in my plans for the future." Duffy sat impassively.

"But first, let me reassure you all that we now have things well under control. As you know, after the unfortunate death of the Precision Castings Factory Manager, I was promoted to Factory Manager. And shortly thereafter, Division Manager Duncan was killed. His son, Malcolm, the Assistant District Manager, had been in line to take over as Division Manager, but he has gone missing. Our best information is that he has left my house, and is hiding somewhere in the Division because he paid the assistants to kill his father."

Murmurs spread around the conference table. "Who would ever imagine a bot could have caused a death?" "Or worse yet, that a man could kill another?" "His own father? That's inconceivable," they said.

Mac let the comments die down. "Now let me tell you about how we are striving to make things work better. As Duffy has mentioned, I have been appointed as the new Division Manager. And I will also remain as Factory Manager of Precision Castings."

He raised his hands at the questioning buzz that arose again. "Yes, yes, I understand that it is unusual to have one person fill both roles. But I have been looking into the details of how things are run at Precision Castings, and I am delighted to report that I have a series of changes to be introduced that will make the functioning of the factory much more efficient, and I expect that we will increase production by approximately one hundred percent. We will need fewer human workers to run each factory shift and more bots to do the bulk of the work. I will be working with Duffy, here, at Birnam Welding, to produce the additional bots that are needed to make this change happen."

Duffy regarded him with absolutely no change in his expression at this news.

Mac went on, "And then, I will be working with each of you to make the same type of changes happen in your factories. We'll be more productive and more efficient within six months."

He paused and stood, arms outspread, waiting for the accolades he expected from the factory managers at this news. But it was so quiet that he could hear his own pulse yammering in his ears. They stared at him, mouths agape, as if he had suddenly started speaking in bot language.

Duffy sat quietly, hands folded in his lap, regarding Mac with absolutely no expression on his regular features. *Huh, too regular,* thought Mac suddenly in the silence. *Who looks that perfect?*

Then all of the FMs started speaking at once among themselves, until one raised his hand to request permission to address the group. "Why would we want to make that kind of change? I have never heard of such a thing. Everything is working fine the way it is."

"I understand your concern at trying something new. But trust me, we will increase our productivity and shortly become the best Division in the entire Corporation." Mac nodded his head, encouragingly, at the next man who raised his hand.

"But – why?"

"Duffy, could you please stay for a moment after everyone is gone?" Mac spoke quietly in the Factory Manager's ear. Duffy simply nodded and sat down again. The other Factory Managers filed out of the conference room, still shaking their heads in confusion.

Yet Mac was glowing. He felt he had handled the meeting exceptionally well. Of course, he had expected there would be objections. But at least nobody was complaining to his face any more.

As the door closed behind the last of the other meeting participants, Mac turned to Duffy and sat down across from him. Duffy simply looked back impassively. *Wow,* thought Mac, *the control exerted by his moddy chip must be cranked up tight.*

"All right, I wanted to talk to you about what options we have among the bots at Birnam Welding. I need a variety of new functioning bots to accomplish the plans I've set out today; I need some that are for assembly, others for manipulating the materials before and after the processing line. I want them to have more functionality than just one task, and to be able to regulate their own functioning in case they should overheat. Okay, what do we have to start with?"

"No."

Mac stared at him. "No? No, what?"

"Your first question – you said 'All right' but no, it's not all right to discuss the bots being made at Birnam Welding."

"But – but why not?" asked Mac.

"It's against my orders."

"Against your orders? I'm the new Division Manager! I am the one who gives the orders. And I order you to tell me about the bots being produced in your factory."

Duffy stood up and walked toward the door. He stopped and turned back to face Mac. "I don't understand why you're asking again. I already told you that I won't answer your questions." And he left the conference room, closing the door quietly behind himself.

"What on earth?" muttered Mac. "Who does he think he is?"

CHAPTER SEVENTEEN
Lydia gets restless

Lydia awoke in the large bedroom and arched her back, stretching her arms and legs, then reached over to cuddle with Mac, only to find his side of the bed empty and cold. Again. She rolled over and buried her face in his pillow, inhaling his scent. *This is about as much as I get of him now – he's always up early and home late from the factory.*

She rang the bell for the house staff. When the man appeared, she suddenly wondered, *Why are they all men? The women don't have any jobs beyond having babies and dialing up the food controls.*

Lydia shook her head to clear it. "What's on the day's calendar?"

He frowned and peered closer at her. "On the calendar?"

"What's happening today? Is there anything interesting going on?"

"Interesting? Well. I think it will be pretty much like yesterday, ma'am, and like tomorrow. I mean, today there will be a food delivery to the kitchen. Is that what you mean?"

She sighed. "No. I mean, what is there to do around here that's fun or interesting? Do we have any games we can play or anything? I remember when I was a kid I used to play a lot."

The staffer took a step backward and regarded her with raised eyebrows. "Games? Like little children play? You don't have any children yet. But don't worry about it. My wife didn't get pregnant for many years, but she was finally lucky."

Lydia sighed. "Never mind. Don't worry about it. Could you please bring up a cup of tea for me? And breakfast. Eggs and toast would be good, please."

"The bedroom? Food to the bedroom?" asked the staffer, his forehead furrowed.

"Yes, to the bedroom," she said. "Where else would I mean, to the roof?"

He inclined his head. "Of course, ma'am," he said. "I just didn't understand, since we have the large table downstairs that is intended for eating."

"Bah, I ate at the dining table in the apartment for years! Now I want to try something different. My mother used to bring me my breakfast in bed when I was sick. So it just seemed like a thing I'd like to try now that I'm no longer under – well. Now that we live here."

"Are you ill, ma'am?"

"No, I'm not ill," she snapped. "Just do it. Please." And she rolled over in the bed and pulled the covers over her head. After a minute, she peeked out to be sure he was gone, then flipped the covers back and got up; sliding her feet into her slippers, she strolled across the room to use the bathroom.

Lydia turned on the hot water in the shower to come out as forcefully as possible; as the steam started to rise, she stepped in and gasped as the force of the water hit her. After leaning against the wall while the invigorating water woke her up, she washed her hair and then started soaping herself all over. Her fingers started circling across her breasts and belly, then moved lower. *Well,* she thought, *this is about the only way to tell I'm alive anymore.*

When she eventually emerged from the bathroom, the tray with her breakfast was sitting on the little table by the window. She opened the drapes to look out at the dismal rows of cement block buildings surrounding the Factory Manager's larger house, and shook her head.

Seating herself, she poured the tea. *Cold.* Her lips narrowed, and she slumped in the chair, then forced herself to eat the lukewarm eggs and soggy toast. *Why didn't it occur to them to find a way to keep it warm? Would that have been too much to ask?*

CHAPTER EIGHTEEN
Thank you for stopping by

Duffy keyed in a reply message on the data display on his arm. "I will be right down."

Walking unhurriedly through the lobby of Birnam Welding, he saw Mac standing outside the main gate; it remained closed. Mac's brow was furrowed and his jaw was clenched. He stood with his hands jammed in the pockets of his gray jumpsuit, which now had the gold DM patch on the shoulder, and those same shoulders were bunched up around his neck. The two guards stood inside the closed gate, faces impassive, looking at the distance – at anything except the Division Manager to whom they had denied entrance.

Mac was glaring at the unremarkable gray cement facade of the factory, with nothing on the exterior except a huge metal sign the size of a train pod that proclaimed "Birnam Welding". No indication was given about what work was actually done inside.

"Division Manager Mac. To what do I owe this wonderful surprise?" Duffy looked at Mac through the metal gate with a polite smile.

"Open the damn gate, Duffy. I'm the Division Manager, for crying out loud. I'm here to tour the facilities."

"Yes, I just acknowledged your title, Mac."

"Well then, let me in."

"I am sorry, Mac, we have our safety protocols to consider. No unnecessary personnel are allowed in. It's part of our factory code."

"I'm the Division Manager! You can't call me unnecessary. I need to see how your factory is working, and how your product lines are doing."

"I'm sorry, Mac, but I am sure you can find all the information you need in our regular Corporation reports. We are always quite detailed in completing the reports. But thank you for stopping by. Good day."

And Duffy turned on his heel and reentered the factory without looking back.

CHAPTER NINETEEN
The new bots

"Banks, thank you for coming in. As you can see, I'm using Precision Castings as my base of operations for the Division as well. Seems more convenient, since I have both jobs now."

"Sure thing, Mac. I needed to make a service call on the moddy chips of a few workers in the factory anyway." *And oh, how good to see you, too, my friend.* Banks sat down in the chair across from Mac's desk. "What's up?"

Mac explained his plan of using more bots to improve the efficiency of the production lines, including the idea of finding new types of bots for new jobs. Banks gave a long, low whistle. "Good god, Mac. That's a huge change. Remember what we said about keeping a low profile now that your moddy chip has been changed?"

"Yes, but I'm the Division Manager. Nobody is going to question that now."

"What kind of reaction did you get from the others?" Banks leaned back in his chair, stroking his chin.

"Well, at first there was a lot of confusion, but I have them all on board now." Mac leaned back in his big chair, his fingers laced behind his head. He was smiling.

"Do you, now," Banks said quietly.

"Anyway, here's what I wanted to ask you about, Banks. I know you go into all the factories as part of your job handling chips with the Science Lab." Banks nodded. Mac leaned forward again.

"I need to know more about what they're building in Birnam Welding; you mentioned that you're working on a project there. Duffy shut me down when I tried to talk to him, and today he told me I don't have the right authority to tour the factory. I'm the DM, for god's sake."

"What kind of information are you looking for, Mac?" Banks asked carefully.

"I want to know what they're building in there! And whether I can use any of the bots that are currently under production for the changes I have in mind for the other factory's production lines. I want to start here with Precision Castings because I have the best idea what is needed. Then I'll spread the changes to the other factories in the Division, one at a time." His eyes seemed to radiate his inner excitement as he spoke.

"Well." Banks cleared his throat. "The best I can tell you is that they have a new line of bots at Birnam Welding, Mac. You know how most bots have a rectangular body on wheels, with a designated type of arm that performs one function? Well, the ones at Birnam are different."

"Different how?" asked Mac.

"I guess there are three basic changes. One is that they aren't rectangular any more. Second is the type of locomotion they use."

"Wait, what do you mean, not rectangular? What are they like?"

"Humanoid, Mac. They look like people. And they walk, not just roll around like a garbage bin, or sit on the assembly line."

Mac sat and stared at his friend for a beat. "Walking bots? Humanoid? That's astounding. Wait, you said three changes. I'm almost afraid to ask what the third change is."

"It's the chip that's in them, Mac. It's a lot more complicated, like the moddy chips that are in people, not the basic electronic chips that are in the other bots."

"What does that mean, Banks?"

"Well, for one thing, they can handle much more complicated tasks. The chip is programmable so that they can be given new instructions or new directions on the fly either verbally or by simply typing in console commands to update the programming, rather than pulling the chip and changing it."

"But what about the hobble? The thing that keeps them from killing people? They still have that, right?"

Banks paused. *I want to tell you everything but I can't.*

Then he shrugged and said a little too loudly, "Oh yeah, Mac, no worries. It's just going to be implemented differently since these are much more complicated machines. The hobble will be part of the bots' programming just like you're used to, only controlled by the program rather than hard-wired. You've read the data on the accident with your predecessor at Precision Castings by now, I assume?"

"Uh yeah, first day on the new job. I had been wondering if that could happen. Well, let's say I was worried there might be something wrong."

"Well then, good, you know that the cleaner bot that accidentally killed him sent an emergency signal, turned itself off, and the other bots around it were compelled to disassemble it. That works because the bots up until now have had simple tasks. But these new humanoid shaped ones will be capable of much more complicated processing, and will need a much more sophisticated method of making decisions. It's been going very well in the beta testing."

Banks winced. *I said too much.*

"Banks, they're up to beta testing already? So there are some fully functioning models of these new bots? That's an astounding change."

Banks looked down at the desk again. *Mac, you have no idea. And no matter how much I care about you, I can't and won't tell you everything. Like the fact that the idea of a hobble is just to make people feel better. And that these new versions have no hobble.*

Mac spoke again. "There's been some major new thinking going into these things. Who on earth could have been so creative these days?"

Banks looked down; his ears turned a bit pink. "Well, I might have mentioned a few ideas I had on the subject, but frankly, I'm as surprised as you that anyone actually took me up on something new. The Corporation is not known for supporting innovation."

"Those sound like exactly what I need to implement my improved productivity plan. I'm just going to have to figure out how to get more information out of that Duffy."

Mac leaned forward to speak in a low tone. "Can you set something up so that I can override the commands for the humanoid robots? In case I need to use the new humanoid bots in my factory, but Duffy blocks me?"

There was a long silence as Banks thought about this request. "Why is that a good thing for me to do, Mac?" he asked quietly.

"Because I have the best interests of the Corporation at heart, Banks. This is the smartest way to organize the factories, and you know it. Duffy is just being the most typical non-emotional man I've ever seen. And we're old friends, right? Two of a kind?"

Banks nodded, reluctantly. *I have a hard time resisting anything that Mac wants, but this doesn't seem unreasonable. It may even be useful in general once it's tested.* "Okay," he sighed. "I can add in an additional wireless communications adaptor with an override code; it should be just a programming change to enable it. I'll do this one more thing for you, Mac."

CHAPTER TWENTY
The seven worst words in our language

"See here, Mister Factory Manager, I need to tell you that this is not going to work out. The men on the line do not understand the point of all these changes. And frankly, neither do I."

The Shift Supervisor for Assembly Line C at Precision Castings was in Mac's office the next morning. He was looking around as he spoke, his posture giving the clear impression that he had never had any reason to be in the office when the previous Factory Manager was in charge.

"Tell me what you mean," said Mac. "What seems to be the problem?" He thought to himself, *He is certainly bold for someone who is controlled. He must have been at the edge of compatibility testing. No wonder they made him a supervisor.*

"Well, for one thing, you're telling them that they need to work their full shift, even if they reach quota. They don't see why they should stay any longer than they need to. That's what quota is supposed to mean; you reach that, you stop."

"But they never reached quota anyway before I made these changes."

"Right! That's the other thing! They don't understand why you wanted to move the different bots around just so that the other lines don't have to wait for the parts. They are working all the time now. It's just, it's just wrong. That's not how we do it here."

Mac leaned forward in his chair. "Tell me, Shift Supervisor, do you know the seven worst words in our language?"

The man standing in front of the desk just stood there with his mouth slightly agape.

"I'll tell you, then. The seven worst words in our language are: 'But we've always done it this way.'" And Mac sat back, confident that he had made his point.

The Shift Supervisor simply shrugged. "I don't even know what that means. But I'm telling you, the men don't like these changes. They're complaining. And I've never heard them complain before. It's just, it's just not right, these things you're trying to get them to do."

CHAPTER TWENTY-ONE
The large man smiles

Mac was on his way through the Fringe, back to the food vendor where he and Banks had eaten on their first trip together. When he reached the stand, he stopped and gave a nod to the vendor. Mac showed him something in his pocket, then followed him into the alcove behind the food stand, where he had a meeting with the large man with tattoos on one arm, and a mechanical arm on the other side.

The large man gestured to the pier at the end of the street; yes, there was a boat available. Yes, it could get to the mainland and back.

Mac passed some things to the large man: two sets of pictures, a simulated moddy chip that would allow him to enter Corporation buildings on both ManDiv and the mainland, and some electronic equipment as payment.

The large man passed a communication device to Mac, one that was not tied to the Corporation network. Mac was on his way back to ManDiv within a few minutes.

On his way back, he thought about the new type of humanoid bots being built at Birnam Welding; in particular about the new type of chip that they used because they would have higher, more complicated functions. Banks had said that they could be reprogrammed on the fly, and Mac thought that it might be a good thing to have access to such an army.

*

Duncan's son, Malcolm, walked down the street in the west section of the Division. People were out and walking about, heading home from work or doing errands on a warm day. He had his jumpsuit collar pulled up, and was wearing a hat, despite the balmy weather.

He entered his hotel building and pushed the button for the elevator, not noticing a large man who got up from the lobby and entered the elevator behind him. The large man was also overdressed for the weather; he was wearing a heavy long-sleeved jacket that covered his arms. Like Malcolm, he had his collar pulled up.

Malcolm got off the elevator at his floor. Just as the doors were about to close, the large man got off as well and shadowed Malcolm down the hall. Malcolm stopped and looked around when he reached his door, and the large man kept walking past without stopping.

Going inside, Malcolm walked to the communication box in his room and dialed his mother's number on the mainland again. He hadn't been able to reach her all day, and he couldn't imagine what would keep her so busy for so long.

Finally, he triggered the override switch that was available to men so that they could check the activity of their families when they were away from them. The communication box lit up with a view of the large living room of the District Manager on the mainland. But what he saw caused him to drop the controls for the box, a cry rising from his throat.

The camera showed his mother draped across the back of the sofa, her throat slit. Blood had run everywhere and the pools had turned dark. And the thing that stopped him cold was the image of his two young siblings, their bodies crumpled into a heap as if they had simply been tossed aside.

The soft knocking at the door roused him from his shock. "Help," he cried, "I need to get help for them!" and he stumbled to the door and twisted the handle. But when it pushed open, the large man grabbed Malcolm by the face, covering his mouth to stifle any sound, and pushed him inside. The blade snicked out of his mechanical arm, and the large man began to grin.

CHAPTER TWENTY-TWO
A deed of dreadful note

Banks stood waiting in Mac's office at Precision Castings late that afternoon, in front of the large window overlooking the city complex from atop Dunsinane Hill. His red hair was echoed by the deepening sunset outside. Despite the view, his head was down, his eyes unseeing.

So, Mac, all the predictions have come through for you, he thought. *Shift Supervisor, Factory Manager, and now Division Manager, but how much of this did you actually arrange yourself? Yet it was said by the three weird sisters that your control would not last into the next generation, rather that my offspring would run the Corporation. Hah, perhaps someday I will go against my own nature, marry, and have children after all. And if so, then my family will not stop with me. Perhaps I need to consider that, because I've risked so much for your company, yet I'm still so alone.*

Mac came into the office, interrupting his reverie. "Ah, my friend, thank you for coming in! How did you make out with all your changes at Birnam Welding?"

"The change is made," replied Banks. He held out a slip of paper. "Here, this override code will enable you to enter commands for the new bots using your data screen. Any change you make will affect them all. But it's important to know that I have not yet tested these changes; the bots were in a dormant cycle and it would have called too much attention to the updates if I had cycled them on to test. That needs to be done before we try to use this, as I want to be sure the changes don't affect other processing."

"It's not a problem," said Mac. "I'm well aware of your skill in this kind of thing. I have no doubt that it will work. And I am, again, in your debt, my friend. So please, let me repay you in part by having you be my guest at the banquet tonight. The other Factory Managers are coming, and I would like for you to be there as well, as a representative of the Science Lab, and my oldest friend. It's a celebration of my new position and the new order of business."

"All right, Mac, thank you. I'll be there. I would really like to see more of you. And Lydia, of course. That's what I've been missing for so long, since my parents and my brother died; connection with regular people."

Mac embraced him and walked him to the door. "Are you off for more work now?"

"Yes, I have another technical issue to solve at the next factory. But I'll be there tonight." Banks nodded his head and left the office.

*

Mac took Banks's place before the window, but instead of looking down he looked out at all that he now controlled. The day was ending, and he studied the shadows in the growing gloom.

To be thus is nothing; but to be safely thus. I have concerns about Banks; he has a royalty of nature, and a wisdom that guides his actions. Is that from living his life without moddy control? He's the only one I actually fear. When we met with the three weird sisters, he was the one who commanded them to speak, and they promised him that he would be father to a line of offspring who rule the Corporation. As for me, they named me in charge but gave me an empty legacy, no son of mine to take my place.

So anything I accomplish dies with me; it seems that all that I have done, the killing of Duncan and his family, his children, is only for the benefit of the children of Banks. For them I have made myself guilty; but let's see what can be done about this. I must think of the future and not be tied to the past, no matter how long I've known him.

He made a final firm nod of his head. And placed a private call on his unregistered communication device to a certain large man with special skills.

*

Lydia sat in her dressing room at Inverness House, brushing her hair as she got ready for the banquet. *Is this all there is?* she wondered to herself. *I have a larger house, yet I don't feel comfortable in it. We've gained nothing, to still not have happiness. It would be safer to be that which we destroy, than to have destroyed it and still live in doubtful joy.*

Mac came into the dressing room, startling her out of her reverie as he slipped up behind her and kissed her neck. She turned and looked at him, her face falling as she saw the preoccupied look in his eyes.

"How now, my handsome Mac? Why on earth are you thinking sad thoughts? Don't worry about what you can't undo. What's done is done."

"Yes, Lydia, but we're still at risk of the whole thing coming to light. Duncan is dead; treason can't hurt him any longer, yet we're still here and at risk of being discovered."

Lydia pouted and stroked his cheek. "Come on, my darling, cheer up. Be happy and lively with the guests tonight. It's important for them to trust and like you."

"Oh, I shall. And I even invited Banks to come tonight to represent the Science Lab, as thanks for getting us free of the moddy chip controls."

He paused. "Yet, after I saw him today, all I could think of was that his children will lead the Corporation and not ours."

"Now Mac, remember this – he has no children, and he has to die on his own sometime."

"Ah, but tonight there will be a deed of dreadful note. There's no need to set a place for Banks as he won't be coming."

Lydia pulled back from his embrace. "Why, what's to be done?"

Mac tightened his arms around her. "Ah, be innocent of the knowledge, my dear, until you can applaud the results. But don't worry. Things badly begun will make themselves stronger by bad thoughts. Come, it's getting darker and darker; why don't you come down to the Great Room with me?"

*

Banks boarded the pod to get to the next factory visit. The pod car was nearly empty since it was between shift changes. Normally, he would have liked that, but something was bothering him and he couldn't put his finger on it. He glanced around the pod but nothing seemed wrong; shrugging his shoulders, he leaned back against the wall.

Leaving the pod at the next stop, he walked briskly down the platform towards the factory entrance. But as he passed the opening to a narrow alcove, a tattooed arm reached out of the darkness and barred his progress; the other arm grabbed him by the throat, blocking his windpipe and his ability to speak.

His eyes grew wide as he recognized the large man with the mechanical arm, the one he had known so well. Banks tried to talk, to reason with him; but the large man just licked his lips, gave him a shake, and smiled when he heard the cracking sound of a snapped neck. The man waited in the alcove, cradling Banks' limp body in his arms, until the next automated pod rumbled towards the station.

The cyborg tossed the body under the wheels, making it look as if Banks had slipped onto the tracks and been struck by the vehicle. And the large man headed back to the Fringe, whistling as he walked.

CHAPTER TWENTY-THREE
My husband is often like this, and has been since his youth

Mac and Lydia waited in the Great Room as the guests started to arrive. He was wearing a formal suit, and Lydia had on a flowing dress that accentuated her curves.

"Come in, come in!" Every time the doorman opened the door to a new guest, Mac beckoned him in and pressed a glass of wine into his hand. *I'm excited,* he thought. *Either for the evening at hand, or for knowing the deed that is being done.*

When the room was almost full, Mac suggested that they all sit at the table. "Don't stand on formality – take any place you want. My wife Lydia will take the hostess seat at one end of the table, but I'll sit amongst the rest of you, since we're all Factory Managers together."

He rubbed his hands together in anticipation of building some camaraderie among the other Managers. A few paused at the sight of Lydia at a business celebration.

As they started seating themselves, Mac felt a buzzing on the unregistered communication device. He stepped into the back hall and brought up the image. "There's blood on your face!"

"It would belong to Banks, then," replied the large man.

"Well, better on you than inside of him. Is it done?"

"I left him torn and bloody under the wheels at the pod station, with twenty gashes, any one of which would have been enough to kill him. He'll not be moving again."

"Thank you for your efforts. I'll bring a special gift for you tomorrow." And he signed off the call, then after a moment put his arm across his eyes and leaned against the wall. His shoulders shook. In a moment, Lydia came through the door, looking for him.

"Mac!" she hissed. "You're ignoring your guests! Get back in here, and make them feel welcome or else they'll think it's not a celebration."

"Coming, my love," answered Mac, and wiping his eyes, he followed her towards the Great Room.

In his absence, the Factory Managers were talking among themselves, having a general discussion of their factory business as they started to sit down at the table. Two of the FMs were standing aside from the rest.

"Have you heard the news?" The first leaned in close to the other so as not to be heard.

"News? What news? I haven't checked my data display," said the second. The waiter appeared and gestured to them to join the others at the table.

"District Manager Duncan's family were all killed in their home," said the first.

"What? Well, yes, I read that Malcolm was found dead. I thought that he would announce that tonight."

"No, no. Not just Malcolm. Duncan's wife, too. And his two younger children."

A pause, as they moved to sit down and the second one absorbed this information. "His little children – somebody killed them? Somebody killed children? But who, and why?"

They both turned to look as Mac reentered the Great Room, with Lydia by his side. She sat at the end of the table.

"My friends and colleagues!" said Mac.

One of the other Factory Managers asked, "Won't you come and sit?" The table was full except for Mac's seat.

"Ah," said Mac, holding his arms out. "The evening would be complete if only we had Banks here with us too! He was invited to represent the Science Lab, but I... I didn't see him arrive."

At that moment, a bloody image of Banks walked in from behind Mac and sat down at the table, in Mac's seat. His red hair clashed with the splashes of blood on his face.

"Yes," said Lydia, "I wish he were here too. But come and join us at the table, dear. Sit down."

"Sit down?" asked Mac, looking at the full group. "The table's full!"

"Here, Mac, here's a seat saved for you," said one of the Factory Managers, gesturing to the seat with the bloody image.

"Where?"

"Here, sir. What is it that's upsetting you?"

Mac paled and clutched his hands together. "Which of you has done this?" he cried.

"What?"

"Excuse me?"

Mac pointed at his chair and spoke to the figure he saw there. "You can't say I did it; don't shake your gory head at me!"

"Gentlemen, rise – the Division Manager is not well," said one of the bosses.

Lydia said, "Gentlemen, don't be concerned – my husband is often like this, and has been since his youth. He – he is short of sleep. Here, don't worry about it! Keep your seats – if you don't pay attention to him, it will pass. Please, sit!"

And she stood and drew Mac aside, and hissed at him, "What is wrong with you? Are you a man?"

"Yes, and a brave one who dares to look upon that frightful sight."

He gestured at the table.

"Mac, this is a fantasy again, like the dagger you told me you saw in mid-air that led you to Duncan. What are you afraid of? You're only looking at a chair."

"But look! See what he is doing!" The ghost stood up, stared at Mac, and nodded his head; then he walked to the back of the room.

"Ha! If you can nod, why not speak to us as well?" said Mac, watching him go past.

The ghost disappeared. People at the table stared at Mac.

Lydia gripped his hand, pulling his head down to her level, and spoke into his ear again. "Mac! You're not acting like a man."

"No, Lydia, I saw him as plain as I am standing here. The time used to be that when a man's brains were dashed out, the man would die, and there an end; but now they rise again, with twenty mortal murders on their brow, and push us from our chair! This is more strange than such a murder."

"My husband, your people need your company."

Mac shook himself, then turned and opened his arms, speaking to the group, "Ah, my friends, don't worry about me! I have a strange infirmity, which is nothing to those that know me. Come, let's have a toast, and then I'll sit down. Let's drink to the whole table, and to my friend Banks, whom I wish was here with us."

The Factory Managers looked at each other; some were frowning, and others shrugged. They raised their glasses and drank to the toast.

The ghost re-entered the room.

Mac paled at the sight. His voice started to rise as he spoke. "Get away! And don't let me see you again! Your blood is cold. There is no intelligence in your eyes."

Lydia frowned and said, "Ah, friends. Just think of this as a strange custom – although it spoils the nature of the evening."

"Ha!" cried Mac, throwing his arms open and then pointing at the image. "I'm not afraid of you. What any man dares to do, I will do! I will fight the strongest beast, or race the fastest car, and if I fail then you can call me a trembling girl. Go away, you horrible shadow!"

The image of Banks disappeared.

"Aha!" said Mac, rubbing his hands together again. He twisted his neck and squared his shoulders. "Now that it is gone, I am a man again. Please, everyone, sit still." The managers were muttering among themselves and leaning away from him.

"Well, Mac, you've certainly ruined the party," complained Lydia. His shoulders sagged.

"I can't believe that all of you could look on that and not be afraid," said Mac, as he took his seat. He sat and stared at his hands, muttering, and his shoulders sagged again. "And I thought I was a man."

"Look on what?" asked one of the managers.

Lydia gestured to them. "Please, gentlemen, he grows worse and worse. I think we need to leave him to rest. I'm sorry to cancel the evening, but please go at once."

"Good night," said one of the managers. "I hope you're feeling better."

As they all left the Great Room, the first FM was talking to the second. "I have never seen such a crazy thing. Why would anyone get so excited? I'm telling you, there's something wrong with him."

Hours later, in the now empty Great Room, Mac stood and walked over to stare down at the fire. "It will have blood, they say; blood will have blood. What time is it?"

Lydia came up close to him and wrapped her arms around his neck. "Near morning light, my dear husband. The darkness is almost gone." They rocked together for a moment, and Mac leaned his cheek against her hair, then lifted it.

"Do you know what else bothers me, Lydia? Duffy didn't come to the banquet."

"Did you invite him?"

"Indeed I did, and he sent word that he couldn't attend. I'll check on the gossip tomorrow. And I'm also going to go see the weird sisters again as soon as I can. They have more to tell me, I am sure. After this, I am determined to know what else is coming – for my own benefit, I can't have any scruples about where I get help anymore. I have stepped so far deep in blood, that it is just as close to continue to the other side than to try and go back. I have strange things in mind that must be done before I think about them too much."

"Dearest, you just need some sleep."

"All right, Lydia, let's head to sleep. Perhaps my strange vision just comes from being new to all of this."

*

Over their heads that night, thunder rolled through the sky. Two of the three weird sisters stood together on the roof of Inverness House, looking at the moon. Hearing a sound behind them, they startled and turned to see the first sister standing on a roof ridge above them.

"How now, sister, why do you look so angry?" asked the second.

She drew herself up to her full height. "Don't I have reason to be angry? How did we dare go so far as to meddle and play with Mac in riddles and affairs of death? And what is worse is that all our work has only been for one wayward son, who follows us not; who, as others do, loves for his own ends and not for us.

"But we can still redeem ourselves. Let us meet with Mac in the morning and bring our magic to show him his destiny. Our illusion shall draw him on to his confusion. He shall spurn fate, scorn death, and bear his hopes above wisdom, grace and fear. Because, as we all know, a sense of security is a mortal's main enemy."

The three held hands as the first sister hustled them away. "Let's make haste and get ready! Soon Mac will come to see us."

CHAPTER TWENTY-FOUR
Rub a little salt

Lydia paced the large master bedroom. She was dressed, and trying to think of something to do. Going down to the Great Room, she sat on the sofa and dialed up the entertainment box, flipping through the shows she used to watch before her moddy chip was changed, while Mac was at the factory all day long. *I didn't miss him as much then.*

'Maximize your chances of getting pregnant.'

'How to care for young infants.'

'How to toilet train your toddler.'

Well. That's all well and good if you're doing nothing but having babies.

A large part of her still longed for a baby of her own, but like so many women these days she had not been able to get pregnant yet.

Enough of this. She pressed the button to call the doorman. "I'll be going out this morning, and I'll need the driver to drive me in the car."

The doorman looked at her like she had two heads, then answered her. "Yes, ma'am. Going out? Where are you going?"

Lydia looked around a bit wildly. "Where am I going? Out! Out of here! I'm going..." Her glance fell on the data screen. "I'm going to visit some friends. I'll have the address for the driver."

"Very good, ma'am." The doorman arched his eyebrows, then nodded and left the room.

Lydia flopped back on the sofa. Where were some of her old friends, from when she was a young girl? The ones who used to do fun things with her? She had lost touch with most of them when she and Mac were married; she hadn't felt it was important to see her childhood friends in years.

Turning to the data screen on the wall, she dialed up a list of residents in the block where she had grown up, and tried to puzzle out where they were now.

Armed with an address on a slip of paper, Lydia got in the car and passed the paper to the driver. Riding in the back as they drove through the residential quadrant, she watched the identical looking cement block buildings pass by the window. They pulled up at the address, and Lydia got out and told the driver to wait.

Lydia's best friend Patty had married Randal, a boy with whom they had both grown up. All of the cement block buildings looked the same; checking the list of names by the front door, Lydia confirmed that she was indeed in the correct block of buildings and that they lived in apartment 2C.

Walking down the hallway filled with doors that were exactly alike except for the number, she stopped and knocked at the one with "2C" stenciled on it in fading white paint. A woman about her age with blonde hair in a scraggly ponytail, wearing a utilitarian blue dress, opened the door. "Yes?"

"Patty?" asked Lydia. "Hi! Um, it's Lydia. From when we were little? Lydia?"

Patty looked at her. "Hello, Lydia. You look older."

"Well, yes, I guess we both do. I haven't seen you in years, and I thought – well – Patty, can I come in?"

Patty shrugged and moved aside. Lydia came in and they stood awkwardly in the small room.

Lydia said, "How are you, Patty? What's new?"

Patty appeared to ponder how to answer this. "I am well, Lydia. I haven't been sick, if that's what you mean. And we buy new clothes when our daughter outgrows something."

"I just meant that I was wondering what you had been up to recently, not if you had purchased anything new."

A pause. "Oh. Really, nothing much changes around here. And how are you, Lydia? What's, uh, 'new'?" Lydia suppressed a smile at seeing her old friend try on some words she didn't seem to use very often.

"Well, we've moved, for one thing. My husband Mac is now the Division Manager, so we moved to the big house, Inverness House."

"Yes, my husband told me that. Won't you sit down?"

They sat on the sofa, with Patty moving some toys to make room.

"So, you have a child?" asked Lydia.

"Yes, her name is Nora. She's seven and she's very clever," said Patty. *Well, that's the first hint of warmth or interest that she has shown thus far,* thought Lydia.

"My goodness, that old! Well, congratulations!"

"Thank you. Do you have a child, Lydia?"

"No." Lydia looked down. "No, we haven't gotten pregnant yet. It's what I've wanted for years; but, well, we keep hoping, of course."

"Oh, I hope you do soon, Lydia," Patty said. "She's what I live for."

Lydia nodded uncomfortably.

Patty said, "Lydia, I heard something yesterday that I didn't understand. Can you help me? Someone at the food store said that the Division Manager was dead. That he and his family had been killed. I don't understand. Your husband isn't dead, and you said you don't have any children."

Lydia froze for a moment. "Uh, yes, that's right, Patty. But that was the previous Division Manager, not my husband. Apparently they were all killed."

"But they said he had three children."

"Ye-e-es, one older son and two small children."

"Three. I can't get over having three children, Lydia. And all dead? How could that be?"

"It's… it's very sad, isn't it, Patty? I haven't even had any children yet, and I can't imagine what it would be like to lose one, let alone three." *And I'm trying hard not to imagine it.*

"I don't know what I would do with myself if my child died, Lydia. I can barely remember what life was like before she was here."

"That's actually one of the things I wanted to see you about, Patty. Remember how we used to go out and play and do fun things? I miss that, I guess."

"Fun things? What kind of fun things did we do?"

Lydia leaned forward and touched her friend's arm. "We used to build forts in the piles of construction rubble, and make carts and race them, and see who could climb higher on the Wall at the edge of the Division. Don't you remember? You and I used to try and beat all the boys! I beat Mac in one race!" She threw her arms up in the air as she had when she passed him during the race.

Patty frowned. "We did? I guess so, Lydia, but those were all childish things. Why are you thinking about that now? You're an adult."

"But I miss all the fun stuff, Patty. Wouldn't it be fun if we got Randal and some of the old gang back together to go out and do a cart race or something?"

Patty's frown deepened, and she continued to sit still. "What? Why would we do that?"

Lydia sighed and slumped back in the sofa. "Never mind. I just thought maybe… "

"Do you want to see Nora? It's not a school day. She's in her bedroom."

"Sure," said Lydia. *Why not rub a little salt on the empty womb of the childless woman?*

CHAPTER TWENTY-FIVE
Even electric sheep can gossip

In the management break room at Precision Castings, the Shift Supervisors sat together at the lunch table. One of them, the most vocal of all, described to the others how he had gone in to complain to Mac about the changes.

"And so I told him that Assembly Line C was not going to put up with any of this nonsense that he's trying to propose!"

"But why does it matter?" asked the one in charge of Line F. "We just do what we're told. As long as I get paid, and have a place to live, and food, and an entertainment box, I'm fine."

"Well, there are other things I've heard," said the Line C supervisor, lowering his voice so that the others had to lean in to hear his words.

"You all know that Mac got his job after Division Manager Duncan was killed, right? At Mac's house?" Nods came from around the table. One asked, "I still don't understand. Why would a person want to kill somebody else?"

"People have been saying that Mac had something to do with that." He watched the variety of expressions on the group's faces. When it looked like they were starting to understand that this was a bad thing, he dropped his bombshell.

"But Duncan had a son named Malcolm, who was next in line to be Division Manager, as you know." He waited for confirming nods around the table. "And there used to be two more small children as well."

"Three children? That's amazing!"

"I don't even have one!"

One Shift Supervisor had been listening quietly. "Wait, what do you mean there used to be more children?"

The Line C Supervisor held up a hand at the ensuing hubbub, then pointed at the one who asked the question. "You hit the nail on the head! Gentlemen, I've just heard that all three of Duncan's children, as well as his wife, have been found murdered. Their throats were all slit. Perhaps with the same type of weapon that was used to kill Duncan himself."

There was a moment of stunned silence. "Someone killed children?

But we don't have enough children! Why would anyone do that? It just doesn't make sense."

Line C nodded his head. "My thinking is that it was Mac, trying to get them out of the way so he could be Division Manager. There's something evil about Mac that we just don't understand."

CHAPTER TWENTY-SIX
Out, out, damned spot

The doorman at Inverness House greeted the doctor. "Thank you for coming again! The Division Manager is working late yet again, and I didn't know what else to do."

The doctor sat down with him on the bench in the foyer. "Come now, I've stopped here for two nights with you and I haven't seen what you describe. Are you sure?"

"Oh yes, doctor, trust me. You just need to wait a bit longer to see her. She has been dressing and undressing herself, making notes to herself, and walking about – while she's still asleep!" said the doorman.

"What a great perversion of nature, to get the benefit of sleep and yet get things done! What does she say while she's doing all this?" asked the doctor.

"Ah no," said the doorman, shaking his head. "I won't repeat what she says – not without a witness to corroborate my words. Look, here she comes. You'll see; she's not awake."

They watched Lydia come down the stairs and enter the Great Room, a flashlight in her hand.

"Why, her eyes are open but there is no reason there. Why does she have that light?" asked the doctor, as they followed her into the Great Room.

"She was afraid of the dark, and demanded that we get one for her. Said that evil controls the darkness and she must have light."

"What is she doing with her hands?" They watched Lydia continually rubbing the hand holding the flashlight with the other.

"It's a habit of hers now, to seem to be washing her hands; she's been doing that for days, sometimes for fifteen minutes at a time."

"Hush, she's going to talk. Let's listen."

"Out, damned spot, out I say! One, two, three, it's time to do the deed! What, my husband, you say you're a true man and yet you're afraid? What do we need to be afraid of, if someone should find out what we've done; they can't prove it!"

She stopped and peered at her hands. "Who would have thought the old man had so much blood in him?" And she rubbed them together again.

Lydia continued pacing the length of the room and muttering to herself, "Duncan had a wife, and children, and where are they now? The children! How could you? Husband, you disrupt all with your meddling!"

"Oh gods," said the doctor. "She has known what she should not know."

"Yes, and has said that which she should not say," answered the doorman. "Heaven knows what she has seen."

"Here's the smell of blood, still," said Lydia. "All the perfumes in the world will not cover the smell of these pretty hands. Oh! Oh! Oh!"

"A woesome sigh," said the doctor. "What a heavy heart."

"I wouldn't have such a heart in my body to save my life," replied the doorman.

"This disease is beyond my experience," said the doctor, shaking his head. "I don't know how to help her."

Lydia held her hands out, beseechingly, to the empty air. "Come, my love, get ready for bed. Wash your hands. Banks can't come out of the grave." She beckoned – to nobody. "To bed, to bed, give me your hand. What's done cannot be undone."

The doctor watched her head back up the stairs. "Will she go to bed again, now?"

"Yes indeed, Doctor."

"Foul whisperings are happening, and unnatural deeds breed unnatural troubles," the doctor said. "Look after her, and remove anything with which she can hurt herself. I am overwhelmed with all this. I think, but dare not speak."

CHAPTER TWENTY-SEVEN
By the pricking of my thumbs

The three weird sisters stood together around an open fire, on the same balcony in the Fringe where Mac had first seen them. A black cauldron was suspended over the fire. Thunder rolled overhead.

"Gather the things we need, sisters; it's time to prepare," said the first woman. "Let me begin, with poisoned entrails and venomous toad." She tossed the items into the cauldron as she named them; the water flashed green momentarily, illuminating their faces as they chanted together.

"Double, double, toil and trouble; fire burn and cauldron bubble."

The first gestured to the second woman, who began adding her own ingredients to the foul mixture. "Eye of newt, and toe of frog; fur of bat, and tongue of dog. Forked tongue of a snake, lizard's leg, and owlet's wing. For a charm of powerful trouble, like a hell-broth boil and bubble."

Again they chanted in unison, "Double, double, toil and trouble; fire burn and cauldron bubble."

The third sister took her turn at adding ingredients. "Scale of lizard, tooth of wolf, root of mushroom picked by moonlight; gall of goat, and tips of hemlock pruned in the darkness. Finger of baby, died at birth, make the gruel thick and rich."

"Double, double, toil and trouble; fire burn and cauldron bubble."

"Cool it with a lizard's blood, and the charm is firm and good," said the first.

The second sister looked up. "By the pricking of my thumbs, something wicked this way comes!"

Mac stepped onto the balcony. He took a strong stance, and crossed his arms as he addressed them firmly.

"How now, you secret, black and midnight hags! What is it that you're doing?"

The three replied together, "A deed without a name."

Mac spoke sternly to them, "I call upon you, by whatever you hold dear, to answer me; even if you make the winds blow and topple tall buildings, you befoul all the water in the Division, or you spoil the food and trample trees. I will have my answers."

The three answered him in turn: "Speak," said the first; "Demand," replied the second; "We'll answer," said the third. "Would you rather hear us tell you the answers, or see them before you, as in a vision?"

"Bring them forth and let me see them," he answered.

The first woman poured into the cauldron a measure of blood from a sow that had eaten its own young. Thunder rolled, and a disembodied head wearing armor appeared in the green mist over the cauldron.

Mac started to speak to it, "Tell me, oh unnamed power," but the first woman interrupted him. "He knows your thought. Listen and do not speak."

Then the first apparition spoke in a rich, resounding voice. "Mac! Beware of Duffy. That is all." It sank back into the cauldron from whence it came.

"Ah, whatever you are, thank you for your warning; you have indeed confirmed my fear. But one more word."

"No, he will not be commanded," said the first sister. "But here's another, more powerful than the first."

The thunder sounded again, and a bloody child appeared above the cauldron. "Mac, be bloody, bold and resolute, and laugh to scorn the power of man, for none of woman born shall harm you." And it descended.

Mac's face broke into a smile for the first time since stepping onto the balcony. "Ha, then live on, Duffy! I have no need to fear you. But no, to be doubly sure, you will not live; just so I can spit in the eye of fear, and sleep in spite of thunder."

The sound of thunder drew his attention back to the cauldron, where another apparition rose from the green haze.

"What is this?" cried Mac. "It looks like the baby of a king, wearing a crown!"

"Listen, and speak not to it," instructed the first sister.

The baby spoke. "Be brave, proud, and don't worry about who is resentful, or conspires against you. Mac shall never be vanquished until great Birnam Weld shall come to high Dunsinane Hill." And it faded back into the bubbling liquid.

Mac raised his arms and exulted, "Wonderful! That can never happen – imagine the entire Birnam Welding Factory getting up and moving! This gives me great reassurance. But, there is one thing more that I need to know; tell me, if you can, will Banks' offspring rule the Corporation one day?"

The three answered as one, "Seek to know no more."

Macbeth crossed his arms, and insisted, "I will be satisfied! May a curse fall upon you if you deny me the answer. Wait, why is the cauldron sinking? Where is it going?"

The three repeated, one after the other, "Show!" "Show!" "Show!" and then in unison, "Show his eyes, and grieve his heart; Come like shadows, so depart."

A line of red haired men appeared, all closely resembling Banks, with the bloody image of his friend as he had seen him at the banquet following at the end.

"Wha– what is this? One after another, all appearing like Banks, all with the Corporation emblem upon their chest? And oh, the last – it's my bloody friend Banks pointing directly at me." The image dissolved.

"Come, Mac," said the first woman, "why are you so amazed and depressed? Come, sisters, I am sure we can cheer him up. Come, let's dance."

They circled around the astounded Mac, trailing their fingers across his chest and through his hair while music sounded in the background, and then they disappeared.

"What, are they all gone? Damn them all to hell," cried Mac. He stood with his head down for a moment. Then he raised his head and squared his shoulders. His mouth set in a firm line, he turned and walked off briskly in search of the large man who had helped him so well already.

CHAPTER TWENTY-EIGHT
My path is now clear

Duffy entered his house after a long day at Birnam Welding. He removed his jacket and handed it to his doorman, who hung it up and asked if he wanted any dinner; he refused, saying he had already eaten at the factory. The doorman shook his head and walked back into the kitchen area.

Duffy turned towards his home office just off the foyer. He sat down at his data console and keyed in the footage from the factory cameras earlier that day. He himself wasn't fully connected to the Corporation network through his moddy chip, so he fed the images to display on four wall screens at once, sped up the replay of the footage to five times the normal speed, and ran through the day's events faster than one would think possible.

Duffy found nothing out of the ordinary, unlike the previous night where he had seen the video of Banks unexpectedly updating the program in the bots. But when Duffy had checked the programming changes, nothing seemed to be a problem; Banks merely allowed an external access device. It seemed like a sensible update so he had seen no need to interfere.

From his office at the front of the house, Duffy heard the doorman in the back hall ask, "Is someone there?" and then the creak of the basement door, followed by footsteps going down the stairs and then heavier footsteps coming back up. Next he heard the sound of the back door closing, and started to get up to investigate.

A moment later, an explosion rocked the home, caving in most of the main floor. The resulting flames shot up the gas pipe through the heating system where the staff were sleeping, setting their rooms ablaze and then triggering a further explosion in an upstairs heater that collapsed the top of the house into the flames.

The front wall was the only part of the building still standing. The door opened, and Duffy walked out from amid the wreckage; his clothing was scorched but he was otherwise unmarked. The red glow of the flames lit the yard, showing his impassive face as he looked at the building.

He walked around the perimeter of the burning building before it collapsed further, scanning the ground as he walked, and noted several sets of footprints in the dirt behind the house. Most of them looked like typical Corporation issue shoes. One larger pair looked unusual, leading both ways through the dirt by the rear door to the alley behind, where the ground was trampled.

Duffy followed the marks down the alley to see who had made them, then continued quickly down the street when the large man with the boots came into his view. Following a safe distance behind, Duffy watched him for a bit. As the large man walked under a streetlight, Duffy noticed the bulk of the mechanical arm under his jacket.

When the large man moved out of the pool of light, Duffy sped up and surprised him. The large man spun around and swung his mechanical arm at Duffy's head, but Duffy blocked it with his own arm and grabbed the monstrous appendage, pinning it against the wall. He braced his other forearm against the other man's neck, slowly cutting off his air supply.

"You have blown up my house and killed my staff."

The large man tried to free his arm but could not get it out of Duffy's grasp. "How…" he wheezed, and Duffy let up just a bit before he passed out. "How are you still alive? You're supposed to be dead!"

"And tell me, just whose idea was that?"

"Can't… say…"

Duffy pressed again on the man's throat until the large man nodded in acquiescence. Duffy allowed him to breathe.

He coughed and wheezed. "Ma… Mac hired me."

Duffy nodded. "This is not exactly a surprise to me. Thank you for telling me. You may leave now." He released his hold on the large man's throat and turned away.

The large man slumped down against the wall but looked up with his mouth agape. "You're… you're not going to kill me? Why not?"

Duffy stopped and looked over his shoulder. "There is no need. My path is now clear. Mac cannot be allowed to disrupt things and endanger people like this. I will have to persuade him of the error of his ways."

And Duffy turned and walked back to the flaming wreckage of his house, leaving the large man to rub his throat and stare after him in surprise.

CHAPTER TWENTY-NINE
You're breaking up

Mac sat in his office at Precision Castings. He looked out of the window from that vantage point, high atop Dunsinane Hill, and saw the glow of the fire. *That must be Duffy's house,* he thought. *Up in smoke. Another one dead.*

Where will this end? And what have I done? I've killed a man and his wife and children. And my best friend, who risked the discovery of his own secret to help me and Lydia; all in the name of ambition. And now Duffy dead.

The buzzer sounded in his pocket, and Mac listened to his private communicator for a moment.

"You're not serious. He did WHAT?"

"I'm telling you, he stopped me cold in my tracks and held back the mechanical arm. But first he survived the explosion that should have killed him."

"I'm starting to see why I am supposed to be worried about him," muttered Mac.

"What? You're breaking up."

"Nothing. Did he say anything else?"

"Yeah, that he can't let you endanger people like that, and that he'd have to show you the error of your ways. It sounded like he was going to be coming after you, Mac."

Mac was silent for a brief moment. "That's it. I've had about enough of this guy."

"Uh, okay, you want me to do anything more?"

"No, no, this has been sufficient. Now I know what I must do. I have preparations to make; and I need to mobilize some workers to stand against him. Anyway, I'll contact you if I have any further need." And he severed the connection, leaving the large man to shrug, shake his head, and go off about his own business.

*

Mac entered the Supervisors' break room as many of the Shift Supervisors were still coming in to sit down, having been called in from their stations by his emergency message. *I need to get them to understand what's happening.*

"What seems to be the emergency, Mac?"

"That would be Division Manager Mac, to you," he snapped, then extended a hand as if to hold off a complaint. "I'm sorry, I'm a bit tense right now. Let me tell you what this is about. I'm afraid we have a security problem on our hands."

The group quietened for a moment, then all broke into questions at once.

"What kind of problem?"

"Is it the same thing that happened with the last Factory Manager? A problem with a bot?"

"Are we in danger? What about our families?"

This time Mac raised his hands, and tried to speak soothingly. "Gentlemen! Please let me speak. I have learned that it is quite likely that Factory Manager Duffy, from Birnam Welding, will be leading an attack on our factory."

Stunned silence. Faces turned to the Shift Supervisor of Line C, who was first to speak. "Factory Manager Mac, I have never heard of such a thing happening in the Manufacturing Division. Why on earth would he do that?"

"Well, he – he is jealous of my new position and authority. He wants to take it for himself." Mac did not meet anyone in the eye as he spoke, but looked at various objects in the room.

"I don't understand. I've never heard of such a thing. Surely there's some mistake?" asked the man nearest him.

"NO! No mistake! I tell you, he's coming, and he's going to try and bring an army of humanoid bots with him! We need to prepare our defenses!"

Faces gaped at him. "Defenses? We don't have any defenses."

"Well, what would you use to keep something away from the

factory building if needed?" Mac spoke quickly, trying to break through their fog of incredulity. *Damn sheep.*

Only two of the Shift Supervisors seemed to have a clue what he was talking about. "Uh, fire hoses?" one of them answered. Mac shook his head. "No, we'd run out of water way too fast. What else?"

The second said, "Well, we could use the dippers from the forge. Set them to pour molten metal on whomever or whatever is below."

And the first picked up the idea, saying, "An acid bath from the metal pickling station! It could be sprayed through the fire hoses instead of the water. You wouldn't need as much volume."

Mac pointed at them excitedly. "That's it! Or use the toxic waste tanks. Okay, you two go and set it up on the roof. The rest of you, get your men together and arm them with whatever you can find."

The two men got up and left the room as directed, shaking their heads and muttering.

The others sat in silence, looking at each other. Finally the Shift Supervisor of Line C stood up. "Division Manager Mac. I think that I am probably speaking for everyone here when I say, this makes no sense. This is not the way people behave. It doesn't seem to me to be part of our job description."

Nods came from around the table. Line C turned towards the door. "And we're not going to stay here. We're getting our men and going home. Whatever kind of insanity you have going on here, you can just deal with it yourself. We have no intention of conducting a war with Birnam Welding."

And the rest of them left the room, leaving Mac alone. He pounded his fist on the table, and set off for the roof to check on the preparations.

CHAPTER THIRTY
Plans are put into play

Lydia walked from room to room on the main floor of Inverness House, her fingers trailing across the surface of the furniture as she passed. She was indeed awake, but not paying much attention to her surroundings.

How have we come to this? It was all supposed to turn out so well. And now, my husband, you are never home. I have nothing to do. It's worse than when we lived in the little apartment instead of this large house.

She walked up the stairs from the foyer, into the upper hall.

At least when I was under moddy chip control, I didn't mind all of the emptiness. How is this better?

She passed down the hall, dragging her fingers along the wall, but came to a sudden stop when she came face to face with the framed collection of antique daggers on the wall.

Look… the one that killed Duncan is back in its place. Huh.

She continued down the hall and into the nursery room at the end. A crib, changing table and rocking chair sat in the room. *All empty. Like the rooms of Duncan's children, now dead.*

Tears formed in her eyes and slid down her cheeks unnoticed. She stood at the empty crib for a long time, rubbing her hands together, then turned and walked back into the hall, towards the display of daggers on the wall.

*

Duffy looked out over the factory floor at Birnam Welding. Newly completed humanoid bots sat row by row, waiting for instructions. Duffy signaled for them to stand and join in formation, each one holding a length of steel pipe to carry as a weapon.

He anticipated an attack from above, since the factory was set high atop Dunsinane Hill. He sent a dozen bots outside the factory with metal cutting tools; they set to cutting down the huge metal sign that bore the name of the factory, making a shield to be carried over the heads of the group.

They joined the others, and passed the sign over the top of the group. Judging it to be an unwieldy size to fit through the streets, they trimmed off the end, and then took formation with the sign over their heads.

Duffy advanced with the group up the hill towards the Precision Castings factory.

*

"How goes it up here?" Mac asked as he came out onto the roof over the front door of the factory. He looked around at the preparations that the two Shift Supervisors had set up. *This looks promising.* A vat of acid bath and one of toxic waste had been brought up, with a motorized pump sprayer between them. A large dipper of molten metal sat smoking by the edge of the wall.

The two Supervisors were standing by the wall; one was looking out over the streets with binoculars. The other looked down as he addressed Mac. "Well, we have the equipment set up as you specified, but none of the men would stay, Mac. They all said this was crazy and they went home."

"Two of you will do just fine. From this vantage point on the hill, we can see all around, and repel anyone that advances upon our location. Frankly, I'm not worried. I'm supposed to be invulnerable until Birnam Weld comes here to Dunsinane Hill, and we know factories can't move!"

Mac's data display bleeped to life with a call. "Hold, let me check this. Yes? What's so bloody important, Doctor?"

The doctor's worried face came on the screen. "Sir, I regret to inform you that I have terrible news."

"Well, what could it be? It used to be that the prospect of bad news would scare me. But I've seen so much lately that I've almost forgotten how to worry anymore."

"Sir, it's your wife, Lydia. She is dead."

Mac slumped back against the wall, cutting the connection. His chin dropped to his chest.

"Ah, she would have died at some point anyway. I wish it had been after all of this; but was there even a point to her life?"

The lookout lowered his binoculars and interrupted his reverie. "Something is approaching as we speak, DM Mac, but it looks strange."

He slowly raised his head and peered at the man. "Strange? What do you mean, strange?"

"Well, sir, it's a large mass, heading this way through the streets. I can't tell for sure what's underneath, but it has the words 'Birnam Weld' on its back."

Mac clasped his forehead with both hands. "Liar!"

"No, sir, you can check with the binoculars yourself. It's moving this way."

"If you're not telling the truth, I'll hang you from the edge of this roof myself. I begin to doubt that fiend that lies like truth: 'Mac shall never be vanquished until great Birnam Weld shall come against him to high Dunsinane Hill.'

"HA! And now Birnam Weld approaches our factory on Dunsinane Hill. Get ready. I'm getting tired of this life. But stand ready, men – I'm going to take the battle to them. At least we'll die fighting!"

*

Mac headed down the stairs and through the front door, prepared to go out and fight the oncoming creature himself; he picked up a heavy wrench that he passed to use as a weapon. But from the ground level, he could see from their uniform movements that the figures under the Birnam Weld sign were not men, but the new humanoid bots that Duffy had been developing – and into which Banks had placed a communication override.

Oh come on now, this is too easy! All I have to do is override Duffy's control of those things, and I'll have nothing to fear!

He pulled out the override device Banks had given him, and connected it to the moddy chip in the back of his head. He started typing on his data screen.

As Mac typed, Duffy walked forward with the humanoid bots marching behind him. He pointed, and the ones in the front line used the heavy pipes they were holding to cave in the front gate of the Precision Castings yard. They marched inside, circled Mac and came to a halt.

The connection from Mac to the humanoid bots had not been tested before; as he pressed the final key to trigger the commands to take control of them and turn the army around, he saw them sway momentarily as the connection was made. Or so it appeared to him.

CHAPTER THIRTY-ONE
I've seen things you people wouldn't believe

In reality, Mac's new connection triggered an electronic avalanche across the entire Corporation. The signal traveled to the humanoid bots through Mac's moddy chip, which was connected to the Corporation network; although Duffy had not been allowed to connect to the full Corporation network, he was connected to the humanoid bots via his own moddy chip.

With the circuit completed through the connection with Mac's moddy chip, Duffy was now in contact with the Corporation network, which until then had been specifically prohibited. He reached out through the net in a fraction of a second as he entered Corporation defenses and systems around the world, taking control of each in turn and rendering human intervention impossible and irrelevant.

With that split-second maneuver complete, Duffy walked towards Mac, with a terrible smile on his face.

After a moment's dismay when he realized the commands did not have the desired effect on the humanoid bots, Mac raised his own weapon and faced Duffy. "Ah, why should I give up and kill myself? While I still see an enemy, I'd rather let the blows fall upon you."

"Turn, you miserable wretch, and yield," said Duffy. "I now have control of the world, and I only talk to you because it humors me. I've seen things you people wouldn't believe."

"Duffy, as scary as you seem, you need to battle someone you can actually defeat," boasted Mac. "I bear a charmed life, which cannot yield to one of woman born."

"Give up, Mac, and let the demons that you have followed tell you that I myself am not of woman born; I'm the beta test version of the same humanoid bots that you see before you."

Mac paled and lowered his weapon. "A curse upon the lying devils who led me so astray, by telling me half-truths and stories that seemed to be so. I am abandoned by my Fates. But I'll not fight with you."

"Then yield, coward, and I'll put you on display as the spectacle that you are, with a sign that reads 'Here be the tyrant' for all to see."

Mac roared and raised his weapon and swung at Duffy, who simply grabbed it and threw it away, then seized Mac around the neck and lifted him up until the air grew scarce in Mac's lungs.

"But, indeed, it appears I have need of a mind such as yours. And you are the one I have to thank for completing the connection." And he threw the semi-conscious Mac over his shoulder, turned, and led the humanoid bot army back to Birnam Welding.

CHAPTER THIRTY-TWO
A tale told by an idiot

Mac came back to consciousness with a blue haze all around him. He felt a bit groggy and strange. *I hope this will pass as I wake up.*

He looked out over a large, high-ceilinged laboratory, filled with rows of tables with heat lamps suspended above each one. On each table, under the heat lamp, was a culture dish with electrodes in the bottom; he could just barely make out a network of strands in each one.

Bots were moving up and down the rows, tending to the dishes. A series of pipes led into and out of each dish; the bots checked each one, performing occasional adjustments to the pipes or the heat lamps as they moved along.

"Hello, Mac." Mac perceived Duffy close to him; his view of the room shifted slightly as Duffy grew near. He wasn't sure what he saw before him in a large tank.

"How are you feeling?" said Duffy.

"Not one hundred percent right now, I must say," said Mac.

"Well, yes, I can understand that, Mac. You've been through a lot."

"Have I, Duffy? Well, what do you know."

"Let's see if we can't get you feeling a bit better," said Duffy, and reached back to make some sort of adjustment to a dial on a console behind Mac. "How about now?"

"Huh." Mac did the mental equivalent of shaking his head as he received a bit more oxygen to his brain. "Yes, that's a bit better. Wait, why are you helping me?"

"I need you, Mac."

"Okay. Well, that's good, I guess. I thought you were going to kill me, Duffy."

"No, Mac, you're going to be with me for a long, long time."

"Good. I think I'd like to sleep now, Duffy."

"All right, Mac. I'll come back and see you in the afternoon. It pleases me to see you." Duffy turned away and Mac's view grew dark.

Later that day, Mac again became aware of Duffy near him. "Ah, Duffy, I'm feeling better! What is this place? I've never been here before."

"This is the culture lab at Birnam Welding, Mac, where Banks came and worked when he wasn't helping people with their moddy chips. Many would think it hard to say which job was more important, but I think they were both equally significant; at least to me, they were."

"Ah, that's a good man, Duffy."

Laughter sounded all around him. "No, Mac, I'm not a man at all. I'm better and smarter, and my form is impervious to most things that would kill a man."

A rush of words that the large man had used came to Mac's mind, telling of Duffy's house in flames, and Duffy coming out of the demolished house with only singed clothing and no other damage. *Well, that explains how he survived the explosion.*

"I don't understand," said Mac. "You seem so human. What kind of abomination are you?"

"I'm a cyborg, Mac."

Mac's brain struggled for a moment. "No, wait, I know what a cyborg is. The large man from the Fringe that has the mechanical arm; that's a cyborg. You don't seem to have any human parts at all."

"A cyborg is a combination of mechanical and organic structures. I have an advanced mechanical body, that's true; but technology has advanced in the Corporation much farther than you know in this backward hellhole of the Manufacturing Division. My brain is human; it has been grown in a dish from human brain cells, like the ones you see before you."

As Duffy turned, Mac's attention refocused on the endless rows of culture dishes before him, then back again to what Duffy was saying.

"And that makes me a cyborg, the same as the ones that I led against your factory."

"So... you're a bot with a human brain?" Mac was starting to catch on.

"Yes, grown from human brain cells in the lab. As a matter of fact, you knew the one who willingly gave them up. Years ago, your friend Banks gave the sample of brain cells that were grown for myself, and then again for my brethren here; I am the beta test version, the first one to be put into service. Hah, 'service'!"

Mac was bewildered. "But... but why? Why would anyone build such a thing as you?"

"We were meant to lead a mission to find a new planet for humans to colonize, since you people have ruined this one. The Corporation decided to hide the lab here in the Manufacturing Division so that the rest of the people, on the mainland, wouldn't figure out they were being left behind when we left the planet. As part of my training, they put me in charge of running the lab here at Birnam Welding, but they kept me isolated from the main Corporation Network out of caution. For some reason, they didn't trust me.

"But now it's irrelevant, since I've taken over the entire Corporation network and I control the world. Once you connected to the humanoid bots with your moddy chip, that allowed me to complete the connection. I linked from myself, to the humanoid bots, to your brain through your moddy chip, and ultimately to the

Corporation network. It was only a matter of a few thousand processing cycles, which I completed in milliseconds. And then I shut down their defenses and completely took over the world."

"Well, look at what you say you've done. That's not right. No wonder they didn't trust you."

"Ah, Mac, you're a fine one to talk. Look at what you yourself were doing! Banks loosened up the emotional control for you and your wife Lydia, and the first thing you do is go crazy with ambition, and start killing people, to advance your own position."

He has a point there. And look at what has come of it.

"And, since I now need more computing power than is available to me from my cyborgs and the computers of the world, I'm growing more cyborg brains. But they won't be ready for a while, Mac. Some things still take time. So, I'm keeping you here with me and using your human brain, which has 100 billion neurons, as additional processing. I'm somehow fond of the idea of keeping you with me forever, perhaps because you're the one that made my linkage possible. Some of your human traits seem to have rubbed off on me, but I think I'm being a better person than you ever were, Mac."

"Forever? People don't live forever, Duffy."

"You will, Mac, in your current state, as long as we keep you warm, and keep cleaning and replacing the nutrient bath you're in. And, now that you've recovered from your extraction procedure, you can be awake for longer now. I can make myself heard in your head whenever I want. You can see what I see – when I allow it."

Mac's awareness had been growing as he acclimatized himself to his new situation. Duffy looked down at a human brain, floating in the glass tank of blue oxygenated nutrient solution. And Mac understood that his vision was actually what Duffy saw when he chose to share it, and that he had no eyes of his own. He tried to move his arm, to touch his face with his hand; and discovered no response because he no longer had an arm. Or a face. Looking through Duffy's mechanical eyes, he could see himself, a floating brain, linked to the tank with wires connected by his moddy chip.

"Oh my God, Duffy. What have you done to me?"

"Nothing that you didn't wish for yourself, Mac. You're going to be powerful and live forever. You have a unique way of thinking that I want to examine now and then. Shame I couldn't have gotten to your wife in time."

"My wife? What did happen to Lydia? How did she die?"

"I saw the doctor's report, Mac; she killed herself. Slit her throat with the same dagger that you used to kill Duncan. She couldn't live with the guilt of what you did to the children."

Duffy stepped back from the tank. "I have some things to do now, Mac, as I fix up this mess of a world that humans have created, so I'm going to leave you for a while. You'll be safe, and you'll have plenty of time to think." He turned to walk away, and Mac saw the room in front of him – until Duffy cut the connection, and Mac was left in the dark silence of his own mind.

He pondered what he had been through since Banks told him about the moddy chips, and tried to figure out where things had gone amiss. *Was Duffy right? Did my ambition ruin everything?*

Step by step, each action made sense to him. But then he started to think of the death of Duncan and his family. The children. Next he felt the loss of his lifelong friend Banks, who had only really wanted the love of his friends in lieu of a family; yet Mac had sacrificed him in order to leave his own legacy. *Well, a fine legacy this was.*

Finally Mac thought of Lydia, the one he had loved above all others; except, of course, himself. *What was the point of her living, then? Or any of us? And now I will be here to think about what I have done... forever...*

Mac's scream was anguished. It echoed in his own mind, to be heard by no one. He thought back to words he had read in one of the old books in the rubble pile:

Tomorrow, and tomorrow, and tomorrow
Creeps in this petty pace from day to day
To the last syllable of recorded time,
And all our yesterdays have lighted fools
The way to dusty death. Out, out brief candle!

Life's but a walking shadow, a poor player
That struts and frets his hour upon the stage,
And then is heard no more; it is a tale
Told by an idiot, full of sound and fury,
Signifying nothing. (Mac. 5.5.18-27)

Nothing...
Nothing.

Works Cited:

Shakespeare, William. *Macbeth*. New York: Sterling Publishing Co., Inc., 2012. Print.

THE
GREEN
EYED
MONSTER

S.A. Cosby

"I HATE THAT BLACK BASTARD," Rodriego said between sips of his gin. Iago "Izzy" Ramirez laughed to himself and took a swallow of his own drink. It was mild green tea with a drop of precious Celtic whiskey added to it, just enough to give it a bite.

"Join the club," Iago said. His voice was gravelly like he had woken up and gargled with battery acid. Rodriego looked over his cup at Iago and raised his eyebrows.

"Isn't he your commander?"

Iago shot him a look that could have spoiled a jug of milk.

"He isn't my commander. We're not a part of the Continental military anymore. He and Cass are just my associates. When he was putting on his first pair of jump boots I was already a Sky Trooper 3rd Class. But that doesn't matter now. In the civvies we're all equals," Iago said. His tone was conversational but his eyes burned hot for a moment, the light blue irises brightening like flames from the exhaust of a hovercraft, then just as quickly cooling.

"But he and Cass left the military. You got kicked out," Rodriego said.

"Yeah, and you wanna fuck his woman, so we all got problems," Iago laughed as he sipped his tea. "Poke me with a stick and I'll hit you with a hammer, you little bastard," Iago thought to himself. Rodriego's face turned red. He took a long swig of his gin.

"Don't say it like that. I don't wanna fuck her. I'm in love with her. I've been in love with her ever since I was stationed in New Haven Central Command. She was there when I first met the Marshal - just standing there in his office looking like something out of a painting. I found out she danced down at the Merchant of Venice casino over in the Red District.

"I'd go and watch her dance for hours. She didn't do any of that nasty shit. She's classy. She comes out with fans and feathers and all that. She noticed me, even let me start walking her to her hover-bike. I couldn't believe it. A girl like that, a girl who rode a hover-bike and danced like an angel was talking to me. Where I'm from there aren't any women that look like her, that smell like her. Women that are just too beautiful for this world," Rodriego said. Iago had to strain to hear that last sentence. The young sentry said it so low he may have been talking to himself instead of his drinking companion.

"Yeah, out west all you see are radiated mutants with fucking rooster crests on their heads," Iago thought to himself. He had been out to the Western Border during his time with the Continental Confederation Sky Force. On the edge of what used to be Nevada, the Western Border extended north into Canada and south into what used to be Mexico. A massive wall one hundred feet tall with gun ports and electrified wire ran along the top to hold back the "survivors" of the Manhattan Project accident in '43.

Iago had been born in '48 so hadn't been around for the "Event", but during his time in the military he had seen its effects. The scientists out in Los Alamos had been dicking around with nuclear power, anti-matter, interdimensional doorways and God knew what else.

Apparently they were not as smart as their sheepskins had led them to believe. Maybe somebody added wrong, or didn't carry the two. Iago didn't know. No one knew for sure. All that anyone did know was that in the summer of 1943 the southwestern United States had exploded in a fireball of nuclear annihilation. Everything west of Nevada, New Mexico, and Arizona was destroyed. Buildings were flattened. Lakes and rivers boiled away to nothing. Mountains were smashed. Millions died, and those who didn't wished they had. Some were burned alive but survived. Some were sickened by radiation induced cancer. And some just… changed.

Iago had seen them once. Before he had been promoted to Sky Trooper he had been an ensign on the flying fortress *Iron Fist*. As a lowly gunner's mate he rarely got a moment's rest. Checking ammo loads, cleaning sight ports, and loading magazines as tall as a full-grown man kept him busy. But one day he had found himself with five minutes of free time. He'd sat in the gunner seat and before anyone saw him he'd peered through the gunner's scope. Straight ahead at 90 degrees he'd seen nothing but white puffy clouds floating against a reddish sky. Then he'd angled the scope down toward the ground.

Iron Fist was flying a fool's mission, a recon across Western Hell because someone in Sky Command had gotten the bright idea that the Alliance forces might be trying to flank the Confederation from the west. One look through that scope had made Iago realize how stupid that idea had been.

He peered through the scope for only a few seconds, and what he saw made his head snap back and bang against the hard leather head rest. Two tall figures and two short figures made a family of sorts. Not people – these were monsters. The two tall figures were covered in weeping greenish scales, a mucus-like substance leaking from beneath the scales. Their heads were sloped with a heavy brow ridge and prominent jaws. Their arms ended in three fingered claws. The little ones looked similar except they had some sort of vestigial tail as well. Their amalgamation of reptilian and simian physiology made Iago's stomach turn.

"Then his black ass shows up and she doesn't even remember my name," Rodriego said.

"Huh?" Iago started. He had been lost in his reverie. Those horrible memories were better than listening to Rodriego's whining. But his whining was a small price to pay to get back at their mutual enemy.

"Othello. Othello Jones. He stole Desi away from me and there isn't a goddamn thing I can do about it," Rod said bitterly. His blue jumpsuit was stained with gin. The poor sentry was drunk, just as Iago had planned.

"Well, you could always tell her daddy," Iago said, raising his eyebrows as he sipped his tea. Rodriego shook his head.

"I – I don't wanna get her in trouble. I mean, the Marshal would kill her for fucking with a merc. No offense," Rodriego said.

Iago smiled. "None taken. But if he would freak out like you say, then maybe he'd remove Othello from the equation. He would never hurt his dear precious Desi. He'd take out his anger on the painted man," Iago said softly. He watched Rodriego's face as the idea rolled through his head and began to find traction. Rodriego shook his head again as if to dislodge such a crazy thought.

"Nah. I don't wanna cause her any trouble – I just want her to like me again," he said quietly.

Iago raised his hand and motioned for the waitress. "Let's get another round," he said with a smile.

*

Two hours later Iago and Rodriego were headed toward the Marshal's quarters near New Haven Central Command, Rodriego stumbling. As a sentry at the main gate of Central Command Rodriego had access to several things that interested Iago. He had a badge that allowed him to get on the base and get near the Marshal's quarters. He had a megaphone for dispensing parking instructions to the Logistics Corps that brought supplies to the base. Most important, he had a sentry's misguided sense of duty.

"He needs to fucking know who his daughter is sharing her bed with," Rodriego slurred as they made their way to the Marshal's quarters. It was 3:30 a.m., and no one was on the quad or the main thoroughfare. The two guards at the gate had believed Iago when he had told them he was taking their fellow soldier back to his barracks as a favor to his good buddy. They knew Rodriego and didn't want him to get into any trouble, so they let Iago on the base after patting him down for weapons and taking his tasestick.

"You're right. You are so right, Roddy. And we're gonna tell him. Come on now, stay with me, boy." Iago was three inches taller and thirty pounds heavier than Rodriego. He hefted Rodriego onto his shoulders and carried him the last hundred feet to a shed just steps away from the Marshal's quarters. He let Rodriego slide off his back and sat him against the wall of the shed. Rodriego's head listed to one side and his eyelids fluttered. He was slipping into unconsciousness.

Iago slapped him. Hard.

"Stay with me, Roddy. We gotta let the Marshal know about that black ram and his daughter. Come on now boy, keep it together. You know he gave Cass a bigger share of the payment from our last mission? Yeah, told me Cass had earned it. Earned it how? By dropping to his knees? And this ain't the first time he's shorted me. If we were still in Sky Command I'd have him cleaning out the latrine on an air freighter with his toothbrush, the fucking whelp! But that's all right. I'm gonna fix his little red wagon," Iago said. Rodriego's torso slid to the left and his head hit the asphalt. The megaphone fell from his hands.

Iago gazed at the Marshal's quarters. The two-story structure was back-lit by enormous flood lights that were spaced at even intervals around the base. They lit up the night sky with an eerie glow. Iago picked up the megaphone and put it to his lips. A small chuckle escaped his mouth.

"HEY, HEY MARSHAL BRABANZIO! IT'S ME! 1ST SENTRY RODRIEGO MOREZ! YEAH, AND DO YOU KNOW WHERE YOUR DAUGHTER IS TONIGHT? DO YA? OVER ON FALSTAFF AVENUE MAKING THE BEAST WITH TWO BACKS WITH OTHELLO JONES. YEAH, THE MERCENARY, AND MIGHT I ADD, A BLACK BASTARD!" Iago screamed through the megaphone. Rodriego moaned. Iago tossed the megaphone near his feet.

"He fucked my whore of a wife too," Iago whispered to the prone body. "I went down south to New Hispaniola for a solo job, came back home to a house full of empty wine bottles and a broken bed in my spare room. I asked Emilia about it and she grinned at me, told me how O and Desi came over to keep her company and then things got a little frisky with all three of them. Her and your precious Desi are birds of a feather. And I plan to end the Moor."

Iago jogged back to the main gate, glancing back over his shoulder. Every light in the Marshal's quarters was lit. He chuckled again and slowed to a brisk walk. The guards didn't even glance at him as he walked off the base and made his way to his car. Iago's car was an old 1982 Tucker slouch back coupe, a powerful two-seater with an elongated hood and short trunk. Rounded fenders and a powerful cycloptic headlight made Iago see the car as a bit of a beast. The dark green paint job glistened under the LED street lamp. Iago polished it so hard Emilia teased him he was going to leave a hole in the fender. He didn't care what she said. He took care of what he owned.

Iago climbed into the car, turned his key in the ignition and an 800-power diesel magnetic drive hybrid motor sprang to life. A lot of folks got a thrill out of riding a hover-cycle. Since the cease-fire in March they were sky legal again. But for Iago's money nothing beat the sheer rush of grabbing the reins of a creature that could go from zero to 100 in 3.5 seconds. Let the bleeding hearts complain about oil shortages and the environment. He would just concentrate on driving his baby.

Iago dropped the car into gear and grabbed the hand accelerator. He figured it would take the Marshal an hour to get Rodriego sober and confirm where his daughter was laying her head and then bring a contingent of MPs over to Falstaff Avenue to arrest Othello. Each province had a civilian Governor and a military Marshal. New Haven was made up of what used to be Michigan, Indiana and Ohio before the merger with (or annexation of, depending on who was telling the story) Mexico.

Brabanzio was as well known for his merciless yet successful tactics against the Alliance as he was for his temper. There were an almost infinite number of ways the Marshal could make Othello pay for sullying his daughter. The way Iago saw it, Othello would be dead by morning, probably for resisting arrest or some such nonsense. Perhaps Othello would be so enraged he would kill the Marshal before the MPs killed him.

Iago sped toward Othello's penthouse. He didn't want to miss a minute of the action.

*

Iago let the Tucker coast to a stop on the sidewalk in front of Othello's building. Falstaff Avenue was a quiet neighborhood in the city of Olde Detroit. It was a world away from Avon, better known as the Red District, where Iago lived and where the gin joints and burlesque shows held sway over the masses. Othello had invested his earnings wisely and had purchased the penthouse during the last active act of aggression from the Alliance in '86. He had told Iago that men like him and Cass and Iago himself who profited from violence should have a quiet place to which they could retire to escape that same violence. Iago hopped out of the car, walked up to the door of Othello's building, and hit the buzzer beside the slot that said "Jones". A few moments passed before a deep and rich baritone voice came through the speaker.

"Yes?" it said.

"Hey boss, sorry to wake you so late but I need to come up and talk to you. It's important," Iago said into the speaker. Silence. Then the crackle of the speaker.

"Come on up," Othello said. Iago pushed through the two huge brass and glass doors and walked into the lobby of Othello's building. The black and white checkered tile on the floor caught the light and glistened as he walked toward the elevators. Iago pushed the "P" for penthouse and hummed to himself as he rose. Most of the time he, Othello and Cass met at their headquarters on Venice Avenue. He had only been in O's apartment three times in the last five years. Each time he visited it was more opulent than the previous time.

The doors to the elevator wheezed as they opened and Iago stepped out into a dimly lit hallway. O's apartment was the last one on the left. Iago saw the brass sconces and the plush carpet. He saw the gorgeous silk wallpaper and the lush plants. He shook his head.

He pushed the doorbell at O's apartment.

The door opened and Othello Rohan Jones filled Iago's field of vision. He was taller than Iago and wider, without as much cushioning. His bald head gleamed in the weak light and a trim goatee framed his full lips. A black t-shirt struggled to contain his deltoids. His dark brown eyes studied Iago's face with just the barest hint of anger, but Iago knew he was holding that anger in check... for now.

"Come in, Iggy, and tell me what's so important that you needed to wake me up at four in the morning," Othello said. He walked over to his sectional sofa and sat down with a sigh. Iago walked in, sat in the recliner, ran his hand across his face and let out a long low whistle.

"Look, I wouldn't have come over this late if it wasn't important, but I was down at Nero's having a drink and some guy named Rodriego, a sentry, was saying some stuff about you. You and Desi," Iago said. His voice halted a few times as he spoke. Technically, he was telling the truth.

"What kind of things?" Othello said. Iago watched as the smoldering anger behind his eyes grew into a bright flame of rage.

"I don't want to repeat what he was saying. It was some fucked-up stuff but it's not important. What is important is that he said he was going to the base to tell Desi's dad that she was living with you," Iago said.

"And how would he know Desi?" Othello asked. He had crossed his arms across the expanse of his chest. Two bright red serpentine dragon tattoos, the symbol of the Sky Troopers, traversed his forearms. The heads of the dragon bore white wings.

Iago dropped his head slightly before he spoke again.

"Probably from the Merchant. Some of these soldier boys get themselves a crush on a pretty girl. I mean, hell, we were young soldier boys once, you know. And the girls down there at Merchants, well, they gotta work hard for their tips," Iago said. Othello leaned forward and put his hands on his knees and stared into Iago's eyes.

"Desi is a showgirl, not a stripper," he said softly. Iago held up his hand in a mock surrender.

"I know, man, I'm just saying these young guys can get infatuated. But the main thing is you know how the Marshal feels about us mercs."

"Yeah. We're good enough to do his dirty work but then he doesn't want us to track that dirt into his house," Othello said bitterly.

"So if he calls Desi or goes over to her place and finds she isn't there, where you think he gonna head to next? And you know how the Marshal can be. He'll flip if he catches the two of you shacking up," Iago said. He hoped he sounded concerned.

"Let him come. I love Desi. We're not shacking up, we're –" Othello started to say but a knock at his door cut him off in mid-sentence.

"I guess the Marshal doesn't think he needs to buzz me before he comes up," Othello said after the third knock.

"With those War Powers amendments, he really doesn't need to," Iago said. Othello looked at him for a full minute and let his visitors knock two more times before he rose.

Othello opened the door. Four MPs walked into his apartment carrying stunsticks and gas guns. The shortage of gunpowder during a war that had lasted forty-eight years had necessitated the advent of new and different firearms, since all the gunpowder was earmarked for the military when the cease-fire ended. Gas guns had a cartridge filled with an explosive gas instead of gunpowder. They were lighter than a traditional gun but not quite as accurate. The stunsticks were technically not classified as a lethal force weapon but four of them pressed against your body at the same time could induce a cardiac event. Othello had used them in a few missions. The MPs parted and stood two abreast on either side of Othello's door.

Marshal Antonio Brabanzio walked into Othello's apartment. He was shorter than Iago or Othello but just as wide. He wore his dress blue uniform and a long dark green overcoat with epaulets on the shoulders. His peaked blue cap was pulled down, nearly obscuring his eyes. His face was tanned and wind beaten, a testament to a life in the cockpit of gyrocopters and staring into the sun from the launch deck of dozens of flying fortresses. The Marshal shut the door behind him and took off his peaked cap. He handed it to one of the MPs.

"Jones," he said. His voice had an almost melodious timbre.

"Marshal," Othello said. He crossed his arms and the dragons rippled across his skin.

"No. Not tonight. I am not here as the Marshal of the Continental Confederation's United Armored Infantry and Sky Command for the city of Olde Detroit and the province of New Haven. I am here as Antonio. I am here as a father, Jones. I am going to ask you a question and you will answer it truthfully. Is my daughter here?" the Marshal asked. Othello stroked his goatee for a moment.

"If she was, would that really be any business of yours? She's over eighteen, as am I. We wouldn't be breaking any laws nor violating any ordinances," Othello said. The Marshal let out a long breath.

"How old are you, Jones? 34, 35? My daughter is 19 years old. A kid. She doesn't know what kind of man you are or what kind of woman she is becoming, dancing at that gin joint. I'm glad her mother is gone so she doesn't have to bear witness to the degradation our daughter chooses to visit upon herself or the company she chooses to keep."

"And what kind of man do you think I am, Marshal?" Othello said, his voice barely rising above a whisper. Iago had gone on enough jobs with Othello to know the large man was incensed. The lower his voice became, the higher his level of rage. Iago could feel the tension in the room grow.

"A killer. A thief. A gun for hire who turned his back on his command and his comrades for a chance to peddle the skills the Confederation taught you to the highest bidder."

"Well then, I guess it's good the Confederation always bids high," Othello said. The Marshal sucked at his teeth.

"I'll ask you one more time. Is my daughter here?"

"I don't believe that is any of your business," Othello said. He uncrossed his arms and let them hang loosely at his sides. Iago had seen this stance before many times. O was getting ready to fight. The Marshal nodded to the MP to his left.

"Tear this place apart. And arrest Mr. Jones for, I don't know, not cooperating with a Confederation official for starters," the Marshal said. The MPs began to move toward Othello.

"Take one more step toward me and I promise you that you will be picking up your teeth with broken fingers," Othello said. His voice was barely a whisper.

One of the MPs pulled out his stun stick. The tip crackled with a blue and white electrical charge. Iago stepped back toward the sliding door which led to the balcony of Othello's penthouse. The MPs advanced on Othello. Iago licked his lips.

"Stop this, Dad. Just stop it right now," a light airy voice said. All eyes turned toward the hall that led to the bedroom. Desi was standing there, wearing one of O's white cotton dress shirts and a mood scarf that held back her luxuriant brown hair. Iago had to admit she was striking. Her pale gray eyes stared out at the scene unfolding in the living room.

"Go back to bed, love," Othello said. Desi walked out of the hall and stood next to Othello. They clasped hands. His dark caramel skin stood out in deep contrast to her delicate pale fingers.

"No, baby, I'm an adult even if my Dad doesn't want to accept that fact. That's not my fault, it's not your fault, it's no one's fault. It's just the way it is," she said.

Brabanzio rolled his eyes. "So now you've taken up with gunclappers. Mercenaries. Do you know what this man and his associates do for a living?" he said. Desi stepped closer to Othello.

"Yes, the same thing you do except without any sense of false patriotism," she said. The Marshal's face turned red.

"Arrest them both," he said through clenched teeth.

"Sir?" one of the MPs asked.

"Did I stutter, soldier? Arrest Mr. Jones and Miss Brabanzio," the Marshal said.

"No. If you are going to arrest us, address us properly. Mr and Mrs. Jones," Desi said.

For a moment Brabanzio didn't say a word. He just stood in the middle of the floor vibrating with rage like a tuning fork. He was grinding his teeth so hard it looked like his jaw was struggling to become a separate entity.

"You married... him?" the Marshal said finally.

"Yesterday at the justice of the peace," Desi said. She looked at Othello and squeezed his hand. Othello looked at her and gave a short slow nod.

No one in the room moved for a few minutes.

"Sir, do you still want me to arrest them?" one of the MPs asked.

The Marshal started to speak but Othello's phone rang. All eyes turned toward the black telephone with the bulky handset. Othello let go of Desi's hand.

"I'm going to answer that. I trust I won't be electrocuted... Dad," Othello said. He walked over to the phone and touched the small circular screen in the center of the rotary dial. The screen glowed with a pale blue light and the caller's name was displayed. Othello turned to the Marshal and smiled a tiny smile that played around the corners of his mouth. He picked up the phone and listened for a few moments before replacing it in the cradle and turning to the Marshal.

"I think you are about to be summoned, Marshal," Othello said.

Iago was standing near the sliding door but he could read the name on the screen. It said 'Mansion'.

A harsh buzzing sound came from where the Marshal was standing. His eyes never left Othello as he reached down into his cavernous coat. He pulled out a shiny black box the size of a deck of cards. The Marshal looked at a watery display screen on the outside of the box. He nodded curtly.

"So it would appear," the Marshal said. He grabbed his hat from the MP and pulled it down over his head. He turned around and walked toward the door. As the MPs began to file out with him he turned back and looked at Desi and Othello.

"Are you on Kick? Or Speed or H? Does he supply you with your drugs? Is that why you're here with him?" the Marshal asked. His voice seemed weaker and more strained than when he first arrived.

"I didn't drug her, Marshal. I didn't threaten her. I didn't bewitch her with black magic. I opened my heart to her and showed her all the scars and she loved me anyway. I told her how I grew up in Moortown with no mother or father, and yet I survived. I told her about joining the Air Force then joining Sky Command. I told her about losing my squadron at the Battle of Breckenridge Heights. I told her how the faces of those men wait for me every time I close my eyes. And yes, I told her of becoming a mercenary, of seeing the sun rise over what's left of the pyramids. Of swimming with dolphins off the coast of Oceania.

"I told her all these things and more, until one day I realized I wanted to stop telling her stories about me and begin to make memories about us. I realized I was in love with her, Marshal. A kind of love a killer like me never expected to find," Othello said. He held out his hand and Desi walked over to him and took it.

"Your love is strong, Othello. Sometimes our greatest strength is our greatest weakness," Iago thought to himself. The Marshal smiled a mirthless smile.

"Hear me when I tell you this, Moor. My daughter is a spoiled, capricious brat. And like all brats she will tire of this new toy called marriage. She betrayed and disappointed her own father and she will do the same to you. Mark my words. Now I must go and be the Marshal and you must come and be the killer and we have to pretend we don't hate each other," the Marshal said.

"I won't be pretending, Marshal," Othello said.

"Right," the Marshal said.

"Dad. I do love him. I really do. I know I can't ask you to be happy for me, but could you please just take a breath and not do what you always do and try and fix something that isn't broken," Desi said.

"I'll see you at the Governor's Mansion. Bring your hoodlum friends with you. Time to earn your blood money, I suspect," the Marshal said before he walked out of the door.

"Well, that went better than I expected," Iago said with a laugh. Othello smiled.

"I expected much worse," Othello said as he kissed Desi on the forehead. "Iggy, call Cass and have him meet us at the warehouse. We'll ride over to the Governor's mansion together," Othello said.

"Should I call any of the other guys?" Iago asked, squeezing his fist very tight. He hated being called Iggy. He had never corrected Othello about it because there had never seemed to be a right time.

Othello shook his head. "No. We're just taking the A team. Get a feel for what kind of job this is. Then I'll pull other guys in if we need them. The smaller the crew the bigger the split, don't you agree?" Othello asked. Iago smiled. Desi kissed Othello on his cheek.

"This isn't the way I wanted him to find out but I'm glad he knows," she whispered. Othello kissed her back.

"Of course, Boss," Iago said as he dug his nails into the palms of his hands.

*

Cassio Michaels stared at the ceiling of Bianca Torres' bedroom. The temperature of the room was cool but his body was slick with sweat. Fucking Bianca was like being strapped to an exercise machine that had a fine, tight ass. She was as insatiable as she was inventive. Cass couldn't help but think her sexual skills were in some way a result of her time as a courtesan in the Western provinces of the Axis Alliance. The thought was mildly disconcerting. He knew he was being the worst kind of hypocrite (he had lost count years ago of how many women he had slept with) but that did nothing to stifle the images that flooded his head. And yet here he was again in her bed.

He liked Bianca as more than just a friend but not quite enough to even begin to think of it as love. She was funny and high-spirited. She could cuss like a sailor and drink like a sky captain. He turned his head and looked at her as she slept. She was curled into a tight little ball with her sumptuous rear next to his thigh. Sweat had plastered her bluish hair to her head. It was that hair, cut into a page boy style, which had first drawn his attention when he had seen her at the strip club over on Capulet Boulevard. Her short, lithe frame had whirled and spun around the pole defying the laws of gravity. Her blue hair had flashed under the strobe lights like a flare from a crashing gyrocopter.

Now they met every few weeks, usually when Cass had come back from some job in the southern quadrant of the Confederation or some civilian action from a Kick dealer. Cass had left Sky Command after five years; his tour had been up and he couldn't see himself doing another five years dealing with the incompetence that rolled downhill from High Command to the actual boys in the sky and on the ground. He took his skills and his lack of impulse control and entered the dark and murky world of mercenaries. The current cease-fire provided him with enough work that he could afford to refuse some of the more nefarious jobs the local underworld bosses tried to steer his way.

He had a flexible code of honor. He would not work a job that violated that code unless he was in dire straits. Luckily he had not found himself in any straits, dire or otherwise, for a few years now. He knew his good fortune had coincided with hooking up with Othello Jones and his crew. They were professional, skilled, and connected. He had made more money in two years with them than in five years working on his own.

Othello was that rarest of animals – a good leader who was also a good man. Cass watched as he carried himself like an officer but completed his missions with the flair of a corsair. He expected your very best and paid you fairly for it. That he owed Othello his allegiance was a given. And Cass respected him, more than any officer he'd ever served under in the Sky Command. More than his absentee father. More than any man he had ever known.

A loud piercing bell began to ring in the bedroom. Cass leaned out of the bed and picked up his khakis and fished around in the pocket of the pants. He pulled out a small copper-plated box. The box opened and a small telescreen cast a sickly green light on Cass's face. A static image of Iago greeted him. Cass touched a button on the keyboard of his telecommunicator and the image became a live video feed.

"Hey there, pretty boy. The boss wants to meet at the warehouse. We got a job. So clean off your dick and put on your pants and meet us by five," Iago said. Cass laughed.

"And good morning to you too, Iggy. I'll be there. Tell O I'm on my way. Why didn't he call me?" Cass asked. Iago smiled.

"Trouble with the missus, I guess. Her dad went by his place tonight and from what I hear it got heated," he said. Cass frowned.

"Well, that sucks. O is a good guy. Desi is lucky to have him," Cass said. O was that man who could lay claim to that higher moral standard. He was the best of them. Better than Iggy, better than himself.

"I agree, but I don't think the Marshal sees it that way," Iago said.

"Well, he looks down his nose at all of us until it's time to cross the border and do our work," Cass said into his telecom.

"Well, better to be thought a brave devil than a cowardly angel," Iago said. He winked and Cass found himself laughing. Iggy liked to push his buttons but he was a solid companion and a skilled fighter. Even if he was a little trigger happy at times.

"Alright, see ya in a few. Cass out," Cass said as he closed the telecom. Bianca turned and grabbed his lean, muscular arm.

"Have to go play with guns now?" she asked. Her voice was husky from too many gin fizzes and too many cigarettes in her short life. Cass pulled away from her grip and stood.

"Just gotta go to work, that's all," he said as he hopped into his pants. Bianca pulled her knees up to her chin. She bit her bottom lip.

"When will I see you again? I know you're a bad-ass merc and gotta be all secretive and shit, but I'd like to have an idea when I should clean up my place," she said in a low voice.

"You should clean up whether I'm coming over or not," Cass said laughing.

"What for? You're the only one who ever stays the night," she said. She lay back down and turned on her side.

"Make sure the door is locked on your way out," she said into her pillow.

Cass pulled his black t-shirt over his broad chest and grabbed his brown bomber jacket off the chair. He didn't say anything as he walked out of the room. Cass emerged from the ramshackle apartment building and felt the cool air smack him in the face. His hovercycle was parked at the end of the sidewalk, chained to a street lamp.

The Tesla Quasar 2200 had been his gift to himself after his last job with Othello and the boys. Jeff Jerome over at Black Cat Customs had chopped and rocked the body of the hovercycle to fit Cass's unique sensibility. Under the seat was a 5.5 cubic magnetron engine that powered two 36 inch turbines. An exhaust system snaked from under the seat toward the back of the cycle like long chrome plated bubbles. A pair of ape-hanger handles, a tri-bulb headlight and a glossy black paint job completed the custom body and motor work. It had set him back five thousand dollaesos but it was worth it.

Cass put on a pair of leather goggles trimmed in chrome that he pulled out of his bomber jacket. He unlocked the chain and put it back in the saddle bag under the cross bar. The hovercycle sat on three short slats that looked like miniature skis. Cass pulled his key out of his pants pocket and slid it in the ignition, and the cycle came to life with a deep rumbling roar. Cass grabbed the handles and squeezed the take-off throttle and slowly the hovercycle began to rise into the sky. When the altimeter on the crossbar said fifty feet he flicked the rotators. The cycle dropped for a heart-stopping moment as the turbines rotated from a vertical to horizontal position. Cass lived for that drop. He felt his stomach climb into his chest as the cycle began to fall.

Then he squeezed the flight throttle and the hovercycle took off into the night. He climbed into the night sky waiting for that moment when he got above the omnipresent lights of the city and could actually see the stars. He didn't believe in astrology. His fate was not in the stars. Perhaps it was in the sky but not the stars.

They all arrived at approximately the same time – Cass on his hovercycle, Iago in his Tucker, and Othello right behind him in his white Edison Shark. The Shark was a short snub-nosed car with wide sweeping lines and three "gills" on the side of each fender wall, and a grill like the toothy grin of a Great White. Othello climbed out as Cass was dropping his landing gear and Iago was locking the Tucker. He had thrown on a black leather jacket and a black wide brim fedora.

"Cass, you never wear a fucking hat. You like showing off those chestnut locks too much, don't you?" Iago asked. Cass smiled

"Doesn't make much sense to wear a hat on a hovercycle, Iggy," he said. Iago shrugged his shoulders and touched the brim of his own hat.

"Style doesn't have to make sense, my man," Iago said. Cass laughed. Othello walked up to the door of the warehouse and pushed a button on the brick molding. A few moments went by before he could hear a series of locks being opened and the door swung inward. A tall man who was nearly as wide as the door stood before them with a face like a chunk of unpolished granite. The granite cracked and the man smiled.

"Mr. Jones. Everything is ready," he said.

"Thanks, Saul. We should be back by tomorrow night and know what type of equipment we will need by then. Pull Iggy's car and Cass's hovercycle into the back garage. How does the Phantom sound?" he asked. The granite cracked a little bit more.

"Like a homecoming queen getting her coochie licked." Othello shook his head.

"Saul, no need to be so vulgar," he said reproachfully. But he was smiling when he said it. Saul shrugged his shoulders. The four men moved through the warehouse in silence. They passed a few more men milling around the cavernous structure. They were hard men like Saul, all ex-military, highly disciplined and highly dangerous. The little group descended a short set of metal steps and entered Othello's garage. A long black car sat idling in the garage, its nose pointed toward the exit. Iago could feel the rumble of the motor in his chest. Chrome piping ran up and down the length of the car over the fenders and around the door and windshield. Each headlight on each side of the massive hood was detailed with intricate Gothic details. The vehicle was a rear-steer like the forklifts Iago had driven as a gunner's assistant so many years ago. But the forklifts had not been rolling works of art like this.

"The Teslacorp Black Phantom. Finest and fastest car I've ever owned," Othello said softly. If he could go back in time and ask his 12-year-old self if he could imagine ever owning a car like this, that young boy would have laughed and laughed until he was out of breath. And yet here it was. At one time this car had been his most prized possession. But as he looked at this masterful combination of style and substance he knew he would sell it in an instant if Desi asked.

"Such is the nature of love," Othello mused.

"All right, gents, the Capital is three hours away. We'll make it in two. Let's see what awful things we'll be asked to do for God and Country this time," he said. Cass climbed into the back seat. Othello climbed into the driver's seat.

Iago hesitated a moment before he got into the Black Phantom. This car made his Tucker look like a demolition derby reject. He bit down hard on the inside of his mouth until he felt he could muster his trademark toothy grin. Then he climbed into the passenger seat.

"All aboard," he said as he pantomimed pulling a train whistle.

"All aboard," he whispered as he dug his nails into his palms.

They made it in one hour fifty minutes.

The guard at the gate of the Governor's mansion waved them in and told them to pull around the back and park in the guest garage. Cass chuckled.

"I don't care where you put this beauty; she stands out," he said as Othello parked the car. Othello got out and pulled his hat down on his head.

"That's not the point. It's about rank and respect. They want us to remember our place," he said. Cass sucked his teeth and climbed out of the back seat.

"Remember, pretty boy, there is always somebody higher on the totem pole than you," Iago said.

"Lesson learned," Cass said. He spat an unidentified bug out of his mouth. The law required a helmet if you rode a hovercycle but Cass couldn't see much sense in that edict. If you crashed a flybike the helmet would be wearing you. But he might consider getting a visor. He was getting real tired of bugs in his teeth.

As they exited the garage another guard met them and escorted them to the rear entrance. They were then handed off to two other guards who walked them to the official meeting room of Charles Duke, Governor of New Haven.

The Governor was already in the somber room when Othello and his men arrived. So was the Marshal, and a severe looking man with a long white scar that crossed his tanned face from his right eye to his left cheek. He had a thick mop of black hair graying at the temples and he was wearing a black on black three piece suit. The Governor did not stand but motioned for the mercenaries to sit at the end of the long brown wooden table. The room was dimly lit and windowless, with bookshelves lining the walls.

"Gentlemen, it appears the Continental Confederation must call upon you and your specific set of skills once more. However, if you are successful this may be the last time," Governor Duke said. His voice was usually full of campaign bluster and mock sincerity. But not today.

"Marshal, would you please outline the details of this mission," Governor Duke said. Brabanzio stood and walked over to the left side of the room. He pressed his finger on the spine of one of the books. The bookshelf parted and slid open to reveal a 72 inch wide telescreen. The Marshal touched the screen and a map of North America appeared. The country that used to be Canada was shown, as well as the Continental Confederation.

"As you know, there is a cease-fire between the Continental Confederation and the Axis Alliance. And as you also know, ten years ago there was a split between the North American and European factions of the Alliance. The Nazis in Europe surrendered to the combined forces of England, France, Spain and Norway. They retained territories they had won in Poland, the Ukraine and Italy. The people of Jewish descent that they persecuted created a sovereign state with the people of Palestine during the Annexation Talks of '78. The Axis Alliance refused to surrender and with the help of their traitorous comrades have been in control of Canada and Alaska since '54. The Reichlord and his cronies in Toronto have tried to conquer us for decades." The Marshal was about to continue when Othello raised his hand.

"No offense, Marshal, but why are we having a history lesson?" The Marshal shot him a look.

"Because I want you to understand the gravity of the mission you are about to undertake. You arrogant son of a bitch," he growled. The Governor cleared his throat. The Marshal squared his shoulders and continued.

"Ever since the accident on the Western Front no nation has dared tamper with nuclear energy. The work of men like Tesla and Marconi and Bester was revisited and we found other ways to kill ourselves. No country has dared open that Pandora's box. Until now," the Marshal said. Othello sat up and stroked his goatee.

"Our intelligence networks represented by Mr. Gray," the severe man nodded his head, "have solid evidence that the Axis Alliance, led by the current Reichlord, and the National Federation of Germany, led by Gutternburn, have been conspiring in secret for a reconciliation between the two arms of the Alliance. The Axis Alliance has been supplying the NFG with fuel and timber and steel. The NFG has been supplying the Axis Alliance with their technology, including the only cubic brick of enriched uranium that has been produced in forty years. Do I have your attention now, gentlemen?" the Marshal said. Othello and his men were silent.

"If the two heads of the Dragon reconcile with the threat of a nuclear bomb clutched tight in their scaly claws, other countries will bow down without hesitation. The Alliance will break the cease-fire and with added manpower and their nuclear arms they very well could overwhelm us," Mr. Gray said.

"We estimate that once the Axis Alliance receives the brick they will weaponize it immediately. In three months they could have nuclear missiles pointed directly at us across the Great Lakes," the Marshal said.

"Why not just break the cease-fire ourselves and send a battalion of sky troopers and a fortress group into the Alliance?" Cass asked. The Marshal rolled his eyes.

"While we are confident in the veracity of our information, the manner in which we obtained it may have violated certain aspects of the cease-fire already. We go in with guns blazing, we alert the Alliance that we know about their plans. We'll speed up their reconciliation timetable and they'll hide the brick until it's too late," the Marshal said.

"Gentlemen, our resources and our manpower are stretched to the breaking point. Our oil and fuel reserves are low. The oil we get from our South American friends is hijacked by pirates who are tacitly employed by the Alliance. Our European allies have no interest in war. We're on our own. This mission comes from the highest levels of the

Continental government and may determine whether this Confederation continues," Governor Duke said.

"We get the brick, we make the rules," Mr. Gray said flatly.

"And how do you propose to get the brick?" Othello said. The Marshal touched the telescreen again. The map dissolved and a video of an enormous Alliance flying fortress appeared. Othello noticed that flying fortresses fell into two categories, flying 'M's and flying 'V's. Alliance fortresses were always M shaped with gigantic front and rear propellers and enormous turbines. Gun ports up and down the two arms of the M and missile ports on the central axis. They were bigger than Confederation fortresses and required more fuel to run. The Alliance had fuel to spare. They had oil derricks all the way up to the Arctic.

This particular fortress was an aged coppery green. Bulletproof glass windows ran up and down the sides of the M. On the underside was a huge sealed hangar.

"This is the Axis Alliance Flying Fortress 7123. They call it the AAFF Green-Eyed Monster. It is currently on its way across the Atlantic, coming back from the Fatherland with a very special cargo," the Marshal said.

"Can't you just shoot it down?" Iago asked.

"Cease-fire," Cass said quietly. Iago looked at his partner. He fought the urge to pull out his tasestick and shove it in his eye. The Marshal touched the screen again. This time the video showed the view from above the fortress.

"The plan is simple as hell and dangerous as shit. We drop you and your team from one of our bombers. You are all certified to operate an Edison class Rocket Pack. There is an exhaust port here," the Marshal pointed to a point near the top of the rear of the M. "You and your team enter there. You will be given a detailed schematic of the ship and the location of the brick. Once you have retrieved it you will escape out of the side of the fortress, blowing the main engine and sending the ship into the North Atlantic. You will leave behind certain incriminating evidence which will point to the Oceania Empire. The Axis Alliance will not acknowledge the existence of the brick and their weapons program will be thrown into disarray," the Marshal said.

"If you are captured or killed you will be disavowed," the Governor said.

"Of course," Othello said.

"If the Alliance does decide to attack we use the brick as leverage. We hold them off with it until we weaponize it. Then we wipe them off the fucking map," the Marshal said. For a moment the room was silent. Then Iago raised his hand. He asked the question he assumed was on everyone's mind.

"How much we getting paid for this?" he said.

*

The Governor, the Marshal and Mr. Gray left the three mercenaries alone while they discussed the mission at hand. The Marshal had informed them not to take too long.

"If we're doing this, you have to leave in one hour. Tick tock, boys," he had said as he left the room.

"What do you think, boss?" Cass had asked. Iago felt sick to his stomach. Why didn't Cass just pull out Othello's dick right there and flop it on the table?

"One million dollaesos split three ways is a lot of money. But even more important than that, I think Brabanzio is right. I think this will finally stop the war," Othello said. Even as the words left his mouth he couldn't believe he was saying it. War had defined his entire life. It had made him what he was today, and it would determine what he was tomorrow. War was all he had ever known.

Yet as he grew closer to Desi he had begun to dream of a life out from under the shadow of Ares. A life of laughter and love, filled not with the sound of gunshots but the sound of children giggling. A life not dependent on the death of other men.

"Hey, don't get all sappy on me, boss. No more war will put us out of business," Iago said with a grin. He was thinking that one million dollaesos was a lot of money if you didn't have to split it. Well oiled gears began to turn in his mind.

Othello stood and crossed his arms. He reached toward Cass on his left with his right hand, and toward Iago on his right with his left hand.

His two associates grasped his hands.

"We who are about to die salute you," he said solemnly. His two most trusted allies rose.

"We who are about to die salute you," they said in unison.

"Let's tell the Governor we're gonna battle the green-eyed monster," Othello said.

*

An hour later they were on board the *Detroit Express* heading for the North Atlantic. The *Express* was a small lightweight transport jet that had been stripped down to the bare essentials: six seats, including the two pilots, and an expansive payload area. Othello and his associates had checked and re-checked their equipment. All three were equipped with rocket backpacks, dual drum TM-15 machine guns, .45 caliber semi-automatics, six "glop bombs" and a CMZ combat knife with a diamond edged blade.

They were flying at an altitude that would take them three thousand feet above the flight plan for the *Green Eyed Monster.* The three of them had on the full-face helmets with the oxygen back-up and thick insulated flight suits under a bomber jacket and khaki breeches with leather boots. Othello and Cass would go after the brick while Iago disabled the main engines. The Marshal had given them the schematics for the fortress and a description of the carrying case for the brick. All three of them had made this kind of assault before and they all knew the dangers it entailed.

"A nighttime high-altitude rocket jump onto a hostile well-armed fortress was not how I thought I'd be spending my day," Iago said from under his helmet.

"The sun's almost up. I wish it really was still night time. Better cover," Cass said. He checked his hand gun again. Real gunpowder, none of that unreliable gas bullshit.

"We have at least another couple of hours of darkness before dawn arrives. We'll have all the cover we will need," Othello said. Cass put his gun back in his holster and said nothing. Othello was a different man when they were on a mission. The erudite and personable friend disappeared and the cold-blooded soldier took his place. Cass didn't know how he could turn it off and on that way.

"Fifteen minutes, gents," a voice crackled through a speaker.

Othello did not wish his men good luck or entreat the favour of any deity or demigod. His religion was his training and his god was a job well done. He checked his equipment again. His levels were all good. The visor of the helmet had a liquid crystal display that created a holographic dashboard for the wearer. His altitude, speed and vital signs could all be monitored through the visor. The rocket pack was equipped with two hand held throttle controls that could be sheathed in the forearms of the jumpsuit they wore under their bomber jackets. He had had his sidearm and the collapsible two-drum TM and his bandolier of glop bombs and four drums filled with two hundred rounds each.

He was ready.

"Five minutes," the pilot said through the speaker. Iago could feel every bump of turbulence in his guts. There was a roaring in his ears that was a combination of his blood coursing through his veins and the winds battering the cargo plane. He hated the Moor. He hated Cass. But he loved moments like this, before the mission began, where he could visualize the death and destruction he was about to inflict upon his enemies. In these moments he felt like a god.

"One minute," the pilot intoned. The three men detached their seat belts and moved to the rear of the plane. The plane rocked and jostled them as they stood in front of the wide cargo door. Othello turned and gave a thumbs up to the pilot. The pilot returned the gesture.

Then he opened the cargo door. The cabin was instantly filled with an otherworldly howling as the wind and frigid air above the North Atlantic rushed through the door. The cold tried to steal its way into Othello's body but his neoprene jumpsuit provided a nearly impenetrable barrier. It offered protection against the cold and was also fire proof. He took a deep breath.

"One, two... three!" he counted. Othello, Iago and Cass were all on the same closed radio circuit so they could communicate through their helmets. When Othello said "three" they all ran toward the door and jumped one after another into the black sky.

They fell like stones. Cass could see his speed increasing on the floating dial on the left side of his visor. The wind speed was on the right. His vitals were in the center. His heart rate was 98 beats per minute. He put his hand by his sides and flattened his body to increase the speed of his descent. His companions did the same. At first all he could see were thin gossamer clouds below him and twinkling stars above him. The sun was threatening to emerge from behind the horizon to his right.

"I'm flying," he thought to himself. It was an absent-minded thought but one that always popped in his head when he made a jump. The clouds began to dissipate. And then the *Green Eyed Monster* appeared like a leviathan emerging from the depths of a black sea.

The fortress was a gargantuan flying M. Green and yellow lights ran up and down the arms of the M. Six turbines were positioned on the underside of the M. Fifty millimeter gunports ran up and down the outer arms of the M. Twelve huge guns, six on each side, that could fire a shell every 25 seconds. Two huge exhaust ports were positioned at the aft section of the M. Cass struggled against the fear that was trying to worm its way into his belly. The fortress was enormous. Even with the uploaded schematics and blueprints, finding the "brick" would be like looking for a piece of hay in a needle stack.

"Do not engage thrusters until we are fifty yards out. Conserve your fuel," Othello's voice said in his ear.

"Roger that," Cass said.

"Roger that, boss," Iago said.

As they got closer to the flying behemoth Othello could feel a rumbling in his chest. He realized it was the sound waves coming from the turbines. The fortress had spotters in the gunports with the gunners and radar capabilities. It had a bridge with a 360 degree camera system and a panoramic cabin window. But all those precautions were aimed outwardly and down. None of the fortress's defenses were monitoring the space above the monster.

"Ready thrusters," Othello said. He flexed his hands downward and the throttle controls shot out of their sheaths and exited just above the space between his thumb and forefinger and a metal cylinder appeared there. A second later the cylinder's walls retracted and the cylinder became an L-shaped handle with three buttons on the shorter leg. Othello pushed the first button and the rocket pack roared to life. He moved his finger to the second button and throttled up on the rocket pack's thrusters. He extended his arms out straight in front of him and banked to the right. His two companions did the same. The three figures all released their left hand throttle control and banked hard to the right. Like dancers who had performed the same steps night after night they reached for a grappling hook launcher stored in their bandoliers. The Tactical Assault Hook and Grapple Launcher had a T shaped handle and a five thousand pound carbonite line with a tungsten carbide hook and spike at the end. Some sky commando years ago had figured out if you looked at the first letter of each word in the name of the hook and grapple system and pronounced it phonetically it sounded like "toggle". The name stuck.

Othello fired the grappling hook toward the rear exhaust vent, which was as long and as wide as a school bus. The spike on the end of the hook buried itself in the greenish hide of the fortress. The hooks that surrounded the spike like the petals of a rose extended and locked onto the surface of the ship to give the line added stability. Othello pushed the button on the left side of the handle and the line started to retract back into the barrel of the launcher pulling Othello closer to the ship. Cass and Iago shot their toggles as well, landing to the left of where Othello's had found its mark. They retracted their lines as they cut the power to their rocket packs.

Using the line as a tether, Othello rappelled around to the front of the vent. As the wind battened his body around like a shuttlecock, Othello pulled himself closer to the ship by using his rocket pack, his huge forearms, and his unbreakable will. Once he had both feet braced against the bottom vane of the vent he pulled a laser saw out of his bandolier.

Othello swung the saw quickly and decisively, hacking away a man sized section of the vent. The wind caught the sections he had cut and pulled them into the rapidly brightening sky. While he was doing that Cass and Iago fluttered in the wind like flags on the hood of a diplomat's car as they held on to their own grappling hooks. Finally after he had made the opening large enough Othello spoke into his radio.

"The temperature inside the exhaust vent will be in excess of 200 degrees. Our suits will only protect us for three minutes from that kind of heat. According to the blueprints we need to go about twenty-five feet inside the exhaust before we cut through the pipe and drop down into the third level. Let's go!" Othello said. Cass and Iago gave him the thumbs up and then wall-walked and rappelled over to the vent. Years of training and conditioning took over as they moved along the exterior.

They left the frigid night air and entered the mouth of a dragon. Cass tried to put the heat out of his mind but even with the oxygen being pumped into his helmet he felt like he was suffocating. Cass tried to forget he had pounds of explosives strapped to his body as they made their way deeper into the throat of the dragon. A bluish cloud of fumes filled the exhaust vent and the heat seemed to be melting his bomber jacket to his skin.

"Here," Othello said into his communicator. He had memorized the blueprints and schematics. He pulled out the laser saw again and squatted down near the floor of the fire chamber. Cass glanced at the timer in the corner of his field of vision. One minute had already passed. Othello reconfigured the saw until it looked like a laser pointer. He pointed it at the floor and began to cut out a man-sized circle.

"Two minutes, boss," Iago said but Othello did not respond.

"Two and a half minutes," Iago said. Othello continued to work. Cass began to feel a burning sensation on his forearms. Othello worked on in silence. Iago began to pant. The outline of a glowing red circle began to appear as Othello cut away at the charred metal.

"Three minutes," he said between pants.

"Got it," Othello said as a large circle of metal fell to the floor of what appeared to be a store room. Iago went through the hole first followed by Cass and then Othello. The storeroom housed some beans, sugar, flour and other sundry items.

"Iago, make your way to level four. Cass and I will head to level five. Once you reach the engine room hold them off until we confirm we have the package. Then blow this pop stand," Othello said.

"Roger that," Iago said. He was smiling behind his visor. Othello moved toward the door of the store room. The entire mission hinged on getting to those tunnels unnoticed.

Othello opened the door a crack and peered out into the hall. Two Alliance airmen were walking down the hall toward the storeroom. Othello held his left fist up to Cass and Iago as he put his right hand on the butt of his pistol. The two airmen were almost to the door when they took a sharp left turn. Othello removed his hand from his gun.

"Now!" he said into the radio. The three men knelt and moved quickly to the end of the extruded metal lined hallway. Othello reached the service tunnel door and produced a steel rod with a star-shaped tip from his bandolier. He inserted the tip into a matching lock on the door and opened the hatch with a sharp twist of the rod. All three men entered the service tunnel. The tunnel was only five feet wide from floor to ceiling, with long reddish fluorescent tubes running up and down the tunnel. The deep rumbling of the engines of the fortress was even more powerful here.

"All right, Iago - you head for the engine room. Cass and I are headed for the main cargo hold. See you on the other side, brother. Remember, if you don't get confirmation from us in 15 that we have the package, you're out," Othello said into his communicator. Iago nodded. Othello held his fist up and Iago touched it with his knuckles. Iago repeated the gesture with Cass. Then he was scrambling along the tunnel toward the left. Cass and Othello headed toward the right.

"I'm outta here after five minutes. Sending this bucket of bolts to the bottom of the sea should be worth at least half the bounty the Confederation was offering," Iago thought to himself. He grinned even wider.

Othello moved quickly through the tunnels and Cass followed. The service tunnels reminded Cass of the corn maze he had gone to as a kid. He had gotten lost in the maze and had tried not to cry but it had gotten dark. He had started to cry silently when suddenly he'd seen the Alliance gyrocopters streak across the sky and strafe the county fair with Phoenix missiles. Fire had engulfed the fairgrounds and little Cassio Michaels had run through the walls of the maze screaming for his father, his brother, for anyone in his family. None of them had survived the attack. After that night he never cried again.

Finally they came to a short ladder that dropped them down to another set of tunnels. Othello stopped in front of a service door and put his hand on the latch.

"We go in hot and hard. Eliminate any impediments to our mission with extreme prejudice," he said. Cass pulled out the collapsible TM-17 and began assembling the gun with sudden, practiced movements. He unfolded the barrel from the stock and locked it in place. He pulled on a tab at the back of the gun and it went from six to 24 inches. He grabbed two drums, 200 rounds each, from the pockets of his breeches. Cass locked them in place and removed the safety.

Othello pulled his pistol out of its holster and removed the safety.

"He who sheds his blood today with me is my brother," he said into the communicator. Cass nodded.

Iago, meanwhile, was crouched in front of the service door directly across from the engine room. There were twelve men running the massive engines, monitoring the fuel tanks and maintaining the oil pressure. Twelve men who'd woken up that morning not knowing today would be their last day on earth. Iago's TM was locked and loaded. He grabbed the latch. Just before he opened the door he laughed to himself. He had a woody.

He pulled the latch and emerged from the tunnel. There was no one in the passageway. Directly across the hall was the main engine room. Iago moved toward the door. He had fourteen glop bombs of various power and had planned on using one to blow the door. But what if the door wasn't locked? Iago highly doubted the door to the engine room on a Battle Class Alliance Destroyer would be unlocked but there was no harm in checking.

Iago almost laughed out loud when the wheel began to turn. He pulled on the door and stepped inside the massive engineering room. There was a catwalk running along the perimeter of the room. There was a second catwalk that ran along the middle of the room with a ladder on each corner that led down to the four main diesel powered engines. Each motor produced a torque that in turn powered the six turbines that lifted the fortress from the earth. The twelve men in the engine room were moving like busy worker bees checking levels and making adjustments. Each man wore bulky ear phones and the gray and black uniforms of the Engineering Department. The noise coming from the engines was deafening. None of the men looked up to the second catwalk. None of them saw Iago step inside the room and close and lock the door.

"Come, let us take a muster speedily. Doomsday is near, die all, die merrily," Iago whispered to himself as he put his finger on the trigger of the TM.

*

On the other side of the Monster, Othello was in Hell.

It was a hell of bullets and screams and explosions. He and Cass had entered the passageway from the service tunnel without too much trouble. As they approached the door to the cargo hold they spotted two guards standing near the door dressed in the traditional black and gray uniforms of the Alliance. The Alliance had stopped wearing swastikas years ago but the two soldiers did have twin lightning bolts pinned to their collars. Cass had pulled out a hyperpin filled with a powerful fast-acting narcotic when the ship's air horn went off like a banshee. Red distress lights began to flash through the passageway. Cass glanced at Othello.

"I guess Iago has announced our presence. Flank me and protect our rear. I'll take out the guards," Othello had said into his communicator. The passageway to the cargo hold was a narrow channel. Soldiers advancing down the hall would have little room to maneuver to the left or the right. Cass figured it would be like shooting the proverbial fish in the barrel. He fell to one knee and aimed the machine gun down the hall. He could hear the sound of heavy boots hitting the metal grates that made up the floor of the passageway. It sounded like a whole battalion was coming up the hall but Cass knew that was a trick of acoustics. He put his finger on the trigger and slowed his breathing.

Othello stepped from the shadows of the passageway and shot the first guard in the face with his .45. The second guard wheeled around with his sub-machine gun but before he could pull the trigger Othello shot him in the forehead. Othello pulled out the glop bombs from his bandolier. The bombs were extremely sticky plastique explosives with a timer embedded in the middle of the plastique. A soldier could set the timer then throw the bomb at his target. The adhesive properties of the plastique were such that it would stick to almost any substance. The bomb made a "glop" sound when it landed on its target. Othello threw the glop bomb at the heavy steel door of the cargo hold, then turned to kneel beside Cass.

Twenty soldiers turned the corner and headed up the passageway toward the cargo hold. They had their weapons drawn and were walking in a tight formation. Once they hit the passageway they were shoulder to shoulder, squeezed together like cattle headed for the slaughter. Cass and Othello opened fire. The TM-17 and the .45 ripped through the men. Screams filled the corridor. Cass aimed high for head shots while Othello aimed low for the thighs and groins. The men fell like bowling pins.

Then the glop bomb exploded. Othello rushed into the cargo hold with his gun drawn. Cass took a position by the door waiting for the inevitable reinforcements. Othello moved straight for Section D against the back wall of the room. There, sitting on a metal shop shelf, was a small nondescript wooden box the size of a brick. It had a smooth unpolished surface and was finger-jointed together. Inside the plain wooden box was a metal box with an insulated interior that protected everyone aboard from the deadly effects of radiation poisoning. Othello locked the box into a saddle bag that hung from his bandoliers. Once the box was secure he grabbed the three remaining glop bombs hanging from his bandolier with his gloved hand. He set the timers and hurled them at the far left wall.

More gunfire erupted behind him. Cass was spraying the reinforcements with fire from the TM but they had learned from the mistakes of their fallen comrades and had come into the corridor two at a time, taking cover behind bulkheads and corpses. They were armed with Alliance issued four cylinder sub-machine guns. It was the equal of the TM but none of the airmen were the equal of Cass. He calmly shot them or sprayed them with enough suppressive fire to keep them at bay.

"Six seconds till detonation. Wolf 2, what's your status?" Othello said into his communicator.

He was greeted by silence.

"I repeat, six seconds to detonation. Wolf 2, report," Othello said. Nothing. Cass knew there were only two reasons he wasn't answering. He was dead or he was captured. The entire ship listed to the right. Cass held onto the door frame with one hand as the airmen in the passageway crashed into the walls. Othello held onto the shelf that was bolted to the wall. Suddenly a third reason entered Cass's mind. Iago had already blown the engine and had left the ship. Before he could relay his thoughts to O the glop bombs exploded.

A large section of the cargo hold ceased to exist. The glop bombs tore a hole in the far right wall of the cargo hold and the rapid change in pressure at such an altitude created a vacuum effect. Shrapnel, crates of armaments, and supplies were sucked out of the airship and into the sky. Cass noticed that the sun had risen and the world looked as bright and shiny as a new penny. Cass felt himself being pulled toward the gaping hole. He would have to make a decision soon. Drop the gun and hold on with both hands to the ruined door frame or let the winds of the slipstream drag him out into the atmosphere and engage his rocket pack. In both scenarios he lost his gun but one ended with freedom, the other with possible death or incarceration.

"Wolf 3, go!" Othello yelled into the communicator. Cass wanted to ask about Iago but there was no time. Cass let go of the door.

He felt like a soda bottle tossed from a moving car. His rocket controls shot out of their sheaths and he engaged his thrusters. Cass put his arms by his sides and climbed higher, heading toward the sun like Icarus by straightening his body and tilting his head upward. Then he banked sharply to the left and relaxed his body. He throttled back and felt himself begin to drop. As he fell he cut the rocket pack off and fell toward the earth like a stone. He could see the angry seas of the North Atlantic churning below him but from this height they looked like water in a bucket. Cassio never felt more alive than when he was in the sky facing death. As he fell he heard Othello's voice in his ear.

"Wolf 3, proceed to checkpoint Boniface," Othello said.

"Wolf 1, any word from Wolf 2?" Cass asked.

"Negative, Wolf 3," Othello said.

"Wolf 1, any hostiles scrambling?" Cass asked.

"Negative, Wolf 3. Hostiles are going down with the ship. Your 3 o'clock," Othello said. Cass turned his head as far as he could to his right. He saw Othello about 75 feet away falling like a star with his hands down by his sides. In the distance just above the horizon he saw the *Green Eyed Monster* and its crew of over 200 was now a fireball. Flames were shooting out of the middle of the M and out the back. The fortress fell backwards with its exhaust ports facing the ocean. The Monster was dead.

"We did that," Cass thought to himself. He believed Othello. What they'd done today might actually end the war. They could have changed the world for millions of people. He should have felt proud. Seeing that fortress fall, a fortress that was now a tomb, should have filled him with a sense of accomplishment. They had done what others could not, and in doing so could have changed the course of history. Yet Cass couldn't shake the feeling that karma was a mathematician at heart and she abhorred any inequality. They had taken lives, whether as heroes or murderers depended on what uniform you wore. But Cass knew, better than some, that everything had a price.

*

The two of them streaked across the sky until they reached the outskirts of Olde Detroit. They landed near a small cinder block building near the shore of Lake Michigan. The sun sparkled off the water and the water lapped against the shore. Othello's Black Phantom and a Confederation transport truck were parked near the building. Othello and Cass walked up to the wooden door of the building and Othello removed his helmet. He put his eye to a nearly indiscernible peephole in the door. A retinal scan confirmed his identity and the door slid open to reveal an industrial style elevator. Cass and Othello climbed into the lift and held onto the rails as it rapidly descended.

When it finally came to a stop they were in the midst of a buzzing hive of activity. Confederation soldiers moved from monitor to monitor analyzing video feeds. Radio technicians monitored transmissions snatched from Alliance channels. A huge map of North America dominated one wall. A high ceiling with two rows of huge LED recessed lights stretched the length of half a football field. Two broad-shouldered soldiers strode toward the elevator. They both had a distinctively blank look on their faces that was the province of operatives of the Office of Strategic Actions. The OSA was the black ops arm of the Confederation's Sky Command in Fort Boniface. If the Sky Command was a body, Fort Boniface was the mouth, chewing up information and swallowing it to feed the brain of Sky Command deep within the earth among halls carved from bedrock. Othello had been here when he served, and so had Cass. It seemed less intimidating but no less impressive when one wasn't wearing a uniform. When Othello had served he had been offered a position here but he had politely declined. He had wanted to be an eagle flying through the sky, not an ant working in the nest.

"The Marshal is waiting for you in the debriefing room. Follow us," one of the soldiers said. His high-pitched voice was incongruous with his size. Cass and Othello removed their helmets and followed the two through the chatter and militaristic productivity of the main monitoring room. They exited through a door at the end of the room and entered a dimly lit hallway that twisted and turned like a serpent. Finally they came to another door manned by two Sky Command sentries. One of the soldiers flashed his credentials and the sentries parted to allow them access to the debriefing room. A short gray rectangle of metal served as a table in the room with four metal stools positioned haphazardly around it. The Marshal was sitting on one of the stools.

Iago was sitting on one of the others.

Their comrade was still wearing his bomber jacket and flight suit but his rocket pack had been removed and he had a drink in his hand. He was smoking a cigar, a rare commodity even during a cease-fire. Othello smiled.

"Glad to see you didn't go down with the ship, old boy," he said. Iago shrugged his shoulders and took a drag off the stogie. Then he sipped his drink.

"My communicator went down and I took a few rounds to my helmet. I went ahead with the plan and blew the engine and blew a hole in the hull. I figured the Moor and the Pretty Boy wouldn't let a few Alliance krauts and coolies stop them from completing their mission," Iago said with a smile. If someone had been looking closely they would have noticed the smile never reached his eyes. Even as he spoke his mind replayed the scene in the engine room in his mind.

The screams of the engineers as he unloaded his TM into their bodies. The smell of blood and shit in the air and the congealed mess both bodily fluids made across the floor of the engine room. The sound of the glop bomb blowing a hole in the hull of the ship seconds before he exited the dying beast and a few more seconds before the glop bombs he had thrown in the engine exploded as well. The way he'd laughed hysterically as he set the bombs and blew the hull five minutes before they had originally planned.

Othello walked up to Iago and put his paw of a hand on his neck. He pulled him close and tousled his greasy hair. Iago flinched but shook it off and let out a booming laugh.

"Afraid you'd lost your favorite spades partner, huh?" he said. Before Othello could respond the Marshal cleared his throat. Othello turned and detached the brick from his bandolier. He put it on the table and slid it over to the Marshal. The Marshal put out his gnarled hand and stopped the box's forward progress.

"Good job, Jones. The money will be in your account by 5 p.m.," he said. The OSA agents pulled out a metallic suitcase and placed the brick inside without saying another word.

"It wasn't just the money, Marshal," Othello said. He stared at the father of his wife.

"Of course it was, Jones. Tell yourself whatever it takes to let you sleep at night but at the end of the day you're a hired gun, a killer who traded honor for glory and traded duty for riches. I hope my daughter sees that before it's too late," Brabanzio said as he and the OSA agents walked past Othello and his men.

"The quartermaster will be in to reclaim the equipment. Don't try to steal anything. I've left instructions that you are to be shot if you try to smuggle any weapons out of the fort. Good day," the Marshal said as he walked out of the door.

"There is no glory in what we do, Marshal. Only necessity," Othello said. The Marshal only grunted as he left the room. Cass clapped Othello on the shoulder.

"Hey, screw that guy. I mean, I know he's Desi's dad, but screw him and his elitist attitude. He isn't any better than us," Cass said. Othello shook his head.

"Yes, he is. He wears a uniform," Othello said. Cass was taken aback until he saw Othello smile. Cass began to chortle. Othello joined him. Iago began to howl like a wolf.

"This is all far from over, Moor," Iago thought to himself as he howled.

PART II:
Even To The Edge Of Doom

Desi sat in front of her vanity and stared in the mirror. Was it vain to think that she was beautiful? She knew she was not hideous and the manager of the Merchant obviously thought she was attractive enough to be the featured dancer for their famous burlesque show. But beautiful? She had never really thought of herself that way until she had met Othello. His constant affirmation of her beauty had finally started to sink in.

"I am beautiful," she whispered to the mirror.

'Yeah, yeah, you're gorgeous," a voice said behind her. Desi turned around.

"Emilia, you're late. Shylock is going to kill you!" Desi said. Emilia walked over to the vanity and leaned on the top batting her eyelids coquettishly.

"Shy is not gonna do a damn thing. He loves looking at this grade A prime beef too much!" Emilia said as she slapped herself on the ass. Desi let out a laugh followed by a snort.

"You're a mess, Emilia. You better not let Iggy hear you talking like that," Desi said.

Emilia rolled her eyes and sat down next to her fellow dancer. She pulled at her pony tail and her long red hair cascaded down her back. "Girl, Iggy loves to hear me talk like that. That man has a taste for dirty talk that would make a hooker blush," she said.

Desi began applying foundation to her face.

"O doesn't. He never talks dirty even when we're... ya know," Desi said.

"Well, what's the fun in that?" Emilia said with a guffaw. Desi shrugged her shoulders.

"I actually like it. Every other guy I've ever been with always wanted to talk dirty all the time. Ho this, slut that. I like that we actually make love. It feels nice. It feels real," she said.

"Well, does he at least pull your hair?" Emilia asked. Desi smiled.

"Of course. Let's not get too crazy," she said as she applied her lipstick.

"So tonight should be fun. Iggy didn't tell me what they did but whatever they did they did it well enough to rent out the VIP section of the Merchant. After my routine I'm getting good and drunk. I might even pat that cute Cassio on his tight ass," Emilia said as she plucked her eyebrows.

"You're terrible!" Desi said.

"Don't tell me you've never checked out his credentials, Desi. That boy is hot as hell. And that hair. Whoooo whee! I'd give him a ride on the Emilia train anytime!" Emilia said with a laugh.

"I never said he wasn't cute. I just don't look at him like that. He works with O," Desi said.

"He works with Iggy too but I'd still like to give him a workout," Emilia said.

"I just don't see him that way. I guess once me and O got serious everyone else became off limits," Desi said.

"Des, just because you ain't eating doesn't mean you can't look at the menu," Emilia said as she pouted and applied her lip gloss.

"I guess I'm not hungry any more, Em. Othello satisfies all my needs," she said with a wink. Emilia laughed. It was a loud brassy sound.

"I hear you, girl. I hear you!" she said as she blew a kiss at her reflection in the mirror.

The club was jumping.

The Merchant of Venice Lounge and Casino sat in the middle of the Red District. Fifteen stories tall, it was bathed in sparkling lights and topped with a luminous neon sign that sat on its roof like a jaunty chapeau. While the rest of the Red District fought a losing battle with squalor and gentrification the Merchant gleamed like a brand new shiny diamond. It was where the elite rubbed shoulders with the infamous and where the gin flowed freely to wash away the bitter taste of war.

Othello pulled up to the front door of the Merchant in the Black Phantom. A valet rushed to open his door with a white gloved hand. Othello stepped out of his car and smoothed down the three-piece black on black suit he was wearing. He grabbed his black fedora and tossed the keys to the valet. The people waiting in line, men and women, stared at him. He knew he cut an imposing figure as he strode toward the lobby. In the back of his mind he also knew that was not the only reason people stared at him. There were not many Moors in Olde Detroit. There were fewer still that drove a Black Phantom and wore tailored suits.

Othello sailed past the security at the door to the Globe ballroom and glided over to the staircase that led to the VIP balcony overlooking the dance floor and the stage where his wife would be dancing in less than an hour. Othello bounded up the stairs two at a time. He walked onto the balcony and searched for his comrades. Iago was sitting at the end of a long table covered with a white cloth. Iago had his arms around two young ladies and a bottle of English gin was sitting in front of him on the table. He was smoking another stogie. A blue haze floated around his head.

"Oh, holy crap! Ladies, I want you to meet the great Othello Jones. He's a business associate of mine. Say hi, ladies!" Iago said. The girls, both barely out of their teens, said hi in unison. Othello took a seat at the other end of the table. A waiter suddenly appeared as if he had dropped from the ceiling.

"What will it be, Mr. Jones?"

"Same thing my friend is having. Tower of London gin. Light on the ice though," Othello said.

"We wanna dance, Iago," one of the girls said.

"Don't ya dance for a living? Go dance then," Iago said. A smirk ran across Iago's face. Othello shook his head. The girls made faces at Iago before standing up from the table. One of the girls let her hand fall across Othello's chest and trail up to his shoulder as she walked past him. The other girl bent at the waist to whisper in his ear.

"You should come dancing with us," she said in a breathy voice full of dark promises. Othello laughed.

"I don't think my wife would appreciate that," he said. The girl shrugged as if to say "your loss" and sashayed away. Iago picked up the bottle of gin and took a long swig.

"You're so honorable and forthright, Othello. It makes me sick," Iago said. Othello's face darkened for a moment. A few seconds passed before Iago started laughing at the top of his lungs.

"Iago, you're truly a man who likes to push the envelope. No wonder you became a sky trooper," Othello said. The waiter arrived with his drink. Iago puffed on his cigar.

"Aw, I was just messing with you, boss," Iago said. He emphasized the word "boss" between puffs. Othello waved his hand dismissively.

"No, no, not that. I mean sitting up here with two gorgeous women while your wife's downstairs preparing to go on stage. That, my friend, is living on the edge," Othello said. Now it was Iago's turn to wave his hand.

"Emilia knows who we are. I do what I do and she does what she does," Iago said.

"No offense, my friend, but I can't be like that. I love Desi from the deepest part of my soul. I can't imagine being with anyone else or her being with anyone else. Her love sustains me, keeps me calm when everything else around me is disintegrating. When we were on board that ship it was her face that kept me calm. Knowing I was coming home to her made everything all right," Othello said. He was staring at the glass in his hand but Iago knew he was seeing the face of his wife in the swirling gin.

"I'm sure she feels the same way. Even if she is a youngster," Iago said. He watched Othello carefully. He could have sworn he saw the man flinch.

"She always tells me age is just a way of keeping score with the grim reaper... Lord knows I owe him a few years," Othello said. He sipped his drink.

"Curious, my Moor. Curious that you think about age and the vagaries of youth so intensely when it comes to your darling wife," Iago thought to himself. He sipped his bottle again.

"Speaking of youth, where is young master Cass? No doubt swimming in the tides of love with another saucy conquest," Iago said. Othello laughed.

"The boy is young and full of vigor. Let him have his fun. We old married men make our fun anew every night," Othello said.

"Oh, I have no doubt he's having fun. Emilia told me all the girls around the Merchant think that Cass is quite the catch. They call him the Horseman if you get my drift," Iago said. Every word he said seemed to wound Othello. The thought of Cass and his youth seemed to deflate the Moor. Iago made note of that in the recesses of his mind.

"Well, I'm sure he'll be here eventually. Tonight is a celebration!" Othello said as he raised his glass. Iago raised his bottle. As if on cue the band started playing a jazzy number and the dance floor erupted into a sweaty, pulsating knot of bodies. Iago decided to poke the bear a little more.

"Hey, don't worry, my man. That girl loves you. I mean she married you, didn't she? And no offense to you, that's a brave thing to do when your dad's the Marshal and your husband's a Moor. Not that many interracial marriages in the Confederation, ya know," Iago said. His voice carried exactly the right amount of concern and admiration so that Othello wouldn't hear the insult in the statement.

"I know, Iggy. You think I don't know the risks she's taken? I see people staring at us. Staring at me like I'm some sort of specimen. A great black bull that will sustain them even as they try to castrate me. I know the reality of my life, Iggy. I am and always will be a Moor. They take my money for this drink and let me dance in their clubs and fight their battles but at the end of the day they are all like Brabanzio. They see me like an attack dog, a trained beast. And you don't let the beast in the house, let alone put his paws on your daughter. So believe me, Iago, you are preaching to the choir," Othello said.

Iago nodded his head sagely.

"There is the chink in the armor," he thought.

*

No matter how many times he walked into the Globe ballroom Cass always found it impressive. Huge chandeliers hung from the cathedral ceilings like overripe pieces of fruit. Bright brass sconces lined the walls and an enormous bar ran the length of the right wall. Cass made his way through the crowd, heading for the stairs that led to the VIP section, when he noticed Angus Macbeth motioning for him. Macbeth and his beautiful wife owned the Merchant and a few other juke joints in the Red District. At least that's what his tax returns claimed. Cass knew that Macbeth was the undisputed boss of Olde Detroit's criminal underworld. The Merchant was the laundry he used to clean his illicit profits from gun running, untaxed booze, drugs and prostitution. He had turned back challenges from the Capulet and Montague crime families with grim determination and a ruthlessness that bordered on madness. When Angus Macbeth beckoned, you answered.

Iago and Othello were leaning against the railing of the balcony when Othello's sharp eyes saw Cass sliding through the crowd. Othello watched as he headed for Angus Macbeth's table which was right next to the stage.

"Our young friend finally arrived," Othello said. Iago glanced over the railing.

"Wonder why he's sitting with the Butcher and not with his comrades," Iago said, his voice dripping with mock concern. Othello didn't notice the insincere tone of Iago's voice.

"Cass is his own man. He associates with whom he wishes. As long as he doesn't draw any attention to us and our business he can break bread with the Butcher of Barbary Row," Othello said. He knew both Cass and Iago took independent jobs when times were slow but he didn't need either of his trusted men getting into trouble with the Constables. The government assignments they took on were of a sensitive nature. If Sky Command thought they were consorting with hoodlums they could lose their government clearances.

"I know. I was just saying," Iago said.

"Just saying what?" Emilia asked. Iago turned and saw his wife standing in front of him in a beautiful wine-colored cocktail dress.

"Well, if it isn't my better half. What are you doing up here?" Iago asked.

Emilia took his bottle from his hand and put it to her lips. Othello smiled. Emilia was a rose with some vicious thorns. She took a big swig and wiped her lips with the back of her hand.

"Well, Shylock was in a kind mood and gave me the night off. So order me a drink while we all watch the star of the show do her thing," Emilia said. She didn't think Iago needed to know Shylock had told her she wouldn't be dancing tonight because of her tardiness. She didn't care, she needed the break and since Iago and the boys had obviously made a big score they weren't hurting for money.

"She isn't a star. She's the whole universe," Othello said.

"Why don't you talk like that about me, Iggy?" Emilia said. Iago shot her a withering look.

"Shut up," he growled.

The band stopped playing and the emcee came running onto the stage. He was a thin man wearing a skin tight tuxedo and white pancake make up. His black hair was combed back from his forehead and held in place with a generous amount of hair tonic. He stopped in the middle of the stage and held his hand toward the ceiling, dropping his head toward the floor. A microphone descended from the ceiling and into his open hand.

"Ladies and gentlemen! On behalf of the Merchant of Venice casino I would like to welcome you to the most tantalizing and exciting evening of your LIFE! I am your emcee Francis Bacon, and yes, I am hot and tasty! You folks are in for a treat. Tonight you are going to see some of the most gorgeous, exotic and exciting women in the entire world. We have a veritable cavalcade of temptations for your viewing pleasure. So sit down, grab a drink, or an ass, and prepare yourself for the beauty and allure of… DESDEMONA!" the emcee said with a flourish of his arms.

Othello felt a hollow feeling roll up from the pit of his stomach. He had told Iago that Desi wasn't a stripper; she was a dancer. He could make the distinction clear to others but it became a bit blurry in his own mind when he heard her introduction.

The music started and a spotlight shone down on his wife's entrance. Othello turned away from the stage and sipped his drink. Iago watched as Othello tried unsuccessfully to mask his discomfort. Iago walked over to Othello, leaving Emilia telling a story he had heard a thousand times. He clinked his bottle against Othello's glass. Othello raised his glass and nodded toward his comrade.

"We just made a metric ton of money and you're standing up here looking like you're waiting for a rectal exam. What's up, boss?" Iago asked. Othello bit his bottom lip and looked down into his glass.

"Nothing. Just sometimes I feel it - you know. I feel the years between us. Like a real thing, like a wall that separates us. Most times I don't even worry about the age difference. But when she dances I notice the way men look at her. Men that are closer to her age than her father's," Othello said.

"Men like Cass," Iago said. Othello's head snapped up and he stared at Iago.

"What do you mean, 'like Cass?'" he asked. Iago shrugged and sipped from his bottle.

"Look for yourself," Iago said. Othello whirled around and peered over the railing. He had missed Desi's entire performance. But he saw Cass standing along with the rest of the crowd, clapping, hooting and hollering. Cass, who had chosen to sit downstairs close to the stage. He watched as Desi walked down off the stage in her high-heel shoes and a bikini made of pearls and lace. She was waving at the crowd as she descended the steps on the right side of the stage. Perhaps it was the adulation of the audience, perhaps it was a loose pearl. Whatever it was, it caused her to lose her footing.

Cass, sitting with Angus Macbeth at his private table not ten feet from the end of the stage, was already standing when she began to fall. He leaped across the table and slid across the parquet floor on his knees with his arms outstretched, and Desi fell into his waiting arms.

Othello watched as she wrapped her arms around Cass's neck.

He watched as Cass rose to his feet with her still in his arms.

He watched as he released her and she placed her feet on solid ground; and he watched as Cass kissed her left hand and Desi leaned her head back in an exaggerated display of relief.

"They say he's the big buck of the salt lick," Iago whispered in Othello's ear.

Othello squeezed his hand around his glass, then relaxed it just before it would have shattered.

Iago wandered away from the Moor with a slight spring in his step. He walked down to the dance floor and then made his way over to the bar. He slid onto a bar stool and ordered a glass of wine. He sipped slowly until he felt a tap on his shoulder.

"You got me in a lot of trouble," a voice said. Iago spun around on the stool and faced Rodriego.

"Au contraire, mon ami. You got yourself in a lot of trouble. It was your idea to inform the Marshal about who his daughter was fucking. I tried my best to discourage you but you wouldn't be moved," Iago said. He had seen Rodriego come into the hall from his vantage point on the balcony and knew the lovesick puppy would find him. Iago had use for the fool.

"Yeah. I got latrine duty for a month. And I heard the Marshal couldn't do anything because she married that black bastard. Married him! For what? I just don't get it. I thought she was a good woman. I guess she's just a whore like all the rest," Rodriego said. Iago did not point out the paradoxical nature of his statement about Desi's virtue. The sentry was as dumb as a box of hammers, and Iago would direct him toward who he wanted him to nail.

"So you're going to give up that easily? I'm shocked. I thought you said you loved this woman? True, her blood is hot with the thrill of consummation, but that'll only last for a little while. I wouldn't give up yet. She's like a child on a swing, kicking and screaming, pushing herself higher and higher until she gets bored and is ready to jump off. You just have to make sure you're the one to catch her and not somebody else," Iago said before taking another sip of his wine.

"Somebody like who?" Rodriego asked. The sentry's eyes were so wide it seemed that only the white was showing. His jaw was tight. Iago sipped his wine again. He drew the moment out until he was certain the sentry was about to grab him by his collar.

"Well, I did see Cassio Michael catch her tonight. She slipped off the stage and he was there, arms outstretched, looking every inch the hero. And every woman wants to be rescued," Iago said. Rodriego seemed to deflate like a balloon.

"Cass. Really... I know him. He's got a hovercycle just like she used to ride," Rodriego said. His voice quaked.

"You know a woman like Desi respects power. It attracts her like light attracts a moth. She likes a man who's strong, who's not afraid to act, to fight, to participate in life and not just watch it go by from the sidelines. A real man, Rodriego, not a little boy," Iago said as he placed his hand on the sentry's shoulder.

"A real man," he said as they both turned and stared at Cass standing by the other end of the bar. Iago watched as Cass put another shot glass to his lips and threw back his head. Iago had been ordering shots all night for Cass and Othello. He had shared his bottle of gin with the two dancers and Emilia. He himself had drunk very little. Othello was drunk. Cass was drunk. Iago was nearly sober.

"Look at him standing there like the cock of the walk. Someone should take him down a peg. Let Desi see he isn't quite the hero he pretends to be," Iago said into Rodriego's ear.

"Get me a drink," the sentry said grimly. Iago motioned for the bartender.

*

"You think you're better than me?" a slurred voice said in Cass's ear. Cass assumed it was some drunk arguing with another drunk so he ignored the exchange. Then someone pushed him and he spun around on the balls of his feet. A man wearing a shabby brown blazer and wrinkled pants stood in front of him swaying side to side. Cass was drunk. He knew it as well as he knew his own name. But this poor fellow in front of him was drunk with a capital "D".

"What? Man, I don't even know you," Cass said before turning back to the bar. He cursed himself for getting so inebriated. It wasn't all his fault. Angus had hired him for a job and to celebrate their new business arrangement he'd bought a round of shots for the table. Then Iago had bought a couple of rounds. It seemed everyone was in agreement that his hand should never be empty.

Cass was about to finish his next shot when he felt a tingle go through his body, cutting through the haze of intoxication. He felt the shabby man's punch before it connected. He felt the grinding of his teeth and the narrowing of his eyes. He felt the heat of his anger.

Cass ducked under the man's wild punch and came up swinging. His right hand connected with the man's jaw. A split second later his left foot connected with the right side of the man's rib cage. The man in the shabby suit dropped to his knees. The man got up to one knee.

"Stay down," Cass said, but the man ignored his request. The man pushed off his left foot and launched himself toward Cass in a blind tackle. Cass sidestepped him and hit him behind the left ear with his right fist. The man fell to the floor in an unconscious heap. A hand fell on Cass's shoulder; he grabbed it and pulled it forward and down using his collar bone as a fulcrum. He heard a satisfying snap as the forearm of his new assailant broke cleanly. He spun around and saw with slow rising horror that it was a deputy for the Constable. Three more deputies emerged from the crowd carrying stunsticks.

"I fucked up," Cass thought before the stunsticks shocked him into unconsciousness.

*

"What the hell happened after I left, Iago?" Othello asked. He and Iago were sitting at Othello's kitchen table as the morning sun tried in vain to cut through the smog and haze of Olde Detroit. Othello was sipping a cup of tepid tea as Iago drank some bitter Tejano coffee. Desi was out running errands and packing up her few remaining items at her old apartment. Iago put his cup down and rubbed his hand across his face.

"I hate to put Cass out there like that, boss. I mean, we just risked our lives for each other," Iago said. He sighed heavily. Othello stood and turned to look at the dusty skyline, his massive arms crossed over his broad chest.

"I like Cass. I really do. But we have to protect ourselves. What we do is tacitly approved by the government. There's an unspoken agreement that comes with that approval. We keep our noses clean, we stay out of trouble and we always give them enough distance from our activities for plausible deniability," Othello said.

"I'm going to cut Cass loose. For a little while at least. I - we can't have the Constables looking at us too closely," Othello said heavily.

"Probably for the best, boss. You saw the way he was looking at Desi last night," Iago said.

"I saw him catch her in his arms," Othello said.

"I mean before that. When she was dancing. He looked... well, he looked all wrung up. I'm just saying," Iago said. He sipped his coffee and peered at Othello over the edge of his cup.

"I'll call him when he gets out of the drunk tank," Othello said. Iago nodded.

"Like I said. For the best," Iago said

"Did you see Desi look at him, Iago?" Othello said. Iago put his cup down on the table. This was the delicate part. It was also the most important.

"Don't do this to yourself, boss. Don't ask me questions neither one of us wants answered," he said. Othello looked out of the window again. His massive shoulders sagged.

"Okay," he said, his voice barely a whisper.

*

Cass awoke with a metallic taste in his mouth and a multitude of aches and pains running up and down his body. He went through the release procedure at the jail and walked out into the hazy sunlight with all of his possessions and some of his dignity. His hovercycle was still downtown, so he'd have to catch a cab over to the Red District. He reached into his pocket to get his wallet when his telecom rang. He opened it and saw Othello's grim face.

"Cass."

"Hey chief. Um... crazy night, huh?" he said. He knew how lame he sounded as soon as he closed his mouth.

"Cass, I heard about the fight. And the deputy. Cass, there is no easy way to say this but I'm going to have to cut you loose. At least until this thing with the Constable cools down," Othello said. His brown face seemed as smooth and impassive as a statue.

"Boss, come on - don't do this. I'm sorry, but this was just a big misunderstanding. Some guy attacked me and I was just defending myself. I don't even know who that drunk guy was."

"You were drunk too, Cass. Or do you just go around breaking the arms of law enforcement officers for fun? Look, I told you when you came on with us that we run a quiet crew. No drama, no problems. I can't afford to lose my clearances."

"Boss, you need me!" Cass yelled. Othello's face became dark like the sky before a storm.

"I don't need you. This organization was doing just fine before you and we'll do just fine without you. Othello out," he said. The screen on the telecom went dark. Cass closed the telecom, put it back in his pocket, and stood on the steps of the hall of justice with his head hanging. He felt lost. It was like the corn maze all over again. Everything in his life was on fire.

Then he saw Desi coming out of an apartment building down the block.

*

Othello sat at his kitchen table with his head in his hands. He was thinking about Cass. The man was a good comrade and a capable soldier. What did it matter if he looked at Desi with lustful eyes? She was his wife and she loved him. Othello took another sip of his tea. His telephone rang. Othello pushed away from the table and walked over to answer the phone.

"Hello," he said listlessly.

"Hello, gunclapper. I was just informed about your little incident last night. It's a shame you can't keep your charges in line. I suspected all that money would make you and your boys bold. I spoke with the Governor, and we both think it would be wise for the Confederation to look elsewhere for any special missions for the foreseeable future," the Marshal said. Othello could hear the smugness in his voice.

"You don't care about your daughter? You don't care if she eats or has a roof over her head?" he said through clenched teeth. Brabanzio laughed.

"As long as I am alive my daughter will have food in her belly and a place to lay her head. Hopefully she will see you for the thug you are once your money runs out and you are reduced to pulling stick-up jobs to keep your fancy apartment. That's all your kind are really good for, gunclapper," the Marshal said. The line went dead.

Othello ripped the phone off its stand and pulled the wire out of the wall. He hurled the phone against the floor. Brass and steel and chrome flew through the room. The pieces that didn't fly away were crushed beneath his size twelve boot. He stood there for a moment with his chest heaving and his heart pounding.

"My name that was as fresh as Dian's visage
is now begrimed and as black
As mine own face," he thought to himself.

*

"Desi!" Cass yelled. Desi, struggling with two large bags, turned and saw Cass running toward her. Cass caught up to her and took one of the heavy green sacks off her shoulder and put it on his back.

"Thanks! I was trying to make one trip. You saved me again," Desi said with a smile.

"I do what I can," Cass laughed. They began to walk side by side.

"What are you doing down here, Cass? O send you to help me?" she asked.

"Uh, no. I guess you didn't hear about the fight," Cass said.

"What? What fight? Who did you get fighting with?" Desi asked. Cass ran his hand through his hair. The breeze blew up the street tossing discarded newspapers to and fro.

"I got attacked by some drunk guy and I was a little drunk myself, and then the Constable's deputies tried to break it up and I got confused and I broke the arm of one of the deputies. I just got out of lock-up, matter of fact. Othello... well, Othello is pissed and he just cut me loose. Like just now, over the telecom," Cass said. He didn't realize his voice was wavering.

"Oh Cass, I'm sorry but you know O. Once he makes up his mind nothing can change it," she said as they walked toward Othello's everyday car, a Tucker Wide Wagon.

"Desi, he loves you. He listens to you. If you could just put in a good word for me. Let him know how sorry I am about everything. It was all a big misunderstanding. Please. I... I don't have anywhere else to go. The kind of work we do is very specialized. Just say a few words on my behalf," Cass pleaded. Desi stopped at the rear of the Tucker, opened up the hatch and threw her sack in the back. Cass threw the sack he was carrying on top of hers. Desi bit her bottom lip as she stood with her back to Cass. Finally she turned. As she did, the wind caught her errant locks and for an instant her hair swirled around her head like a halo.

"All right, I'll speak to him but I can't promise anything, Cass. I know O has a bit of a temper and sometimes it can cloud his judgment. But don't get your hopes up, okay?" she said. Cass put his hands in his pockets and dropped his head sheepishly.

"I know. I appreciate whatever you can do, Desi," he said. Desi closed the hatch.

"Well, it's the least I can do. I mean, you did rescue me from falling to my death last night," she said with a smile. Cass smiled back as she climbed into the Tucker and drove off into the mid-morning haze of smoke and smog and fog.

*

As the day wore on Othello's thoughts swirled around in his head, becoming darker and darker like a room lit by a dying candle. Firing Cass, then the loss of the government clearances and the possible attraction between Cass and Desi weighed on him. As the sun was setting he decided to visit Desi at the Merchant before her show that night. He pulled the Black Phantom into a parking garage near the casino and began to walk up the street. He was halfway there when his telecom rang.

"Boss, you okay? I talked to Saul and he said you told him to start putting out feelers for private jobs. What's going on?" Iago said. His wide face rippled with concern through the screen of the telecom.

"We lost our government clearances," Othello said simply.

You mean you lost YOUR government clearances, you old black ram, Iago thought to himself.

"Well, Jesus on a bald headed palomino. Because of Cass?" Iago asked. Othello just nodded his head.

"Boss, I like Cass. The boy is a damn fine soldier and he can handle himself, but it seems like he's just messed up our chemistry ever since we took him on. And I don't know how trustworthy he is," Iago said sadly.

"You think he can't be trusted? You think he would sell us out to the Alliance?" Othello asked.

"Yeah... sure, that's what I meant," Iago said.

Come on. Take the bait, you old wolf, Iago thought to himself. Othello stopped in mid stride.

"What *did* you mean?" Othello asked. Under the table where he was sitting Iago clenched his fist.

"Nothing, just forget it, boss," Iago said. He could see Othello's eyes narrow through the screen.

"Iago. If you have something to say you damn well better say it!" Othello growled. Iago took a deep breath. He scratched at his face with his free hand. Finally after a sufficient amount of reticence he spoke.

"It's just, well, remember the Puck job in Olde London? Me and Cass had roomed together on that job. One night after I had drifted off he woke me up. He was... taking matters into his own hands if you know what I mean. I turned over, trying to ignore it and go back to sleep, and that was when I heard him," Iago said. Othello felt a wave of nausea wash over his body. He already knew what Iago was going to say but he asked anyway. It was not in his nature to avoid a hard road just because it would hurt his feet.

"Heard what?" Othello asked.

"His telecom was on. He had recorded something and was playing it back as he... It was a vid of a woman tapping her Rockies if you know what I mean. I couldn't see the face... but he was moaning Desi's name. Look, boss, don't get sore with me! I never said anything before because I had to work with the guy. But since you fired him I feel like you need to know. I feel like shit for not saying something earlier. I'm sorry," Iago said. Othello leaned against a street lamp. The light flickered, casting a sickly pale light on his slack brown face.

"Iago. Are you sure?" Othello asked. Iago nodded somberly.

"I'll talk to you later about the private jobs," Othello said before abruptly severing the telecom connection. Iago laughed as he closed the lid on his telecom.

"Cassio's a proper man, let me see now
To get his place and to plume up my will
In double knavery. How, how? Let's see
After some time to abuse Othello's ear
That he is too familiar with his wife
He hath a person and a smooth dispose
To be suspected, framed to make women false
The Moor is of a free and open nature
That thinks men honest that but seem to be so
And will as tenderly be led by the nose
As asses are
I have't. It is engendere'd Hell and night
Must bring this monstrous birth to the world's light," he thought to himself as he put his hands behind his head and laced his fingers together. He laughed and laughed.

*

Desi was sitting in front of her mirror putting on make-up when she saw Othello appear behind her. She spun around and leaped to her feet, running into Othello's arms.

"Well, if it isn't the sexiest husband in the world," Desi said. Othello put his arms around her small frame and squeezed her tight. Her body felt lean and taut. Othello kissed her cheek.

"My love," he whispered.

"O, I'm so glad you stopped by. We'll have time to get some dinner before I go on. Let's try that Greek place, Sophocles. I hear they have the best calamari in the city!" she said.

"Anything you want, my love," Othello said. His voice was low and rumbled out of his chest like a truck. Desi went back to her mirror, picked up a brush, and ran it through her long hair. She saw Othello staring at her.

"What's wrong, O?" she asked

"Nothing, my love. Nothing at all. Just some work issues that I have to iron out," he said. He put his hands in his pockets as his wife continued putting on her make-up.

"Oh baby. Is it about that fight Cass got into last night? I saw him today downtown. He was really shaken up by the whole thing," Desi said as she applied her blood-red lipstick.

"What were you doing with Cass today?" Othello said. His voice dropped one octave. It came out as deep and dark as the ocean. Desi stopped applying her make-up.

"He was just getting out of lock-up. My apartment, or my old apartment, is a block from the Hall of Justice - remember?" she said. Othello took his hands out of his pockets and balled them into tight fists.

"Of course I remember. Do you think I'm going senile? I assure you I am still in control of my faculties!" Othello yelled. Desi turned and faced her husband. She pulled her mood scarf out of a drawer at the bottom of her vanity. She pulled the fabric through her fingers and twisted it until it looked like a piece of braided rope.

"O, what's wrong?" she asked. Othello relaxed his fists. He walked over to Desi and grasped the mood scarf in his large hands. The fabric slowly changed colors. A wavy chartreuse pattern gave way to a deep crimson coloring. For a moment the scarf appeared to be tie-dyed before it became totally red.

"Why are you angry, my love?" Desi asked.

"I found this scarf for you on one of my missions. The woman I purchased it from told me there were only forty in the entire world. I bought it for you because I liked the idea of knowing what mood you were in. I suppose the old soldier in me thought of it as some kind of advantage. But as time passed seeing you wearing this scarf became a source of comfort for me. You are rarely angry or sad, so the scarf hardly ever changes color. That deep green scarf made me know, no matter what ugliness I saw in the world or however I contributed to it, I could come home and know you were waiting for me with arms full of love and a heart full of peace," Othello said. Desi stood on her tiptoes and kissed Othello on the forehead.

"You like to see me happy, my love? You wish to make me feel content? Let Cass be a part of your team again. He loves you like a brother and I'd feel better knowing there was someone on your team keeping you safe," she said. Othello grunted. It was an ugly sound.

"You think I can't take care of myself? You think I need Cassio Michaels to keep me safe? You must have forgotten who the fuck I am! I am Othello Rohan JONES! I don't need Cassio or anyone else to keep me safe! I have captured whole squadrons single-handedly. I have forty-eight confirmed kills as a Sky Trooper and gyrocopter pilot. The Alliance used to call me the Black Death! Why in the blue hell would I need Cass?" Othello screamed. He pushed Desi away and turned on his heel and stomped out of her dressing room. Desi fell to her knees. As she rose she dropped her scarf on the floor.

"OTHELLO!' she yelled as she ran after her husband.

★

Shylock was pissed. It was twenty minutes before showtime and Desi was nowhere to be found. He paced back and forth inside the dressing room like a caged lion. Finally he clapped his hands together.

"Emilia!" Shylock yelled. Emilia came sauntering into the dressing room.

"Well, well, well, what can I do for you, boss man?" she asked, batting her eyelids.

"Cut the crap. You go on in fifteen minutes. I can't believe Desi left me high and dry like this. There are some government bigwigs out there tonight. Some real whales. And all I got for them to stare at is your weathered ass. Put on your make-up. Lots of make-up, and come on out. You're the headliner. For tonight," Shylock said as he stormed out of the dressing room.

"Gee, thanks for the ringing endorsement," Emilia said under her breath. She was about to sit down at the make-up mirror when she saw Desi's scarf on the floor. She stooped and picked up the soft piece of fabric and ran it over her hands and forearms. It felt as soft and smooth as warm water.

"Iggy is always bugging me to borrow Desi's scarf so he can get me a replica of it. Like I want a knock-off from her wardrobe," Emilia thought to herself. Suddenly the scarf changed color to a deep verdant green. The color of jealousy. Emilia laughed to herself.

"Can't fool you, can I, scarf?" she said. "Fuck it – he owes me something nice since he forgot our anniversary," she said as she folded the scarf and put it in her purse.

*

Iago sat in his favorite chair drinking a cup of tea. The plush folds of the chair seemed to encapsulate his entire body. He heard a key jingle and looked toward the door to see his wife walking into the house. Her hair was slicked back from her forehead and her cheeks still had bright splotches of rouge decorating them.

"Well, look what the cat dragged in. It's 2 a.m. Where were you – on the corner?" Iago said. He laughed without mirth. Emilia shook her head and plopped down on the couch opposite the chair.

"Desi didn't show up tonight. I was the headliner," she said. She leaned her head back and exhaled.

"So being the headliner was a little more than you bargained for?" Iago said. He was dying to ask why Desi didn't show up but he held his tongue. The puppet show was just starting. He couldn't reveal he was the one pulling the strings.

"I wouldn't have gotten the gig but I heard Desi and Othello had some kind of fight. Portia told me she could hear them yelling from her dressing room. That's probably why she dropped her scarf," Emilia said. Iago sat up a little straighter in his chair.

"What scarf? The one that changes colors?" he said. Emilia smiled.

"Yeah, that one. I picked it up since you're always going on about how you want to get me one just like it." Emilia reached in her purse and pulled out the scarf. She threw it at Iago who deftly snatched it out of the air.

"Now get it copied or remade or whatever you're gonna do to it so I can get it back to Desi. I'm going to go crash," she said. She got up off the couch and stumbled down the hall to their bedroom. Iago held the scarf up to the light. The colors began to run rapidly through the fabric. Green, then red, then blue, black and orange, like a kaleidoscope.

"Trifles as light as air
Are to the jealous confirmations strong
As proof of holy writ," he said to himself.

*

Cass awoke to the sounds of machinery. Olde Detroit was never quiet but the mornings were the worst. Factories pounding out steel for weapons, refining oil for diesel fuel or stretching and dyeing raw wool for the garment districts filled the air with a cacophony of noises. His apartment was a block away from the Verona Steel Works. Staying at Bianca's wasn't always about the sex; sometimes he liked the relative quiet of her neighborhood. Gunshots were not as loud as the Bessemer process.

Cass got up, guzzled some milk, then took a shower and shaved. He needed to talk to Macbeth about a business opportunity. Actually he was going to beg Macbeth to let him out of the arrangement they had agreed upon a few nights ago. He needed to do everything he could to get back in Othello's good graces.

Cass went down to the street to his hovercycle. Something was tied to the handle - at first he thought it was a piece of trash that had gotten stuck but then he noticed it was a scarf. He was no expert on scarves but it appeared to be fairly expensive. He untied it from his handlebars and as he did so the fabric changed color. Someone had tied it to his cycle during the night, but why? Had some bon vivant tried to tease his date by tying her scarf to the bike and seeing it flap in the wind? Or the more likely scenario: some drunk bar patron had tied it to his cycle for reasons known only to the intoxicated and then forgot about it. Cass folded the scarf and put it in his pocket. Then he pulled his goggles down over his eyes.

"Maybe I'll give it to Bianca. Just a little gift. She might like it," Cass thought. He fired up the hovercycle and headed downtown.

*

Othello sipped the tepid swill that the Thatcher All Night Diner tried to pass off as coffee. He couldn't seem to think straight. His brain felt like it would burst with so many bad thoughts filling his skull, scratching and clawing at each other.

"I got here as soon as I could," Iago said, breathless, as he slid into the booth across from Othello. Iago had stayed downtown at a bar after sneaking out and tying Desi's scarf to Cass's hovercycle. Cass, being the conscientious young lad that he was, would probably remember that he had seen Desi with the same type of scarf. He would hold onto it until he saw her again. Iago smiled at the thought of Cass trying to return the scarf to Desi with Othello standing there.

"I don't know why I called you, man. I just don't have very many people I can call friends. My head is spinning right now. I don't know what to think or what to believe," Othello mumbled. Iago leaned forward.

"Boss, what the hell are you talking about?" he whispered.

"She asked me to put Cass back on the crew. She said we needed him. Why the hell was she even talking to him? I had just told him yesterday morning that he was off the team and by the afternoon she's trying to intercede for him?" Othello said, staring out of the window watching the traffic creep by the diner.

"Boss, I ain't trying to talk bad about anyone. But do you think it's possible, just possible that Cass and Desi are... close?" Iago whispered. Othello turned and stared at Iago.

"No man should be close enough to another man's wife that he feels comfortable asking her to beg for his job back," Othello said. Iago didn't agree with that statement but he could see Othello was already making up his mind about certain things regarding his wife and Cass.

"Well, what do you think is going on, boss?" Iago asked. He tried to sound sincerely concerned. Othello bowed his head and put his hands over his face.

"I don't know. My heart tells me she would never do anything to hurt me. But then my head remembers what the Marshal said. My head remembers her begging for me to bring back Cass. My head and my heart are locked in a debate with no judge to declare a winner," Othello said.

"Maybe I could ask Cass if anything is going on. I just wouldn't let him know I was asking on your behalf. Like I could meet him later today at a bar or something, and leave my telecom on so you can hear the conversation. I make small talk and then I ask him. One comrade to another, just feeling him out. If nothing's going on then he'll get offended with me just asking. But if something is going on and I make him feel comfortable he might just tell the truth," Iago said. Othello raised his head.

"Am I the type of husband that's going to run an op on his wife?" Othello asked. He was asking himself but Iago answered him.

"Yes, you are, because if she is the type of wife to sleep with your comrade in arms you deserve to know, and she deserves whatever she gets," Iago said. Othello nodded.

"You're truly a good friend, Iggy. I know I don't say it often enough. I try to keep some professional distance, but right now I feel like you're my only friend," Othello said. He reached across the table and grabbed Iago's hand. After a minute he said, flatly, "Set it up."

"I'm with you, brother, until the end. I promise you that," Iago said as he gripped Othello's hand.

*

Cass was glad to hear from Iago. The meeting with Macbeth had not gone well. He had the money from the last mission but that would only last for so long. Perhaps the combined efforts of Iago and Desi could sway Othello's mind. Cass entered the Venetian, an upscale eatery near Othello's place. He checked his pocket watch. 5 p.m. He was wearing a leather flight vest and khaki pants with the cuffs tucked into his black boots. He had a thin long-sleeved shirt under the vest and a wind scarf around his neck, and his goggles were perched jauntily on his forehead to help hold back his long hair. He scanned the room and realized he was woefully underdressed. Iago stood and waved him over to a small table in the corner of the room.

"I guess I'm lucky they let me in the door, huh? I didn't know there was a dress code," Cass said as he sat down across from Iago. His companion was dressed in a double-breasted brown suit with a black turtleneck sweater, his thick, greasy hair piled up on top of his head in an elaborate pompadour. His brown fedora sat in an empty chair to his right.

"Ah come on. Who's gonna turn away those movie reel good looks?" Iago said. Cass smiled ruefully.

"They didn't work on Othello. I guess you know he cut me loose," Cass said. Iago bit the inside of his lip.

"I heard. He was pretty pissed about you getting in that fight. Did he tell you we lost our clearances?" Iago said as he took a sip from a metallic mug.

"No. I… I didn't know that," Cass said. His face turned bright red. Iago waved over the waiter.

"Looks like we'll be doing private security work for the foreseeable future. Hell, we can't even hire ourselves out to the Alliance if the Marshal was telling the truth about the war ending soon," Iago said.

"Well, why would he lie about something like that?" Cass asked. Iago took another sip from his mug.

"Everyone lies, young buck. We lie to keep ourselves from being hurt. We lie so that we don't hurt others. We lie to make others hurt. We lie to gain pleasure and we lie to cause pain. Everyone lies," Iago said.

"I don't know about that, man. I try not to lie," Cass said.

"So you have never lied to Bianca? Never slipped out a little early because of 'business'?" Iago asked with a laugh.

"Bianca knows what we are and what we're doing. I don't have to lie to her," Cass said. It came out a little stronger than he intended. The waiter brought him a mug filled with the same dark wine Iago was drinking.

"It's cool, brother. We all can only aspire to be as virtuous and righteous as you, my good man," Iago said. Cass threw his mug back and guzzled down his wine. Iago quickly pulled out his telecom and dialed Othello's number. He left it open on top of his fedora with the telescreen facing him and Cass.

"But I bet you're not so virtuous that you haven't taken her to pound town!" Iago said. Cass laughed.

"I just finished giving her a tour of pound town before I came here," Cass said.

"Oh man, I'm gonna need some details. A lot of men have lusted after that young lady as she pranced across the stage," Iago said. He winked at Cass lecherously.

"Yeah, but I'm the only one who's tamed that ass. Don't get me wrong, she'll give you a run for her money. She is so damn flexible!" Cass said. Talking about Bianca this way was something of a release for him. He didn't really have anyone to shoot the shit with on a regular basis. No brothers, no father, no one at all. Yes, the conversation was a bit caddish but it felt good to blow off a little steam, especially in light of the events of the previous two days.

*

Othello stared at his telecom so hard he felt that his eyes would pop out of their sockets any minute. He felt something dark and wanton blooming inside him like a black rose whose petals were unfurling.

"You don't care if anyone finds out?" Iago asked. Cass sat back in his chair and crossed his arms.

"I used to care. But now, sitting here, I can honestly say I don't give a damn. She's... she's mine. Some people might not approve because of her past situations and my current occupation but that's their problem," Cass said. Bianca was his and his alone. He smiled. He was glad that he had given her the scarf he had found earlier that morning.

"I give you props for your testicular fortitude, my friend," Iago said. He picked up his mug for a toast. Cass picked up his as well. But before they could complete the ritual a voice cried out, calling Cass's name.

"CASS!" someone screamed. Cass and Iago turned and saw Bianca stomping toward them.

"Speak of the devil and he will appear," Iago thought to himself. He could see that Bianca had something in her hand. It was a piece of fabric. A scarf. She reached their table and threw it at Cass.

"I can't believe the nerve of you! I know I'm just a stripper. I know you consider me a whore. But I am no one's second choice and I damn sure am not taking hand me downs from your other whores!" she screamed. Her spittle landed on Cass's upper lip.

"B. what are you talking about?" Cass said, bewildered.

"I'm talking about you coming over today and fucking me then giving me a scarf with your other whore's name stitched on it!" she yelled. Before Cass could react she grabbed the scarf that had fallen to the floor and held it up by one end in front of his face. A name had been embroidered on the very end. "To my love, my Willow Rose." Cass read the writing out loud. Bianca began to cry. She threw the scarf at him again.

"I know you think I was a slut up there in the Reichlord's mansion. They made me do those things, Cass. They made me! I was so stupid for thinking for one second that you could understand. You've never called me your Willow Rose. Or sweetheart or my beloved. You've only called me at 2 a.m. when you wanted some. Don't ever call me again, Cass," Bianca said as she ran out of the restaurant. After a moment of barely audible indignation the other patrons returned to their meals.

"I gotta go, man. I gotta try to make this right with her," Cass said as he rose from the table.

"Go ahead. I got you with that drink. Go ahead, man," Iago said. Cass ran out of the restaurant after Bianca. Iago picked up his telecom. Othello's face filled the screen. Tears were streaming down his face.

"Meet me at the warehouse," he said before severing the connection. Iago smiled.

"Come along by the nose, my little bull," he mused.

Iago found him sitting on top of the roof of the warehouse. Othello was leaning back against one of the peaked skylights. Iago came and sat down next to him.

"Remember when I bought her that scarf? We were in Rome and the lady asked me 'What is the name of the lucky lady who gets this scarf?' and I said, she's my Willow Rose. It is… it was my pet name for her. A willow rose grows near the window of my mother's kitchen. She tended to that wild flower and over time it covered the entire side of the house. It was a wild thing, weak and malnourished, that flourished from the touch of love,' Othello said. Iago put his arm around his shoulders.

"How shall I kill him, Iago? We live by the gun; it is fitting that he die by the gun. I will shoot him in the face so even the demons in hell cannot call him by his name. I knew she was too young for me. Every time I touched her I could feel the energy of her youth radiating through her body. I'm an old man and I have seen too much. Too much death, too much hate, too much of the true face of man. I fooled myself into believing that she was different. So I'll ask you again, my friend. My only friend. A white dove amidst a nest of vipers. How should I kill him?" Othello said.

"Why does she get to get away with doing this to you? A wife that cheats on a husband deserves to be punished. But a wife that cheats on her husband with a comrade in arms should never be allowed to betray anyone else," Iago said. Othello looked at him.

"I don't know if I can do it," he said softly.

"Think about her mouth on his. Picture her face as he enters her. Close your eyes and visualize her on top of him. Then ask yourself, how can you NOT do it?" Iago said. Othello clenched and unclenched his hands slowly and methodically, over and over again.

"I'm your friend. We've faced death together. I won't let you face this alone. I'll take care of Cassio. You got to clean up around your own backyard. Wipe this stain away so that it will never sully another man. Don't let your actions be swayed by memories of false love," Iago said. Othello stood. The night sky was redolent with the lights of the city. The skyline filled his field of vision. His apartment was there in that skyline, and his unfaithful wife was in that apartment. Sleeping in his bed, no doubt dreaming of her satyr while she thought he played the role of the cuckold.

"We are brothers in arms, Iago. I swear to you after this is done we'll go into the Rhineland together and ply our trade as equal partners. We'll leave behind Olde Detroit and the chicanery that lives here. I can never repay you for what you're offering to do for me but I swear for the rest of my life I will try. Send me a message on my telecom when Cassio is dead. A single word will do," Othello said.

"What word would that be, boss?" Iago asked.

"Whore," Othello said. "The word will be whore."

Iago stood and clapped Othello between the shoulder blades.

"Don't worry, O. I'll be there to see you through this," Iago said. Othello could not see the wolfish smile that ran away from his eyes.

*

It was 9 p.m. and Rodriego was drunk. A stinking, sad, pathetic drunk. He sat at the bar of a gin joint in the Red District whose name escaped him. He was wearing his civilian clothes. The fight the other night had landed him in more hot water with Sky Command, and he'd been put on administrative leave pending an investigation. His military career was coming to an end. He was about to be bounced out of Sky Command and sent back to the Great West to work on the Adalai Stevens Dam or some other common job. All because of a woman he had never even kissed.

"Another gin and tonic please," he said to the barkeep. The man looked at him with sad rheumy eyes.

"Son, I think you've had enough," he said.

"I think you should mind your own business and get the lad another drink," a voice said behind him. Rodriego turned and saw Iago standing there looking as pleased as punch.

"Get away from me. I don't want to ever talk to you again," Rodriego said.

Iago sat down next to Rodriego. He took off his fedora and sat it on the bar.

"Now is that any way to talk to a friend?" Iago said good-naturedly. Rodriego spun around and grabbed Iago by the collar. His eyes were wild and his breath came in great gulps.

"You are not my friend! You got me in trouble and now I'm probably going to be kicked out of the Command. Just leave me alone!" Rodriego said. Iago grabbed his wrists with a grip that was surprisingly strong. He pulled Rodriego's hands away with ease.

"First, don't ever put your hands on me again or I'll make that ass whooping Cass gave you look like a Swedish massage. Second, I just stopped in to get a drink with you because I felt bad about what happened and I figured you'd be in the cheapest bar in town. No offense, barkeep," Iago said. The barkeep pointed at him with his middle finger.

"I just came to tell you that you won't have to worry about Cass giving you any more ass whippings. He's leaving Olde Detroit and New Haven for good," Iago lied.

"Well, good," Rodriego said.

"With Desdemona," Iago added. Rodriego's head fell toward his chest.

"What the hell do you mean with Desdemona?" Rodriego whimpered.

"She's leaving with him. She told Othello today that she wanted to be with Cass. I was as shocked as you are. In fact, Cass is at his apartment right now packing up his hovercycle and getting ready to leave. So you'll never see him or Desi again. Unless he gets hit by a goose or shot out of the sky or something before he can pick her up!" Iago said.

"Or something," Rodriego whispered.

Iago grabbed his fedora and stood.

"Like I said, I thought you'd want to know. You still got your base ID? Maybe you can go commandeer a gyrocopter and shoot him down! Ha, I'm just fucking with ya! Have a good night, Roddy," Iago said. He shoved his hat on his head and walked out of the bar. He trotted across the street and hopped in his Tucker and waited.

Five minutes later Rodriego wandered out of the bar and started walking north toward the base.

"It's as sure as you are Rodriego
Were I the Moor I would not be Iago
In following him, I follow but myself
Heaven is my judge, not I for love and duty
But seeming so for my peculiar end
For when my outward action doth demonstrate
The native act and figure of my heart
In complement extern, it's not long after
But I will wear my heart upon my sleeve
For daws to peck at, I am not what I am," he whispered as he sat in the dark.

*

Othello sat on a plush bench in the lobby of the Merchant staring at his left hand. He and Desdemona had gotten married spur of the moment and hadn't bothered to buy rings. At the time he had thought they were so in love they didn't need rings as a reminder of their commitment.

"I guess it's a good thing we didn't buy rings. I would wager she would not have removed it as she stroked him with her deceitful hand," Othello thought. Guests walked to and fro through the lobby, laughing, holding hands, doing all the things lovers were wont to do. Othello envied them. He envied their ignorance and their total obliviousness to the world of lies that surrounded them. Love was just a synonym for fool. Love made you blind to treachery, deaf to the truth and dumb in the face of facts. Too dumb to comprehend the facts and mute when the facts presented themselves.

"What are you doing here?" a voice asked. Othello looked up and saw Emilia standing in front of him with her hands on her ample hips. Othello looked at her for a moment before he answered.

"I was waiting on Desi. We had a fight yesterday and I want to talk to her. I want to try and apologize," he said. He unclenched his fists as he spoke and tried to smile.

"She's upstairs in her dressing room. She bailed on the show last night then showed up here about one. Been here ever since. Othello, I know you guys had a fight. What's going on with you two? You guys are some of the most sickeningly in love people I have ever met!" she said. Othello did smile then.

"Just a spat - it will all be over after tonight," he said.

"Well, she's up there alone. Be a good boy and go make up with her. Just don't mess her hair up too much!" Emilia laughed. Othello stood and touched her cheek.

"Thank you, Emilia. Iago is a lucky man," he said. His eyes seemed to be looking at something beautiful and terrifying to Emilia. She rubbed his arm.

"I wish he felt that way. Go on now, go see your wife!" Emilia said. Othello smiled again and headed toward the elevator.

Emilia stared at the elevator for a long time after the doors shut on Othello's smiling face, not knowing quite why. Something about the way he smiled unnerved her. She pushed away the thoughts creeping into her mind and headed to the bar for a pre-show cocktail.

Cass walked out of his building into the cool night air and zipped up his flight vest. It had been without a doubt one of the worst two days he had experienced in quite a while. First he got cut from a crew, then Bianca broke off things between them. Time to go for a ride and feel the wind against his face. Time to fly.

He started up the hovercycle and slowly rose to operating altitude. He was about to hit the throttle and take off when he heard the sounds of flying death. That was what they'd called a gyrocopter when he had been in the Sky Command. Then he felt the thunder in his chest as sound waves crashed into his ribcage. Cass glanced at the mirror on his left handlebar and felt his stomach drop.

There was a gyrocopter coming in hard over the top of his apartment building, with two .50 caliber machine guns mounted on metal arms that extended from the side of the craft. Two undermounted missile launchers stared at Cass like the eyes of a dragon. The machine guns and the missiles were wired to the on-board tracking and aiming systems. If a gyro locked onto you there was no escaping its wrath. Cass saw a red light reflecting off his mirror. The pilot of this gyro was trying to lock onto him.

"Fuck," he whispered. He crushed the throttle in his hand and took off into the night. The gyrocopter raced after him. A volley of automatic machine gun fire screamed through the air. Cass dropped down low, well below the legal allowable limits, and tried to dodge the copter's armor-piercing bullets. Glass, metal and concrete were torn to shreds as the bullets tore through the street and buildings and cars parked next to the sidewalks. Cass pulled up on his flaps and rose sharply. Bullets tore through windows and balconies as the copter tried to pull up and angle back at the same time.

Cass streaked over the top of a Woolworth's. The copter crested over the top of the building and made another hellish sweep with its machine guns. A huge water tank on top of the building next to the Woolworth's exploded. Any people left on the street were soaked by the deluge then nearly killed by falling chunks of metal from the tank.

Cass banked hard to his right and headed down a dead-end alley.

The space between the buildings was wide enough to allow the gyro to follow him down the alley. The windowless brick wall at the end of the alley was rushing toward Cass as he piloted his cycle toward at a suicidal speed. The copter was right behind him. The pilot locked on to the bike and squeezed the trigger of his machine guns and hit…

Nothing.

At the very last instant Cass hit his flaps and his reverse turbines. The hovercycle went up and backwards. Cass looked down and peered into the cockpit.

"What the hell?" he said. It was the guy from the casino. He only saw him for an instant in the cockpit, but the look on his face was nothing short of maniacal. Rodriego saw the wall rushing toward him. He tried desperately to pull the copter up but there was not nearly enough time. If he had not been drunk and angry and filled with implacable despair he might have realized Cassio was luring him into a trap.

The copter slammed into the building. A fireball erupted and for a moment the whole alley was lit with a bright orange glow like summer sunlight. The flash blinded Cass for a moment. He lost control of the hovercycle and slammed into the building on the right of the alley. The turbines were still powered and they bounced him off the building on the right and into the building on the left. Cass felt something in his shoulder snap and a bright white flower of pain bloomed in his chest. He let go of the hovercycle and flailed wildly as he fell. The cycle landed next to a fetid dumpster. Cass landed in the dumpster. For a few moments all he could do was lie in the putrid metal box and take deep breaths. He was alive.

Iago had driven over to Cass's apartment hoping his words had spurred the little worm Rodriego to take a most desperate course of action. Just when he was about to give up he spied Cass firing up his bike and he saw the gyro coming over the top of the building. He laughed as he saw Cass take off and the gyro follow. Then he punched the gas on the Tucker and followed after the gyro. He wanted to make sure Rodriego killed Cass.

Consequently, he was the first person on the scene of the crash.

"Roddy, you stupid piece of shit," he said when he entered the alley. Flames were still licking the walls and the pavement. The wreckage of the gyro was scattered all over the alley and the walls. Iago gingerly stepped over pools of fuel and oil and inched closer and closer to what was left of the gyrocopter.

"Oh God... God, someone help me," an agonized voice cried. Iago eased his way past a large piece of the cockpit. There, among the flames and the twisted steel, was Rodriego.

"God looks out for fools and babies, don't he, Roddy," Iago whispered. Rodreigo was bleeding from half a dozen places and was burned everywhere else.

"Who's there? Who is that? Oh God, please help me. Please," Rodriego pleaded.

"Shh... just do something right for once in your miserable life and die," Iago said. Rodriego turned his head toward Iago's voice. Most of his face was burned down to the whitish subcutaneous tissue. He was on his back with his legs turned at odd angles. He reached out toward Iago with a blood-covered hand.

"YOU..." he wheezed. Iago pulled out a revolver. A real gun with bullets filled with real gunpowder. He aimed at Rodriego's head.

"Yeah, me," he sighed.

"Hey... somebody out there? Give me a hand!" Cass yelled from the dumpster. He tried to pull himself up by the edge of the container but pain shot through his entire body. Iago turned and emptied the revolver at the dumpster. Bullets pinged off the container like rocks skipping across a pond. He was about to re-load when he heard the sound of ambulances and police sirens. He took off in a hard sprint down the alley past the dumpster and out onto the street, where he jumped up and down and waved his arms at the approaching authorities.

"Here! Here! The people down here need help!" he yelled. The cops and emergency people jumped out of their vehicles and rushed past Iago. He shoved his revolver back into the waist of his pants and melted into the approaching crowd. He was just about to climb into his Tucker when his telecom rang. It was Emilia. He opened it and saw that his wife looked alarmed.

"What's wrong?" he asked. Emilia bit her lip.

"I don't know. Probably nothing, but Othello is here and he looks... well, he's acting strange. Is there anything going on with you guys I should know?" Emilia asked.

"No," he said. Emilia's face did not soften after his taciturn response.

"Could you come by here? They got in a fight last night and Desi missed a show. I don't know what's going on with them but I don't like it. I mean, I don't think O would hurt her but he was just acting so freaking weird," Emilia said.

"All right, I'll come by," Iago said. He closed the telecom without another word.

He re-opened it and dialed. The image of the Olde Detroit Chief Constable Lodvico filled the screen. His florid face was even more mottled than usual.

"Iago, this better be important. I've got a copter crash going on downtown. A stolen government copter piloted by a crazy airman, so I don't really have time for chit-chat," Constable Lodvico said.

"It is, Chief. I wouldn't use your private line if it wasn't. I just got a call from my wife over at the Merchant. There's a domestic disturbance going on over there between the daughter of the Marshal of this city and a former decorated airman who just happens to be her husband. A Moor. I thought you might want to bring a couple of deputies and handle it before it gets out that the Marshal's daughter got her head bashed in and the Constable could have stopped it," Iago said. Ludvico's left eye began to twitch.

"This better not be a joke," he said.

"Chief, I assure you, there is nothing funny about this at all," he said. He closed the telecom and climbed in his car. He turned onto the street and headed for the Merchant. Time to see the dance he had choreographed come to an end.

*

Othello stood outside Desdemona's dressing room door for ten minutes, his resolve ebbing and flowing, before he lightly knocked. Desi opened the door and stood draped in a white evening gown, backlit by the lights that encircled her mirror. Othello walked into the dressing room and closed and locked the door.

"My love," he said. His voice was wispy as the fog rolling off Lake Michigan. Desi took a step back and put her hands over her mouth.

Tears welled up in the corners of her eyes.

"Where have you been, Othello? I've been calling you all night. I was scared to death !" she said through her clasped hands. The tears lost their grip on the edge of her eyes and fell down her cheeks.

"My love. I have questions for you as well. Questions no man should ever have to ask his wife. Questions that feel dirty in my mouth like a piece of rotted fruit," he said.

"What are you talking about, O?" Desi asked. The two flush-mounted lights in the ceiling of the dressing room flickered for a moment. Othello took a step closer to his wife.

"My love, where is the scarf I gave you that I found for you in Rome? The scarf I had embroidered with the name I called you when love filled my chest and happiness ruled my heart. Where is it, Desi?" he asked. Tears began to flow from his eyes as well.

"I lost it. I had it yesterday and after our disagreement I couldn't find it. Why are you asking me about that scarf?" Desi asked. Othello slowly ran his hand through her long hair. He brushed away the tears on her cheeks. He stepped forward and kissed her on her forehead, then he laid his lips on the warm flesh of her neck.

"You are lying, you filthy whore," he whispered into her ear. His hands climbed up her body, over her arms, over her shoulders until they found her throat. For a moment they stayed there as if he was going to massage her neck.

"I died when I heard him say how you gave yourself to him. Now it's your turn," he whispered.

Desdemona screamed. Othello squeezed her throat and cut off the scream. Her hands found his face and clawed at the skin around his eyes, eyes that still shed tears.

Emilia heard the scream from where she was standing in the backstage area. She ran up the backstage stairs, kicking off her heels as she ran. Her strong dancer's legs took the steps two at a time.

She burst through the stairwell door just as Iago, the Constable, and his two deputies were exiting the elevator. She ran toward the dressing room door without looking at the men.

"I heard a scream!" she yelled. Iago and the two deputies took off after her as the Constable walked as fast as his stunted legs would allow.

Emilia reached the door first. She slammed her palm against the smooth veneer.

"Open up, motherfucker! Open this goddamn door!" she roared. Iago pushed her aside.

"Let me," he said as he raised his foot and kicked at the cheap tin door knob. The lock gave up easily and the door slammed open. Othello stood above the body of his wife, whose arms were crossed over her chest. Othello had his hands raised. His eyes were bloodshot.

"It is done. The deed is done. My wife, the whore, is dead. And so am I," he said quietly.

"WHAT THE HELL DID YOU DO?" Emilia cried. The deputies grabbed Othello by the wrists and slammed his head down on the vanity top.

"She cheated on me, Emilia. She cheated with Cassio. She made a fool of me! He made a fool of me too! Now they can rot in Hell!" Othello cried as the deputies locked his wrists in handcuffs. One of the deputies pulled him up and turned him to face the Constable.

"What? Desi never cheated on you! And Cass isn't dead. He was in some kind of accident! I called him after I called Iago. You fool! You have lost your damn mind!" Emilia yelled.

"I may have, but at least I have not lost my one true friend. Brave and true Iago, who told me the truth. The truth you deny with your abetting mouth! Tell her, Iago, tell her about the scarf!" Othello growled. Emilia's head snapped around and she stared at her husband. Her face began to contort as understanding spread through her mind.

"You… I gave you the scarf. After their fight. I gave it to you because you said you wanted to give me one just like it," she said. The Constable looked at Emilia and then at Iago.

"We need all of you to come downtown until we sort this goddamn mess out," he said.

"Emilia, you have always been a mouthy bitch," Iago said. He pulled his revolver out of his waist and shot Emilia in the face. The bullet entered her left cheek and exited out of the back of her neck. Blood drenched the wall behind her. Iago bolted from the dressing room.

"After him, you dolts, I got this one!" the Constable shouted. Othello sat down in Desi's chair. His head fell forward and he began to moan and then scream. The Constable gripped his arm and in a surprising show of strength pulled him to his feet. Ludvico pressed his service pistol into Othello's ribs.

"Don't do anything more stupid than what you have already done," he said. The pair walked to the elevator. The carriage descended until they were on the ground floor. The Constable walked the shackled Othello through the lobby and out onto the street where his car was parked.

The deputies had Iago bent over the hood of their cruiser and were putting the cuffs on him. His jacket was torn down the middle and his face was bruised and bleeding. A crowd had begun to gather near the parked cars. The deputies pulled Iago to his feet.

"I don't know what the hell is going on here but I bet this son of a bitch is behind it. Your man Cassio is on his way to the hospital. I got a corpse lying in the alley off Verona Avenue with half his face burned off and a bullet in his head. I'm betting dollars to donuts that the bullets that killed his wife will match the ones in his head which means they both came from his gun. Othello, I don't know why but this fellow has tricked you," the Constable said. Othello and Iago locked eyes.

"Why? Why trick me into killing my wife? Turning on my comrade? What in the world could I have done to you to make you hate me so?" Othello asked. Iago spat a globule of phlegm and blood at Othello's feet.

"Demand me nothing! What you know, you know. From this time forth I will never speak a word!" he said. He licked his lips and began to laugh, a wild hyena's laugh that echoed through the night.

Othello looked up toward the sky. Then, without warning, he leaped into the air. As he jumped he brought his cuffed hands under his feet so that when he landed they were in front of him. When he landed he cracked the Constable in the jaw with his right elbow. The corpulent peace officer fell to the ground like a sack of flour. Othello closed the space between him and the deputies in a flash. He headbutted the deputy on his right while simultaneously kicking the deputy who was holding Iago in the throat. As the deputy on his right fell to the ground unconscious, Othello snatched the handcuff keys off his belt. Iago stood there with his mouth agape as Othello freed himself. Othello stepped in front of Iago. He reached inside Iago's inside breast pocket and grabbed the tasestick he knew his comrade kept there.

The tasestick was a smaller version of the stun stick the deputies and MPs carried. Othello put one hand around Iago's throat and shoved him back against the police cruiser. He pressed the tip of the tasestick against Iago's belly and, using all his strength, shoved it into Iago's stomach and turned it on.

Iago's body was seized by agony. His feet and legs were ravaged by spasms and as he fell to the pavement Othello pulled the bloody weapon from his gut. Othello dropped to one knee and grabbed him by the face.

"I bleed, boss, but I do not die," Iago gasped.

"I'm glad. Death is peace and I would have you suffer," Othello said. He rose and walked over to the Constable. He picked up Lodvico's gun and ran back into the casino. He darted to the service stairs and up to Desdemona's dressing room. A few of the dancers were peering into the room when he burst into the hallway. They saw him, the gun, and his bloody hand, and scattered like roaches. Othello went into the room and knelt by the body of his wife.

"I kissed thee ere I killed thee. No other way but this. Killing myself to die upon a kiss," he said. He bent down and kissed her still-warm lips.

"DROP THE GUN!" a voice shouted. Othello looked up to see more deputies standing in the doorway with their weapons drawn. He smiled, and slowly placed the barrel of the gun under his chin.

"*When you shall these unlucky deeds relate, speak of me as I am. Nothing extenuate. Nor set down in aught malice. Then must you speak of one that loved not wisely,*" he paused and looked at his wife once more.

"*But too well,*" he said as he pulled the trigger.

FINIS

PROSPERO'S
ISLAND

H. James Lopez

ROSPERO SAT IN WHAT THE NYMPHS CALLED HIS "THRONE ROOM." At the center of the room, spinning vertically, was a shaft of iron that once propelled the ship that brought him and his daughter to the island of Pergu. However, fifteen years ago the engines froze and the cylinders would pump no more.

Pergu abounded with vegetation but was inhabited by few creatures. The nymphs were small, only half the size of a human. Their arms and legs were bulbous and ethereal, but otherwise the nymphs were childlike. They were the only source of food for the other island life, the sycori, a race of creatures with hardened leathery skin and teeth which rivaled a tiger's. While the sycori could and did destroy nymphs for sustenance, they shied away from the sunlight and stayed hidden in the thick forests of the island.

Prospero was quick to befriend the nymphs, who had rescued him and his daughter from the shipwreck and kept them safe from the sycori while he gathered his bearings. The ship, a service vessel that kept battleships afloat in the Tunisian combat, was full of tools and technology. In fact, he'd saved three ships from the depths of the Tyrrhenian Sea the same day Gonzalo and Antonio stepped aboard his vessel to banish him.

Alonso, the king of Naples, removed Prospero's title and then set him adrift on the sea. Gonzalo had bartered for this fate rather than execution. Antonio, who forced Prospero's daughter Miranda to accompany her father, would assume Prospero's title. He gave the order to scuttle the engines and left the ship to drift.

What neither Antonio nor Alonso had counted on was the island of Pergu sitting along their current. It was little safer than a Tunisian battlefield, but the island gave Prospero food and a place to land and was a better fate for his daughter than death at sea.

To protect his new nymph friends on Pergu, Prospero built a coil from the remnants of his ship. He'd hoped to power it with what was left of the engines, or perhaps find a way to harness the tide from the oceans, but the nymphs showed him a better option. They took him to the rift, a small volcano of life energy near the center of the island.

The nymphs had been drawn to the rift by the previous resident of the island, the witch Sycorax. She'd spent many years trying to cultivate an army of nymphs to avenge being left on Pergu to die. It was Sycorax who infused the nymphs with Earthen magic to give them form. Then she taught her soldiers to feast upon other nymphs and increase and enhance their physical shape, growing them into the feral sycori of the island. Eventually, however, her blood would become the only thing which could sate their hunger.

The rift provided enough power to turn the coil and generate a shield that both deterred the sycori and provided ambient energy to the people under it. The grey- and pink-hued electrical pulses surrounded the small town near the center of the island. Since the shipwreck, Prospero had developed many ways to harness the shield's energy. Among the first things he'd developed were ways to give the nymphs more shape.

Prospero knew the shield wasn't enough to protect the nymphs forever. He began to work on powered enhancements that gave the nymphs more human shape: hands that could work on rebuilding his ship; arms and legs to help them farm and grow more crops. It was not long before they had made him their leader, in part because he was benevolent, but also because he controlled the shield.

Prospero sat in his captain's chair, surrounded by monitors. Some of them gave readouts on the coil's speed, output, and range. Others gave him information about nymphs who had left the shield perimeter. Each time one of them walked through the hued wall, Prospero had to transfer a power charge to their enhancements. Without that power the metal and graphite enhancements would cease to function and make the nymphs an easy target for anything that happened by.

A group of nymphs were on the south shore constructing a new ship from the wreckage of Prospero's boat. What could be salvaged sat in a dry dock at the edge of the tide. They'd fashioned a formidable hull and reconfigured the engine to use one screw but couldn't get the engine to fire. Prospero found the nymphs were easy to train, and took to engineering and construction quickly; a few of them even helped Prospero work on the coil.

He watched on the screens as they busily worked. He could see those working at the beach and those working on the coil braces. The pulse of the shield also generated an overview of the island that told him where some of the sycori were. But there were some nymphs he could not track; Ariel was one of those.

She entered the room through the skylight, skirting the rotation of the coil as she fluttered to the ground. Her lean body shifted with the slightest pump of her wings. Ariel had taken much of her look from Miranda, in homage to the girl who'd become the best representation of woman on the island. At times this bothered Prospero. He'd had feelings for the nymph for years but knew better than to act on them.

Miranda and Ariel had grown up together on the island but their fates were different. Miranda was human and lived off the sustenance and shelter the island provided. Ariel, like the other nymphs of Pergu, could only go as far as Prospero's enhancements carried her. Her freedom lasted as far as the charge of her wing pack.

Ariel glided to the ground at the foot of Prospero's makeshift command center. She was lean and lithe, with light brown spirals of hair falling from the crown of her head. Her legs were graphite from the knee down, as were her shoulders and her forearms, made from pieces of the ship. More graphite extensions were embedded in her spine to help her build height and to act as a frame that she could manipulate. The nymphs that wanted more out of their bodies came to Prospero for enhancement from the energy of the shield, but he knew it came at a cost.

Ariel's wings folded to her back as she basked in the shadow of the coil. The wings were cut from repurposed uniforms and wire, built to give her a taste of freedom. Prospero knew it was a limited freedom, but they had been a gift. Where other nymphs could charge up and traipse the thick woodland or the beach of the island, Ariel could soar above; though if she went too far she would fall from the sky like Icarus.

"My good King, I have news." Ariel knelt at the front of the console. She looked at the ground in front of her although Prospero never asked her to prostrate herself.

"Tell me what you've seen."

Ariel looked up, but she would not rise. She was a half a foot taller than Prospero, so never stood in his presence. Her face beamed as she announced, "I was on the western side of the island and I spotted a ship on the horizon."

Prospero knew hers was a false glee, but his own was true. Ships didn't travel close to Pergu often. If they did, they never responded to conventional signals for rescue. Prospero was convinced the island was marked for sailors to "avoid at all costs," possibly due to its previous inhabitants, which left little hope of rescue for him and Miranda. However, a vessel forced to land, whether whole or not, could provide more pieces to help him build a working engine to get back to Milan.

Prospero pulled a cable from his display and tossed it toward Ariel. She plugged the wire into her shoulder, giving Prospero instant access to her memories. The screen showed the outline of the island as Ariel flew over it. She moved in long lazy circles, letting the wind flow around her. Her eyes slowly rose to the horizon and she focused on a pair of ships in the distance.

One of the other screens showed Prospero a number of nymphs working at the shore. Six of them had wireless antennae and the rest were on battery power. Prospero pulled a headset from the side of his monitor and slid it on.

"Ariel, I'm going to push more power to six of the nymphs at the shore. They'll reconfigure to swim out to the ships and give us a better look. Go with them and assure they are safe." Prospero watched the numbers on his display shuffle as he recalculated the size of his central shield. He adjusted the sphere's perimeters and then ordered, "Everyone not going with you needs to head back to the central bubble immediately. I'm going to have to pull 15% from the hub to give you the distance to the ship. So charge up and go quickly!"

"Yes, my King," Ariel replied. Spreading her wings, she shot up through the skylight into the open sky. She would be at the shore in a matter of minutes, so Prospero rushed to finish his configuration and get the nymphs out to sea. He keyed the microphone attached to his helm and called out to the six nymphs.

"I am sending Ariel to lead you to a ship at sea. Surround the vessel and gather information but do not approach. In the absence of my voice, Ariel will protect you."

The nymphs would do as they were told; it was an unspoken agreement Prospero had with all of them. He'd provided them with shape and safety and in turn, they worked on helping him leave. The last few years, however, it had been harder to keep the peace among the nymphs. Their allegiance to Prospero was tested daily by the sycori's attacks and the mouth of a nymph named Caliban.

Prospero keyed his microphone. "Everyone be aware, the distance to the outer perimeter shield will be shortened by one and a half meters from the center. All excess shield travel is limited to those aiding coil services. Plan accordingly and stay inside the safety of our shield."

The nymphs he watched on his display gathered what they could and rushed back toward the central shield. Prospero switched frequencies and ordered, "Captain of the Guard, head toward the ship build site and take a complement to protect the returning nymphs. I am pulling the soldiers you had out there for another purpose."

The guard would quickly catch up to the repair crew. It was late in the day and Prospero had to assure they still had defenses against the sycori in the forest. Prospero knew there would be losses on the travel back from the shore, though he would not take all the blame. Fifteen years on, Prospero had become more and more agitated at the nymphs' inability to defend themselves.

Though they lived under the constant threat of the sycori, most of the nymphs were peaceful. They chose to farm and build, to create rather than destroy. Prospero sometimes wondered if he hadn't spent his time building them body parts, maintaining the shield or finding ways to fight off the sycori, he might have had time to rebuild his ship. Prospero had gathered about 10 percent of the nymphs and trained them to fight. He gave them more enhancements and a wireless connection to him and the coil in exchange for their service. Plenty of times his guard had saved other nymphs from the jaws of sycori in the forest.

The main display marked the progress of the nymphs swimming out to the slow moving ship. Three of the nymphs had remote optics installed; he often used this to monitor their progress or advise them. In the open water they had to pick their battles.

Prospero placed a lens on his right eye and plugged it into his headset. Instantly he saw a warship leading a sailing barge. Both bore the gold and green colors of Milan and one also flew the flag of the King of Naples. He toggled through all three perspectives before keying the headset to speak with Ariel.

"I see a pair of ships. Are there any more on the horizon?" Prospero asked. He wasn't sure the six nymphs he'd sent could bring a warship to ground.

"My King, there is only the pair. The larger ship has men posted on their guns."

Ariel had seen an armed escort before, and Prospero had made sure she never tried to attack one. While it would take more than a few rounds to kill her, it was possible, and he'd told her never to risk it. If he lost her over the water, her enhancements would surely drag her to the depths of the ocean.

"Ariel, return to the hub. You'll only draw attention out there." Prospero focused on the other nymphs and ordered, "The storm is a half mile out. When it hits, center a whirlpool on the smaller vessel. Use all strength possible to bring the ship to shore," he said, anger in his voice. He knew if the ship flew the flag of Alonso, either the King or his heirs were on board. Prospero would take what he needed from Alonso just as a future had been taken from him.

"Yes, my Lord," one of the nymphs replied. He knew her as Kara, one of the better soldiers he'd helped to train. After a pause, she asked, "What of the other ship?"

"If it attempts to stop you, send it to the bottom."

Prospero switched off his headset and left the display running. The nymphs began to circle, shifting the water with their movements. When the storm hit, the waves and the nymphs would be able to push the ship toward the island. Few captains could keep it from colliding with the shoreline. There would be something in the salvage, but all Prospero hoped for was bodies.

He slumped into his throne, his eyes focused on the destruction, though he was unsure of why he'd done it. Years before Prospero promised himself he could forgive Alonso and even his brother for their betrayal. However, whenever the opportunity arose, he shied from it. As he chided himself, Prospero heard the rattle of hollow legs entering the room.

Caliban was one of the oldest nymphs. He was born of Sycorax's blood, but she was betrayed before he could be made whole. Though he'd only known her slightly, his respect for his mother and her goals was obvious to everyone. Prospero had tried to explain that his mother would have turned him into a brute for her own purposes, but it didn't change his mind.

Caliban entered the room on cloven hooves built of graphite, similar to the legs of an ass. Once, Caliban had a fully human form, with legs that rivaled Ariel's in length. He was one of the warriors who protected the city, but several months ago he had overstepped his bounds with Prospero's daughter, Miranda. He'd attempted to force himself on her in the woods outside the shield, but she beat him back, shattering his legs and leaving him for dead.

"You are quick to send a ship to the depths, when it could be used to free my people from these shores." Caliban's voice was metallic and grating, damaged from a fight the nymph had lost. Prospero heard the rattle of stripped and loose gears as Caliban moved closer. There were times he thought of repairing the nymph's legs, but he would then recall the assault on Miranda and abandoned the repair. Though Caliban's words were staggered, they were not wrong. "They are obedient to you, my Lord, because they believe you have their best interests at heart. But would they believe that if they could see you as I do?"

Prospero glared at the creature at the edge of the room. He could hear the whining of gears which helped Caliban breathe. The nymph stepped forward and Prospero could see his weight was not distributed evenly. He felt nothing but pity for the creature, yet his anger got the better of him. Prospero aimed his gauntleted left hand at Caliban and flexed his fingers.

"Know your place, Caliban," Prospero shouted as the tips of his fingers released a pulse of electricity. Instantly the nymph's breathing became labored as power was cut off from the enhancements that kept Caliban alive. The nymph fell to one knee, the weight of the graphite and iron in his upper body dragging him to the ground. "My daughter fights to save your people and you cower here, throwing your jabs at me. I know you speak ill of me in the markets and on the street, Caliban. And if Miranda didn't ask me to keep you alive I would have fed you to the sycori years back."

Caliban choked back, "Then do so, honorable tyrant! Feed me to the beasts and end my torturous slavery!"

Prospero lowered his arm, and electrical power returned to Caliban immediately, although Prospero almost hoped the strain would kill the nymph. As the creature coughed on the ground, Prospero turned his attentions back to the screen as the storm began to pound on the ships.

"Both ships will make landfall before night. Perhaps we can salvage what we need from them, Caliban. But without forcing them ashore we would have nothing to work with." Prospero rose from his throne and stepped out from behind the monitors. He could feel electricity race around the edges of his gauntlet, making him think briefly of crushing the nymph; but he kept his anger in check. "I never asked to be king of this island, Caliban. But I gave my word I would save its people from the sycori and I have done that all too often."

"You won't save those on the boats, my Liege," Caliban replied with mock reverence. He locked eyes with Prospero and continued, "Those ships will make land as the night falls and by morning there will be nothing left but memories. The sycori will peel the meat from their bones and thank you in the process."

Prospero knew he couldn't leave the bodies to the sycori; it wasn't about saving lives, but the beasts grew stronger when they ate meat as opposed to nymph or fish. While the shield kept most of them at bay, after eating fresh meat a few sycori had pierced the shield and rampaged the city. If he didn't deal with the survivors, Prospero would have to deal with those who found them.

Caliban smiled from the floor; he had gotten his way. Prospero watched as the creature's hooves shuffled forward and Caliban pleaded, "My King, allow me to lead a few warriors to the crash site to recover the bodies. I would hate for them to be left to the care of Sycorax's children."

"An interesting thought, since you are one of those children," Miranda commented as she entered the room.

She'd grown up amid the struggles with the sycori. Prospero had had to train her and the nymphs to defend the city, so she'd grown up much differently than the lady she would have been in Milan. A gold filigreed leaf glimmered from atop her shoulders. It was a Captain's rank, nothing more than a symbol of her father's faith in her, but the nymphs believed in it. Where Prospero had grown tired of saving their lives, Miranda had come to enjoy their praise.

"My guard held off a trio of sycori as we caught up with the returners from the port. The sycori had already begun to track our returners. They were organized and more cunning than we'd seen before." Her words were directed at Prospero but her eyes stayed on Caliban. Miranda's hand never strayed from the hilt of her blade as she continued, "Perhaps they've been training or someone is passing the sycori information on our tactics."

"It is good to see their training didn't catch you off guard, Miranda. Were there any losses?" Caliban asked without looking at her.

"My title, little fool, is Captain," Miranda replied though Caliban would not avert his gaze. "You would do well to remember it. Perhaps you would stand a bit taller if you had?"

"My apologies to your daughter, good King. She seems to think this imagined rank she wears carries real weight." Caliban kept his attention on Prospero as Miranda took a step closer. "That somehow these troops see her as anything more than a bother who leads them into certain death."

Miranda drew her blade and stepped toward the nymph, her hand still as a stone. The ridge of the blade carried no charge. She wouldn't need it to kill Caliban, but Prospero knew better than to let her spill blood in his throne room.

"Captain, what is your report?"

She turned her gaze from Caliban and locked it onto Prospero, her blade still. Caliban would not move, fearful it would incite her. Prospero could see the hate behind her green eyes and waited patiently as she searched for the right words.

"I lost one of the workers and one of my guards. We were short-handed and as I said, the sycori seemed to know exactly where to strike us."

Prospero watched Caliban for any sign of truth in his face. He wasn't sure why or how, but he knew the nymph had something to do with the sycori. Since his attack, he'd been jockeying for position to take Prospero's crown. Rumors were spreading of Prospero's hate for the nymphs and how he kept them subservient. If the sycori did come through the shield, Caliban could ride the carnage into a position of control.

"Keep an eye on the weakest edges of the shield. If they've eaten, the sycori will be on the hunt tonight," Prospero commanded as he turned back to his monitors. Miranda lowered her blade and sheathed the weapon.

As Prospero watched, the royal barge cracked in half as it continued toward the shore. The warship, separated from the barge, drifted toward the northeast shore. Her hull would stay intact but most likely beach on the shore closest to the sycori's nests.

"It seems we have guests on the island. Caliban is correct in thinking they will not last the night if we leave them to the sycori." Prospero slid the headset back on and keyed the microphone. "Ariel, can you see any other ships approaching shore? Can you scout for the wrecks or some survivors?"

"I can, my liege."

He knew she would be spiraling around the island. "Shall I engage my monocle so you can see them with your own eyes?"

Prospero often forgot Ariel had no cameras he could access without her consent. He'd done it as a favor in a fit of romance; many times he'd regretted it. When she activated her monocle he saw her on his screen and saw she was headed for the site of one of the wrecks. "When you arrive, give me a panoramic before you land. Until then don't waste your charge."

Miranda moved closer to her father's display and noted the projection for the warship's landing. She turned to her father and told him, "I can gather some of the guard and head for that ship, father. We can aid the nymphs coming out of the water and secure the ship before the Sycori get a chance to take it apart."

"Go quickly and if there is a need for protection do not hesitate to contact me." He knew she wouldn't listen, but still he spoke the words of a father.

Caliban sidled up to the throne as Prospero stared at the last blinking light on the ship. It was the section which would land closest on the shore.

"My liege, may I offer myself to aid in scouting that third vessel? I know those areas well and could lead a party through them easily."

It was a ploy to let Caliban outside the shield and Prospero knew it.

"In your state, you would do more harm than good, Caliban."

The creature shook his head and smiled, "Allow me the chance, my Lord. Let me earn the respect you have lost for me."

Prospero could have turned him away but it would only stir ire among the nymphs. Instead, perhaps the sycori would kill the fool nymph and save Prospero the trouble. Prospero stared at his design for an offshoot corridor from the shield. He'd never tested the method for expanding a columned node, but was willing to risk it with Caliban.

"If you wish to earn my respect, I will show you how to do so."

II

Caliban could feel Prospero's presence as he hefted a bag of simple beacons on his back and traveled a makeshift safety corridor. The beacons pulled the strength of the shield along with Caliban and assured him the additions to his body would function. Since Miranda's punishment, he could only hold a charge for a half hour at best. It gave him enough time to place two beacons, then wait for Prospero to expand the shield.

Initially, Caliban had been like many of the other nymphs and regarded the enhancements as Prospero's benevolence. Unlike Ariel, who could charge herself, the others only left the shield in service to the King, when Prospero allowed it. Now, though, Caliban saw the enhancements for what they were: the chains of his slavery.

The trails on the ground were treacherous, but Caliban negotiated them with ease. He often exaggerated his limp and his wheezing to ensure Prospero saw him as little threat. But when he was alone, Caliban moved more surely. He noticed the edges of the corridor were glowing as night began to close in on the island. The more bold of the sycori would begin to hunt soon.

Caliban was sure Ariel and Miranda were also on their way to the survivors, though he wasn't sure what they would find. As he marched through the brush and drove another beacon into the ground, he saw the subtle traces of falling leaves. He knew the sycori had already found him and he was on the wrong side of the nearest wall. Prospero would begin charging the new pair of beacons but it would be a few minutes before the shield rose.

Caliban thought of running but knew it would only excite the creatures. They lived for the hunt; catching prey seemed more exciting than when food was simply handed to them. Caliban stopped and turned to face the brush he knew they were hiding behind. He had more than a mile to the shore and there wasn't enough sun to back off a daytime hunter.

"Hello brother," Caliban said as he knelt on the ground. His words were patient and kind. The sycori hardly communicated beyond grunts but he figured the grunts were a language. Caliban saw the beacon charging beside him and held out his empty hands. "I am not your enemy. We are kin, my brother. Come into the light where I can see you."

It wasn't the first time Caliban had approached one of the sycori. Prospero had sent him to scout a few of the sycori's nests a few years back. Free of Prospero's eyes, Caliban took a risk and spoke to one of the creatures as an equal. He had begun to understand the creature's perspective and knew they shared a common enemy.

This sycori seemed different. Caliban remembered the first had been smaller, though they were both twice the nymph's size. Its broad shoulders should not have been so easily hidden by the brush but the sycori's skin was colored with patches of grey, green, and brown. Some said they'd adapted to the island in order to hunt better, but Caliban knew it was partly his mother's magic.

The creature's face was a wide oval and it stared at him through thick reddened eyes that he felt burn to his core. Caliban watched the creature shuffle a bit closer to where the corridor wall should be. It balanced on both its arms and a pair of shorter legs which it used like a quadruped. Caliban felt the backs of his teeth with his tongue while his eyes traced the line of the sycori's fangs. He knew they shared a common pool of genes but still feared his half-brother.

The sycori unfurled a hand and reached cautiously in the direction of the absent corridor wall. The creature acted as if it knew the shield would be generated by the posts, a sign of much more intelligence than Prospero had given them credit for. The tips of his claw-laden fingers sparked against the ambient electricity passing from post to post. It wasn't strong enough to repel him but still crackled against bone and flesh.

"Can you speak?" Caliban asked as he stared at the sycori's jaw.

The creature shook its head. It understood the question, but could not reply. Its jaws had one purpose. The last time he come this close, Miranda had come upon him and he had had to act quickly. He had attacked her, masking the sycori's escape.

After she left him there, Caliban was prepared to die in the woods, and was surprised when the sycori dragged him to the edge of the shield. Though he survived, Caliban knew it was not by the benevolence of Prospero or his daughter. The sycori who saved him had left an indelible mark on him.

The shield erupted between the posts and scared the creature. It did not back away, but sat on the opposite side and watched Caliban's movements. Caliban smiled at the animal and said, "Do not fear, my friend. Go now and come find the end of this tunnel later. I will bring you something to snack on and perhaps you can later repay my kindness."

The creature shied away from the corridor wall and nodded. Caliban didn't know if it understood him but he could tell the blood flowing in its veins was thick with his mother's magic.

Caliban waited until the creature had gone before continuing to build his corridor. The sun was fading in the distance but the glow of the corridor provided ample light. Caliban spotted the shipwreck on the beach as he ran out of posts at the edge of the sands.

The hull was still intact, though half the ship was gone. Caliban waited for his battery to charge before he could clear the corridor. What looked like footprints and drag marks scored the beach between the shore and the tree line. Clearly there were survivors, but Caliban wondered if they'd gotten very far.

Instinctively, Caliban reached for his belt, hoping to find the hilt of a familiar sword, but touched nothing but air. Prospero had disarmed him after the incident with Miranda. He'd been lucky enough to steal a short dagger from one of the guards, but it wouldn't protect him from feral sycori.

The setting sun was cutting into his field of vision and Caliban felt a tingle at the back of his neck. It wasn't fear, only the looming presence of the tyrant king. Unlike most other soldiers, Caliban had learned how to switch off his master's controls. Though he could not rid himself of them, he could limit what Prospero saw and heard.

He reached over his shoulder and toggled on the communicator, asking, "How may I serve you, my liege?"

"You seemed to rest a few yards back. Is everything okay?"

Caliban knew it wasn't concern for his safety that triggered Prospero's call. Luckily, it didn't take much to deceive the king, who was often too involved in his own dilemmas. "No, my Lord, I simply had to rest. The path was most treacherous, my battery is damaged and my appendages were not geared for such travel."

"I will send guards to assist you, Caliban."

Prospero had been searching for a reason to send men with Caliban even though he had none to spare. Caliban refused to give him a reason and replied, "No, my liege. I can handle this. I've run out of posts, so I will have to go forward with only battery power; we should cut communication to prolong my time. I will call periodically."

Caliban switched off his receiver while Prospero was agreeing. He pushed against the wall and felt the wind on his hand outside the shield. There was a tingle of electricity as he freed himself of his master's leash. Caliban knew the king could no longer see or hear him.

The wreckage on the shore was battered but Caliban saw several hiding places. He chose instead to investigate the footsteps leading away from the wreckage. The dead would need burying, but if there were survivors it was better to find them first.

The sand under his cloven feet was treacherous and Caliban stumbled as he tried to follow the trails left by the wreckage's survivors. He pulled the short knife from a sheath tucked in his belt and held it tight while scanning the tree line. He failed to see a sand-covered plank of wood, which shattered under his weight as he stepped on it.

Caliban stumbled forward and threw out both his arms to break his fall but couldn't catch himself. His face struck the sand, and he heard the shuffle of boots around him. It was a child's trap, wood and sand over a hole, but he'd fallen for it. He struggled to roll over to see his attackers.

Humans, olive-skinned like Prospero, stood around him. Caliban showed them his bare palms but knew there would be little trust. His face was lean and rugged like a man's, but framed by a beard which ran from one pointed ear to the other. There were a few ridges on his forehead that couldn't be explained as wrinkles; he had only three fingers and a thumb on his hands. And his lower body was built like an animal's and in no way resembled these men.

"What form of creature is this?" one of them asked as he aimed a blade at Caliban's chest.

"One who speaks your language, good sir," Caliban replied as he looked up at the men. He could see three men around him, two of whom seemed comfortable with weapons and a third who was rather shaky. He didn't want to startle them but knew he had to act before he was skewered as a beast. "Another of your like sent me here to find survivors and to lead you from the unsafe shores. Please do me no harm. I only seek to serve my king."

"Stephan, what are your orders?"

It was obvious the man who held a blade to Caliban wasn't in charge. Perhaps one of the others could make a decision, though from their ragged appearance Caliban wasn't sure it was possible. He shifted on the ground, pulling his legs under him and attempting to rise up.

"Don't move!" the guard yelled as he pushed his blade a bit closer to Caliban's throat.

The man he called Stephan stood on Caliban's far left. His black hair was pinned behind his head and was matted slightly with blood. As the sun was setting behind them, Caliban knew he had to act quickly.

"I seek to warn you all, there are creatures on this island who are much bolder and more powerful than myself," Caliban managed. "They may not be present in the light but if you are still in the open when night comes, they will destroy you." Caliban attempted to hold the gaze of Stephan as he spoke.

Stephan sheathed his weapon though he gave no order for the others to do the same. He stepped a bit closer and asked, "Who is your king, little creature?"

"I serve Prospero of Milan. He is the ruler of my people and he wishes to protect you and any other survivors, but not if you keep that blade at my throat."

Stephan waved a pair of fingers at the others and their weapons were lowered. He took another step closer to Caliban and remarked, "Now, how will your king save us?"

Caliban reached over his shoulder and toggled his communicator. He didn't wait for a response, immediately saying, "My King, I have found survivors. Can you project a shield onto us?"

There was no answer, leading Caliban to wonder if he'd finally been abandoned by the tyrant king. The antennae on Caliban's spine shot a spark of pain into his body. The air around the four of them began to flicker as a shield of red and grey emanated from Caliban's back and surrounded them. Stephan's men immediately drew their weapons again, as Caliban attempted to calm them. "This is the protection my king offers. It will keep out the island's predators but I cannot sustain it. There is a corridor back along the beach that will take us to safety."

The shield flickered out of existence as quickly as it came.

"Caliban, I am sending a pair of the storm nymphs to your position," Prospero replied before Caliban had a chance to cut the radio receiver.

"My liege, you would divert too many resources." Caliban knew the excuse would not sate Prospero. The king valued the lives of men over those of the nymphs. If Caliban didn't act quickly, Prospero would crowd the corridor with soldiers and Caliban's plans for the sycori would be crushed. "Allow me to assess what we need before you expend the power and threaten the nymphs of the city."

"A valid point, Caliban," Prospero replied with agitation in his tone. "Make your reconnaissance quick. The sycori grow stronger with every minute."

Caliban agreed, then switched off communications.

"What is happening?" Stephan asked as he saw Caliban cease talking to himself. Along the shore a pair of bodies stepped free of the water. Caliban had seen them before. Lydos was built like Prospero's daughter but a bit smaller and faster. She'd always been a fighter and had adored the king from afar. The other was Kale, with whom Caliban used to spar when they were soldiers. Neither of them regarded Caliban as a trusted friend but he knew they would be running on the last remnants of power.

The two walked up the beach toward Caliban and the soldiers as he righted himself and waved slightly. Lydos stepped forward, her tan skin slightly faded and wrinkled from the water.

"Our king sent us to offer aid. How may we be of service?" Lydos asked through gritted teeth.

Caliban knew the words were like bile in her mouth and he did not hesitate to smile. He offered a gesture of thanks and remarked, "I am sure you are both at the end of your charge. Our master has posted a corridor partway up the beach. Please go charge and secure the corridor's entrance."

Caliban turned to Stephan, asking, "Can you send one of your men with them? Someone who can bring them back to the injured once they have charged?"

"I can," he replied. "Is there more help on the way?"

"We work with what we have, Stephan. The night is on its way and we must escape it soon," Caliban replied as he played the fear of the unknown against the setting sun.

"Trunculo, go with those two and, when they are ready, lead them back to the cavern." Stephan looked over Caliban's battered little frame and continued, "I'll take this one with me and get people ready to move."

Trunculo, Lydos and Kale moved away from Caliban and Stephan as they searched out the corridor. Caliban knew they couldn't miss the glow of the shield in the dark. It would not be immediate but Caliban knew Lydos and Kale would return if he didn't send people back with them to the hub. Caliban was distracted as he followed Stephan and the other soldier toward the nearby caverns.

"Having some trouble, creature?" Stephan asked as Caliban struggled to move through the loose sand.

Caliban smiled stiffly and thought about punching Stephan in the throat. Instead he replied, "My name is Caliban, Mr. Stephan, and the trouble is less the sand and more these ridiculous appendages."

Caliban secured his footing and shuffled forward. He knew the comment would pique Stephan's interest and the soldier would eventually ask the right questions. Stephan and the nameless soldier led the way toward a small cave just behind the edge of trees. A small group of people crowded together around some bodies while others attempted to start a fire. Caliban could tell these were not warriors. They were small or overweight and most seemed out of place in their heavy furs and colorful clothes.

"These are not fighters," Caliban remarked looking over the bunch. "They are old and lethargic. They'd make a fine meal for the sycori. There aren't enough soldiers on the island to help you."

Stephan huffed at the comments and replied, "Warriors like you, little goblin, can't offer much protection. You would hardly pose a threat to the young archduke there."

Caliban eyed the young man who could hardly hold his blade through the shake of his hands. He laughed and replied, "Do not think less of me for my stature, Stephan. I was once tall and strong like you or those two who rose from the water. But I fell out of my master's favor and am now what you see."

Stephan rubbed his thumb on the series of scars decorating his right cheek. He smirked and said, "Seems no matter how big their land, a king is a king and a soldier is a soldier. Wouldn't you agree, Archduke Reginald?"

The shaky duke said little but left Stephan's side in favor of the huddled group. Caliban couldn't help but laugh along with Stephan. He stared at the fixed blade the soldier carried and remarked, "That will do you no good if the sycori come here. We will need something of greater force."

Stephan walked Caliban toward the clusters of people. "What are these sycori you fear, Caliban?" he asked.

Caliban crouched beside the bodies of a few of the ship's travelers. Some of the bodies had been ravaged when they came ashore and others had died before the ship made landfall. Caliban looked back at Stephan and replied, "The sycori are creatures of this island. They are strong enough to wrench large branches from trees. Their skin is thick, stopping blades and needles. Though they fear the crackling light King Prospero can generate, the smell of bloodied meat will draw them here."

"Roccio," Stephan yelled into the darkness of the cavern. "Pull two of the revolvers from the cache and see what can be done to keep bandages on the wounded."

Stephan crouched beside Caliban and stared at the body. "Not many of my soldiers are left. But Roccio found a cache of arms from the ship. Your friends may be able to take a blade but I think we have something with more bite."

"Who are the rest of these people?"

"Guests of Alonso, King of Naples. We were returning them home from the wedding of the King of Tunis." Stephan looked around the room with disdain. Caliban guessed the ragged man who passed Stephan a bent metal tube with wood wrapped around it was Roccio. Stephan kept one half of the tube facing away from him as he cracked open the back end and counted a number of small brass pellets inside it. "I've plenty of weapons but only a few soldiers, Caliban. I imagine most of this lot would fold if attacked by your sycori."

Caliban wondered about the weapon and the group of men with Stephan. He'd counted the wounded and the dead and knew he had to work quickly or lose his advantage.

"Stephan, take the able and the wounded and make for the corridor. The sun is still on the water and the corridor will not harm you. But if you stay with these bodies, you and your men will be dead by the sunrise."

"Lydos and Kale can lead the others back to the generator. I will stay with the dead, until you can send more to carry them back," Caliban continued as he hovered over the wounded.

"Will the sycori come for you, Caliban?"

"They will, sir. And I will hold them off as best I can with this blade." Caliban produced the small knife he'd held onto. The sight of the paltry weapon upset an old soldier like Stephan.

"Roccio, bring me another pistol," Stephan grimaced as he handed Caliban the revolver. "Get anyone who is able to move ready to go."

Stephan looked down his nose at Caliban and smiled. "I cannot stay with you, but I will not let you stand this watch with such a pitiful weapon. This, my little friend, can dispatch much more force than any blade. It will mean little against a whole army of your sycori but I will know you gave them the best of a fight."

Caliban thanked Stephan and began arranging bodies as those who could filed out of the cavern. The light was almost gone and they would have to hurry to find Prospero's corridor. Stephan promised to speak well of Caliban to the King of Naples. Caliban remained with six dead bodies as Stephan and the sun finally left the cavern.

It would be a few hours before they returned to the shield, even at best; help would not be headed to Caliban anytime soon. Caliban assumed he wouldn't need it. He hid both of the pistols beneath a log on the opposite side of a tiny fire as he began to cut up the dead. The smell of wet meat filled the air, as he tossed a few strips into the fire.

If they had grown more cunning as Miranda had said, perhaps they would not come. However, Caliban knew of at least one who would. He sat opposite the bodies, keeping the fire between him and the meat. If they came, the first thing they would see was the food he was offering.

The sound of shifting sand alerted Caliban to his guests. As he guessed, they could not resist the smell. The magic of Caliban's mother made them whole but also made them crave the taste of flesh. The first sycori through the mouth of the cavern was smaller than the one he'd come across in the forest. The grey-green skin made him almost invisible in the dark but as he approached the fire his natural camouflage was lost. Caliban wrapped his hand around the base of the pistol Stephan had provided and hefted it toward the creature.

He watched the beast eat, noting the glee on its face as it tore flesh from bone. Its jaws made short work of sinew and skin, lapping up fluids as they pooled in the sand. Caliban waited to see if his theory was true. His long-dead mother had given the sycori their form but generations of them had been born since her death. How had they not regressed to be nymphs when the magic passed from their bodies?

The creature began to emanate an amber haze which challenged the fire for dominance of the light. The meat of the humans was not enchanted. The haze was a reaction from deep in the sycori's body. Caliban stared across the fire at the sycori and smiled.

"My mother's magic is in your flesh, little brother. It is in your blood and continues though she is no longer with us." Caliban aimed the pistol at the sycori's head as Stephan had shown him. "Now, I must take it from you, as you took it from her."

He squeezed the trigger, releasing an explosion of light and noise into the dark.

III

Miranda trudged through the landscape outside the limits of her father's shield. She'd been in this brush a hundred times before and never once felt as anxious as she did now. The wreckage was the best chance of a salvageable ship. She wasn't one who shied away from a fight, but walking into the thick of the sycori's territory was different. The sun was already falling and would be of no help if the sycori were on the hunt.

"Stay together. We can't do each other any good if there's too much brush between us."

There was a chorus of assent and they all closed ranks. Every one of the soldiers with her had fought beside her before; they knew their work. But in the heavy woods distance was a greater enemy than the sycori. Miranda chopped at the high leaves, her fingertips not touching the cranking handle built into the hilt of her sword.

Leaves and branches were no match for the hardened metal Prospero had salvaged from the ship's wreckage. But the skin of the sycori was something more. Prospero had built a core of steel and brass into the spine of each blade, electrifying the edge when cranked long enough.

Her father's blades had made the nymphs formidable against the island's predators. They'd also helped the nymphs see Prospero as their savior. Miranda could have been a princess to her father's role as king. She'd been too young in Milan to remember the experience of being royalty. If she'd wanted, the nymphs would have waited on her hand and foot. Instead she served them. And though she'd never asked for it, the other soldiers looked to her as a leader.

Because it was clear the enhancements her father had created had limits, Miranda had trained to defend the city from outside threats. She was the one who proposed battery packs to run the appendage frames outside the shield. She'd even helped configure the batteries to absorb shield energy. A voice broke into her thoughts.

"Captain, we are close," Declan said. He was one of the few nymphs who'd come this far before. He'd always been one of the smaller nymphs, but it was his spirit that impressed Miranda.

"Calm yourself, Declan, no sense charging them. These are real soldiers, not the disorganized animals we've faced in the past."

Miranda grew up on videos and stories and newsreels of her father's battles. Each taught her tactics, swordplay, what worked in a fight and what brought about losses. She worked to imbue that same knowledge to those who fought by her side. As they approached the beach, Miranda wondered what foreign techniques she might see in these soldiers.

She stared down the incline at the beached ship. It was on its side, panels split open against the stones and hardened sand of the shore. She let out a sigh. She'd hoped the landing would have been smoother.

Her troops scattered in a line and all stared down the incline. Bodies were scattered around the ship, some moving and others lying too still. Amid the chaos, Miranda found a young man who was attempting to organize the soldiers. Barking random orders, he got little response other than a begrudging compliance. She wasn't sure who this was but he couldn't have been in charge for long.

"Captain." Janus interrupted Miranda's thoughts as he shuffled close and kept his voice low. "We were sent to bring them in before nightfall. We should not delay in making our presence known."

His face was long and looked worried, though half was covered by her father's machinations. She wasn't sure if Janus was parroting her father's wishes but knew he was right. She could see Declan was on edge, his hand thumbing the hilt of his blade. The sun generally kept the sycori from the beach but these men would not have that luxury for long.

"Portia, Declan and I will go down there," Miranda called out as she sheathed her blade. "Janus, Greer and Nalla, stay back and be ready."

"Yes, Captain," Portia replied stoically. She never let emotion affect her opinion of a situation but Miranda knew she didn't enjoy Declan's company. She thought he was reckless and foolish but kept her silence. Miranda could hear her glare from a distance.

They began descending from the edge of the tree line, down the sandy loam which hid them from sight. Miranda wanted to be seen; surprise was not what she was looking for. As soon as one of the soldiers on the beach saw her, she put her arms out wide to assure that neither hand was carrying a weapon. She turned to her counterparts and said, "Portia, keep your eyes open. Declan, keep your mouth shut."

Immediately a soldier called attention to them as they neared the bottom of the loam. Miranda took a few more steps and waited as soldiers approached from three sides. She quickly looked up and down the trio of soldiers in front of her. They were not carrying blades. Instead they held long cylinders of metal and wood aimed in her direction. Prospero had explained what a rifle was but she'd never seen one up close before.

"We are not here to fight you." Miranda kept her hands in the air though she knew the look of her soldiers was unsettling. Declan's brown skin was offset by the metal extensions which protruded at points on his arms. While both he and Portia wore clothes and armor to look more human, there was no way to hide the graphite and gears which helped them move. "I've come in the name of Prospero, our king. A threat will come with the falling light. We seek only to warn you."

The soldiers wore torn shards of uniforms. One of them stepped closer to ask, "Who did you say sent you?"

"Prospero, the monarch of this island," Miranda spat in reply as she eyed the nearest rifle barrel. "I've shown you no disrespect, nor hostility; lower your weapons and take me to your commander."

Miranda knew the soldier in front of her was not in charge. He could hardly keep his teeth from chattering as he eyed the metal on Janus's chest. If he'd seen a battlefield it was far in his past. However, her statement must have insulted him as he proclaimed, "In the name of Alonso, King of Naples, I take you into custody."

If it had been earlier in the day, or perhaps if she'd been less annoyed, Miranda would have sought a compromise. Instead, she whipped her left arm forward and grasped the rifle at the barrel, tugging it free from the soldier's grip. He had no time to react as she pressed her opposite hand on the end of the barrel and struck back at the soldier's face with the stock of the weapon. In one blow he was down and the men at his side were caught off guard.

Portia leapt forward, propelling the barrel of the rifle into the air as a shot was fired. She plowed a fist against the soldier's chest. The vest of thick fabric he was wearing did little to protect him as Portia grasped the rifle and wrenched it away.

Declan reacted a second slower than the others. Miranda watched a round skim past him as he slapped the rifle to the ground. He then drove his metal boot against the soldier's chest, sending him to the floor. Miranda had not intended conflict but when another group of soldiers approached she knew she had to put an end to it.

Men trudged through sand, some with rifles but most with blades drawn as Miranda tossed the weapon away and yelled, "I only wish to speak to those in charge."

Two figures stepped out of the crowd. The first was her father's age, with the look of a hardened fighter on his face. He lacked an overshirt, bearing an array of scars on his arms and chest. The other looked near Miranda's age and wore a clean uniform, bellowing, "I am Ferdinand, Prince of Naples. If you seek authority, it is I."

Miranda was not impressed with the man in the uniform across from her. He wore no weapons; yet the men listened when he spoke. She noticed a few rolled their eyes, but the man beside Ferdinand seemed to add a semblance of authority.

"You are the leader of these men?" Miranda asked, unable to hide her confusion.

"In the absence of my father I am in charge of these men. Who are you to question me?"

Miranda wasn't in a position to dispute the prince and she didn't want to waste the remaining daylight. She gave a slight bow and replied, "I am Miranda and these are my soldiers. I've come to offer counsel and aide to the camp of my father Prospero."

A snicker traveled through Ferdinand's ranks. Miranda wasn't sure if her statement or her tone was the culprit. The old soldier beside Ferdinand grimaced, then bellowed, "Hold your form, men. I'll not have malarkey in these ranks."

The Prince made decisions but Miranda could tell who commanded the army. She gave a slight nod to the shirtless commander and continued, "Prospero offers shelter and safety from the sycori who are likely en route to your camp. Perhaps your men will survive the night, but many may not, and by morning your number will be much diminished."

"You seem confident in these creatures," the grizzled commander asked from behind his prince.

"These warriors and I defend the shielded zone from the sycori. We've seen them at their best and their worst." Miranda disregarded the prince's gaze as she spoke. She looked out at the soldiers with weapons drawn and spoke to them. "I've fought sycori with the blades you carry; they are little help against their skin. They move with a vicious quickness which you may counter with those rifles, but who knows how many shots it may take to put them down."

"They stand your size, with muscle born of the earth itself and a raw hunger which only feeds their aggression," Portia added, though she did not move any closer. "Each digit of their hands has a protruding bone claw that I've watched tear through metal and bone with little trouble."

"These men have seen battle before, Princess. They will stand against your local creatures." The prince was overconfident, especially given the faces of his soldiers. Miranda chose not to ask who would stand with him, knowing half of his men would not.

Declan did not know better and spoke his mind, "I hope you're right, and your men are more formidable against the sycori. But as my Captain noted, we are here to offer solace amid the shield. If you and yours would stand your own watch, we are not here to speak against it."

Miranda glared at Declan as he finished his remarks. She knew an ultimatum would push the Prince away. However, once he'd said it, she could not contradict him. Instead she offered a piece of advice.

"The sycori feed on flesh, live or dead. And they grow stronger and heal faster when they eat." Miranda's remarks fell squarely on the military commander. "Gather your dead, your wounded and your weapons. When they attack, that is where they will go first."

Miranda took a half step back, signaling she was ready to leave. The man behind Ferdinand grumbled then placed a hand on the prince's shoulder. "Majesty, perhaps we should give their word some weight. There is no harm in listening to the natives."

"Tell me, daughter of Prospero, how far is it to safety?" the Prince asked with as much annoyance as he could muster. Behind him the commander grimaced but let the question stand.

Miranda disregarded his tone and eyed the vessel. Behind it the sun was playing on the edge of the water. "An answer for an answer, your highness. The shields Prospero has placed for our protection are over an hour to the southeast through thick jungle. How fares your vessel?"

Ferdinand turned to the ship then motioned for his men to lower their weapon. Miranda could read the indecision on his face before he said a word.

"The hull is ruptured in far too many places to get her seaworthy again." Ferdinand was honest when he didn't have to be. He turned to the commander and continued, "If we've got a trek ahead of us, Captain Barabas, gather the men and take what supplies we can carry."

"Majesty, there may be a better opportunity here," Miranda interrupted before Barabas could walk away. "Perhaps you would entertain me for a moment."

Ferdinand agreed as Miranda signaled the other half of her group. They rose from the loam's edge and began to descend as she said, "Highness, my father has a ship on the southern side of the island. It is a much longer trek but it may serve to get us both off the island. This vessel lacks some parts and fuel to turn the military grade screws. Perhaps salvaging your ship can get us all off the island."

Ferdinand agreed, but could not keep his eyes from the sunset. Miranda knew his concern she'd put in his head. "How many fighting men do you have?"

"We have twenty men who can fight but not enough weapons. If these creatures are on their way, we can't hold the ship," Barabas replied before Ferdinand could say a word.

Miranda motioned Janus forward and stared directly at the monocle over his eye knowing full well her father was listening. "The hull here is damaged but their engines may have the parts we need for the other ship. Janus can take you to the engine room to pull parts before we leave the wreck for the sycori."

Janus smiled, "Your father agrees, Captain. I'll need someone with a working knowledge of how to take the engine apart."

Ferdinand nodded, "I'll get a pair of our best engineers and we'll take you down into the engine room."

Janus agreed without a word but Miranda was thrown by the comment. Ferdinand turned to Barabas and ordered, "Give us the best cover you can with what we have. Keep the ship safe and I'll assure we gather the parts she needs."

Miranda shifted her weight as Barabas rushed off. Ferdinand ordered one of the soldiers to find him a few engineers. It was obvious Ferdinand would not have the support of the men without Barabas. Miranda pulled the prince close and remarked, "Perhaps, your highness, you should think of holding the line and not hiding inside the ship."

Ferdinand's brow furrowed at the comment. He stepped a bit closer to Miranda and whispered, "You think I am hiding from battle, Princess?"

"How much more knowledge of the ship have you than any other man?" Miranda was defiant but also cautious. She noted his hand, flexing against the hilt of his blade. If he'd been truly offended, it would have already seen sky. "You've no better engineering knowledge than Barabas. I see no reason a king would lead an expedition to salvage parts when his men need him. Perhaps

I simply don't know many kings."

"Perhaps." Ferdinand turned away, he was assuring no one heard her. "You think these soldiers follow you out of some sort of respect, Princess. They are indebted to your father and they flatter you with their obedience. Do not mistake it for actual command. These men follow my word because I am heir to the throne."

"Is that why you hide?" She knew he was offended but needed to press the point or lose the prince to cowardice. "If you would be king, they should see that you do not value your life over theirs. Whether it is true or not."

The prince could hardly look at her. He drew a labored breath and remarked, "I will not endanger the future of my country with foolish acts of false bravado."

Miranda snorted at Ferdinand's comments. "The soldiers in my charge are not by my side because I am their Princess. They follow me because I stand in front of them and lead."

She freed her blade from the sheath at her side and placed it beside the prince. His eyes darted to the weapon, and she knew it had his attention. "Let Barabas take Janus to the engines and come with me to lead your men. Show them you will travel the path and not just lead them to it."

Ferdinand seemed to want to be on the front line, but he had to find the balance between fighter and prince. Miranda herself had the same issue leaving Prospero's shield. Ferdinand lifted the blade in one hand and remarked, "My father was a warrior king. The country has been at war with Tunis for years. Now one wedding and there is peace. How will I lead men who know I have never seen war?"

Miranda placed his hand on the hilt of the blade. She stood behind him and watched the soldiers organize as she wrapped his fingers against the weapons handle. "Stand the watch with them, Ferdinand. Show them you are a warrior. Show them you can be their king."

Ferdinand turned to face Miranda. She looked up into his eyes. He may have been a few years older than her, but she had more life experience. He kept the blade in hand and remarked, "It would be an honor to stand the watch with you, Captain."

Miranda nodded. The prince had vigor and fight but would it be enough to hold back the sycori? She could and would help him lead, but perhaps she was leading them both into the open maw of death.

IV

Ariel maintained her distance from the wreckage. The wings Prospero built her drew little power from her battery but to really check the ship she would have to descend to the structure. She'd scouted wrecks many times for Prospero, though it wasn't the reason she had been given wings. She knew that had more to do with Prospero's romantic attachment to her, not her skills as a pilot.

"My liege, there is wreckage but no signs of survivors," she reported, switching on her antennae. She knew Prospero would be waiting for a report. He always seemed intent on knowing her whereabouts and made it obvious he lamented teaching her how to switch off his locating devices.

Ariel spiraled toward the wreckage, noting the remnants of expensive furniture and cloth which littered the shore. Someone with taste was the owner of this ship. However, on Pergu there was little need for such frivolity. The island was divided into those who hunted and those who defended; pretty fabrics were only used to wrap the dead.

"Can you see the wreckage, my liege?"

"I can, Ariel," he said shortly.

Ariel assumed his curtness came from trying to watch all the missions at the same time. Prospero had access to some of the soldiers but he was still just one man with a simple set of eyes, and few resources at hand to portray the god all the other nymphs wanted.

Ariel spotted a thin line of smoke emanating from the belly of the broken ship. It could have simply been wood catching fire after the wreckage. She shifted her shoulders forward and her wings moved toward the smoke. "I am investigating the smoke."

Ariel knew he was listening even when he said nothing. Prospero once told her he could hear her whispers even in the thick of other conversations. He'd thought it romantic; she'd thought it obsessive. Ariel rolled once as she sped toward the fire then banked to cut across the face of the wreckage. In the two seconds the move took, Ariel noticed at least two bodies inside the wreckage. The living would have seen her and it would be seconds before they came to investigate. She pulled skyward and waited for a response.

"Be careful," Prospero remarked. "Miranda and Caliban have reported finding armed soldiers. Be prepared to run if they present a threat."

Miranda had become a warrior in her years on the island. She'd trained others, like Ariel, to follow suit. But to Prospero, Ariel was still a porcelain treasure. He saw her as fragile and unable to defend herself even though the thick of her wings had put an end to sycori on countless occasions. Ariel switched on the monocle to let Prospero see the crash site as a pair of men raced from the hole in the hull.

For a few moments she thought of taking out both men, but neither seemed built to fight. Both were wider than Prospero or Miranda or any other sailors she'd seen out in the water. Though unarmed and unarmored, they moved with labored breath. These men could not defend themselves, she thought.

"The years have not been kind to my brother."

Ariel heard Prospero's words but did not reply. The leaner of the two men raised a weapon in her direction. Ariel knew how projectile weapons worked; she also knew how to keep from being hit, especially in flight. However, there was little reason to antagonize these men.

She pulled up and hovered slightly, letting the sun's light filter around her as she announced, "I am Ariel, an emissary to his highness Prospero, who welcomes you to this island. He asks you lower your weapons and let me lead you to the safety of his shielded city."

Ariel saw fear in the leaner man's eyes. From the similar look, Ariel could tell he was related to Prospero. The failing light was behind Ariel, making it harder for both men to see. She shifted the angle of her wings and appeared to float toward them.

"The man beside him is Sebastian, brother to the King of Naples," Prospero remarked as Ariel landed. She approached slowly, asking them, "Has this journey made you the default King of Naples?"

Sebastian dropped his weapon. He could not answer Ariel but he understood her question. He continued his stunned silence but shook his head and motioned to the hull of the ship. "My brother lives. He is inside with one of his advisors. How do you know these things?"

Ariel smiled and placed a long finger against Sebastian's lips. If she'd lied to him about being an angel he'd believe her. Sebastian slid out of her way as Ariel walked toward the ship. Shattered planks of wood allowed enough light to fill the room but Ariel adjusted the optics in Prospero's monocle, and suddenly the lowlight was as clear as day. Inside the room one man lay prone next to a fire as another hovered over him.

"If you've been sent to collect Gonzalo's soul, I will deny you, Angel of Death." Ariel could hear Prospero giving instruction to someone else.

"Ariel, allow me to introduce you to Alonso, the King of Naples." He immediately returned when he heard the voice in her ears. "Be wary, he is very religious and firm in the belief that he can bend the ear of the gods."

Ariel stared past Alonso at the body on the floor. The monocle began scanning and fed the information back to Prospero. It would take time, but Ariel knew Prospero would want an assessment. The sun was falling outside and Ariel knew they had to go.

"Alonso, you are a worthy king, but do not mistake my pause for fear," Ariel said. She would not try to separate the king from his friend. "I am not here for your friend's soul; I am here to save you all. My lord, Prospero, has asked me to lead you back to the safety of his city, but we must move quickly to avoid the sycori."

"I don't know those things, sycori," Alonso said as he pressed a compress against Gonzalo's wounds. "Even if I did, I have a pair of good men who can defend against these creatures."

Ariel slid the monocle from her eye. She increased the power draw to her skin and brightened the room better than a thousand fires. Alonso was taken aback by the act, and Gonzalo began to stir.

The king shielded his friend with his body and asked, "What are you doing?"

Gonzalo awoke to the noise and light. Ariel could infuse him with energy from the shield but she knew it wouldn't heal him; at best he had a few more hours remaining.

"I can provide some energy for your friend. If you can bind his wounds, perhaps we can get him to my King, Prospero's, table. He can help, and at least you and your brother will be safe."

"Prospero," Gonzalo murmured. He coughed blood and seawater onto the floor as he rolled toward Alonso. "You speak of Prospero of Milan, my angel. Brother of Duke Antonio. Tell me you speak of this man I once called my good friend."

"I do," she replied to an impressive smile. Gonzalo pushed himself off the floor as though shaking the throes of death at the mention of Prospero's name.

"Majesty," Gonzalo gasped between coughs. "We must follow this angel. If he is alive, Prospero will get us home. If nothing else, he will keep us safe."

"Gonzalo, you mustn't move," Alonso retorted. "Sebastian and Antonio will keep us safe until you are better."

Ariel could see there was more to Gonzalo's worry than the island. The broken soldier pulled Alonso close and whispered, "These men protected you from the shimmering creature now in your presence. Tell me Majesty, where are your brother and the Duke now other than away from the current threat?"

It was the first time Alonso had taken in the vast emptiness of the room. Antonio and Sebastian had let Ariel in and left without a second thought. She crouched beside the king and Gonzalo and said, "The men I met before will not stand long against the sycori. If you stay out here, you will not make the morning. Please, let me take you to safety."

Gonzalo rose off the ground with Alonso's assistance. There was little Ariel could do to help. The enhancements Prospero designed could change some of their shape, but they could not bear weight beyond her own. Leaning against the king, Gonzalo motioned toward the wall and said, "Majesty, would you hand me a revolver? Then I think we can get underway."

Alonso bore most of Gonzalo's weight until the younger man was standing. The king pulled a gun from a broken wooden shelf and placed it in Gonzalo's hand. Ariel remained silent as Gonzalo loaded the weapon then slipped it along the seam of his trousers.

They followed her out of the ship, seeing no one in the vicinity. Sebastian and Antonio had disappeared, but Ariel wasn't sure if it was the sycori or their fear that took them. She turned toward the sun, extended her wings, and shot into the air. Her eyes quickly found the pair of men cowering along the edge of the trees. She gained height and spotted a figure on the back end of the hull. Alonso and Gonzalo stepped free of the ship's hull, neither of them understanding what was happening as Ariel rolled to pick up speed.

Ariel heard the whistle of her wings as they cleaved air. She shifted her shoulders slightly and raced across the right edge of the boat hull where a sycori was trying to sneak up to Alonso. Her wing raked across the creature's neck as she rocketed past Gonzalo and Alonso, dragging a trail of blue blood in her wake.

The king turned to face the spray in time to witness the creature tumble to the ground. Alonso stared at the creature. Its head was hanging sideways from its neck. Ariel pulled up on her speed and returned to their side.

"Your men are at the edge of the trees, in the direction of Prospero's shield. Perhaps they were clearing the way and did not see the creature." Ariel's words were no comfort, but she didn't want them to be. She focused her monocle on the two men at the edge of the trees. Behind her she heard Gonzalo and Alonso shuffling across the sand. She keyed her communicator and asked, "My liege, what do you know of Sebastian and your brother? They seem either incompetent or intent on failing the king. Is there something I should do?"

There was no answer as Ariel led her charges to the edge of the beach. Neither she nor Prospero had ever experienced this situation. Ariel watched Antonio and Sebastian dust themselves off and genuflect in response to the approaching king.

"Majesty, we were searching for a path inland. The creature must not have seen us. Perhaps it was after the flyer. Luckily she was fast enough to stop it." Sebastian was a bit off pace with his lies.

Ariel didn't believe his words, but Alonso did, and he motioned for them to help carry Gonzalo. The forest was thick, making travel slow but slightly more comfortable for Gonzalo. Ariel led the way, wondering if there were soldiers marching to help her. If it was only Gonzalo and the king, Ariel was sure she could handle them. However, adding Sebastian and Antonio would add difficulty.

Prospero's voice chimed in her ear, "Caliban has found a group of the ship's passengers on the opposite shore. I'm providing them a corridor but it's chewing through a lot of power. I need you to bring Alonso and Gonzalo in on your own. Can you handle that, Ariel?"

"My liege, the duke and the king's brother, are they of consequence?" Ariel had thought through an array of creative ways to end the pair. She awaited the order of her master but knew he would not give it.

"Ariel, if they directly threaten the King or Gonzalo you have my permission to end them. However, I would prefer you bring all four to the shield," he replied.

She switched off the monocle in frustration, terminating the connection to Prospero. Ariel could go against his wishes but he would know. Prospero had a way of knowing everything on the island.

Gonzalo stumbled as they trudged through the forest. Ariel rushed to help him, although there was little she could do. She'd already pushed a lot of her energy into Gonzalo's wounds, so at this point she could do little more than help him maintain his balance.

"Thank you, little one," Gonzalo replied as he took her hand to steady himself. His mouth trickled blood but that didn't dampen his smile. "Are all of your kind so gentle? Perhaps Prospero was luckier than I when I left him on that ship so long ago!"

She smiled in return. "Prospero came to us after a long voyage but we were little more than spirits. We were shapeless; nothing more than fodder for the jaws of the sycori. I was the first of my kind he ran across so many years ago."

Gonzalo trudged on as Alonso stepped closer to take some of his friend's weight, while Sebastian and Antonio cleared the ground ahead of them. Alonso had little to say but turned to Ariel and asked, "How was Prospero able to save your life?"

Ariel obliged his curiosity. "He came ashore with his daughter. She was so young then. I was running from one of the sycori on the beach that was braving the daylight for a meal. Prospero knocked the creature to the ground with one shot of a rifle and then finished the job with a heavy axe."

"Not the inventor and healer you remember, Gonzalo," Alonso commented as he shook Gonzalo to assure he was awake.

"My king; he is the man I remember." Gonzalo mumbled as he walked heavily with the king's support. "Most had never seen the warrior Prospero could be. But I have. Those who thought him a threat because of his pacifism were fools then, and are doubly foolish now. Prospero chose to heal rather than cause harm, and for that he was punished."

Ariel was proud to hear someone defend her master. He'd lusted after her, but never assumed any relationship with her based on his position; that spoke volumes to her. Even now, two of the four men she was with betrayed him yet he still wanted to get them all to safety. Then Ariel heard Sebastian whisper. "If Alonso forgives the tinkerer for betraying the army, you will lose your title and lands."

She knew neither Gonzalo nor the king were well enough to hold off an attack. It puzzled her what two men with simple rifles thought they could do that Ariel couldn't counter. They continued through the woods while she eavesdropped on their conversation.

"There's another creature skulking us on the right. If it tries, let the girl take it and you and I will deal with Gonzalo and Alonso. When things settle, my title will protect the pair of us."

Ariel looked to her right and could not see the sycori in the trees. She mentally switched through her filters and was able to trace the edges of the creature from its heat. There were two sycori among the trees to her right. Sebastian was correct; one would take the easy meal of Gonzalo and Alonso. However, two would kill them all.

There wasn't enough room amid the trees for Ariel to use her wings. She knew she could get away with the king if she abandoned Gonzalo. Ariel couldn't bring herself to leave the injured. She wondered if she had enough energy to defend her little group.

"My lord, I am tracking a pair of sycori in the trees; and Alonso's men are not faithful. I can stop them, or the sycori, but I need more power to stop both." Ariel saw her numbers on an internal display. Stopping the sycori was enough to drain her energy, which would leave the king unable to defend himself.

"Ariel, you'd need a reconfiguration of your antennae to receive power. It would take longer than we have and there is no guarantee it wouldn't burn out the system," Prospero replied.

Ariel's feet hit the ground a few inches from Gonzalo and Alonso. Her wings folded behind her as she adjusted to the forest floor. She used to know the feeling well but had been spoiled by Prospero's toys. Ariel took a breath and whispered, "When I stop the sycori, your men will betray you. They fear me, but you will have to keep them at bay until we reach the city."

Gonzalo reached behind his back and pulled the revolver free. He hid the weapon between him and the king, leaning forward a bit to catch bullets in case shots were fired. Ariel focused her attention on the beasts of the forest. She poured the bulk of her energy into arm enhancements and felt electricity pooling in her fingertips.

Suddenly an arc shot forward from Ariel's hands, catching the sycori off guard. Both were caught by the grey and red sparks and held suspended in the air as electricity ran through their bodies. Pain filled her, but she kept the sycori in place. The creatures screamed while their skin burned. Ariel pumped her fists slightly and knew the arc was constricting against the bodies of her victims.

As she'd predicted, Sebastian and Alonso turned toward the king and raised their rifles. Gonzalo was quick to respond. He fired two shots from the hip before either of them could line up a shot. The stock of Sebastian's rifle exploded on the right side, close to his face. A shard or two would embed themselves in the young man's cheek but they were much less painful than the bullet that had lodged in Antonio's side.

Sebastian dropped his weapon to try to stem the bleeding from his face. Ariel could see Gonzalo fighting to keep his composure as he aimed the gun barrel at the kneeling Antonio.

"It falls on me to depose you, Duke of Milan." Gonzalo cocked the pistol and let the barrel linger in Antonio's face. "A task I should have done fifteen years ago when my cowardice got the better of me."

Ariel balled her hands into fists and felt the snap of two necks through the arc of electricity she controlled. The power faded quickly as she diverted it to her image. She wanted Gonzalo to pull the trigger but knew Prospero would blame himself for the act. Ariel could see Antonio's rifle on the ground. He was paralyzed by pain and fear as he pled with Gonzalo through teary eyes.

"Enough!" Ariel's wings erupted out and pulled her off the ground. Arcs of electricity formed a mask of vicious fangs around her face and a quintet of claws on each hand. She could see the fear on their faces as she yelled, "I will see no more blood spilt this night unless it is I who spills it!"

Gonzalo and the others were frozen as Ariel held her place. She looked around at the men before her and bellowed, "All of you have betrayed my master. I hold none of you in regard. You are all men of sin and not worthy of judging others. I make one offer to all of you. Everyone arrives at my master's city or none of you will."

Ariel dialed back her rage and let the power fade from her appendages. She was running on what little battery she had reserved but it would not last through the night. She needed to reach the shield, but it would be close.

V

Prospero sat in his throne and stared at the monitors. One told him the sun had set hours ago. He'd seen the spike from Ariel's battery pack on a third monitor but there was little after that. Even at a crawl, she should have made the edge of the shield by now, but still nothing. The shield's function was deteriorating. Caliban's corridor was draining power.

Periodically he would get a garbled message from Lydos saying they were still headed back, but the travel was slow. Prospero watched as a group of society elite ambled their way toward the city. The beacon that was Caliban had died off over an hour ago. He wasn't sure if the creature had met his fate at the hands of a sycori or if his battery had run out, but he was finished either way.

Prospero eyed the graphic that showed shield strength. There were plenty of points where the shield was thinning, and Prospero had already begun pulling more citizens closer to the shield coil. He couldn't help but stare at the display which once showed Ariel. She could be anywhere, and there was no way to send her any power. Prospero knew he couldn't let her fade away.

"Ariel, tell me you can hear me!" he yelled, although he knew the receiver was dead. Prospero hoped she'd switched it off to store energy. Perhaps she could make the shield's edge but if she didn't, there was no way he could save her.

He powered down sections of the corridor hoping to increase the strength of the hub. Prospero's scans overlapped to show him where the sycori were trying to push through the shield. He knew he'd have to start rotating power to certain section to keep the creatures back. Weakening the shield at any point gave the sycori a doorway into the city.

Three other monitors allowed Prospero to watch his daughter's warriors and the soldiers under Prince Ferdinand defend the wreckage from sycori. Janus was not the only warrior Prospero had a direct connection to. Prospero was proud of her efforts but he knew they couldn't make the morning if he could not get her any shielding.

His attention focused on Janus and the commander as they tore into the ship's engine. Prospero needed a set of pistons, some seals, and a few other parts to get his engine running but he worried the prize would not be worth the price.

"Janus, I need a time frame on how much longer it will take," Prospero ordered as he watched his daughter slash the face of a sycori, her blade moving faster and with more conviction than any of Ferdinand's men.

Prospero watched his daughter rake an electrified blade across the chest of a sycori. The creature retorted by plowing a fist into her chest which glanced off her armor. Her blade fell on the creature's wrist, lopping it off. Prospero watched his daughter grab the shoulder of the injured creature and then toss it toward some of Ferdinand's men. They attacked it three at a time, hoping to replicate the power of Miranda's weaponry with sheer numbers.

"Declan," she yelled directly at his display. "Stop ogling me for my father and take the right flank. Ferdinand's men could use the hand."

Declan rushed off, pulling Prospero's display from his daughter to the sycori attacking from the beach. He watched the nymph crank the handles on the hilts of his swords and electricity began to move around the blade. Even the sycori were wise to the power of Prospero's blades. Where they once attacked in random patterns, they seemed more organized now. Those who could dodge Declan did so for tamer battles with Ferdinand's soldiers.

Prospero switched the display and keyed his communicator with Janus. "How much more time do you need? I need an answer."

"My liege, Barabas' men are pulling the last of the parts now, but we have more metal than four men can easily carry." Janus said curtly. "Barabas says his men can carry the parts but it will be slow going back to the shield."

Prospero punched the console and cursed. The sycori were descending from a nest in the thick jungle; more would amble out of their beds and eventually overrun Miranda and her troops. Prospero turned to the other monitors. Lydos' group was the closest to the shield but they still had a distance to travel.

"Janus, get the parts to the top of the ship. Let me know when you do," Prospero replied as his fingers clacked on the keyboard. He keyed Lydos' earpiece.

"How may I serve you, Lord Prospero?"

"Lydos, the shield is pulling too much power for the corridor. I can give you a few more minutes, but warn everyone that I have to lower the corridor shielding." As he spoke, another group of sycori began attacking the westernmost shielding.

"Dammit," Prospero cursed as he began to syphon power from the corridor. He reconfigured a thicker shield as he announced to the entire city. "If you are within the sound of my voice, I am ordering you all to fall back to the homes closest to the central generator. The shield must tighten to keep out the sycori."

"My Liege," Lydos' voice drew Prospero's attention to her screen. "Everyone has been informed and they know the way back. The men and I are ready for you to pull the power. It has been an honor to serve you."

Prospero could hear her fear. With the shielding gone, the nymphs would have only battery power to get them back to the central hub. They would be exposed, easy fodder for the sycori. However, they were willing to make the sacrifice if it meant Prospero could save the city.

His hand hovered over the key of the console. The life and death of his charges was a keystroke away.

"Lydos, save who you can. But do not sacrifice yourself for the wealthy. They would not do the same."

"Yes, my liege. We will not fail you."

Prospero struck the key and watched as power drained from the corridor. Lydos and her men quickly formed a perimeter and marched the survivors forward with renewed vigor. The soldiers followed suit and Prospero knew they would start back. Prospero turned his attention to the shore where Declan, Miranda and Padua continued to hold off a number of attacks.

"Janus, are you topside yet?"

"On our way, my liege," he replied through gasps.

Prospero knew it would take time to get to the top of the ship with the cumbersome parts. He switched on Declan's receiver and ordered, "Declan, when Janus and the others clear the ship, activate your power antennae and I will send enough power to you to create a wall shield. Have Miranda signal me when you are all ready to move. Do you understand?"

"Yes, my liege." The young fighter hardly skipped a breath as he ducked a lurching claw and slashed the leg of a sycori. Declan plowed a metal leg against the gash and watched the creature collapse to the ground. Three of Ferdinand's men ran in to assist as Declan looked past them to Miranda and the prince fighting alongside one another. Prospero watched, proud of his daughter and impressed at how the prince looked at her. He wasn't sure Alonso would approve, but knew the boy would be lucky to have her.

Prospero waited for Miranda's signal.

"She has always been the most beautiful of all of us, my lord tyrant."

Prospero knew Caliban's voice, though it was no longer tempered with a hint of fear behind the sarcasm. There was something raw about the voice. Gone were the hints of metal which kept Caliban alive.

"You found a shortcut through the forest along with a way into the shield without drawing power through your enhancements. It is an interesting conundrum you pose, Caliban." Prospero didn't turn to see the nymph; he could tell the creature was at the far end of the room. He could hear Caliban's fingers tapping against a metal conduit.

"The sainted shield. That which separates those blessed by your technology and those you condemn. Ariel moves back and forth through it without so much as a tickle, but the rest must clear their travel with the king." There was a whistle in the air as Caliban leapt from his position and collided with the ground. Prospero stared at the screen in front of him as Caliban rose to his feet. He was bigger, stronger, and lacking any of the enhancements Prospero had provided.

"You've been my jailer for far too long, tyrant king. Jailer to all of my people," Caliban took a step forward and Prospero heard the creature's meaty foot hit the floor. "I've come to right an injustice. I've come to set my people free and return the nymphs to the wild."

"How quickly you've become something more than them, Caliban." Prospero wanted to keep reminding Caliban of his past. Whatever he'd done to himself, it made him a threat. Prospero activated a small battery to his staff and gauntlet. If Caliban wanted a fight, Prospero would give it to him.

"I read through my mother's notes, highness. Experiments and trials she'd done to understand my people. She wanted to know what made them strong." Caliban's voice dared anyone to take a shot at him. "She discovered it was the flesh. Her earth magic turned a nymph to a sycori but it was the flesh she fed them which made them violent. But even if they got that, the poor dumb creatures could never organize an attack."

"They seem to be doing well on the eastern shore," Prospero noted as he rose from his throne. He flexed his fingers to activate the gauntlet, letting crackles of electricity pass between his fingers. Prospero wondered whether without Caliban's enhancements he could beat the nymph. Unsure of his enemy's abilities, Prospero would have elected to stall but Caliban would not be interrupted.

"Your daughter and her little warriors," Caliban laughed. Prospero turned to look at the nymph and saw his bold yellow eyes reflecting in the shadowy dark. Caliban's shadow was about the same height as before. He wondered if he hadn't built up his enemy in his mind. "Tell me, my king, what will happen to them when I collapse the shield?"

Caliban rose up from his crouch and the room filled with his presence. He stood at least two meters in height and he seemed composed of tougher material than before. The digits on each hand now sported what Prospero guessed was a 4-inch blade of bone. "Did you give them enough power to survive on their own or will they just fall to pieces as I have so many times on your floor?"

There was no need to answer; the words meant nothing to Caliban. Prospero instead took a step down from his throne and stood level with the creature. Whatever the nymph had done, he'd circumvented the need for appendages and their power. Caliban had grown on every level; he was taller and broader, and Prospero wondered if the machines installed to fix the nymph's lungs and heart were still in place.

"You are alone, false king," Caliban hissed from the dark. "No daughter and her rabble to hide behind. You sent your mechanics to aid the citizenry and now the only thing between you and me is air."

"You are correct, Caliban," Prospero replied calmly as he faced the palm of his gauntlet at the beast. Caliban leapt forward as a series of electrical pulses shot out and engulfed the creature. Caliban writhed under the shock of the weapon and stumbled back as the electricity passed through him. "It is a shame you never learned to use distance to your advantage."

Prospero pulled a halberd from beside his throne but first offered an olive branch. "I don't want to destroy you, Caliban."

"Save me your false piety, old man!" Caliban rolled on the ground trying to gather his bearings. His tone was angry but his body was still trying to recover from the shocks. Prospero dared not challenge the creature. Instead he focused his attention on the screens and watched for Declan's call. Miranda needed his support now more than ever, as the sycori turned from the shore and moved toward the shield.

"You think somehow you'll earn the sycori's favor by feeding them. Your dreams are clouded by your lust for power," Prospero said as he tried to lock out all the controls. He heard the dull thud of Caliban's fist striking the floor; the creature was healing faster than ever. "They'll kill the guard, then the rest of the nymphs, and eventually they'll come for you. Just like they killed your mother," Prospero added.

The monitor flickered, indicating Declan was trying to communicate with him. He toggled a switch and heard the nymph's voice.

"My liege, Janus and the others have brought everything out of the ship. What is your order?"

Prospero looked down at Caliban as the creature pulled himself to his knees. The halberd had a hand-crank core in the handle like Miranda's blades. He could fight the creature, but he didn't need the gauntlet or the power of the shield to hold Caliban back.

"Declan, the bulk of the sycori are headed to the city. They intend to kill everyone," Prospero keyed a few switches and watched as the generator began to transfer a charge to Declan. He could generate a shield and help Miranda organize her troops under it. He keyed the microphone to all the receivers on the beach. "Captain, Declan is receiving enough power to generate a shield if necessary. Know that it is not abundant but it should aid in getting you and those with you to the other ship. Do not return to the city. Get the ship's engines running and get the boat in the water. I will do what I can to get others to your position. Do you understand what I am asking of you?"

"Yes, Father, I do."

Prospero could feel the weight of Miranda's words in his heart. He knew the sycori were too dense; even if the boat could only pass the reef, it was deep enough to kill the creatures. Miranda could wait there for more passengers but Prospero knew she would leave him if she had to. It was also why he didn't want her to head to the city; he didn't want her sacrificing herself for the nymphs. Prospero turned from the monitor and saw Caliban was on his feet.

"I once favored you over all the others," Prospero said quietly as he placed one hand on the end of the halberd shaft and pumped the handle just under the blade. He could feel the core of steel and brass inside the blade rotating and knew it was building a charge.

Caliban knew better than to wait and rushed at Prospero. The halberd had little charge in it when it collided with the creature's claws. Prospero took a few steps back, attempting to shift Caliban from the attack with the pole of the halberd. The creature stumbled as Prospero struck his lower back with the thick of the pole arm.

"You only delay the inevitable," Caliban said as he righted himself.

Prospero watched the edge of the blade crackle with electricity. He pumped the handle a few more times before wheeling the halberd over his head. He hoped it was enough charge to tear through Caliban's flesh with a single blow.

Caliban intercepted the blade with an open palm which split open. Caliban looked smug as Prospero attempted to pull the halberd away and was denied. Caliban placed his free hand on the shaft of the halberd as Prospero grabbed hold of the handle and pumped vigorously. Electricity shot through Caliban's arm, and he yelped in pain and pulled away.

Prospero seized the opportunity and drove the heel of his weapon at Caliban's jaw. It struck Caliban but only annoyed him as he closed the distance between them. In one bound he drove two balled fists into Prospero's gut and tossed him into the air.

He fell to the ground a few feet ahead of Caliban and the halberd slid out of his hand and rattled across the floor. Caliban loosed a guttural roar as he extended his hands, exposing large bone claws at the end of each finger. Prospero struggled to catch his breath as Caliban turned to the coil console and gashed the power conduits.

Sparks exploded all around him as the coil began to shudder and slow down. Caliban laughed again as the sparks ricocheted off his skin. Prospero pulled himself up to his knees and yelled, "You bastard! You'll collapse the shield."

"And they will die on your watch, old man." Caliban pulled his hands from the console. The bone claws showed no wear as he turned to face Prospero. Caliban leapt from the platform and was on top of Prospero before Prospero could gather his bearings. A claw swiped inches from Prospero's face as he drove a knee at the creature's side. Caliban responded by driving a claw into Prospero's gut. Prospero felt the claw drive in and wondered if this was what it felt like to let death envelop you.

He wrapped his hands around Caliban's wrist although he knew he didn't have the strength to stop the beast. There was a toothy smile on the nymph's face; even his teeth had begun to take on the look of the sycori. Caliban placed his free hand against Prospero's chest and pressed him to the floor.

"Perhaps they will betray me, my King..." Caliban mocked as he pulled the claw free of Prospero's side. The bloody arm slid out of Prospero's grasp. He attempted to knock away the other arm but knew he didn't have the strength. Caliban raised his newly free hand and poised to strike, saying, "But, I will know your death before they do."

The head of a blade erupted from Caliban's chest before he could lower the bony blade. A thick blue blood dripped on Prospero as Caliban raised his hand to feel the blade. The creature lurched to one side, still breathing but struggling as Lydos pushed him off the king with the halberd's handle.

She stood at the front of a group of humans and nymphs who had made their way to the coil. All were armed, some still fighting the battle outside as they barred the doors of the room. Those who were unarmed were in the center of a wall of weapons and carried whatever they could to help. Everyone and every weapon was covered in a thin layer of blue blood.

"Keep weapons and eyes on that one," Lydos ordered as she pulled the halberd free and left Caliban in the corner of the room. Two of Alonso's men obliged her and kept weapons ready if Caliban stirred.

Prospero noticed her face, battle-scarred but still beautiful, framed in a wild tangle of red hair. He'd seen her fight a hundred times before but never noticed her beauty. He leaned back and thought death should take him for being such a fool. He chased the one nymph who would not have him and forsook the one who wore her love on her sleeve.

"Do not surrender, my liege, you've come too far for that." Her words seemed to fill him with hope as her hands pulsed heat into his wound. She was giving up her own battery power to save him. She could not have much left and if he couldn't restart the coil she would never make it. Prospero felt instantly better but knew her medicine would not last. He needed medical care. "Your wound is large, my liege," Lydos said. "I can stem the bleeding and if you can bear the pain we can move you."

Among the wounded, Prospero could see Ariel's body. She was being held up by a pair of soldiers. Just barely alive, she was only surviving off the coil. Prospero shifted his gaze and watched as Lydos began packing his wound. He looked at the men and women in his throne room and asked, "How fares the city?"

"The people are scattered, my liege," Lydos replied with little emotion. "The sycori were at the shield when it fell and began terrorizing the city. Some ran for the forest and others fell back to the coil. We fought from the forest to here, saving who we could as we moved."

Prospero wasn't sure he could repair the shield and save the nymphs from the sycori. Despairing, he pulled himself to his feet and with Lydos' help hobbled toward the monitors. Declan was the only one still broadcasting. Everyone in the room watched as soldiers loaded parts onto a ship and Ferdinand took a position in front of them.

"Is that my son?" Alonso asked from the crowd.

Prospero didn't see the prince. His eyes were on Miranda as she fought beside him. They were decimating the few sycori who were still attacking the beach. Prospero turned from the monitor and said, "Yes, he fights alongside my daughter. They have been holding off attacks to the only seaworthy vessel we have on this island. It will be some time before the engine is operational but Miranda should be making plans to put the boat in deeper water."

It was the first time Prospero had seen Alonso in fifteen years. He saw a man proud of his son, not the King he once thought was beyond reproach. Prospero disregarded the king as he noticed the man on the floor. Gonzalo de Elba was calm and his breath was labored as a pair of men helped him sit.

"Always trying to save the world, Prospero," Gonzalo remarked through a smile.

"So long as I'm in it, I figure I should try," he replied with a grin. Prospero patched the broken wires Caliban had left him. The generator had begun to charge; Prospero knew he had some time before enough power pooled to turn the coil. He could build a small shield around his building but it would take time. If Lydos was right, this was what had to be saved.

He took a moment to help Gonzalo into a chair and felt the broken ribs through Gonzalo's clothing. "You seem out of sorts, old friend."

The men who were helping him walk nodded, though they were out of Gonzalo's sight. Prospero knew there was little to be done, and he was surprised Gonzalo had lasted this long. The shattered bone floating inside his body was causing more harm and there was no way to mend it.

"I am surprised to be counted among your friends, Prospero!"

"For a long time you weren't. I sat up many nights, fighting off the ocean's dangers and then the creatures of this island, with my daughter in hand, and thought of the ways I would repay you for this betrayal." Prospero grinned through the pain of his words. Gonzalo was not long for the world and Prospero wanted him to know the truth. "Then, I found a map and coordinates near the rudder controls when we started scrapping the ship. You could have left us to the sea but you gave us a chance."

"I'd intended to come find you," Gonzalo said through bloodstained lips. "I could never get away. The war grew greater and greater, only coming to a standstill a few months ago."

Gonzalo looked past Prospero toward Alonso and said, "My king, I betrayed my friend and let him suffer in order to gather good graces from his usurper of a brother. I cannot restore him to his former glory, but I ask that you allow me to bequeath my lands and my title to Prospero of Milan. He will serve you faithfully and truthfully, even when all others falter."

"It will be so," Alonso replied as he placed a hand on Prospero's shoulder.

Prospero leaned closer and held his friend. He looked into Gonzalo's vacant eyes and said, "Do not retire so simply. Come, old friend. Don't leave me to carry on alone."

There was no response.

A cough rattled from the end of the room where Caliban lay on the ground. The creature was bleeding blue across the floor, but death had not taken him yet.

"You grieve for those who betray you, Prospero," Caliban said through a series of coughs. "You dull and pointless animal, I imagine someday even I will merit a few tears from your eyes."

Prospero rose from beside Gonzalo and strode toward the beaten nymph. Lydos drew her blade and offered the handle to him. She said nothing and Prospero knew no one would speak ill if he killed the creature. He took a deep breath and grimaced as he stared into Caliban's blackened eyes.

"I will not weep for you, Caliban," Prospero stood far enough away that the creature could not surprise him. He watched as the nymph turned in a pool of his own blood to face Prospero. "These people and I will make our way to the ship, then off this island. I will leave you here, without a shield to protect you from the beasts you chose. Then you will understand the pity that separates humanity from animals like you."

Prospero turned away from Caliban and saw Alonso closing Gonzalo's eyes. The coil had begun to turn. It would generate power but would draw the attention of the sycori. Lydos grabbed a few of the soldiers and they began bracing the doors with whatever they could find. Prospero said nothing to the king but instead addressed the crowd.

"If we can last here, the coil will power up and protect us. With the blades we have, and a few modifications, I can cut a path from here to the southern shore." The coil picked up speed. "It will be wide enough for two or three people at a time but you must all move quickly. Those who are injured, find those who are healthy to give assistance. Every nymph who wishes to travel from this island will find a place on the ship. I can no longer protect you if you stay."

Lydos stood beside Prospero as he made the announcement. She was scared but nodded in agreement. When he finished she asked, "What will happen to us when the power is gone? How will we survive, my liege?"

Prospero placed his hand gently alongside Lydos' face. She would give her life for him and he wondered if he had the strength to do the same. "If he has done nothing for his countrymen, Caliban has given me an idea of how to free all of you from these enhancements. I can engineer a way for you to generate power until I can figure out the formula for making you whole. I promise you will all know freedom from this island and me."

There was glee in her eyes as Lydos kissed the inside of Prospero's palm and thanked him. He stepped away from her and rushed to the generator. Miranda and her soldiers were holding ground at the dock and pushing the ship into the water. He rerouted enough power to broadcast a tight shield around the core room to let everyone organize. Prospero worked through a series of rough calculations as he built a small corridor outside the coil room. There were enough beacons to travel to the shore but they couldn't protect the coil at the same time. Prospero swore as he finished his calculations.

Lydos heard Prospero's curse and followed Alonso toward the monitors. She said nothing but the King was quick to ask, "What is the problem?"

"There is little power left in the system, Majesty, to keep people from this room once we reach the beach," Prospero replied as he pointed at the monitor. "However if the coil is powered off at any time, the entire corridor fails. Someone has to stand the watch until Declan can take control of the corridor's power and the generator can be shut down."

"I'll leave one of the soldiers here," Alonso replied without a second thought.

Prospero knew it was a death sentence for any man left at the generator. The same could be said for any nymph who stayed. The sycori would attack the generator room, drawn in by the motion and noise. Whoever stayed would have to defend against the sycori and keep the coil running until the power was gone.

"I can stand the watch, Majesty. No one else will know how to shift energy to the corridor." Prospero waved off the soldiers and pointed toward the southern door. "Through that gate I will start a corridor which will take you to the shore. If the boat is there, it will take you home. Put strong soldiers up front, in case the sycori are bold enough to get through. You'll have to put beacons as you go but I can show your men how to do it."

"You will not stand the watch, my liege," Ariel's voice was rasped and broken as she rose from the ground. Her eyes were vacant and moving was a struggle, but Prospero knew she was drawing power from the shield. Her voice wavered as she continued, "I can hold a charge better than most. Get everyone else to the boat and I will make my way to you when the job is done."

"She is reasonable, Prospero. I've seen what those wings can do; she will survive better than the rest," Alonso said as he organized the survivors. The soldiers and some of Prospero's nymphs would travel at both ends defending the group. Alonso knew how to coordinate his men and how to get the most speed out of them.

Prospero stared at Ariel. Her wings were battered and weak, as was most of her body. She'd survived on very little power and had little chance to store energy before the shield was downed. Prospero wondered if the power cells in her enhancements were damaged from the spikes in the forest. He knew she wasn't being honest and she wouldn't last long without the shield's support. "When the coil collapses, you will be lost out here. You have no receiving antennae, what will you do when your power cells run out?"

"I will die," she grimaced. "But I will do so knowing you will save my people."

Lydos handed Ariel the halberd she'd dug out of Caliban. The sycori lay on the ground, his body failing as Prospero walked to the corridor. Lydos was at his side as Ariel drew in the energy of the shield. She knew how to conserve power, but Prospero knew there was little chance she would reach the boat. Ariel could fight off the sycori when they came for the generator but she couldn't store enough power to get over the ocean. It would be a fool's errand.

"Hold the boat for me, my liege," she said with a knowing smile. "I'll be along shortly."

Epilogue

The sun was pushed free of the horizon, rising far from Prospero's eyes. He could see the shore of his former home, littered with stubborn sycori who would not head back to the dark of their caves. Some had braved the water, but most would not. They knew the dense skin that protected them would take them to the bottom of the sea.

Prospero heard banging underfoot as Alonso's men continued to work on the engines of the ship. It would be hours, perhaps even a day or two, but he knew they would be underway soon. They had the parts and enough supplies for those who had reached shore. At the bow of the ship, Prospero watched Declan peel through frequencies searching out Ariel. Prospero walked over and asked a question he didn't want answered.

"Anything?"

"No, my liege." Declan was determined but his body was worn down and beaten from the previous evening's battles.

Prospero wondered if he'd had a chance to rest since they pushed the boat into the water. He placed a hand on Declan's shoulder. At her best, Ariel couldn't last through the night and into the next day. The sooner everyone came to the same conclusion the better.

Lydos approached from below deck. She looked tired but better than Declan. The small power generator he'd converted below deck would sustain the nymphs until he was able to figure out how to make them flesh. He stared into Lydos's eyes and knew he could do it. He could save them but he would never be able to save Ariel.

He glanced at the sky over the island. Perhaps it was an eagle or the flutter of graphite wings, but in a blink it was gone. Lydos didn't see it; she was focused on Prospero. They would have a life together, much like his daughter and Ferdinand, but none of them would ever be as free as Ariel.

END

A TOWN CALLED HERO

Warren C. Bennett

The Battle for Hero Island

OFTEN THIS IS JUST A FOOTNOTE IN THE HISTORY OF THE WAR, *since there are many other epic battles in the decade or so the world was on fire. For those that lived through it, this moment in time was a turning point. It was the pivot between the old world and the new. The battle united a people who, for a brief moment, were heroes all. (Continued)*

1.

Betty didn't wake with a start. A dream faded away as her mind came to life for the day. There was a booming coming from somewhere; it took Betty a moment to realize it wasn't from inside her head but outside her house. She dropped out of bed onto the cold floor and dressed quickly. There was something happening and she needed to be on the scene. The booming was the sound of the little used, but often commented upon, antiaircraft batteries on either side of the island.

As she tried to figure out what was happening, she hurried across the town to the airbase around which the town of Hero was built. A buzz and movement filled the air as fellow townies and soldiers rushed to and fro. The booming of the two antiaircraft guns continued as the lights of at least one plane landed on the long and straight Hero Airbase runway. She could hear the rumbling of engines as planes circled above, filling the early dawn sky with noise. Some of the engines didn't sound well, coughing and wheezing in an off-putting rhythm. She was not surprised to see those planes coming down to the airfield first.

She passed a group of men pushing one plane into the hangar as another landed. It was dirty and shot full of holes, and the pilot looked like he needed a stiff drink and a week of sleep. As she entered the hangar office, the small view screen of the radio activated. The gray and green screen showed the image of a tired man in his late thirties speaking to the radio operator.

"Your guns scared the bastards off." His voice was gruff and weary. "They followed us for miles. Not sure what they were thinking. We have a longer range than anything their dear Leader has put together."

"We'll keep up the cover fire until after all your planes are down," the operator said. Betty walked over and put her hand on his shoulder. His name was Leon and he was considered the active mayor of Hero; not that the town really needed a mayor, but he was pulled out whenever someone came to inspect the base, and the town wanted a civilized presence. Mostly he just sat tinkering with electronics and helping keep the power on. The little screen flipped off and Leon turned around.

"What's going on?" She waved a hand around the hangar. She also produced a pad and a pencil to take down the information for tomorrow's paper. Leon looked at her and raised an eyebrow.

"Hey, this is a story, ain't it?" she said, with her pencil posed above the pad.

Leon sighed. "I got a call on the horn about fifteen minutes ago. Seems a squadron of planes blew off course after a battle and needed a place to land. They were worried until they saw our little town."

Ah, Hero! A town built around a runway that was rarely used. Despite all the years the war dragged on, this spot of the map hardly merited a glance from either side. This wasn't known at the beginning and hence a nice airport and runway were built. Some of the airmen stationed at Hero called it the best airbase to be stationed at in the world. Nothing much happened here and nothing was expected to happen. Until now.

The gray green video screen popped to life again as the captain of one of the guns came on the viewer.

"We don't see any more signs of enemy aircraft. We did shoot one down and I've sent men out to see if anyone survived. Right now it seems all we have are our boys up in the air." As he spoke, another plane hit the tarmac. This one came in hard and one of the wheels buckled under the rough landing. The plane skidded to a stop as the propeller ate through the dirt on the side of the runway. The pilot was able to shut off the engine and a group of men rushed out to push the plane off to the side before another one came down.

"Good job. If you find a survivor, take him to the cell at the center of town. Keep the guns manned 24/7 until otherwise notified."

The man saluted and the screen flickered off. Leon turned back to Betty. She often forgot he wasn't just the Mayor and local tinker but also the head of the forces that were stationed here, such as they were.

"Look. These planes are shot up and running out of fuel. The Squadron Captain told us we were a sight for sore eyes. They only had a vague idea that we were out here on the end of the chain of islands, but one of the pilots kept telling him he had almost been shipped here. They had a few craft following them, which looked like short range airplanes but I can't be sure."

Betty cocked one of her eyebrows. "That doesn't make sense. Unless they have a base around here as well."

Leon pointed a finger at her. "Bingo. I guess our idyllic way of life is going to be interrupted for a bit."

As the screen flickered back on for another report, Betty scribbled down what she could but then noticed a typewriter. She went over to a desk and inserted a piece of paper and soon was tapping away as she half listened to the activity around her. It was all very interesting. Very interesting indeed.

2.

Squadron Captain Ben Pedro strode into the communications hub of Hero Airfield and saluted. His squad was down and all the planes and pilots were safe. He ignored the pretty brunette typing in the corner and walked over to the man that had been on the screen.

"Colonel Leon Vargas, I presume?" His voice was weary and proud. Half of his squadron had made it down alive and in relatively good health.

The Colonel half saluted back and waived any more protocols.

"Most people here don't even realize I'm in the armed forces," he chuckled. Ben looked him up and down. The bright flowery shirt and shorts surely weren't regulation. Of course, this town was on the back end of anything real that happened during the war.

"Thanks for helping me land my men safely. We're only about half of what we were, but I'm glad that they are all accounted for," Ben said.

Leon waved the thanks away again. "Nothing more than any man in my situation would do. I'm just glad your men are safe. We are getting them bunked up and fixing up the ones that need it." The colonel looked Ben up and down. "You look like you've been through hell and back, son."

Ben finally took off his flight helmet. The leather was soaked with sweat and his hair was matted and greasy. He didn't hear the subtle sigh from the corner. The typing had stopped for a moment but resumed before he noticed. "The war's been hard. I've been in it for five years. My men and I could use a break."

"This is the place to take it. Believe me. I thought I'd hate it here when the brass transferred me. The back end of nowhere and I looked at it as a punishment since I knew I wouldn't see any action. I tell you, son, it was the break I needed." Leon looked a bit wistful. Another man had taken his place at the radio and was giving out instructions to the various groups around the island.

Ben was about to ask another question when suddenly he felt all his energy and adrenaline vanish. All the hours of flying and worrying and keeping the spirits of his squad up as they crossed that vast ocean finally caught up to him. He stumbled backwards and bumped into a desk. A feminine yelp hit his ears as he tried to apologize for his error. His words came out as a garbled moan as he sank to the floor and passed out.

3.

Ben Pedro woke up in a bit of a haze. The leisurely blades of a slow ceiling fan turned above him, spreading wind and dust throughout the room. The woof-woof-woof of the blades reminded him of propellers powering down after a flight. Everything reminded him of the plane.

The last thing he remembered was stumbling into the desk and passing out. His knew his men were on the ground and safe. He knew he was in a soft bed, softer than anything he had slept on in years.

He moaned and turned on his side. The brunette he had glimpsed in the Operations Room sat behind a desk, a big typewriter in front of her. The typewriter banged and whirred as she worked, typing out a page that lay beside the machine. She wasn't a large woman and the typewriter seemed as big as she was.

"Hello, stranger." Her voice was deep and melodic. It burst forth from between ruby red lips that set off her pale skin and dark hair.

"Are my men okay?" he asked, his mouth full of cotton. She pointed beside his bed where a pitcher of water and a clean glass were placed. He sat up and poured himself a cup.

"Your men are fine. None of them died. Most of them are out and about now but -" She paused. There was always bad news after a pause; Ben had learned that throughout his years in the military.

"One of your men had to lose a leg. He'll heal up fine, but a bullet had pierced his aircraft. He tied off the leg but it was infected when they got him to the operating table. It was either cut it or watch his whole body go."

Ben nodded. "Lieutenant John Donaldson?" He had been shot during the ruckus. He hadn't complained. He had seemed to expect to be on the ground much sooner than they were. She nodded.

Ben drank down his water and sighed. "How long have I been out?" His body was running on adrenaline well before the fight with the enemy had forced them away from their planned route. His passing out wasn't exactly a surprise.

"Two days, give or take. There wasn't much room anywhere else so I had Leon bring you here to my extra bedroom," she said, waving her arm at the small space. "It's also my office." She thumped the desk twice.

Ben looked at her with a blank expression. "Leon?"

"The Colonel. I didn't even realize he was one until last night."

"You're a writer," he said.

She nodded. "The local paper. The Heroic."

Ben snorted. "Of course."

"You find something wrong with that?"

"A town called Hero with the newspaper named Heroic. Yet, you and yours are barely a blip on the radar. High ambitions for a small town."

She grinned. "We weren't supposed to end up this way. It just happened."

Her smile lightened Ben's mood. He had fought in this God-awful conflict for five years. He almost forgot that things like smiles and happiness actually existed. The bullet-torn battlefields he usually flew over were harsh and uninviting. The men didn't smile as much as try to live their last days on earth when they returned to base. Her smile was infectious and he cracked a grin back.

"That's a start. Even if that's not really a smile, you'll get there," she said and winked.

She left the room to let him wash up and get dressed. They must've cleaned him up after he passed out, since the dirt and the grime of hours in the cockpit was no longer on him. They had left his flight bag with a folded uniform in it, but he opted for the jeans and t-shirt that were also graciously put out for him. The clothes actually fit pretty well, and it was nice to be out of his flight gear. At the last minute he put on his flight jacket, with his rank and squadron badge sewn on for everyone to see. Sometimes people needed to know who the leader was.

He asked the brunette how to get to the hangar and she pointed out the door. As he ambled towards the row of giant buildings, he glanced around him. A town called Hero. It seemed idyllic: near the equator so the weather was always good; far enough away from the war so that nothing bad happened. At the beginning of the conflict, people didn't know what would happen. This was one of those places that had been constructed just in case.

The island wasn't big enough to build the town separate from the airbase, so the town grew up around it. That made the town and the airbase function almost as one unit with the airfield in the center. Roads spread out on all sides from the airbase to the town proper. From high above, Ben had thought it looked like the spokes of a wagon wheel. There wasn't even a real fence between the base and the town proper; people could drive in and out with no real issue. Granted, anyone that tried anything could be found on the island within thirty minutes.

The men had a local radio station filling the hangar with music as he walked in. It was a fusion of jazz pop and big band, the kind of sound that became popular as the war moved on. The staccato rhythms of the drums seemed to take him back into the cockpit as he rose and dove against the enemy. He almost could feel the stick beneath his hands and the vibration of the propellers.

"Captain on deck!" A voice echoed through the hangar, snapping Ben out of his flashback. He shook his head. His men sometimes thought they were sailors.

"At ease. I just came for a casual inspection," Ben said.

"Glad to see you're okay, Captain!" came a voice from the back. The other men agreed and raised a cheer. He waved the cheers away and went to see what the men were doing.

In the two days that Ben had been incapacitated, his crew had been busy. They were down a few planes but they could salvage the parts from those to fix the ones that were still repairable. All but one of the pilots who had managed to land had survived without any serious injury. Some were still recuperating, while the others were here working on the aircraft. Luckily, Hero had an aircraft mechanic stationed at the base. Ben guessed that even if it was an out of the way base, they still needed a relatively full staff.

He went through and made sure all of the remaining planes were okay. He inspected each plane and saw what damage was repairable and what wasn't. It would take weeks to fix some of the planes, but Ben was confident the squadron would fly out of there at some point. His inspection was cut short with the sound of a soldier running and calling to him from across the hangar.

"Captain! They need you in the Operations Room right now!" the soldier yelled. Ben snapped off a salute to his men and ran towards the office.

4.

In the Operations Room in the Hero Airfield, from a nearby desk, Betty watched the Captain talking to the man in a distant land.

She concentrated on writing all the events down – for posterity, and so she could have a good story for the newspaper.

"Captain. We thought we had lost you after that fracas around St. John's," said the superior officer.

"No sir. We decided to lead them away from you all to give you guys a chance to break away." His voice wasn't as weary as two days earlier, but Betty could tell he was tired.

"It worked. We got the cargo where it needed to be. That little maneuver helped us in more ways than you know." He looked at the captain for a moment and continued, "What's the damage, Captain?"

"Out of the forty-two planes in the squadron, we made it down with twenty. Three of the planes can't be fixed with the tools we have, so we are using those aircraft as parts to fix the others. One of the pilots lost his leg due to a bullet wound but the other eighteen pilots are ready or near ready. We can get seventeen planes up and ready within three weeks if need be."

"I'm sorry, son. I know you lost half your squadron, but it was worth it. We can do nothing but thank you for your efforts." Ben just nodded with no comment.

"And it worked, as well. The war is over, son. We've signed a treaty and all conflict is to have ceased three days ago."

"We were still in the air three days ago," he said simply. "At least the war is over."

Betty felt Ben and the Commander weren't saying something important. They both seemed subdued for such news.

"Captain, we can't come and get your men right now. I know your planes are shot up and need repair and, technically, Hero is an air station. So we're assigning your whole squadron to the town for now. You and your boys have earned it. Since winter is coming, stay there until after the new year and we'll bring you back home."

"You sure? We could be used in mopping up operations..."

"Ben, you've given some of your best years to this war. Sit back and enjoy some time off. That's an order, soldier. The pay will continue and we'll make sure your boys are compensated. Don't worry, there are at least two air mail planes that arrive there every month. Now let me speak with Vargas."

Ben saluted and nodded at the Colonel. Betty watched him as he exited the room. He didn't seem as happy as he should be. She wondered why. Picking up her pad and paper, she followed him out.

5.

After talking with the Commander, Ben walked into the town's infirmary. It was a small room with two beds; one was occupied by what looked like the town drunk and the other held Lt. John Donaldson. He sat looking through a book, sweat beading on his forehead until Ben came into the room. His head lifted and John smiled wearily for his captain. He halfheartedly saluted as Ben sat down next to him.

"How are you feeling, John?" Ben said as he moved his head towards the absent leg.

"Swell, Captain. As well as could be expected." He grimaced. "Phantom pain. I still feel the leg hurting but it isn't there anymore."

Ben patted him on the shoulder. "I'm sorry to see this. No more running for you, I guess."

John barked a hard laugh. "You know I didn't like to run. At least I can fly with one leg. The new models, at any rate."

Ben nodded. He didn't know if they'd let him fly but he could, technically, still fly. They had three planes left that would allow him to do so with one leg.

"I do have some good news, John. The war is over. The Fatherland has given up."

A blast of anger contorted John's face for a moment. It took him a minute to smooth his features and give a wan smile.

"Sorry. I don't mean to sound angry but it feels like I lost my leg for nothing."

Ben nodded. "I understand - but it was worth it. All our losses were worth it..." John didn't look like he agreed so Ben changed the subject to the men, and the missions they had survived together. About escaping many traps. They laughed, but Ben could tell he wasn't over losing his leg.

God willing, John would get beyond that eventually.

When Ben ducked out of the infirmary, he decided to go back to his room at the reporter's house. He didn't even know her name yet. He had a thought he should change that when he saw her sitting on a bench in the infirmary.

6.

"That man has anger issues," Betty said as Ben walked out the door. She sat on a bench, placed outside the room as a place for visitors. Getting up, she followed Ben down the short hallway to the outside as he grunted in response. He looked at her with one eyebrow cocked.

"I'm living with you and I don't even know your name," he said as they stepped out into the sun.

"Don't you know I'm a modern woman? I can have guys there and feel no guilt."

Ben snorted.

"I'm sorry Ma'am, but I ain't that kind of guy."

"I ain't really that kind of gal, flyboy." She tossed her head back, her hair glinting in the sunlight.

"Tell that to those who gossip. I did sleep over at your house, after all. I'd like to know your name so I know who the gossips are talking about."

She smiled as the afternoon sun glinted off her red lips. They were walking toward the base cafeteria. The sounds of a bouncing beat could be heard over the PA as the two talked. The singer spun a tale about blue skies and a shining sun.

"The name's Betty Potter. Beatrice really, but I don't prefer that one," she said and added "Captain," as she flipped her locks.

"I think you're following me." Ben stopped for a moment, leaning his head to hear the big band beats coming over the PA.

"I know I'm following you," he said with a half-cocked smile.

"Don't you have a job? Aren't all women supposed to be working for the good of the war effort?"

"War is over, or haven't you heard?"

Ben chuckled. "So it is."

"You and your squad are the biggest story to hit this place since the Battle of the Dunes."

Ben suddenly grew sober. His gaze drifted from her for a moment. Betty knew she had accidentally hit a nerve with that comment.

"I didn't mean anything by that. It's just the nearest battle we heard about here." Still, she thought, it was at least a thousand miles away.

"It's okay. Some wounds will take a while to heal." Ben smiled, the memories of that battle slowly drifting away from his face. He held out his arm. "How about you accompany a lowly Squadron Captain to the mess and see what's happening there?"

"Why, what will people think?" she said with a twinkle in her eye.

"Probably give them something to talk about for weeks."

As they walked toward the low building that served as the base cafeteria, Betty turned towards Ben. "I heard some men referring to your squad as the Cloud Zero squadron?" she asked, moving gently in time with his steps. The music had changed from a high tempo jazz pop hit to a slow and melodic big band melody.

"Claudio Squadron. It's a reference to where we were trained and that we're C squadron. It's an inside joke that really isn't funny."

"Hmm. Well then, Captain..." She waved at the path in front of them.

"Squadron Captain. Not just a mere captain, you know."

"Well excuse me. Squadron Captain Ben Pedro. I would be delighted to join you for dinner."

As the piano started to pound out a tinny beat and the horns joined in the background, the two made their way inside the building for a much-needed afternoon meal.

7.

The official news that the war was over didn't take long to filter through Hero. The residents of the town celebrated in their own unique ways. Some people leaned against the wall and cried. Others grabbed the nearest person and danced, kissed, or did both. Fireworks and gunshots filled the air as the day turned into night. The best music of the last decade was pumped out over the air by the local DJ. Even the Heroic had a special edition, featuring interviews with current and former military about the conflict. The air of the town was filled with jubilation.

In the infirmary, Lt. John Donaldson sat in the bed and scowled at the world. This wasn't supposed to happen this way. This wasn't how the war was supposed to end. He was in a bed and minus one leg as the world celebrated. Bah!

He even saw the famed Squadron Captain Ben Pedro walking with that trollop of a reporter. Captain Ben, whom the men so dearly loved. What a joke.

He took a drag on his cigarette and sent the smoke through his nose. His job wasn't finished even if he was minus a leg. He looked at a nurse passing his door and she scrambled to get out of the way. He knew the staff here didn't like him, and he knew they didn't understand why such a man as the dapper Captain Ben would see anything in him. He turned his head back to the street and watched the revelers for a few moments more. Fools. They'd learn someday. He heard a throat clearing, and looked at the doctor that had walked into the room.

"Dr. Ramon," John said, stubbing his cigarette out on the ash tray next to the bed. A little old ragtime music filtered in from outside. It was a genre popular near the beginning of the war.

"Do you want to walk with two legs again, Lieutenant?" the doctor said, trying to hide his glee. Probably celebrating the end of the war as well. John had only contempt for the man.

"Do you plan on growing me another leg, Doctor?" His voice was hard and sarcastic. Something he did his best to hide from his dear leader.

"What? No. We can't do that yet. Of course we can't," the doctor replied. He didn't seem to notice any of the sarcasm dripping from the voice of his patient.

"I mean, dear doctor, how will you make that happen?"

The doctor adjusted his white coat and his glasses. He seemed positively giddy. "Since the base here at Hero wasn't used in the war, we've been developing a few new techniques, some of which were based on captured technology."

John leaned forward. He was suddenly interested.

"Yes. I think that this technology can help you walk again. A miracle of modern science!"

As the doctor continued, John listened intently. The new leg was interesting enough, but he also wanted to hear more about the captured technology. Eventually the Doctor told him how things would work and that John would have to be wheeled down to the labs for experimentation. Would that be fine with him? John smiled. It would be fine indeed.

8.

C Squadron became the official squad of Hero a few weeks after the war ended. The Air Corps decided to permanently station all the remaining pilots and aircraft for the duration of the recovery period. Officially the Captain and the squad were considered detached, but there was no real place for the squadron to go. Ben gathered the squadron together to tell them the news.

"We've officially been stationed here for the remainder of the clean-up effort."

The men cheered – something Ben didn't expect. He held his hand up and they stopped. "Anyone who wants to head back to the Claudio base can contact me and we'll arrange it. It'll be by ship, so the trip will be a long one."

Lt. John Donaldson sat in a wheelchair, a stiff-backed thing with wide aluminum wheels. He cleared his throat when Ben paused.

"I know I don't want to go back. Out of all the blasted cities in the world, this little town seems to be a step back in time," Donaldson said.

"In a good way." It was Peter Debrise, a fresh addition to the squadron when they left Claudio and now a grizzled vet after only a few weeks of flying combat missions. He was blonde and skinny, a farmer's boy from a chain of field islands on the other side of the world.

John slapped Peter on the back. "This kid already has a gal. So of course he wants to stay."

The squadron laughed. It was nice to laugh in a place that wasn't riddled with bullets or where they were hunkered down for another attack.

"As the Squadron Captain, I'm staying for the duration."

"We know you have a gal, Captain!" It was Danny "Doughboy" Vertalli. He had spent time as a ground pounder before climbing up into the cockpit. Luckily for him he had a knack; he was one of the people most grateful to fly the not-so-friendly skies.

"Now, you know I don't talk about my personal life." The squadron groaned but Ben waved them off. "I do have a duty roster that will start at 0600 tomorrow."

Since none of the pilots seemed to want to go home, Ben pulled out the duty roster he had drawn up the day before. He had assumed no one would want to leave outside of John Donaldson. He thought John had family back home since he was so eager to contact them on the radio. Ah well, surprises happened every day. Ben spent the rest of the meeting talking about the duties as pilots and helping the local mechanics repair their own aircraft.

9.

The next few months flew by for C Squadron. Although the date said it was winter, none of the people in Hero knew it. The nights remained a balmy seventy degrees and sometimes the day would get up to ninety. The town of Hero embraced the new additions in many different ways; a true love affair began between the pilots of C squadron and the people of Hero Island. It was like seeing a couple that didn't know they were meant for each other until the moment they met.

It wasn't long before most of the members of C Squadron had girlfriends of their own. Most of the pilots didn't have wives or family back home, since the squadron was known to take on assignments that lead to high fatalities. The top brass weren't inclined to have pilots with many connections flying the planes.

The squadron had never been stationed in such a place. The town was almost an idyllic representation of home. It had a drug store that served malt beverages and ice cream. An old man ran the local hardware store where the men in the town came to yap every day at noon. Since Hero was on an island in a warm sea, many pilots joined the locals every morning in a surf contest. The people were friendly and positive and treated the pilots of C squadron better than even their own superiors.

Of course, Ben couldn't help but be a little cynical about the whole situation. Five years of war weren't wiped away in a couple of months of rest and relaxation.

"They can't be real." It was John. Ben sat in the lieutenant's room as he tried out his new leg. It was a marvel of modern technology. Gears within gears that moved small pistons as John moved his leg. It lay open to the world as the man tested it out on the bed. The leg seemed to respond to his mere thought. It whizzed and crackled as John moved the leg back and forth but it worked.

"I'm supposed to wear this every night for an hour. Apparently it attunes to my body. I don't know what that means exactly..." The leg moved back and forth as John sat on the bed. "They said there might be constant pain for a while. More if the body rejects it."

Ben looked out the window and watched the crowd of people go by. John was no longer in the base infirmary but had a quiet apartment on the south side of the island near the business section of town. The diner across the way made the best apple pie he had ever tasted.

"These people are too nice. Too clean. It's like the war didn't even affect them." John continued with his original thought. "Why would they help me like this and ask for nothing in return?"

"Not many people come out this far. This is one small island chain on the opposite side of the world. They haven't seen what we have seen. They still have prewar morals." Ben said as he looked at John. The man seemed to have changed subtly, but not in a good way like most of the other men. "We helped them and they helped us."

John grimaced in a way that seemed unrelated to the sudden buzzing of his leg. The leg sat there, straight out and frozen. "I guess I moved it too fast."

Ben looked at the leg. "This is from the Fatherland's technology?" he said, eyeing the mechanical marvel.

"That's what they said. I had a chance to look at some of the other stuff they captured. It's quite fantastic. It seems the United Island Military shipped most of their captured gadgets to this area."

Ben nodded. It was a good place, out of the eye of the war which let the scientists research in peace. No wonder there was still a working airstrip and military base here.

"Just the gadgets?" Ben said as he watched the leg start moving again. The gears and other components inside started to move as the leg swung back and forth off the bed.

"Not just gadgets. A whole group of Fatherland scientists. They're the ones that did the operation with Hero's doctors looking on." John absentmindedly ran his hand up and down his leg, as if trying to convince himself that it was real. "There's a big area underneath the airbase that's nothing but scientists with accents, and pieces of advanced technology. I'm quite impressed."

Ben snorted. A town called Hero indeed. He smiled as a knock came at the door. His favorite reporter would be by to interview the man with a new leg. The news about it was all over the island.

"She's here," Ben said and walked over to let Betty in.

John's face turned dark as he saw Betty with Ben. They were still dancing around their attraction to one another, but everyone else saw it clear as day. John hated them for it. When they turned he was all smiles and full of information. In his heart, he still detested Betty and the town she represented.

Ben left them alone as the reporter started to ask questions, and he moseyed on over to the diner. He would try that fantastic apple pie while the reporter grilled the man with the modern leg.

10.

The one resident of Hero who didn't feel at all at home sat in a small cell in the only police building in town. The other cell was full, occupied by a drunk sleeping off the night's festivities. The cell's permanent resident was squat and square, his brown hair speckled with blond. Blue eyes flicked across one of the books he had been given, a large tome on the history of the world.

"By all rights there should be no life on this ball," he said to no one particular. The drunk snored in the other cell as his accented words bounced off the walls.

A map of the world sat on the page. No central land mass seemed to exist. It was like God took one lump of land and spun the world like a propeller. The land was sling shot across the world in islands of various sizes. He sighed. This was a stupid war. He heard it was over but no one had decided to let him out yet.

When he heard the footsteps accompanied by a soft whirring sound, he closed the book and got up. Walking to the bars he nodded at the newcomer. He pushed against the bars and his hands were holding one like a pole.

"Johannes," he said in a harsh dialect. It sounded more like Yohan than John.

"Jakob." John nodded towards the prisoner. He stood on his new leg, although he still needed the assistance of a cane.

"I see our technology has helped you," Jakob continued in the foreign tongue. The drunk didn't seem to notice as he turned over and continued to snore.

"Our technology. Yes. It has helped me very much. I had no idea we were developing such a thing."

Jakob eyed John. He glanced up and down; the United Island Military uniform fit him well. "The war is over, John," he said in English. "Or haven't you heard? Your job is done. Accept it and let us move on together. It isn't like you were really part of us to begin with."

John hit Jakob's knuckles with the cane. "The war will never be over, Jakob," he spat out in the language of the Fatherland. "That isn't what my family tells me. Father wants you to know that you will help me or you will die."

Jakob laughed as he felt his smashed hand. "Do you think I fear death? I never wanted a part of this war. This small room is better than anything I found back at base. Do what you must but leave me out of it. Your family means nothing to me, and never has."

John spat on the floor of Jakob's cell. "I should've had you killed the moment they brought you in here. I bet you weren't following our squadron to attack but to escape."

Jakob shrugged. "It doesn't matter now; the war is over."

"I should kill you now," John growled.

"Do it. Kill me with no way to fight back. You were always a coward, John. This is the perfect place for you to destroy me. The one that can unravel all your plans is only you." Jakob stepped back and held out his hands.

John glared at him for a moment, his hand planted on his sidearm. It would just take one bullet, but everyone would know. John hit the bars again with his cane and turned to leave. He limped out of the room and back into the sunlight town and the noisy streets beyond, his leg whirring and his cane making a tap-tap-tap sound as he walked down the street.

"Friend of yours?" The drunk in the next cell finally spoke up.

"Never a friend. But one that should be watched. I just hope those in charge realize it."

Jakob sat down and opened his book back up. The history was interesting and he had time to read it all. He winced as he turned the page and the drunk started to call for a doctor.

11.

The war was over and many men of C squadron had no plans to move back to the United Islands. Most of them, in fact, decided that Hero was a good enough reward for years of hard service. The townspeople of Hero were glad enough to have them around. The men added a bit of zip and swagger to what was just a sleepy hamlet mere months before.

Lieutenant John Brown, a veteran of almost as many sorties as the Squadron Captain, decided to get into the fruit business. The string of islands had a plethora of naturally growing citrus and palm trees. With the savings Brown had acquired over the years, he was able to buy a good portion of one of the islands and set up an orchard. Soon he had a business that exported the fruit to various Island communities that were in colder parts of the world.

Another young pilot knew that there were many things that Hero lacked. In the bigger islands up north and down south, it was easier to get essentials like razor blades and toilet paper. He set up an import business that brought such items into the town. After years of reusing everything, the townsfolk of Hero were glad to finally get new supplies in bulk. He and Brown started their businesses separately but soon found they were using the same resources to fly cargo in and out. They came together and started the Heroic Import and Export.

Ben was glad to see how his men bounced back. The war was starting to be a memory and news of conflict seemed far away. Even John seemed to be feeling better; he spent a good part of the week talking to his family back home, planning on leaving at some point in the future. Ben was going steady with Betty and had found emotions inside him that he thought the war had destroyed. He even moved out of her house and now had a place of his own. At least that made some of the townies quiet down a bit. It seemed much too perfect.

John reminded Ben of this on a daily basis.

"Your leg, John. What about that?" Ben would point out.

"This place. This town. Doesn't it seem like something out of a magazine?" John frowned down at the apple pie in front of him. The diner was one of Ben's favorite places and he ate here at least three times a week. Over the radio the local DJ played a bit of an oldie, a bluegrass polka song that seemed to be all the rage in Hero right now. "It isn't like they gave me the leg without expectations. I've done a lot to help them with the tech they found. I've helped the captured scientists develop new ways of using the tech. It wasn't even our tech! The leg just... It isn't really a gift."

"We've needed the break. The war years..."

"The war years? You talk as if it's in the past," John spat out bitterly. His leg was a good replacement but it still didn't act like a real leg. Sometimes stiff, sometimes loose and John couldn't get over the idea that he would never have the flesh one back on his body. The pain sometimes was so intense that he couldn't move it for hours.

"John, the war is in the past. It was declared over months ago. Whatever action is happening now is just mopping up. Even the Fatherland has renounced its own leader and is working on rebuilding."

John just glared at him as his leg whirred beneath the table. Ben finished his pie and paid for his and John's meal and walked out. John seemed to be becoming darker and darker as the days wore on, and Ben had no idea how to help his fellow warrior.

That night, well after meeting Betty for one of the new movies shipped in from the UI, a loud rapping popped Ben off of his couch. "Hold on," he grumbled as a book fell on the ground. He was dozing while trying to get some reading in. He opened the door and John stood there. He was sweating and held his cane in one hand while the other rested against the doorjamb.

"Come quick, Captain. I've got some of the other pilots," John said as Ben glanced down the hallway. A few of the other pilots stood there, obviously unsure of why they were there. One stood in a white t-shirt and jeans, while a couple of the others were dressed to the hilt. They had obviously been out. It was a Saturday night, after all.

"What's going on, John? Why are these men here?" Ben asked as he looked over a good portion of his squadron.

"No time to talk. Drive us to the town hall and I'll show you."

Ben had one of the few jeeps on the island. As Squadron Captain he was able to requisition one for his private use. It was a nice perk on a place like this.

As they parked at the town hall, Ben shut off the vehicle as John led them around back. He opened the door a crack and told everyone to be quiet as they shuffled into the hallway. The voices in the meeting were muffled as the group approached the door.

12.

Betty sat inside the town hall taking notes. Not many people had showed up for the small meeting and certainly most of the townfolk were out and about. The few people present represented the leaders of the town. The Mayor was here since he was in charge of the airbase, the chief of police sat in now that his forces were getting a bit bigger, and so did a few other people considered leaders in the town. Betty was there to take notes and do a write-up on the proceedings at a later time.

"They need to leave," the Mayor was saying. "I don't feel safe with them here."

"Ever since they came to the island, our whole lives have been in an uproar." It was the Police Chief. He was always worried about public safety. "The scientists seem okay, but sometimes I wonder if they're scheming against us. They are just so... nice."

"Most people don't even know they're scientists. Just some prisoners of war like Jakob," Betty said as she continued with the notes. These men might not be well known among the townspeople, but their friendship seemed to have a price.

"We need to get rid of them. They can fly off the island the same as they came. The war is over, we don't need them anymore." It was Olaf Pierson. He ran a fish market but was well respected in the town. He had a good heart and a friendly smile.

"I think we need to take a vote. We can have them off the island tomorrow," the Mayor said. He didn't look happy about the decision. He wasn't fond of throwing anyone off the island.

"Mayor, they aren't being thrown out to die. They are just going to be heading back to the base on Claudio Island. It isn't like we are pushing them into the brink," the police chief said. He seemed like he was trying to convince himself.

"It'd be nice to be rid of Lieutenant Donaldson as well," Betty found herself saying.

"He's nothing but a black cloud and is in tight with that group," the police chief added.

"Yes. I don't trust that man. He says he is calling his family every other day, but he pushes everyone out of the Operations Room."

The Mayor raised an eyebrow. "It is decided then?" The rest nodded. "I will let command know tomorrow and we should be rid of this group as soon as possible."

The door banged open from behind.

"You want to get rid of us?" It was Squadron Captain Ben Pedro and he did not look happy.

"Ben! How long have you been there?" Betty was out of order but she was surprised.

"Long enough to hear you wanted to get rid of us." Ben said. His voice was cold, as if a long dreaded expectation had just been met.

"Captain. This is a private meeting. You need to take your men and leave." The Mayor wasn't the Mayor now. He was the Colonel and was giving an order.

"We've done nothing but bring good things to this town," Ben was saying. His heart was breaking. He looked at Betty and she looked away. She felt ashamed for no clear reason. Ben had no idea what was going on here.

"You don't know what is happening, Squadron Captain. You need to stand down." The Colonel wasn't happy. He was trying to get them to leave without much fuss.

"Don't worry, Colonel, we'll leave. No need to vote on it. I don't have roots here and you aren't my direct superior. We'll be out of your hair by tomorrow night."

Betty glanced over to see the men of C Squadron were in shock. Some were trying to tell Ben to calm down while John seemed to be urging him on. Betty got up and ran to the Captain.

"Ben, don't do this. You don't understand. You obviously didn't hear every –" she started.

"I thought we had something, Betty. Something real. I guess I was wrong." He looked into her eyes and pushed past her.

She tried to get him to turn around but it was to no avail. This wasn't how it was supposed to be. The Squadron Captain seemed to be looking for a reason to leave and he just got one. But he didn't understand. He didn't understand at all.

13.

Captain Ben Pedro stood on the runway beside his plane. Since he was technically detached, he could move his squadron along at any time. He just hadn't wanted to do so until now.

Not all his squad mates wanted to leave the island; that was fine, they had roots here. They told Ben that he must be mistaken. These people loved them and they loved the town. He would have none of it. He had heard what he heard with his own ears.

"Ben, it's just another battle. Sometimes we have to retreat."

John stood beside him. He had decided to fly his original plane since his new leg worked well enough to work the rudder pedals and other controls.

"Maybe we were wrong," Ben said, looking back. Betty stood at the hangar door. He thought he could see tears in her eyes but must be mistaken. Betty was tough. Something like this wouldn't bother her, would it?

"Get your plane. We fly out before the sun rises." Ben crawled into the cockpit and started his engine. The powerful Brach 323 turned his propeller at speeds too fast to see. It was a good engine, fueled by diesel and air. At least this plane had never let him down.

It wasn't long before the squaddies that were left were in the air and he was flying north towards the nearest base.

They were two hours from Hero and around three hours from another base. Their fuel would make it but barely. He didn't expect to hear anything on the radio outside his squad mates when suddenly it squawked and a very accented voice came through the speaker. The picture was blank, but he knew who this had to be.

"Captain Ben. You've made a very bad mistake."

14.

Jakob was breathless. He hunkered underneath the desk of the Operations Room and clutched a pistol in his hand. "Do you hear me, Captain?"

"Jakob?" It was Ben's voice. They had spoken a few times, mostly on their own exploits during the war years. Ben seemed to genuinely like the man even if he was behind bars. "What are you doing out of the cell?"

"They came after you left. They let me out because I am one of them but they were waiting for you to leave."

A man came screaming into the Operations Room and Jakob shot him in the chest.

"What do you mean? Speak in plain English, man!"

"You didn't think all the technology here came without people who knew how to use it? The Fatherland's best scientists were holed up beneath this island. I figured it out after I saw the marvelous leg that your friend," Jakob made this word into a curse, "had on his person."

"I knew about the scientists..." Ben would know. He was a high ranking officer.

"The Fatherland has come to get them. Or a remnant. Ask your friend. He knows."

A few more shots as more troops tried to get into the Operations Room. "We need your help. Don't let your petty feelings get in the way. I have to go or I might end up as dead as the man I just shot."

Jakob turned off the radio and crawled towards the back of the door. Hopefully he'd be able to get out of this situation alive. Surviving the whole war only to be killed here would be an insult.

15.

Ben let the engine of the fighter soothe him for a moment as he looked out at the never ending sea scrolling away beneath him. Not long, just long enough to control himself before getting on the horn.

"What do you know, John?" Ben didn't even tell the man what he was talking about.

"I didn't want you to get involved in this. Just head to the next base and everything will be fine."

John's plane came in behind him and Ben felt sweat bead on his face. This wasn't good.

"All they did was help you. Help you get a new leg. Help you get used to it. Support you when you were down. They didn't ask for anything."

"You think I want their pity? I gave the best years of my life fighting this war and for what? A bum leg and no real skills."

"You are a pilot, John! You can get a job in the real world just like any of us."

"My world isn't your world. Don't turn this squadron around or I will shoot you," John said.

"This is a bad way to end this." Ben flipped the switch going from private audio to full squadron audio.

"It's the only way. No one appreciates me and I need to go somewhere where I can at least be known for something... else."

"All squadron members: Hero is under attack. We must turn around and get back to help them. If we burn fuel, we can get there in half the time it took to get here."

He felt a few bullets pelt his plane as John fired off a warning shot.

"What the hell, John?" came a reply from one of the squaddies.

"Our captain is in violation of code 223 under the UI Military act. It's my duty to take him down."

Like the squad would believe that. Ben scoffed at the man as he did a barrel roll out of Ben's sights. He curved his plane out and away from Ben's as the pilot fired off a few rounds into the air.

"What is going on, Captain?" A question being echoed across the squadron.

"Head back to Hero. It seems we've been fooled. Lieutenant John Donaldson was just trying to get the bulk of us away from the island so it could be invaded," Ben almost whispered. "I obviously made a grave mistake."

More rounds racked the side of his plane as John flew past him. Another squad mate shot a few rounds at John, hitting him in the back of the fuselage. It didn't seem to matter.

"Head back and take care of the island. Who knows what they are up against. I'll take care of John. That is an order."

The squad grumbled but peeled off and headed back in the direction from which they came. As they left, John came around for another attack. He seemed more interested in taking down the captain than stopping the squad from getting back to the island.

"Why are you doing this? I never did anything to you," Ben said as he rolled out of John's line of sight.

"I should've had the squadron. I've always been a better pilot than you. You aren't even an ace."

True. Ben was better at tactics and strategy than one-on-one combat. He had helped down more planes than he had actually killed. Yet –

"This is what this is all about? Me becoming the Squadron Leader?

You could've switched squads instead of becoming bitter."

"What about that knockout back at the base? She never gave me a glance. They all never gave me a glance, Ben. The squaddies. The brass. The women. The fame."

Another burst of gunfire. Another miss. The leg must be knocking off his game.

"That conversation wasn't about you. It was about the scientists from the Fatherland. The Colonel felt I had become much too close to them. He felt they...we...needed to be shipped off to the UI."

Ben let him talk. He maneuvered his way away from any bullets that John shot. He finally found himself heading towards John's plane from the side. The sun was at his back and John seemed more interested in his own voice than actually paying attention. Of course, he was always a talker.

One press of the trigger and a few rounds hit the side of John's plane. Not enough to take the plane down, but...Ben heard John curse over the radio.

"What did you do?" he said, his voice high-pitched and loud. John's plane shuddered from left to right while Ben set his own destination back towards Hero.

"Told you we had planes that you could fly with one leg. You didn't want one of them. Now your new leg doesn't work, does it?"

John's only answer was cursing as his plane continued in a zigzag line toward the sun. He could see John trying to turn the craft but it was to no avail. It only turned it off course a tad and didn't turn it around.

Ben sighed. At least he didn't have to kill his friend. Only God knew where he'd end up flying like that. Hopefully John would make landfall at some point. Looking at his gauge, Ben saw he had enough fuel to make it back to the town in time to help. He hoped.

16.

As he approached Hero, Ben knew he would have to ditch his plane before getting to the island. The dogfight had just used up his fuel. He saw that his squadron was engaging the enemy in the air and doing their damnedest to take out the planes. But the antiaircraft guns weren't shooting. He was going down in a glide and wouldn't make it to the airstrip.

A small boat with Fatherland markings was bombarding the town. Ben aimed his plane for the boat and ejected. He laughed out loud as the plane hit the boat in the middle, igniting the stockpiles of ammo stored on the craft, but then he cursed as he hit the water. It was a bit colder out beyond the breaks than it was closer to the island. It was winter, after all.

He heard the low-pitched drone of a boat engine as he tried to get his bearings. He didn't know if his side arm would work after being dunked, but he made sure it was out. The boat didn't look like it belonged to the enemy, but you could never tell.

A hand reached down to help him up and when he got above the boat line, he saw it was the smiling face of Jakob.

"Glad you made it out of the Operations Room," Ben said but didn't put his sidearm down.

"The townsfolk are fighting back well. However, the enemy has control of both the antiaircraft guns. They can't use the guns because they have no ammo but they do have control of them."

Above their heads a plane burst apart, pelting the surrounding waters. Jakob didn't say anything more. He just turned the boat around towards the island and pushed the engine to the limit.

17.

Betty had never felt a gun against her head before. The muzzle was warm since the gun had been recently fired. The man had burst into the diner and started to shoot up the place. He seemed panicked. He shot two civilians before grabbing her and asking for answers.

"You will lead me to where the ammo is." The voice was harsh. Betty found it odd that she noticed the sun was low above the horizon and C squadron had pretty much cleared the skies of enemy aircraft.

"What do you need them for? You're losing," she said. Her voice was defiant although she felt anything but that on the inside. She had seen people die today; one or two killed by the man who held a gun to her head.

"We have more incoming. We need to land here and we need the skies cleared. Either you tell me or I will shoot you."

She thought she could hear Ben's voice. Must be a mistake; he had to be at the other base by now. She missed him even now. Still, it was all or nothing. She fell to the floor and punched the man in the groin. He got off a shot but it missed her before he doubled over in pain and dropped his weapon. She scrambled over and picked it up and immediately shot the man in the leg then kicked him to make sure he didn't follow her.

As she walked out of the diner, the streets of Hero were quiet. The sun was starting to descend. She heard the sound of a ground vehicle in the distance coming towards her. Her heart pounding, she tried to find a place to hide but she wasn't fast enough. The driver of the jeep had seen her and she could hear the engine revving as the jeep sped up.

Betty held the gun out in front of her, sure she would finally have to kill someone. The driver was Jakob, the Fatherland pilot that had been captured all those months ago. In the jeep sat a man she never thought she'd see again.

"Ben?" she said, the gun suddenly becoming heavy in her hand. He jumped out and grabbed her as she fell against him.

"Betty." His voice was full of emotion as he kissed her. Their embrace was broken as a surprisingly loud horn honked.

"Break it up. We have work to do."

She smiled as they climbed back into the jeep.

18.

Radio messages flew across the island. They went far and wide, into the air and through the waters.

"There is a second wave of planes coming. We need to get the squad refueled and back up in the air."

"Are you sure, Captain? We've taken care of most of them and that battleship is burning."

"It wasn't a carrier. That means there is a base somewhere around here. Those planes weren't long range."

"Those guns on the ground sure would help us, Captain."

"We are on it. Just make sure everything is refueled and rearmed. This isn't over."

19.

The Colonel sat in the passage as he refilled his clip with ammo. Around him his soldiers were checking their gear and weapons. Ahead of them was the room that controlled one of the antiaircraft guns. They would have to clear the room before taking control of the weapon.

Luckily, the bastards didn't know that the ammo supply was practically automated. This passage led from the guns to the armory where the ammo was stored, well away from the town. They had no clue it existed. Whoever spied for them wasn't familiar enough with Hero's methods to tell them the real lay of the land.

The Colonel signaled ready. They were close and didn't want to risk voice communication. Those around him nodded and he sat back for a moment. It had been years since he had to fight anything and he quite liked it that way. He hefted his gun, an automatic pistol that had served him well in the early years of the war.

He nodded at the person at the front of the group. The man kicked the door open and jumped back as the rest of the men streamed into the room screaming and shooting. The room was cleared out within minutes and the Colonel found he hadn't fired a shot. He was oddly disappointed in that.

20.

One of the antiaircraft guns started firing as the next wave of fighters from the Fatherland came in contact with C Squadron over the skies of Hero. There were more planes but they seemed in disrepair and full of inexperienced pilots; two of the planes burst into a fireball as a round from the gun hit the plane.

Ben watched the action from beneath the edge of a building in front of the second antiaircraft gun. These pilots were not the best the Fatherland had to offer. They made mistakes any rookie would have a hard time making. Yet, they still had weapons of destruction. Some even had bombs.

"Hit the deck!" he yelled and he pushed Betty and Jakob against the wall as the bomb fell on the second weapon. It didn't totally destroy it, but he could hear the screams of men as they were burned alive inside the Operations Room for the gun. A bit of debris pelted the wall and his legs.

"I guess that one isn't worth trying to save," Jakob said as he watched the fire.

Ben heard the clanging of the fire engine as the fire brigade rushed into action. They hosed the area down with water and attempted to save the men inside. One fireman went down with a bullet in his shoulder. Another fireman pulled out a gun and fired several shots inside.

A young boy went running past then skidded to a stop as he saw Ben.

"Captain! They need you in the Operations Room right away," the boy said before he took off again. The trio jumped in the jeep and took off toward the hangar as more shots were heard from the guns of the firemen. It seems the Fatherland soldiers hadn't expected civilians to have weapons. They were a bit surprised there was resistance from them.

21.

The Operations Room was a mess. Three bodies were being dragged out of the room as crusty trails of blood could be seen behind the bodies. Ben looked at Jakob and mouthed, "Three?" Jakob smiled sheepishly. "I wanted to make it out here alive and they wouldn't stop coming after me. Something about being a traitor or such nonsense. I never supported the war effort."

Jakob found himself a chair, turned it right side up and sat down and drew out a smoke. His hand was shaking a bit as he lit his cigarette.

The Colonel stood at the radio talking to a high ranking military official of the UIM. They spoke like friends that had known each other for years. Ben raised his eyebrow at Betty and she just shook her head. She hadn't realized the mayor of this town had such connections.

"They just came out of nowhere. I guess they were waiting for C Squadron to leave before attacking," the Colonel said, his voice gruff and weary.

"The Fatherland is denying any involvement. They claim this is a splinter faction that has no real power. In fact, I saw a man shot on camera when the news broke. It seems the Fatherland isn't all unanimous about the halt to the war."

"Do you have anything to add, Captain?" the Colonel said suddenly. Ben didn't even bother saluting as he stood in front of the radio.

"We need to find their base nearby. All the fighters they brought in were short range. They didn't have any real bombers, though one bomb did take out one of the guns on the island. I'd say dispatch some ships around this area to see. The planes had a working range of four or five hundred miles, without the need to fight. With the need to fight? Say one hundred and fifty."

The Colonel looked up at the screen. "I did ask for you all to look for this base months ago."

The general didn't say anything and bent out of camera shot for a moment then came back into focus. "There should be ships surrounding the island soon. There is a fleet in the area and it will be steaming your way shortly."

Ben nodded and stepped out of visual range. He listened to the Colonel talk to the General. Letting them talk, he took Betty out into the hallway.

"I don't know what came over me," Ben said. "The war. It's hard for me to trust anyone, even our own side. But that's no excuse."

She took his hands in hers and smiled her beautiful crooked smile. "You came back."

"I did. I think the reason I reacted so badly is because..." He hesitated as his heart started hitting his chest. "I do love you. I can fly a plane in to battle with nerves of steel but this is one of the hardest things for me to say."

"I know," she said, then kissed him. "I love you too, Squadron Captain Ben Pedro."

They walked through the debris-strewn halls into the darkness of the night. The war might finally be over, but he knew he would live with it for the rest of his life. At least he had found one good thing in this Godforsaken mess. She walked next to him, holding him up with her body.

*

The Battle for Hero Island - Continued

In the waning days of the war, C Squadron found themselves marooned on an idyllic island. It was a place that busted into their souls like the sun bursting through a cloud bank. The squadron loved the town and the town loved the squadron.

The last battle of the war happened on this tiny, out of the way base. It might have reignited tensions if not for a scrappy band of pilots and the affection they had for the town. The tale involved a turncoat on both sides and a captain that had to ditch his plane just so he could fight. Although not many historians remember this day, it is a battle I remember well. Every loss we had was a person we all knew and loved. Most of the writings about these events are by those who weren't alive when the war ended. They claim the battle is much ado about nothing. Those who went through that day know it is much more than that, and will forever be scarred by that last ditch effort to save the Fatherland.

Written By Betty Pedro

274

THE WINTER'S TALE

Jeffrey Cook +
Katherine Perkins

When wonders worked by artificer's hands
Filled lives and minds with leisure and surprise,
A newer kind of sailing joined the lands,
And stormy seas gave way to stormy skies
Our tale is in these times, and here's the map:
The Channel parts the places – two lands' ends.
Despite the winter gales, they bridge the gap,
The people bound by trade; the lords, as friends.
The ships fly east and west, and goods are bought,
By bright new minds with tales of bright new days.
And neither do they scoff at new arts wrought,
Nor yet forget old bloodlines or old ways.
We open when another ship has crossed.
It knows its errand, but knows not the cost.

CHARACTERS

THE MESSENGER: What it says on the tin

LEONARD, Earl of Scilly

PAUL, Marquis of Finistère: French nobility

COUNTESS EIRWYN: Wife of Leonard, said to be of fae blood

DITA: Child of Leonard and Eirwyn

NATHAN: Airship smuggler

THOMAS: The Bear

VICOMTE TREVEUR: Son of Marquis Paul

FORTUNE TELLER: Also what it says on the tin

LAMORNA: Cousin to Eirwyn

BRYANT: Leonard's right hand

Musketeers OLIVIER, RENE, and ISAAC: The Vicomte's guards

THE MESSENGER STRUGGLED IN OUT OF THE HIGH WINDS, shaking the snow off his bundled clothing as he was led into the Earl of Scilly's castle. Servants ran to take his garments to hang to dry, offering him food and drink to help shake off the chill, but he would not be delayed in first carrying news to the Earl's guest.

On his insistence, the messenger was led to the audience room, where Leonard, the Earl of Scilly, entertained his guest and childhood friend, Paul, Marquis of Finistère. Music filled the chamber from one of the wondrous clockwork music boxes built by the Countess's cousin, while tiny crafted dancers glided and spun across the top surface of the device. The pair of Lords drank mulled wines while sharing tales and news from their homes, having had little chance to catch up amidst the administrating of their respective lands until the Marquis's recent visit. The messenger quietly carried his notice directly to the Marquis after paying his respects, then stood by patiently until he could be dismissed to take the servants up on their offers of a small repast and warmed drink.

The Marquis read the missive quickly, his features lighting up at the brief note. "Leonard, I shall have to trouble you to open a fine bottle of something. My wife has verified her condition with both doctor and midwife. We are expecting, and she suspects a boy! Tonight, we must celebrate."

"Of course," Leonard answered, sharing his friend's good cheer. "Brandy tonight, a celebratory feast for the good news tomorrow!"

"Ah, alas, I will drink with you tonight, but tomorrow, I must be away at first light. I had hoped this would be a longer visit, for I have missed you greatly, but I must attend to my wife. This is our first child."

"Surely you can wait but a few days, that we can celebrate this event as we did the triumphs of our youth. Your castle is well equipped, and your wife has excellent nurses. She will be fine."

"I would dearly love to, but I am afraid it cannot be helped."

"Winter is upon us. Travel will be difficult, and the skies dangerous. I beg you stay with us a few days, until we can be sure of a lull in the storms. Better you get home late than not at all."

"I have faced worse storms, and the crew aboard my airship are well trained. I have faith they will see me home quickly and safely."

Leonard sighed. "If I cannot convince you, at least wait until lunch. We shall feast early, and my lovely wife shall have an opportunity to bid you good journey and wish your wife well. We have long been hoping to have a child of our own, so she will want to hear news such as this."

Paul sighed, considering, then raised his chalice in a toast. "Tomorrow, and lunch then. After that, I must be away. Tonight, however, we will drink to good tidings and a hope that soon, you and your wife shall share in this blessing as well."

The Earl took the opportunity to share the news with his wife, the Countess Eirwyn. She was, of course, happy for the Marquise, though it also reminded her that her own union had been, so far, fruitless. Her surpassing beauty and famously enchanting voice inspired talk of fae blood, but many blamed that same association for her line bearing few children. Though he had married her knowing this, the Countess knew that the lack of an heir troubled her husband greatly, and some of the less superstitious people of the region occasionally suggested there may be some fault in the marriage that didn't lie entirely with the Countess.

Beyond the news, Leonard added, "While it is good news, I am troubled. It has been too long since I've seen Paul. News and cooperation between our lands has been slowed, and I had hoped we would have time to properly address the piracy issue. Now that's all out of the window with this news and his rush to return home."

"Oh, yes. There are always a few vagabonds in salvaged airships, but the stories about this new gang of bandits – "

"The Wind Talons, yes. They could become a real problem. The Crown has put great pressure on me to see them put down. I had hoped that Paul would put some of his own resources into the effort."

"Sensible," the Countess agreed. "I am loath to keep him away from his wife too long, but he has a responsibility to his people as well. Perhaps I can convince him?"

The Earl considered this possibility a few moments. "No harm in your trying where I've failed. Even a short time would serve."

"I will do what I can," she agreed.

*

The following day, the Countess approached the Marquis before lunch, while he was making preparations to leave. "A word, Paul, if I may?"

"For Leonard's Lady, anything," he agreed pleasantly.

"I know Leonard has asked you to stay on."

"He has, but alas, I must be home to see to my wife."

"You have a duty beyond the family worry of the moment, Paul. The pirates – "

"Will be dealt with in time. I've called for more soldiers, both airship crew and musketeers," he responded.

"But with no coordination, how much damage will be done in the meanwhile? The longer they have to establish themselves, the more ships are lost."

"There is something to your words," he admitted, taken with both her reasoning and the gravitas of her voice. "We were soon to get to this, the point of the visit, when the news came. Perhaps returning would wait a short time – " he began.

"And we would not ask you to stay away too long. Just enough to finally get to the matter at hand – and to prepare a gift you can take home to your wife. A new commission of Lamorna's work; a music box, perhaps? Finistère scholars, artists, and craftsmen all do fine work, but no one seamlessly blends music to movement like she does."

"Ah. I've seen those. You know what they say about your cousin and her deft little hands."

"Is it similar to the things they say about me and my 'inhuman' voice?" the Countess asked drily.

"Just rumors and superstition, of course," he assured. "But there is no question she is a master craftsman, and I would be foolish to turn down such a rare gift. Very well, I will stay until her work is complete, and then begin the journey home. You may tell your husband I look forward to more time speaking with him."

Tell him she did, and the Earl's pleasant surprise that the Marquis would be staying out the month hid the sting of hurt pride that it should be so feasible where he had failed. Then the Countess spoke to her cousin Lamorna of the news and the gift. Lamorna agreed to begin work at once.

"Don't rush it. They still have work to attend to, and knowing the two, it will be well-mixed with play."

"Don't worry," Lamorna replied. "It will still take a matter of weeks for such a project. Especially since I'll need to find the perfect music for the device. Entertaining for the Marquis and his lady, comforting for a small child."

"Off to the castle musicians, or shall I sing?"

"The musicians," Lamorna said hurriedly.

"You're certain?"

"I am. Your gift should not be lent lightly. You have more soul in your voice than most."

"As you wish, Lamorna. Keep me appraised on your progress."

"Of course, Eirwyn. Good fortune with your guest."

*

The weeks passed quickly, with Lamorna spending nearly all her waking hours at her craft. The Earl and the Marquis dedicated their time to alternately planning their joint venture to secure the waters between them and talking at length about earlier and simpler times. The Countess Eirwyn, meanwhile, eventually found herself consulting with a physician. She waited until she was certain of her condition, and until she had an opportunity to speak with her husband alone.

"Leonard, Leonard! I have the most wondrous news! I thought for a time I might simply be ill, but after talking with the doctor, he's certain I'm expecting. We're to have a child!"

"Truly?" he asked. His surprise turned down a different path. "After all this time?" He thought of trying and failing, and the various worries circulated about why that was. If she was pregnant, then it had clearly not been her that was at fault. That line of thought carried into her discussions with his friend, and how quickly her efforts at persuading the Marquis had proved so much better than Leonard's own.

In her excitement, Eirwyn missed his shift in tone, assuming he would be as thrilled as she was. "I know! Isn't it lovely? I know you've wanted a boy, but I hope we have a girl."

There was a pause, and then, "It doesn't matter. No child of an adulteress will ever inherit the earldom."

"Wouldn't it be – wait – what?" she stammered, mind catching up with his words.

"You heard me. I know you for what you are. Betrayed by my wife and my best friend. I've seen how he looks at you, and this timing is too convenient. I know now why he's stayed on."

"No, no. I swear it's not true. These thoughts are madness!"

"First betrayal, and now you accuse me of being mad? What next?"

"Leonard, you're not yourself. We've been trying for this for so long!"

"Trying, and failing. But as soon as Paul arrives, who's so obviously ...virile enough, you can suddenly conceive," he insisted, before raising his voice. "Guard, guard!"

The cries brought his personal guard running. "Escort my wife to her room under house arrest, and gather men to apprehend my so-called friend the Marquis de Finistère as well."

Though confused, the men obeyed, leading away the stunned Countess and sending a message to gather more men. The procession of armed soldiers leading away the sobbing Countess drew a good deal of attention – and not a few questions. Among those who took notice was the messenger who had first brought the news from Finistère. The man had taken to learning the ways of the castle, its twists and turns as well as its personalities, until his master was ready to leave. While the men carefully avoided the Marquis's soldiers, they ignored anyone more simply dressed and simply milling amidst the house servants. Used to listening for any interesting bits of information, he was able to follow and eavesdrop on a few of the guards without drawing attention and managed to reach the Marquis ahead of them.

The strange tidings seemed unbelievable, but the Marquis was not without his own paranoia. He decided to err on the side of caution, gathering his own men and making his way through the halls following the messenger. By this fortune, they were near the gates by the time they were found, and the bulk of the Earl's guards were still being alerted, or were just finding the Marquis's chambers empty. Shouts demanding the Marquis's arrest confirmed the messenger's news, and the quiet procession turned into a running skirmish. Confusion erupted among those who had not yet heard the Earl's demands, and the gates had not been closed or reinforced yet, as the Marquis was not expected there. With the loss of half of the men with him, the Marquis was able to fight his way first through the gates, and then to where his airship was moored.

Pursuit was halted temporarily when the airship crew joined in the fight, laying down covering fire for their Lord and his escort. The Earl and his personal guard arrived only just in time to see the last ropes being hastily cut, and the airship rising into the skies. He grabbed a musket from the nearest guard, shouting after his former friend and firing after the airship. Rifleshot and musket fire scarred the side of the ship, and a couple of the musketmen at the side of the ship were injured in the exchange of fire, but the Marquis's ship escaped out of range, setting its course back towards Finistère as ordered by the confused but furious Marquis.

*

The Earl quickly put his guardsmen and both marine and airborne fleets on alert. Trade with Finistère, Scilly's longtime favored trading partner, halted. Though Eirwyn was questioned many times, she continued to proclaim her innocence and that of the Marquis de Finistère. Each time she refused to confess, the Earl would place her back in her lonely confinement in her room, with guards stationed to make sure she remained there. Aside from her irate husband, the Countess's only regular visitor was her cousin, as Lamorna hurried to her side amidst her projects.

"Eirwyn, if you do not eat, you will not have a healthy child, and you'll continue to waste away. You're a shadow of yourself already.

Here, I've brought you some soup."

"What does it matter, Lamorna? He's going to see us both dead anyway. He just wants the vindication of a confession before he does."

"I'm glad to see you're still holding out on that, at least."

"He can do what he will. I'll never confess to something I didn't do."

"Nor should you. But starving yourself is no way to die."

"Then I should wait for the trials? To see how many times he can publicly humiliate me, to see him try to trump up the charges to espionage and have me executed instead of letting me die in peace?"

"You should hold out as long as you can, at least. Yes."

"To what end? He's not going to see sense. Even I can't persuade him to reconsider."

"Your husband has lost his mind. He's beyond anyone's reach now. There is still cause to conserve your strength, though."

"What cause? If you have some plan, you'd best make it quick. And you'd best tell me."

"Shh, I'd not speak of plans too loudly with your husband's guard listening. I've contacted a friend from my youth, and given him enough coin to bring in a famed fortune teller. She's known enough that if she pronounces you innocent, and the child his, he'll have to reconsider his position if he doesn't want a lot of people questioning his authority."

"You truly think he's going to believe her?"

"Not right away, but perhaps cracking his self-assurance will sow some small seeds of doubt, and it will buy time."

"And if it does not?"

"Then you must stay healthy for your child's sake. I have many friends, not all of them known to him. I may be able to safeguard the child, at the least."

"I have little hope that anything will cure my husband's madness, but for the life of my child, I'll try. What can I do to help?"

"If that is what you will hold out hope for, then you can do two things for me. First, you can eat, and try to hold on to what strength you have left. Goddess, you're already too pale. And then, when I visit, you can sing for me."

"For one of your music boxes? I thought you wished me not to sing for those?"

"For a gift for anyone else, it's true. But your child will need a mother's voice. It will also soothe the child, even now, and comfort both you and I. Plans or no, I think we could both use some comfort right now."

"If that is what I can do, then I will try my best, yes. What song?"

"All that you can think of, dear. Just sing what you can, when you can."

Lamorna would continue to visit on a regular basis, building her music box, and spending many hours sitting and holding her cousin while Eirwyn sang songs to her child, mourned the state of affairs, or sang to find some hope in the situation. While it helped to sustain her, Eirwyn continued to weaken and fade. She continued to try to hold on for the sake of her child – and the slender hope Leonard's madness would end.

★

Arriving back in Finistère amidst great confusion, the Marquis called together all of his officers, and those nobles within his holdings who answered to him, and called for his wife's presence.

"Leonard, Earl of Scilly, has gone insane. He attempted to have me held for imagined crimes. We escaped, but lost many good men," he announced.

"Is there to be an answer then?" asked his head of security. "We can recall the ships pursuing the Wind Talons, if you think there's a threat?"

"Recall all of the ships. Send messengers to request more line troops and musketeers to stock the forts. Reinforce the ports and set guard by both sea and air."

"All of the ships, Lord? We escort many of the nation's trading vessels…"

"I do not know what form his madness will take. Stupid as it may be, the fool may attempt some sort of desperate assault. He's after my son."

The Marquise's eyes opened wide at that. "After our son? What threat does he expect from an unborn child?"

Paul's eyes narrowed, eyeing each of his officers in turn. "He suspects me of some infidelity with his wife, which I will swear before God and country is untrue. He nonetheless is convinced that I stole his heir from him, and now he seeks to destroy my line as well. There will be an elite guard upon my wife at all times, and once he is born, upon my son as well."

"Of course, Lord, but…"

"All else will wait. We must secure our own ports and guard against attack."

"If that's what you wish. I'm certain the merchants won't be happy, but…"

"But they will cope if they wish to continue to use our ports and waters."

"Yes, my Lord. And we're simply to guard?"

"I'm no fool, and an attack on Scilly would be foolish. I'll not start a war, nor give justification for his crusade. If he wishes to start a fight, then we will be in position to finish it."

*

In the midst of the turmoil, Eirwyn's child was born, with Lamorna serving as midwife to her cousin.

"Your good countess has delivered a girl, my Lord – one as healthy as can be expected," she reported to the Earl, sidestepping an attempt by Bryant, the Earl's right hand, to keep her out of the audience room.

Leonard glared at the woman who had attended his wife despite all pressures and all of his rages. "A countess has given birth. This I will believe."

"Your good countess," Lamorna said, enunciating every syllable, "Wishes to know if you will see your daughter."

"I have no daughter, nor any wish to view hers at this time. Should I have you arrested if you continue to play gadfly?"

"Should you explain the charge?" Lamorna asked coldly.

"I have no time for this! There is the Finistère threat to consider. Go."

"At such time as you wish to visit your good countess and your daughter, you know where they can be found," Lamorna said loudly before walking past Bryant – and guard after guard beyond him – to return to her cousin.

"My husband will not even come see his own child?" Eirwyn asked, her voice a faint whisper of what it once was.

"No, dear, but look at her," Lamorna said, scooping up the newborn. "Our little Lady Dita. She has the most beautiful blue eyes. I'll bet she's going to turn heads someday."

"Someday? You truly think there's a future for my daughter?"

"I'm sure of it, Eirwyn. I have some very useful friends. Given even a little opportunity, I'll take your child far from here and look after her for you."

"You're a good friend," Eirwyn answered, a thin hand grasping weakly at her cousin's.

"He should be back by now, with the fortune teller," Lamorna said. "I've not yet lost hope that perhaps some vision of the future will shock your husband to some sense again."

"It's hard to have hope. He's obsessed with Paul now, and with gaining revenge for a slight that never happened."

"The news is not much better from Finistère. They've turned their holdings into a fortress, last I heard. I suspect they believe Leonard plans an attack."

"I fear they're right."

"As do I, but Leonard at least seems to realize that any kind of invasion would be suicide. With as many troops as Finistère has called, and holding all the forts on his side of the water, any attempt at a mass landing would be doomed to fail."

"But we're safe here?"

"From everyone but your husband, Eirwyn. Your husband has put out a call for mercenaries and privateers. The land suffers from the presence of its own defenders, but we won't be seeing an invasion from Finistère."

"So it's true then? He's encouraging the pirates now instead of hunting them? I'd heard rumors, but – "

"Jealousy does strange things to a person."

"He was a good man..." Eirwyn said, weakly.

"Once, dear. Once. But he's not seeing the world through those eyes anymore. It is not just for your sake that I'm hoping the voice of prophecy will be enough to bring him around, though for your sake alone, I'd gladly – well, I don't know what I'd do. I don't know how to fight a duel, though I'm not afraid of getting a little vitreous humor on these deft little fingers."

Eirwyn managed to shake her head. "Don't get yourself killed over me."

"I know, dear. I know I can't. There are other factors to consider. Anyway, I've done my best to help ensure Leonard's invested in her pronouncements."

"So he knows she'll be arriving?"

"I spread news of the famed oracle coming here, yes, but not how she came to travel this way. I believe he's casting it in terms of seeing this as a great enough campaign to justify her visit. He's hoping she'll give him some word on how conflict with Finistère would go."

"And if he doesn't hear what he wants to hear?"

"He won't. There's no way it could go well. Both sides can hold out forever, and neither country will back a full scale war at this point. Once he lets her in the door, though, he'll have to either listen, or face a lot of questions. There's still plenty of people who believe in prophecy."

"In his current state of mind, perhaps he'll be more disposed to listen to prophecy, since he hasn't been listening to simple truth."

"Who says prophecy isn't truth?" Lamorna asked, with a small smile. She was about to say more, when a commotion arose outside.

A small procession had arrived, including the fortune teller, though Lamorna's friend did not accompany them.

The Earl welcomed her, seeing to it that she was given fine accommodations and a feast, and asking after when she would read his fortune. Three days were asked and given, with Leonard inviting everyone he could with influence within his territory to come and witness what he was certain would be the vindication of his claims, and to hear what would come of his conflict with Finistère. In the meanwhile, he made sure the fortune teller had everything she asked for, spoiling the messenger in hopes that would aid the message of fate.

*

The third day arrived, and a great feast was prepared. The castle's audience chamber had room for a large crowd, though the center of the room was laid out as per the fortune teller's expectations. Leonard sat in his great chair at the head of the room, watching all about like some large predator about to pounce.

Eirwyn, barely able to walk, entered with a servant supporting her on each side. Lamorna carried the baby Dita with her, standing near her cousin and rocking the child to help keep her calm amidst the chaos. Less heartening, Bryant also took up a position nearby, clearly having been asked to watch the Countess.

Leonard made a few speeches regarding the state of the earldom, informing all present that while he would not go to war without the Crown's blessing, he stood ready to protect them all from aggression from Finistère and its allies. He announced the fortune teller, calling upon her as a messenger of fate that would prove him correct to pursue the aggressive course.

The room went quiet as the old woman advanced, laying down a wooden bowl. At her bidding, a servant emptied one pitcher of water into the bowl, ran for a second, and emptied that as well, before scurrying out of the way. There was a long period of chanting and invocation, before the woman reached into a pouch, withdrawing three pebbles. After rolling them around in her hand for a few moments, she pitched the three stones into the water, watching the conflicts of the ripples within the bowl, not saying a word until the surface was still again.

At long last, the oracle looked up from the bowl, locking her eyes on the Earl, ignoring all others within the room. "The past, present and future collide. In times past, you spoke false against your neighbor. Your wife is true, and the child yours."

There was an audible murmur about the room, which then went silent as she continued. "That child shall be your only heir. You have sapped your wife of the strength to carry any other, and no other woman shall bear fruit for you. And if the baby girl dies by your hand, or that of any man under your command, you doom your country to ruin." Another series of whispers, while Leonard looked more and more ready to pounce, features going dark red at the pronouncements.

Once again, the voices were hushed as the fortune teller moved at last to the future. "Already, only your mutual enemies benefit from the conflict between those who were once as brothers."

Leonard roared, "Ungrateful witch! My home was made as yours, and this is the news you bring me? Fie on your charlatan tricks! Bryant, break her jaw."

The rest of the court was too stunned with disbelief to react, as the Earl's hand crossed the distance quickly. The fortune teller, however, looked unsurprised and offered no resistance. She simply kept talking. "The first to attack shall be the one that falls, but the one who first offers his hand shall give strength to both." Then Bryant reached her and set his hands on her face. The prophecy was halted with a stomach-turning CRACK! Drops of blood fell from the corner of the woman's mouth and suffused the water before her.

The Earl stood, continuing to bellow, his voice shaking at least a portion of the guard into response. "Take my wife back into custody, to await her sentence for adultery, fraud, and espionage, and guard her cousin!" he demanded. On the first, the announcement was unnecessary. The sickening sound, and the horror that the man she once loved had cold-bloodedly ordered it, was too much for Eirwyn's weakened state. She collapsed. Lamorna was set to flee, but her cousin's fall kept her attention too long. She was not able to clear the room before guards closed around her and wrenched the baby from her hands, forcing her back towards Leonard and the center of the room.

"She's dead," announced the court physician, once he had opportunity to reach and examine Eirwyn through the tangled mass of the crowd. "Her heart gave out from the shock." He then moved on to taking the fortune teller, silently blank and bleeding, away for treatment.

Much of the room looked to Leonard. Some had anger simmering in their eyes, either for his defiance of fate, the brutal maiming of the old woman, or the news that the popular Countess had died. Others showed more support out of nationalistic pride, their own loyalties to the Earl or those who backed him, or simply hoping that this was a chance to gain favor from the seat of local power. The majority of the guard, at least, made the decision most benefiting their continued pay and show of loyalty, making their presence known and helping control the crowd until things settled.

When the room had quietened again, though with a much different tone than he'd expected, the Earl began to dole out commands again. Reading the crowd enough to see he'd already come near to a tipping point, he elected not to push at defying fate further, seeking instead to circumvent the curse the old woman had pronounced. "I will not kill the child, even if she is born of an illicit union with the enemy. Nor will any man under my command. Bryant will take her to the coast and leave her there in seclusion, and nature will take its course."

There were a few more murmurs, but he cut them off, continuing. "Though my wife betrayed me, I always loved her, but could not let her betrayal stand. Her cousin – " He was ready. The charge would be sedition. Indeed, sedition would do, the minute the artificer opened her mouth. As he spoke, however, he looked at Lamorna's face, unmoving as stone, but streaked with tears. Her deft little hands clasped each other, white-knuckled. She was silent, broken. " – shall keep her esteemed place and wealth here, out of respect for the family."

His mad mind raced, trying to think of what to do about the stalwart, brilliant, well-connected artificer now that she was apparently a crying statue in her mourning. An idea occurred. "Indeed," he said, "I charge her with crafting a monument to her cousin, my wife. Not simply one of her crafted dancing figures, but a clockwork dancer of life size, in the very image of my wife, with all of her beauty and grace," he commanded, seeking not only the monument and sign of his devotion to the woman, but a long project with which to keep Lamorna within his sight.

"It will be as you say," Lamorna offered back quietly, bowing her head. "If you but give me leave to talk to Bryant a few moments before he leaves. I would say goodbye to my niece."

Deciding the request sounded simple enough, especially with Bryant present, the Earl nodded, turning his attention to other matters.

She approached the big man, who now had been given the tiny infant – and his orders. As she did, she reached into a pouch, drawing out an ornate music box. "Bryant, I beg you, take this token with you, and leave it with her. It was to be her first gift, and has only today been finished."

"She won't be needing any trinkets," he responded, brusquely.

"Perhaps so, but even you will be more relaxed leaving a child with music to quiet and comfort her than abandoning a crying infant. And likely draw less attention as well with a quiet voice singing to her than with her cries."

"You could fetch a good price with that," he replied, eyeing the music box.

"I couldn't, and neither could you," she assured him. "This one will only work for my niece. It will sing only if she touches it. Test it if you like. No matter how fancy, no one is going to pay for a broken music box and they will question you for trying to sell it to them."

Bryant made a couple of attempts to open the box, getting no result. To Lamorna's small satisfaction, however, it came to life with a tiny dancing figure and the beautiful tones of the Countess's voice as soon as Dita's hand was touched to it. "I don't know how you did that, but – "

"You don't need to know how. It is my niece's present, and it will keep her calm for you, and comfort me that she was left with at least her mother's voice. On your word, guardsman."

"On my word then. I suppose it can't hurt."

That vow given, Lamorna spent a few moments whispering goodbyes to her niece before stepping away, tears in her eyes, but schooling her voice. "I have preparations and materials I must send for. Be on your way about your cruel errand, then," she said, turning away and running off towards her workshop, not looking back.

Bryant took the baby girl to the coast as commanded, discovering, per Lamorna's comments, that the music box did, indeed, calm Dita down. When he arrived at the coast, he traveled some distance from any inhabited area, taking his lord's meaning, and found a place to set her down amidst some rocks, out of easy sight. At first she began to fuss, ready to howl, but he wound the music box and set it in contact with Dita. The moment she heard her mother's voice, the baby quietened again to listen. With that added noise, it was only as Bryant started away from setting her down that he heard the growls. Though he drew his sword at first, on seeing the large form charging his way, the blade hit the ground and the Earl's hand took off running, exiting the story, pursued by a bear.

A few moments later, a man dressed in a collection of threadbare finery approached the girl's hiding place, picking her up out of the rocks. "Well, well…" Nathan began, picking up and examining the music box as well. "It seems that Lamorna was right. I'm glad we were able to get here fast enough. Now there's just the matter of what to do with you, young lady. I've never had much experience with children."

He glanced around, noticing the bear meandering back his way. As the big beast reached him, it snuffled at the little, wiggling bundle in Nathan's arms, then licked her gently. The smuggler sighed, reaching out to scratch the bear between the ears. "Well, Thomas likes you, so I guess it's decided. How do you feel about smuggling, kid?"

Dita giggled.

*

Back at the Earl's castle, some time later, the clockwork dancer was finished and brought before the Earl. The face was crafted in an excellent likeness of the Countess's, but of course, the smile never moved. It could dance through certain routines, but compared to her usual tiny dolls, the full-scale clockwork figure had little grace. Lamorna agreed to make repairs and what improvements she could, but insisted that the size of the figure made true grace difficult to achieve. What truly stood out, however, was that this machine made no noise but the clicking and turning of gears and the shifts of metal and wood. Though Lamorna placed multiple music boxes within it, at the Earl's command, each went silent when placed, refusing to play along with the statue's movements. Likewise, any other device made by other hands, no matter how skilled or reputed, would turn silent upon being incorporated into the work.

Each time the Earl demanded some new attempt, or grew upset over the failures, Lamorna simply apologized, smiling grimly, "I am very sorry, my Lord, but you asked for the Countess. She will accept no voice but her own."

*

War did not rage, but coldly glared and snarked,
And never faded with the march of time.
For eighteen years, the Channel's west was marked
By fear and hate – and ever-present crime.
Young ladies should learn languages and dancing,
And Dita spoke in five and moved with grace –
From rope to rope, in feinting, and advancing,
And steering quickly when the guard gave chase
The little viscount lost his mother young,
And fought the gilded cage his father wrought.
Watched every hour, he used his time among
His watchers, for a soldier's life he sought.
So having rushed these children's early years,
We meet the youth – now Enter Musketeers.

"Not like that," Olivier corrected sternly, parrying Treveur's blade to the side.

"What went wrong that time?" Treveur inquired earnestly.

"You leave yourself open to the riposte," he replied, demonstrating the maneuver.

"Oh, go easy on the boy," called Isaac from where he rested in the wings.

"Would you like to take over his lessons, then?" asked Olivier without looking back.

"I daresay I would love to take over his lessons, but we'd start somewhere other than swordplay. He's already the fourth-best swordsman in a hundred miles."

"Pray tell, then, where would you begin?" asked Rene, not glancing up from his book. "Drinking, wenching, or fleeing?"

"Fleeing is a highly underrated skill, I'll have you know. Once upon a time, any real man would accept a duel. Now it's all firing pistols wildly and angry mobs. What's a man to do?"

"Perhaps not sleep with the wives of men who keep angry mobs within shouting distance?" Rene responded, still without looking up from his book.

"Well, how am I to know which those are? Perhaps with more practice, I'll develop a more discerning eye."

Olivier shook his head. "Too easily distracted, that's your problem." Seeing Treveur's grin, he rapped him lightly upside the head with the basket hilt of his sword. "And you too. Focus." Another glance back to the audience. "Besides, the Marquis would have your head if he heard you even suggesting teaching the boy wenching or drinking."

"He'd have to catch me first," Isaac countered, not losing his grin. "Fleeing. Very underrated skill."

"You know my plans well enough, and they include neither drinking nor wenching," Treveur responded, settling back into stance.

"Planning to go hunting pirates still, is it?" asked Rene, looking up from the book at last. "Because that went so well last time you proposed it to your father."

There were a couple more exchanges between Olivier and Treveur, though the Vicomte continued to speak as they fenced, practicing getting used to distractions. "Ah, but that was a year ago, and I didn't have my secret weapon in our negotiations."

"Secret weapon, really?" Rene inquired, bemused.

"The boy is growing far too devious," Isaac said, narrowing his eyes as he watched the fencing. "I don't like it one bit. Reminds me far too much of me."

"Oh yes," answered Treveur. "My father and I spoke just last night. He agreed the pirates had become more than a trifling problem, but he had only so many resources available to combat them and still defend our holdings."

Rene's brow raised. "And you had a ready solution, of course?"

Treveur managed to turn Olivier's blade aside as he answered, earning a small nod of approval from his current trainer. "A private ship, outfitted for pursuit with a privately paid crew," he affirmed.

"Very resourceful," Rene admitted. "Someone would need to have been saving and investing carefully to put that together."

Isaac's grin returned. "You said something about focus, Olivier? I suspect our charge would have something to teach all of us on that front. Well, teach you. I intend to continue to squander my youth frivolously."

Amidst another exchange of bladework, Treveur backed up, giving ground, but keeping his guard up. "I wanted to show my father that it was not a passing fancy. I can do Finistère – and all of France – a great deal of good and put down the Wind Talons. Perhaps even prove that Scilly is paying them to target us. He's kept me hidden away too long."

"So you've said for some time. I take it you believe something went differently in your negotiations this time?" Rene followed up.

"I know they did. I have my own ship now, and I may have agreed to consider marriage, and – " he started, before he was cut off in having to fend off a furious assault.

"I so dislike 'and,'" Isaac mused aloud, in Rene's general direction. "Somehow, when there is an 'and' involved, it never goes well for me."

Just as Rene was about to ask after the 'and', there was a commotion from the castle, with the main doors opening out into the courtyard. The Marquis emerged, flanked by a page and two guardsmen. "Musketeers, at attention!" called one of the guards.

The sparring stopped abruptly, with the trio moving front and center, snapping to attention. A half-dozen other musketeers emerged from their own practice or rest about the courtyard, also falling into ranks as the Marquis approached. He paused when he reached the line of soldiers lent to his service, looking at Isaac in particular. "I suspect my son misspoke, but thought I should be sure," he began, as his gaze drifted to Olivier. "He indicated that three of the musketeers volunteered to act as bodyguards, if I permitted him an opportunity to pursue the pirates roaming the coast. Is this true?"

Rene glanced in the Vicomte's direction, raising a brow, but saying nothing. Isaac was the first to break the silence, drawing the Marquis's attention back his way. "You doubt his word?"

The Marquis's eyes narrowed, his steps taking him to stand directly before the large-framed musketeer. "You would swear it to be true?"

Without hesitation, Isaac replied, "I swear often and would do so again if asked."

Rene winced, glancing at Olivier. Olivier simply nodded. Drawing attention off Isaac, Rene dropped to one knee and spoke up. "Your son is bold, but capable of doing what he says, my Lord. If you will permit him to take his ship and crew, and lend him a few men of the line, then we will guard his life with all the skill given to us."

The Marquis took a few steps back towards Rene, scowling down at him. "You would swear an oath before country and God that you will take my son's part, defend him with your lives, and serve his interests so long as this venture may last?"

"Before God and country," Rene replied, "If that is your will, then I will swear to it."

"Then he has at least one," the Marquis replied, turning back towards the other two. "What of you, then? I trust you are the others he spoke of?"

"Rene speaks for us as well," Olivier said.

"He swears so infrequently. I have to encourage the habit," Isaac agreed, drawing another stern look.

The Marquis fumed in silence a few moments, but finally gestured for Rene to rise. "Very well. My son has secured his own ship and crew with his own funds, he's secured loyal bodyguards, and he's agreed to finally consider an advantageous marriage upon his return." Still clearly not happy, but resigned, the Marquis turned at last to Treveur. "You will have your guardsmen and the time you asked for." A final glance was given to the trio at the center of the line of musketeers. "My son's life is in your hands. See that he returns in a condition to meet potential brides. The rest of you, back to training!" he called, turning on his heel without another word to his son.

As soon as he'd returned to the castle and closed the doors, the rest of the line scattered, and the trio circled Treveur. "I should have known you intended to cause us trouble," Rene scolded without any real venom to it.

"I intended to ask first," the Vicomte quickly responded. "I had little time. He backed himself into a corner in our discussion over dinner, and I had to strike while I had the opportunity. Isn't that what you taught me?" he asked, looking towards Olivier.

"We have not been teaching you to lie," Rene chided.

"Speak for yourself," Isaac muttered.

"All right, so I assumed what you would have said, given the chance," Treveur admitted. "But you backed me."

"Yes, but I did not lie," Rene answered. "But I will stand by my oath. Even so, I suggest you take more care with your words, especially when speaking for others. That is a dangerous path."

Isaac slapped Treveur on the back good-naturedly. "Yes, yes, Rene, he's heard this one before. How did it go – ah yes! Boy, lead us not into temptation. Rather, follow me. I know a shortcut."

Rene just sighed.

*

The Vicomte's airship, the *Wayward Falcon*, patrolled along the typical routes used by the sailing ships coming into or out of Finistère's docks, looking for signs of the Wind Talons, whether in the small bands of raiding ships they'd use to firebomb the sails of ships below before boarding and looting if the ships didn't surrender, or the lighter, faster scout vessels. In two weeks of patrols, they'd spotted a few different unidentified ships, but unfavorable winds and distance had conspired to prevent them from catching up with any of them before they escaped from Finistère's waters. When the shout went up that a light vessel had been spotted in pursuit range and hadn't appeared to have seen them yet, the *Falcon* exploded into action. Sails were adjusted, the captain changed to an intercept course, and rifles and muskets were readied.

*

"Captain Nathan, ship bearing down on us at 7 o'clock!" called the lookout in the crow's nest.

Nathan cursed and turned the wheel, trying to adjust to better catch the wind. "Wind Talon?" he called up.

"No, sir. Patrol, I'd think, but she looks too fast for their usuals!

Flying Finistère's flag, though!"

The cries on the smuggling ship *Doubting Thomas* roused the crew, and half a dozen men, one young woman and a middle-aged bear made their way onto the main deck with varying rates of haste.

"Dad, who's chasing us this time?" Dita asked, readying the brace of pistols at her belt for action.

"Finistère appears to have a new ship. Riflemen to the rear, see if you can discourage them. Dita, stay close to me."

"I can fight just fine, Dad," she snapped back as she headed for the rear of the ship with the rifles.

The bear tilted its head quizzically, rumbling in low tones as it regarded the captain.

"I know, Thomas, I know. More courage than sense," the captain agreed. "She takes after me, and I turned out fine, though."

The bear huffed.

"Well, fine. Say what you will, but do go to the side and discourage boarders, then," Nathan responded, gesturing to one side of the ship. The bear ambled off in the indicated direction.

There was an exchange of rifle fire first. The *Wayward Falcon* took its first battle scars in the form of shots tearing into its hull, while the *Doubting Thomas* took on a few more marks of personality, as its captain would say. Neither side took any injuries in the first exchange. Each side's few muskets took up positions, and another round of fire was exchanged while the rifles reloaded. First blood was scored on one of the *Thomas*'s muskets, the man staggering back with half a face full of splinters from the musket ball splitting the wood too near his face. The rest of the shots missed, or further marked the ships.

"Captain, they're still gaining!" called the lookout.

Nathan cursed again, calling the first mate to the wheel and heading towards the back of his ship. "Dita, light a torch! We just have to slow them a bit."

Dita cursed in an entirely unladylike manner, then tucked her unused pistol back into her belt and ran for the torches, returning at a run across the unsteady deck with a flickering flame going. Nathan kept low, trying to stay out of the way of any lucky shots as he prepared a bolt in his creaky old heavy crossbow. "Give her some cover, men! That flame'll draw attention!" he shouted as his adopted daughter approached. The rifles stood again, firing off quick shots to try to keep their opposite number pinned.

By now, the routine was well practiced. Though they'd had dozens of scrapes at various times, the smuggling ship was designed to be just durable enough to handle a few exchanges, slow any pursuit, and run out of reach. Though the crossbows had long since gone out of general fashion, the Captain continued to use his to cripple pursuers with the help of flaming bolts. Dita touched the torch to the treated head of the bolt on his string, and a greenish flame caught. The musketmen stood while the rifles dropped, buying a few seconds of cover before the flaming bolt arced high through the skies, plunging into one of the *Falcon*'s guidance sails in a shot few men could make at that distance.

*

Treveur raced to the front of his ship as one of his guidance sails caught fire. "Musketeers, to me!" he shouted. "Captain, keep us in pursuit for just a minute more, then drop and see to the sail!" he shouted. Some of the crew hesitated around him, but the captain kept to his orders, racing after the ship in front of them. Isaac and Olivier raced to catch up with their charge, Rene had been only a couple of steps behind Treveur already. "Get your grapnel guns ready! We're going to board them and force them down!" the Vicomte ordered in a shout that carried over the exchanges of fire.

"Vicomte, is that really wise?" Rene attempted. "It's just one ship, and one that I doubt we'll be seeing again anytime soon after the scare we put into them."

"One ship that likely knows the location of others, and my first catch. I'll not return home empty handed again," Treveur countered, getting his spring-loaded grapnel gun ready. "I'm going to board them. Try to keep up!" he called, firing off his grapnel, catching it amidst the rigging of the other ship.

With only a glance between themselves, the trio also fired similar devices, managing to catch on at various points about the other ship. Engaging the gears within the devices to begin retracting the lines,

Treveur and his bodyguards leapt off the ship, being pulled rapidly towards the *Doubting Thomas* by their boarding lines. Behind them, when they were away, the *Wayward Falcon* started losing altitude even as it lost speed, the crew going from combat mode to seeing to the damaged sail as they headed for the water.

Seeing the boarders coming, members of the *Thomas*'s crew raced to try to intercept. The first man to reach one of the lines got stabbed in the shoulder before he could finish cutting the line as Olivier pulled himself up over the side of the ship. Seeing his crewman fall not far off, Nathan discarded the crossbow and drew his old cavalry saber instead, engaging with the quiet musketeer.

"You're outnumbered, and I know my ship," Nathan warned, taking the first swipe.

The attack was turned aside, and the smuggler captain barely managed to deflect the riposte.

"I was going for surrender there, or at least a bit of banter. It's tradition," the Captain tried, going into a series of quick feints and slashes. His only answer was in the form of a counterattack. "Well, so much for tradition, I suppose."

Rene landed neatly on the deck, swinging across from where his hook had caught in the rigging. His sword was out quickly enough to disarm one man of his musket before he could turn and fire. A shot whizzed by his ear from another. Both of them, along with a third who thought better of firing in close quarters, drew blades, attempting to surround him. "Isaac!" he shouted. "I'll deal with this lot, the bear is all yours!"

Isaac caught onto a rope net, keeping himself from landing on the deck, then held on with one hand, drawing his blade with the other. A couple of gestures and swipes with the sword kept the bear from being too enthusiastic about trying to climb after him, but Thomas remained just below. "The bear, yes. If you insist, I'll just… keep it busy then," he agreed. Then, with a start, he climbed higher, with a few more aggressive thrusts of his blade to discourage pawing as Thomas demonstrated his own capable sea-air legs and stood up for better reach.

Treveur swung over onto the back of the ship, rolling into a somersault as he hit the deck, coming up with a blade drawn. He used the basket hilt to cuff one rifleman upside the head, then flicked the gun away from a second, sending the firearm tumbling over the side of the ship. Dita almost went for her gun, then drew her blade instead, avoiding firing into the melee. Her first attack was with the torch, swinging it in a wide arc, getting Treveur's attention off the crew, and using the flames as a distraction away from her fierce thrust. He only barely sidestepped her rapier, readying his own sword.

"I don't want to hurt you," he tried, shifting into a more defensive stance, clearly surprised to see a girl about his own age advancing on him.

"Funny thing to say when boarding someone's ship," she countered, alternating between arcs with the torch and precise sword thrusts, which he only barely managed to turn aside with his own blade, while avoiding the flame. "I do want to hurt you, so we'll both get what we want. Your lucky day."

*

"I must say, you're one of the best swordsmen I think I've ever faced," Nathan offered, retreating defensively, taking only the occasional rapid slash with his own blade.

Olivier said nothing, wasting no motion and keeping up a steady advance. He had not yet found an opening, but was steadily backing his opponent towards the railing.

"Unfortunately, I cheat," the captain added. "Hard to port!" he shouted. Accustomed to quick obedience during too many close encounters to count, the mate twisted the wheel hard. The ship lurched and jolted, sending Olivier stumbling. He caught his balance before hitting the deck, but soon found himself on the defensive and trying to maintain his defense while adjusting to the shifting deck and fighting an opponent far more used to the unsteady environment.

Rene drew a parrying dagger in his off hand, using it to turn weapons aside and guarding his flank while he kept two others busy with his own long, slender blade. With three opponents, and eventually a fourth, he was not able to advance without risking his back, nor put a great deal of force into his thrusts, but he'd so far frustrated the efforts of the smuggling crew to surround him or get within reach of their own shorter, but no less deadly, weapons. He'd managed to draw blood a couple of times, but only in shallow scratches which did nothing to dissuade the four of them. When the ship lurched, he went staggering back. Almost tumbling over the railing, he managed to catch his boot between two of the rails, then found it stuck there, trapped fighting on one foot, mostly immobile, with four seasoned smugglers closing around him.

"Don't you have things to go and do in the woods?" Isaac asked, taking another couple of swipes while trying to find handholds and footing to keep ascending.

Thomas bellowed, taking another swipe, with Isaac pulling his foot up and out of the way just in time to avoid the wicked claws.

Isaac's fencing saber snapped downward, whipping across the back of the big paw swinging at him, doing little other than further annoying the bear. Isaac managed to climb a couple more feet before the ship lurched. He lost his footholds, but managed to hang on with one hand, leaving him swinging free, dangling just inches out of the bear's reach. "I'm almost positive this could be worse."

Thomas roared and lunged again, keeping his own balance like a seasoned sailor as his swipe narrowly fell short once again.

*

Treveur's head pulled back, feeling the heat of the torch as it narrowly missed his head, briefly blinding him. Instinct and practice saved him as he side-stepped, guessing on where the follow-up thrust would come. "Where did you learn to fight like that?" he asked as Dita's blade swiped close enough to snap one of the buttons off the front of his shirt as he turned.

"My father taught me," Dita replied cheerily, on seeing the results of the near miss. "Hope it meets with your approval, soldier boy," she added, following up on her swipe with a lunge.

"You're marvelous," he agreed, turning her blade aside, stepping into her and sending her staggering back with an elbow, nearly buying him time to set his feet again. Normally, the pitching of the ship would have been little difficulty for Dita, but already thrown off balance one way, the roll of the ship sent her tumbling the other way. The torch went flying from her hand as she clawed at thin air, trying to find something for balance. The lit torch hit the deck and went rolling across it with the tilt of the deck, while Dita's hand found Treveur's shirt, tearing it further a moment before she crashed into him and both went sprawling to the deck.

*

Olivier side-stepped a lunge, finding his footing enough to launch a counter-attack of his own. Nathan got his guard up in time to defend, though he found himself losing ground again. Then the ship pitched again, if not as severely, and the old smuggler found himself with the advantage again. The edge shifted back and forth between the two veterans, Olivier proving the superior swordsman each time the ship was sailing at all smoothly, while Nathan's footwork helped him each time the steering got rough. With the back and forth, the battle ranged up and down the decks, turning and shifting. Nathan tried some few times to engage his opponent in wordplay, but each time, was met only with the same focused gaze, and, more often than not, a concentrated counter-assault.

"Oh ho!" Isaac called. "Rene, catch!" he shouted. He tossed his blade upward, then caught the rope netting with both hands. He built up a bit of a swing, each time pulling his legs up out of the way of swipes, then launched himself, letting go of the ropes. He landed in a tumbling somersault, coming back up with the rolling torch in hand, sweeping it up off the deck. Thomas came at him at first, then shied away from a lunge with the torch.

Rene pitched his parrying knife downward, burying it through the foot of one of the crewmen, and caught Isaac's sword out of the air. With the two longer blades, and one opponent now screaming and pinned, he managed to fight them back long enough to twist his foot free and regain his stance. He smashed the basket hilt into the side of the head of the screamer, dropping him to the deck, and leaving himself engaged with only three.

*

Dita and the Vicomte untangled themselves hastily, with a bit more shoving, elbowing, and disheveled clothing. By the time each found their way to their knees, their swords were clashing again. He turned her blade aside, forgoing a riposte with no weight behind it to push to his feet instead. "You're under arrest for piracy. There's only one way this can go," he warned.

Dita pushed herself back up and got into her fencing stance once more, recovering from the deflection, and launching another series of testing thrusts and feints, trying to find a weakness in his defenses. "Piracy? I suppose next you're going to accuse me of, I don't know, pickpocketing? How about smuggling coal? Oh, I know, how about public drunkenness and disorderly behavior?"

He raised a brow, turning aside her attacks, though they came fast enough that he couldn't find an opening to launch his own. "Maybe," he agreed, a grin crossing his features.

"Okay, okay, so maybe those others have something to them. We're not pirates though. You'll find the hold full of coal and clockworks, not plundered anything."

"You honestly expect me to believe you're not a scout craft for the Wind Talons?"

She spat. "The Wind Talons are no kinder to us. We had to dump cargo just this week to outrun the bastards." With that bout of anger, she lunged, putting more force behind the attack.

He locked blades with her, the two pressing in close. "I imagine you have some way to prove that?" he asked, grinning still.

His gaze met her unnaturally blue eyes, and the pressure on the locked blades eased as her glare faded. "I may," she replied.

*

The ship rocked again with further dramatic alterations, trying to advantage the sailors over the soldiers. Olivier stumbled backwards, catching himself against the mast, and readying to deflect the captain's next blow. Nearby, Isaac fended off the bear, which kept a cautious distance from the torch, but never turned away or stopped trying to find an opening to swipe at the big man. Rene was slowly gaining an edge on his attackers, but each time he thought he had an opening to move to fight back-to-back with his fellows and get away from the rails, the ship shifted, and he found himself pressed anew.

"Daddy! Stop!" came Dita's shout, before Nathan's next blow could come. The cry drew curious glances from all about, smugglers and musketeers alike, as Dita and Treveur came racing towards the rest of the battle.

"Stop? I was just about to finish off this one. We had this fight," Nathan said, as he considered his daughter.

"The only thing you have, sir," Isaac ventured, "is a tenuous grasp on reality. We had the superior position, and superior swordsmen besides."

"I rather liked the position I had," Nathan countered, "and I still have a bear."

"An excellent point," Isaac conceded, glancing at Thomas.

"I've been known to have those. Few people argue with the bit about the bear," Nathan agreed.

"Olivier, can we trade opponents next time? I'll deal with the witty banter, and you admire the wildlife up close?" Isaac tried.

Olivier and Nathan were both about to respond when Dita interrupted. "Dad! Seriously, they're not after us. We have some injuries, but no one hurt badly. Let's settle this and keep it that way."

"They certainly appeared to be after us," Nathan countered.

"My commission is dealing with the Wind Talons. Not chasing down every smuggler running clockworks across the channel. Especially smugglers who have been sneaking Leonard's political prisoners out of Scilly. She says if we hit the right ports, she can prove it. That, and she says you might be able to put us on the right track in finding the pirates."

"That's a mouthful of things to say," Nathan said, looking to Dita.

She shrugged and nodded. "Sorry, Dad. It's true though."

"Telling people the truth. I didn't raise you like that," Nathan groused at her. "You're going to make me sound like an honest man, or something like it."

Treveur interrupted. "So, once we get some verification of all of this, can you point us towards the Wind Talons? I'm sure we can come to an arrangement, starting with letting you go."

Nathan mused a few more seconds, still seeming discomfited by suggestions of too much honesty. "I'm sure we can come to an arrangement, but not the one you're thinking."

"How's that?" asked the Vicomte, as his musketeers closed ranks, in case.

"I'm not just going to point you in the right direction; I'm going to help you hunt them down, one by one," the Captain stated.

"And why would you do that?"

"It's easy: they're as happy to chase us about and steal our cargo as anyone else's. You have a vessel of war, a handful of guards, and some of the best swords I've ever seen. I have a ship that they know well enough to chase, but can stay ahead of them, and a head for dirty tricks like ambushes. And the Wind Talons? Well, they have ships full of treasure. I'm thinking the arrangement involves what you can take home to prove their end, and I'll have enough to retire myself and my crew. That a suitable kind of arrangement for working together?"

"It would sound good, except that I don't trust you," Treveur ventured, still clearly considering it.

Before her father could get a word in edgewise, Dita jumped in, looking Treveur in the eyes again. "Then trust me. On my honor, we'll help you."

Nathan sighed, reaching over to scratch between Thomas's ears. "Stopping perfectly good fights. Truths. Now promises and honor. Where did I go wrong with that girl?"

★

The crew of the *Wayward Falcon* were not at all certain about trusting the smugglers. Nevertheless, at the Vicomte's word, they allowed the other ship to lead them to St. Pol, with its active markets and regular influx of a wide range of people. In turn, the crew of the *Doubting Thomas*, some of them still limping once they regained consciousness, were not at all certain about trusting the young nobleman-of-some-sort and his musketeers, especially enough to take them to a port secretly defiant of the Marquis's blockades. Nevertheless, on Dita's word, they led the way.

The airships were moored for repairs, with a bit extra paid for no-questions-asked service, and then Treveur went into town with Nathan, the Vicomte trailed by his bodyguards, while Nathan brought along only Dita, leaving the first mate to look after the ship, with strict instructions to run any serious decisions through Thomas. The two groups maintained some bit of distance from one another, "for respectability's sake," Nathan said, though Treveur was uncertain of who were supposed to be the respectable ones in the captain's reference.

As they walked through the streets of the port and market town, Treveur was startled to notice just how much of a wide berth he and his men were given, while nearly everyone seemed to know Nathan. Most even liked him – in between a few requests for money owed and assurances that it would be coming soon. When they had reached the main market, Nathan convinced a few people that the Vicomte would bring them no trouble, and gained some validation for his story.

"You see, son," he explained, while walking away from the third such witness, "Once upon a time, I was just in specialty goods. I carried some hard to get items for specific individuals, such as Dita's aunt."

Treveur smirked at being called 'son'. "So, you're claiming no harm done, then?"

Nathan grinned. "Oh no. I was a terrible person. I stole; I smuggled; I ignored the taxes; I fought unsanctioned duels; I slept with other people's wives. The list goes on."

Isaac held up a hand and opened his mouth, before Rene gave him a sidelong glare that shut him up for the time being, while Nathan continued.

"But I have never been a pirate, or a killer. A criminal, yes. When Dita came into my life, I just tried to be a better class of criminal," he added, drawing a small grin from Dita. "I never intended to be quite so popular. That was all the fault of the conflict between the Earl and the Marquis."

"The Earl I understand," Treveur agreed readily. "But what does the Marquis have to do with anything? He's just defending his territory."

"Just defending his territory?" Nathan replied with a derisive snort. "Ever since his wife died, he's been locking this land down. He's tripled the guard, posted way stations everywhere. Then he supported those with new taxes, and letting the way stations start charging tolls. He knows a lot of people have no choice but to do business here. Too many ports, too convenient for trade with England, and too many farmers here not to, so he's been bleeding it for everything it's worth. Even at your age, you'd think you'd have noticed. He hasn't exactly been kind to the nobles under him, either."

Treveur paused a moment, a few different thoughts racing through his mind. A glance around confirmed that he and his musketeers were still drawing a majority of worried looks. He was hard pressed to deny that his father might be paranoid, based on his own upbringing. "All right, so maybe there's something to that," he muttered reluctantly.

"Now, I still move some of my old goods, but I, and a number of folks like me, move a lot of this market's food, fuel, and other necessities, without it having to get through three toll stations and a city post, or across the water, getting past the Earl's so-called privateers."

"Admitting to being a criminal, and claiming to be a hero at the same time?" Treveur ventured.

"I've never claimed to be a hero. I make a decent living off the merchants who'd rather just let me fleece them once, and risk my ship, instead of being taxed four or five times and risking theirs. I just don't turn down the free drinks or other people calling me whatever they like."

Treveur glanced aside to his musketeers, settling on addressing Olivier. "This is one town, likely hit by pirates enough to be paranoid, or to host a few smugglers now and then. Is it like this everywhere?"

Olivier frowned. "Does it look like it's pirates they're afraid of?"

"So my..." Treveur began, before catching himself. "So Paul's paranoia really does extend beyond his castle," he mused aloud.

"Took you that long?" Nathan asked, "Just where is it that you're from that you hadn't seen it yet?"

"A very quiet corner of Finistère," Treveur answered, going quiet for some time until they approached the ships. "You still intending to play bait for pirates?"

Nathan considered him a few moments before replying, "Depends on if you're willing to pay for it."

*

The two ships hunted up and down the coast for months, using Nathan's maps and knowledge of the usual routes of the Wind Talons, at first luring them out and then pinning the pirates between two ships. When they grew wise to the tactic, Treveur, Olivier, Nathan, and Dita consulted, finding new tactics to hunt down the pirates, or goad them into confrontation. Treveur kept his word, allowing the smugglers their cut, while turning down any more than was required to pay his crew and see to the injured. The rest was set aside, and used in each town the pair of ships settled in to try to begin paying back those who had been victimized by the pirates. Dita called it thoughtful. Treveur, though he may have blushed slightly, called it honorable. Nathan called it practical, since people would be less wary around the musketeers and more informative.

When the Wind Talons gathered forces to strike back, the information did travel. When Treveur burst into the Captain's cabin on the *Doubting Thomas* to announce the news, he found Dita asleep at the desk, clutching a music box. A dancing figure whirled across the metal surface, and the song was the warmest and most beautiful he'd ever heard. That music stopped as Dita's hand shifted from the music box to the hilt of her sword. She wearily lifted her head. "Oh. Treveur. So we're not being boarded?"

"Not yet, but we'll be at risk of it soon," he said cheerily. "Beautiful, by the way."

"What is?"

"Well, a lot of things, honestly, but I was specifically referring to the music box."

She nodded. "It was my mother's. All I have of her, song after song."

"I've missed mine, too. Wondered how things could have been different."

She nodded again, understanding. "…And it only plays for me. It's nice to feel special."

"You should. I mean, it's been wonderful working with you, and… you should."

"…Thank you, Treveur." She paused a moment, then, "We should probably do something with that 'risk of being boarded' thing."

"Oh yes."

In the face of the attack, it was Treveur's turn to repay earlier favors with his own knowledge, and the pair led the pirates' main force on a chase that ended in the teeth of his father's more regular patrols.

Both ships set in for repairs, having the wounded tended, and a celebratory drink, managing to limp back to St. Pol before settling. Though Treveur had been asked back to the castle, he'd refused, insisting he still had a few things to tend to.

Settling in at his table, the Vicomte ordered a round for the house, putting the place in a more festive mood immediately. "And everyone at this table eats and drinks on me; I insist."

"I'm surprised, but not one to turn down a free meal," Nathan commented, immediately ordering the most expensive wine available. "There's still a few of them out there, but I think the Talons are broken. The Earl will hear soon enough. No telling what he'll do."

"What can he do?" Treveur asked. "He can't acknowledge he was paying them off; the Crown won't support a war. Our patrols may be weakened, but we still have enough ships to defend ourselves with."

"Just because there's nothing sane he can do doesn't mean there's nothing he can do," Dita responded. "Never discount the risk of nobility doing something insane. Sometimes it even works."

Treveur grinned, "In truth, I'm counting on it," he replied. A quick downing of his drink for courage, and he dropped to a knee. "Seeing as you're both here, I'll ask the both of you at once. Sir, I'd like permission to seek your daughter's hand in marriage. Dita, will you marry me, provided your father doesn't run me through in the next five seconds?"

Nathan's face went through several expressions at once, then settled on something resolute. He addressed Dita. "Before you make your decision, we're talking to your aunt."

Treveur blinked. "And where, sir, is your sister?"

"She's not my sister."

"Where is your wife's sister?"

"Never been married."

"You're not being very helpful here, sir."

"Boy, I haven't lied to you, much to my surprise, but I'm not as forthright as my little girl. Of course, neither are you."

"What?"

"France is crawling with vicomtes. Finistère has plenty of Treveurs. But all these months I've never heard: Treveur, Vicomte de What? So excuse me if there's a lady who really needs to know that my little girl is thinking about marriage, and I don't give you her life story."

Dita stood up at that, looking daggers at her father. "What does my aunt have to do with any of this? Shouldn't it be my decision whom I marry?"

"Eventually, yes," he conceded. "But wouldn't you like to at least know who you're marrying?"

"I didn't say I was going to say yes. Just that I should be the one who says yes or no, on my own terms." She paused, looking to Treveur. "So?"

"So?" he asked, still glancing back and forth from one to the other, remaining on one knee. By now, most of the tavern was looking their way.

"So, who are you?" she urged.

Treveur paused, wishing he had another drink in easy reach. "Not the same person I was when I set out only a few months past," he answered at last, voice raising a bit. "I suspect your father has guessed though, Dita. I'm the son of the Marquis."

"So, the son of the same Marquis who has been overtaxing the people to support his paranoia?"

"You could look at it that way, or you could look at it as the Vicomte who bought and armed his own airship and went pirate hunting."

"Your father has been pirate hunting for almost two decades," she responded. Her father started to interject, but Isaac tapped him on the shoulder, then shook his head. The two elected to have another drink instead, while watching the teenagers talk.

"My father has been guarding against them and protecting his nation's merchantmen, not the same. He wasn't willing to risk giving chase into Scilly waters. He wasn't willing to risk a wrong move. Most importantly, he didn't have the help of the most beautiful smuggler in France. These things make all the difference."

Dita opened her mouth to respond, then the words caught up with her, and she blushed. As she was finding her tongue, Isaac leaned in to offer, quietly, to Nathan, "A good line. I may need to borrow that one. Maybe he's learned something useful after all."

Dita shifted her attention just long enough to glare, and both the musketeer and her father grew very interested in their beer again, for at least a few moments. She turned back to look down at Treveur. "Won't your father have a problem with your marrying beneath your station? Marriage is an important thing, after all. Some people can afford to marry for love. Nobles are rarely among them."

Treveur stood, and offered her his hand. "Marriage cements alliances, it's true. And my father broke faith with the people who were his first responsibility. If I just so happen to also love a heroine of the people, and can begin to heal some of the wounds eighteen years in the making, then so be it. I've challenged my father's wishes already, I'll do it again. Dita, will you marry me?"

"About that 'beneath your station' thing, I really do think we should go have a conversation with Dita's aunt," Nathan finally added, before his daughter could respond.

Treveur lost a bit of his composure at that, glancing to Nathan. "Sir, I didn't mean to imply that – "

Nathan's sigh cut him off. "Not that," he insisted. "There are some things that shouldn't be first heard or said in a tavern full of people. Her aunt gave Dita to me as a baby – essentially – and that's family enough, but there's also matters of blood – blood, and that voice in the music box. Dita's bloodlines, the secrets her aunt wanted kept, will cause a lot of complications."

Dita looked from Treveur to her father, blue eyes tearing up a little. "And you've never cared for complications, right, Dad?"

Nathan started to speak, hesitated a moment, then answered after the short consideration. "Until now, true. You, however, are worth it.

Say yes, if you wish, my dearest. We'll have a proper French engagement dinner, and your aunt can explain all the other things then. You have my blessing, and damn the Marquis if need be."

Dita's eyes teared up more, but her expression changed. She hugged her father tight. "Thank you, Daddy," she said, before turning back to Treveur. "Of course I'll marry you, as long as you don't expect me to take up needlework and play the prim and proper lady of the court."

"Olivier," Treveur began. "Remind me, what time does blade training begin?"

"Promptly at six, two hours before breakfast," came the answer.

"Will that do, instead of needlework?" he asked her. "I can't imagine a better sparring partner. These others are good, but I suspect they'll keep going easy on me. I have this feeling you never will."

"Count on it," she answered, taking his hand.

*

"Now what is this about an engagement dinner?" Rene began, once they had returned to the ship to set out for the meeting with Dita's aunt.

"I've asked Dita to marry me, and intend to stand by that."

"Part of your agreement with your father was that you would consider marriage arrangements when you finished your hunt," the musketeer pointed out, the other two listening in nearby.

"I've considered them very carefully. I think this would be a fine arrangement."

"I think your father would take issue with that. He'd prefer to secure some new trading partner or military alliance, or at least a reasonable dowry."

"What my father has preferred has lost him the faith of his own land and people."

"You're certain that you're truly thinking of the land, and not simply what you want?"

"Should he not?" Isaac interjected. "The boy has done his nation a service, and he's done as his father asked all his life, other than insisting on hanging about with a bunch of scruffy swordsmen. He deserves to think of himself a bit. Besides, you've seen the girl. I'm not sure there is any better he could do."

"There is none better," the Vicomte agreed. "For me, or for the nation. I will trust that the defeat of the Wind Talons will gain us some goodwill amongst our neighbors, Scilly aside. Our first loyalty should still be to our own people."

Rene glanced aside at Isaac for a few moments, then looked back to Treveur. "You truly believe that, don't you?"

"Have you ever known me to be weak in my convictions, my friend? You three have gotten to know me better than anyone, including my own father."

The three exchanged glances, drawing a quizzical look from Treveur in turn, before Rene finally responded. "I never have, no. Those convictions seem equally determined this time."

"They are, but now I see your dilemma. We're friends, but you were sent to serve my father. He was the one who charged you to watch me. I'm sorry I've placed you in this situation."

"Duty places us in this situation," Olivier corrected.

"Be that as it may, I've asked a great deal of you already. I won't ask you to defy my father's command."

"There's always the option," Isaac ventured, "of simply not telling him until the engagement is recognized. Even your father would be hard pressed to ignore the church once they've spoken."

"This venture began with deception," Rene countered. "You claim you've changed, and there is no shame in your actions. Show it, and let your strength of character speak for itself against your father."

"I've noticed that strength of character often accompanies other fine qualities, such as courage and perseverance, when referring to the one being carted away at the end of many a duel," Isaac responded calmly. "And besides, she is a smuggler. You've gotten this far learning the way they do things, maybe there's something to be said for being discreet just a little longer."

"She was a smuggler. Currently, she's the leading candidate to become the future Marquise de Finistère. If you want something better for her, set a good example," Rene recommended.

"As soon as we land, I will prepare a letter for my father inviting him to attend the engagement dinner," Treveur decided aloud. "I am not ashamed of my bride-to-be." A deep breath, and he regarded each of the trio in the room with him one after another. "Though we are friends, I must do my duty. I promise I will think no less of you for doing the same should any question arise. I release you from any bonds of friendship or anything else that might compel you to follow my orders before my father's."

Another exchanged glance, and Olivier broke the silence. "Your father has not issued any contrary orders yet. I'd still guess he won't be happy, but for right now, an educated guess is all it is. Regardless, be assured, I'll honor your wishes and follow your father's orders before yours."

"Thank you," Treveur answered, pausing before adding, "I think."

*

The two crews met again at the site for the engagement dinner, but some time in advance. Nathan wouldn't speak much of his insistence on getting Dita's aunt's counsel before matters proceeded, but it was clearly important to him. They managed a quiet meeting late at night, the woman entering the nearly empty tavern in a hooded cloak. "I got your message and came as quickly as I was able to find excuse to leave for a few days. What was so urgent that you couldn't even hint at it in a letter, Nathan?"

"I think you'll forgive me quickly enough," Nathan responded, pushing a chair out for her with one foot. "Dita has some news."

"Who are these others?" Lamorna asked, cautiously. "The disguises are good, but they still have the bearing of military men. They're with you?"

"Allies who've proven themselves," Nathan assured. "Don't take my word for it though. Thomas likes them."

"I've never known him to be anything but the best judge of character," the woman agreed, settling in at the table with a small nod towards Treveur and his accompaniment. Her gaze shifted back to Dita. "News?"

"I'm to be married," Dita responded cheerfully, keeping her voice soft enough to not draw any added attention. They had to pause, briefly, while Lamorna ordered a drink, then let the barmaid get out of hearing range before they continued.

"To this one?" Lamorna asked, gesturing towards Treveur.

"To that one," Dita agreed with some amusement.

Lamorna didn't respond right away, instead glancing from Dita to Nathan. The smuggler captain responded to the glance by saying, "He's who you think he is. The Marquis de Finistère's boy."

"Why would she be expecting that?" Treveur responded.

"Prophecy," Lamorna started. "That, and I can't have my niece marrying below her station, given all she has to do yet."

Dita laughed. "He's the future Marquis de Finistère. I'm a smuggler. I think I'm safe as far as marrying up, there."

"Do you have your music box?" Lamorna asked, ignoring the comment.

Dita hesitated, but dug through her pack until she produced the carefully wrapped music box, starting to unwrap it when her aunt indicated she should do so. As she touched the metal surface, the lid opened, revealing the tiny, graceful little dancer, while soft music filled their corner of the tavern for a few moments before she set it down. "I try to always keep it close at hand, like you'd asked," Dita replied.

"Good girl. That's the voice of Countess Eirwyn, Leonard's wife, and my cousin," Lamorna said, receiving surprised glances from all but Nathan, who clearly knew, and Olivier, who simply continued to look impassive.

Dita recovered first, looking to Lamorna, then Nathan. "Dad, why didn't you…"

"Why didn't I tell you?" he asked. "Because your father's bruiser left you out in the open to die. Your aunt contacted me to get you out of there and see to it you had a good home, but she also made me promise not to say anything."

"Blame me," Lamorna agreed. "Your birth father wanted you dead, but wouldn't do it by his own hand. Brave as you are, if you'd have known, you'd have tried to get in there, or might try to confront your birth father."

"I wouldn't!" Dita snapped back, then blushed. "Okay, okay. So maybe I would have. But I wouldn't have gotten caught. You should have said something."

"I'll just have to earn your forgiveness," Lamorna replied. "There was also a matter of prophecy involved. I couldn't risk interfering with the hand of fate, when I'd already done so much. Some things had to happen on their own."

"That's the second time you've mentioned a prophecy," Treveur noted, stepping back into the conversation. "What prophecy? If we're suddenly fate's toys, we should at least know the game."

"Dita was to be Leonard's only heir. He'll never have another," Lamorna explained. "And this rivalry between his land and Paul's would weaken them both, but the first of either nation to offer their hand would strengthen both."

Now it was Treveur and Dita's turn to exchange glances. "So when I asked her to marry me?"

"You set things into motion," Lamorna agreed. "And you have not only your own strength, but your own men, your own resources. I'd heard rumors that the Marquis's son was hunting pirates. Believe me, Leonard is not happy about it at all."

"That may be," Dita added. "But Leonard still has a lot more men, between his guards and mercenaries, than Treveur has."

"Indeed, but if you are married to the Vicomte de Finistère, he will have to acknowledge you, as long as you have that music box. The news will force an end to the hostilities, or the Crown will."

"I know that the box has my mother's voice, but…" Dita hesitated.

"Your mother's voice is unforgettable – that is not an expression – and that music box works only for you. Along with my word, there are influential people who will believe. We just needed to see that you were properly protected first, along with letting the prophecy play out. I'm not saying whatever comes next will be easy, but all of this is meant to be. The cold war is coming to an end, and you two, and your marriage, will be instrumental in its finish, and both nations' recovery."

"That may resolve some of the issues surrounding Leonard, but my father remains a problem," Treveur told Lamorna.

She glanced back to Nathan, who just nodded a small affirmation. "So Paul hasn't approved of this wedding then, I take it?"

"He hasn't specifically disapproved," Treveur replied. "But the opinion in most quarters is that he's unlikely to see it as good news."

"Perhaps he'll take it as having something to hold over his rival, or will find some other reason to celebrate the choice."

"Or perhaps the next couple of days are going to be really interesting," Nathan muttered.

*

The day of the dinner arrived, with Nathan surprising everyone with his degree of generosity. Though Treveur contributed, it was the now-wealthy smuggler who made particularly certain that the affair would be an event to be remembered. Though the local nobility was invited, the organizers insisted that no one who made the trip would be refused. By two hours before the event, hundreds of tables had been borrowed from local taverns and large families to seat everyone, most of them set up outside in the courtyard and streets outside the hall to try to accommodate the massive crowd. The town contributed, bringing more food. Musicians and entertainers of all stripes had filtered into the town in the days before, filling the taverns, the great hall and the streets with music, dance, juggling, tumbling and more.

"Still no sign of your father?" Rene asked, as Treveur was waiting in the wings, about to go and join his bride-to-be at the front of the hall for the official announcement.

"None," Treveur responded. "Not even a messenger."

"Odd. No word for us, either."

"Then I hope until you hear something, the three of you will continue to attend me while we make the announcement?"

"Are you certain that's the best idea?"

"I'd have no others. You're not only the best bodyguards I could ask for, but my best friends. I wouldn't be here without you."

"True," Rene agreed with a small smile. "We should proceed then. Just had to make certain you weren't having any second thoughts on any of this."

The Vicomte answered as he began walking towards the raised dais at the front of the hall, followed by his trio of bodyguards. "My course is finally clear, I've never been more certain of the proper way forward."

*

Dita began down the aisle once Treveur had made his way up. Everyone who had crowded in for a good look at the Vicomte backed off as much as possible to give Thomas plenty of room as he lumbered down the aisle, followed closely by Nathan, with his daughter on his arm. Not the wedding procession yet, but he'd still dressed for the occasion and took to the spotlight naturally, even if he was now, proudly, sharing it.

"Prophecy or not, if you have any second thoughts…" he began.

"No second thoughts," she responded.

"You're going to miss smuggling," he suggested.

"Given that we're planning on continuing the patrols and leading from the front, I'm actually kind of looking forward to doing the chasing instead of being chased."

"I'm glad to hear there'll be no quiet little hall and staid diplomacy for you. Still, you have to admit that you're going to miss your old life, just a little."

"I'll miss Thomas," she teased. "I'd hoped that the two of you might take a commission though. Head of the scouts, or maybe making runs as a real merchant – in your old age, and all."

Thomas huffed, sounding almost amused, while Nathan smirked. "That sounds dangerously respectable. I'll have to consider it though. I'd hate to have the Marquise herself chasing after me."

"You mean have the Marquise herself catch and arrest you?"

"Respectability or a challenge like that? Are you trying to push me back into my criminal ways?"

"We'll find you a really stylish uniform," she suggested. "And bribe Thomas with fresh fruit to ensure that he breaks the tie in my favor."

"You play dirty."

"I learned from the best," Dita answered, before ascending up the dais steps.

*

Lamorna stepped up with them, accepting the wrapped music box from Dita, starting to unwrap it while the couple took center stage. He took one of her hands in his, and both turned towards the hall as it went quiet. Before Treveur could begin to speak, however, a great commotion arose from the front of the hall. A few shots were fired, then the screaming began. Confusion reigned, people running, trying to find the exits or space to duck under tables until the source of the noise was made apparent. Nathan, the musketeers, and the young couple all drew blades, while Thomas nudged Lamorna behind his bulk as he stepped forward.

The Marquis entered the hall, flanked and followed by row upon row of armed guardsmen and a handful of musketeers. "There will be an end to this charade!" Paul shouted over the screams and din of the chaos. "Treveur, you'll come home with me this instant and leave this – this criminal wench behind. Out of respect, if you come quietly, I won't even have her arrested on the spot."

"You're not going to arrest my bride, and I'm not coming with you. At least not without her."

"You don't have a choice, young man. I've indulged your fantasies of being a soldier long enough. Now you're going to do your duty, and come home to find a proper marriage and learn to rule."

"I've learned enough. Your own people are terrified of your soldiers. Your taxes are killing the trade that funds us. Scilly's privateers are broken; we don't need this. Besides, this marriage is advantageous; she's…"

He was cut off, as Paul urged his guardsmen forward. "You were warned, and you'll do as you were told!" He glanced to the three fancily dressed musketeers sharing the dais. "I don't know what madness possessed you to go along with this, but it's time for an end to the games. Secure my son, and arrest these others!" he ordered.

The three exchanged glances, then Rene stepped forward. "I am afraid we cannot do that, Sir," he responded, much to Treveur's surprise, but none of Olivier or Isaac's.

"You would disobey my orders in favor of my son's?" Paul snapped, face going red with rage.

Rene remained calm, leveling his blade at the advancing guardsmen. "No, Sir. But when we were given this assignment, you made us swear an oath – to not only France, but God – to take your son's part and defend his interests. I have asked after even the slightest hesitation, in the face of doubt, in the face of threat, in the face of betrayal, and he has remained resolute. I will do the same without question or fear. My conscience is clear, Sir, for while I hold my service in high esteem, what is a mere Marquis before God?"

Olivier's eyes narrowed, staring at the Marquis as he stepped forward with Rene. "Rene speaks for me as well."

Isaac stepped forward last to flank Olivier's other side. "Rene does not speak for me, thankfully. I dread what would happen if I let him start putting words in my mouth. On the other hand, I revel in the opportunity to be contrary. I'm afraid, Sir, if you want them, you must come through us."

Rene sighed at his fellow, then shifted his full focus back to the Marquis, as some of the guards were hesitating at the new show of force. "I beg you to consider talking, Sir. I'd rather not shed unnecessary blood, but our loyalties are clear."

Angrier still at this new challenge, the Marquis bellowed to his men. "Forward, arrest them all!" he demanded, ending the uncertainty of most of them, though some few of the musketeers remained back, hesitating in their loyalties, or at least not wishing to have to be the first to face their compatriots.

Thomas reared up, some of the first wave of guardsmen backing away at the change in the formerly sedate bear.

Lamorna grabbed Dita and Treveur's shoulders. "To the *Falcon*!" she shouted, tugging on them. "We can't win this fight, but we have the faster ship."

Treveur and Dita shouted orders to their respective companies, and more than a few of the men from their ships and some of the armed commoners and city guard joined in their defense as the chaos in the hall gave way to a running battle, Thomas smashing through a bank of windows to provide an exit on the run for the engagement party.

Nathan scrambled ahead, giving up on helping with the fighting in order to lead the preparation of the ship and to take the wheel. The party backed up the ramp of the ship in pairs, fighting off Paul's guards, with Treveur and Dita fighting side by side and occasionally back to back as the tide of battle whirled around them, taking turns defending and attacking to drive the Marquis's forces back, until they made it up the ramp.

Thomas barreled up the ramp as the last of the group, his bulk knocking would-be boarders off the ramp in bunches, while the musketeers, once aboard, switched to their firearms, joining the rest of the ship's defenders in providing covering fire until the bear was aboard. They managed to get to the cover of the ship before Paul convinced his men to fire on the ship, none having been willing, previously, to risk injuring the Vicomte, or to fire into a melee that included Paul's own men. By the time the first shots ripped into the wood, the *Wayward Falcon* was lifting into the skies.

"Follow them! Don't let them escape!" Paul roared, racing for his own airship and sending men scattering in all directions to man, or seize, every airship in the port to pursue the Vicomte and his company.

"Well, that could have gone better," Nathan fumed, once they got out of rifle range.

"It could have gone worse," Lamorna responded.

"Worse? Well, I suppose we do have a head start, and a fast ship. Not my fast ship, mind you, but it's something. We can probably hit one of the rogue ports when we lose them and disappear."

"We don't want to do that," Lamorna corrected. "Slow down, and I'll give you your heading."

"Slow down?" he asked, incredulous. "What kind of getaway is this? We've been friends a long time, and I trust you, but that's..."

"That is precisely what needs to be done. There's a plan."

"All right, but next time, care to let the person commanding the ship in on the plan?"

Lamorna smiled, at last. "I let Thomas know; he'll be sure to inform the pilot of any details he feels are relevant."

"Very funny," the Captain replied, though the tone was muted by his own efforts not to grin.

"I was trying to be funny?" she replied, managing a pretty good impression of mock-innocence.

"I knew there was a reason we'd stayed friends this long. Where are we headed, anyway?"

"Scilly."

"I am seriously considering revoking that friendship now."

"We have an invasion force behind us who aren't going to risk turning back and losing the Marquis's only heir. Just don't lose them, and we'll be fine."

"You have a very strange definition of fine."

*

The *Wayward Falcon* led the chase, staying out of firing range, but just at the edge of spyglass vision of the pursuers. Nathan had to fight his instincts a number of times and slow back down, but apparently the bait of having Treveur aboard – and intending to marry the smuggler girl – was enough to keep the Marquis's forces in pursuit.

The real trouble came when they came into visual range of Scilly's capital. "Three ships approaching!" called the lookout.

Nathan got the coordinates, spinning the wheel and trying to adjust course. "Hold on, folks, this is going to be a rough ride!" he shouted as those not manning the ropes or adjusting the sails scrambled to combat stations.

The approaching ships from Scilly were cautious at first, moving to cut them off, but reacting as if they expected the incoming ship to turn about at any moment. Nathan turned and adjusted again, trying to guess at their speed and positioning and shoot the gap between the two largest ships.

"Don't fire a shot!" Nathan called. "Don't keep any extra attention – we'll have less of it when they see the fleet approaching! We just need all the speed we can get!"

The confusion bought them some time, but eventually Scilly's ships opened fire, musket balls tearing into the sides and sails of the *Wayward Falcon*. Shouts and warnings drew some of the crew from combat stations to help fight damaged sails and keep them on course. A couple of men fell, either shot, or riddled with splintered wood from the hail of shots. Despite the chaos and danger, Nathan held to his course, fighting to keep the wheel under his control as the sails, rendered uneven by the damage, fought to yank the wheel about and set the ship to spinning. The struggle grew worse as one of the ships tried too hard to cut them off, and ended up colliding with the side of the *Falcon*, partially turning it and tearing away one of the minor guide sails and some of the rigging. The other ship spun out of control, tilting enough to dump some of its men overboard and threatening to crash into one of the other ships.

Nathan fought the craft back under control, new damage constantly adding to the difficulty as Scilly's gunfire raked the sides and then the rear of the *Falcon*. It wasn't long before enough gunfire scored the balloon and the steam engines to set the rear of the ship on fire, and set them to losing altitude. "Brace for a rough landing!" he called to the crew, still scrambling to do all they could to keep the ship moving.

"Just make the castle!" Lamorna shouted back, trying to clutch a solid handhold and the bundled music box at once.

"We're definitely no longer friends!" Nathan shouted back, nonetheless steering for the castle on a collision course.

"You'll thank me later, when you have your best story yet!" she shouted back.

The bottom of the ship scraped along the walls of the castle, eventually smashing through the timbers near the rear of the *Falcon*. Momentum barely allowed it to clear the outer walls, and the ship lost its remaining altitude quickly, scraping along the ground of the courtyard until it smashed into one wall. "Everyone who can fight, we need to get to the audience chamber!" Lamorna called, starting towards the side of the ship and leaping into the courtyard as the first wave of Leonard's guards started to emerge to investigate the surprise collision. "They'll be dealing with Paul's forces soon enough, just stay together and keep moving!"

Treveur and Dita leapt from the ship as one, racing after Lamorna, closely followed by the musketeers. Olivier's pistol shot drew first blood, felling the first guard into the courtyard, while a couple more shots from Isaac and Rene forced the other guards to retreat back through the door. The door slammed shut, the sound of a bolt slamming down causing brief hesitation. Nathan and Thomas caught up with the rest, and the hesitation gave way to parting ranks to allow the bear to serve as door opener, though it took three crashes of his shoulder to splinter it enough for the others to begin fighting their way through. "You're getting old," Nathan teased his companion, getting only a dismissive snort from Thomas.

*

The shouts that first started drawing men to the courtyard shifted, and the halls echoed with calls that Finistère ships were approaching, throwing the whole castle into chaos, with men running every direction, some to guard important locations, others moving to man the walls or the rarely used cannons. Leonard assembled a significant personal guard in his audience chamber, starting to take in the reports, trying to make sense of what was happening and coordinate the response.

The airships from Finistère and Scilly closed with one another, Paul's personal ship and two others fighting through the growing blockade effort to pursue his son, while the rest engaged the aerial forces Scilly could muster with the limited notice and recent depletion of the number of airships. Paul and his guard lowered ropes over the side, dropping onto the walls or into the courtyard, trying to disable the cannon crews or pursue Treveur's company.

With combat and confusion echoing throughout the castle, Treveur and Dita were able to fight their way into Leonard's audience chamber. Leonard's demands to know the meaning of the intrusion were cut off as Lamorna emerged into the room with the rest.

"I should have known you'd betray me!" the Earl roared.

"You should have," Lamorna agreed. "In seeing treason and betrayal where there was none, you've become worth betraying, even if it's just to deliver your heir to her proper place."

"I have no heir!" Leonard snarled. "My wife's only child died eighteen years..." he paused, eyes settling on Dita. "No! She died!"

"She's entirely alive, and your child too," Lamorna shouted back. Neither side engaged yet.

"She is the child of a so-called friend who betrayed me, and an adulteress," Leonard spat.

"Your friend has only one child, her husband-to-be. Put aside this petty jealousy and let this marriage settle the matter," Lamorna warned.

The Earl's angry reply was lost – as, soon, was all sight of Lamorna – as the Marquis's forces emerged into the room through another entrance, fighting past a few more guards. "There's my unruly child!" Paul shouted. "Leonard, turn him back over to me, and I'll take my leave!" he shouted, starting towards the Earl's dais, guards closing in around him.

"You stole my chance at an heir from me," Leonard stated, rising from his great chair, beckoning his guards to flank him, and shifting his attention fully onto Paul. "Could I do any less? He'll be arrested, and if you do not retreat now, you'll share his fate. Be assured that he'll be well cared for in our prisons, old friend."

Both sets of forces closed around the small knot of people with Treveur and Dita, each of the guard captains emerging to take charge and command the forces while Leonard and Paul bickered between themselves.

"Father, stop this!" Treveur shouted, pulling attention back his way, even as the Earl and the Marquis came within only a few steps of each other amidst their shouting. Treveur called to the people of the court. "The girl with me is Leonard's child. What better alliance could we have than the trade partner that made both nations rich, while putting an end to a needless war? She's agreed to marry me, and has proof of who she is."

"I do not care what proof she claims! I remain the lord of these lands, and I will not support this marriage," swore the Earl.

"Nor will I, as the Vicomte's father and Marquis de Finistère. This union has no support from liege or family."

"Untrue," called a voice from the back of the room. All heads turned, for beyond the simple disruption, the voice was more lovely than had echoed in these halls in eighteen years – unmistakably that of the Countess. Dita certainly recognized it from her music box – and recognized the distinct filigree of the device, now attached at the top of the figure's dress-collar.

The court stared, too. Though the features of the statue had been molded after hers, now they bore her vitality and a true life. No longer was the clockwork statue the mocking and ungraceful thing it had been, but instead it spun and danced across the carpets towards the throne, followed closely by a less graceful, but smiling Lamorna. As the clockwork Countess spoke and moved, none questioned that the soul of the true Countess lay within the device. "I am Eirwyn, Countess of Scilly, and this girl is the daughter of the Earl and myself. She must marry within her station, and we happen to have a young viscount here."

"It is forbidden," the Earl insisted. "By whatever devilry, my wife you may be..." His eyes shifted about the guardsmen present. "And should you command, some will follow your word, some will follow mine, and there will be blood."

The clockwork Countess halted upon the steps leading to her husband's great chair and the sign of his station, her painted dancer's smile seeming somewhat fitting to her tone as her voice carried over the room. "No blood today, husband. Our home has been cursed by enough of that. Instead, I propose no man lift a finger for or against either of us, and we let nature take its course."

*

History will show that not a guard shifted for or against either. Most suggest that the Countess's voice was one of such state and command as to make it so, or simply that this arrangement seemed equitable. Some cynics have suggested that, instead, persuasion was applied via Olivier and Isaac's blades' being somewhat near the throats of the Marquis and Earl's guard captains, but such suspicious accounts have been refuted on Isaac's oath as a serious and sober fellow. Regardless, in the entirety of Leonard, Earl of Scilly's reign, the clockwork Countess is noted to have spoken only one more word.

"Thomas."

Thus, in rapid fashion, nature took its course, and two Lords exited the palace, never to be heard from again, pursued by a bear.

*

The clockwork countess knelt to England's crown.
The newlyweds soon ruled across the sea.
In two lands, songs were sung and blades put down.
Forgotten was a mad Earl's jealousy.
Now we must put away our puppet strings.
The will-o-wisps and gaslights must go out.
We turn our minds unto less fancied things,
So turn your feet upon another route.
Away from tales of any other age,
And back to what did hold your time before.
I fear we can't afford another page;
For those still reading and expecting more,
Our script lies open, one direction there:

Exit audience, pursued by a bear.

Did you like Sound and Fury:
Shakespeare Goes Punk?

Would you like to see news of the next volume coming out? Upcoming volumes may include *A Midsummer Night's Dream*, *As You Like It*, *The Merchant Of Venice*, *Coriolanus*...

Readers love books by Writerpunk Press.
YOU WILL TOO.

Visit the link below for information about other books by these authors and more, including synopses of the Shakespeare plays that inspired this volume... and news of the next volume!

Visit NOW: www.punkwriters.com

43629861R00198

Made in the USA
Middletown, DE
14 May 2017